Just Like
Heaven

ALSO BY LACEY BAKER

Homecoming

Just Like Heaven

Lacey Baker

St. Martin's Paperbacks

This is a work of fiction. All of the characters, organizations, and events portrayed in this novel are either products of the author's imagination or are used fictitiously.

JUST LIKE HEAVEN

Copyright © 2013 by Lacey Baker.
Excerpt from *Summer's Moon* copyright © 2013 by Lacey Baker.

For information address St. Martin's Press, 175 Fifth Avenue, New York, NY 10010.

ISBN: 978-1-250-01923-3

Printed in the United States of America

St. Martin's Paperbacks edition / December 2013

St. Martin's Paperbacks are published by St. Martin's Press, 175 Fifth Avenue, New York, NY 10010.

10 9 8 7 6 5 4 3 2 1

To Ms. Bonnie Russo, my tenth-grade history teacher for telling me that everyone deserved a second chance.

And everyone who wasn't afraid to go for second, third, and fourth chances until they found exactly what they were looking for.

Chapter 1

Preston Cantrell opened the door after the second knock. He wasn't sure where his sisters were and could hear the puppies playing in the backyard. Since he was back in Sweetland, lounging in the parlor with a glass of iced tea and the trial transcript his secretary had overnighted to him, he figured it was the least he could do.

What he hadn't considered was that that simple act would end with an armful of woman falling into him the moment the door was opened: arms flailing, a small gasp escaping her lips, and Preston stumbling backward to keep them both upright. Over his shoulder he spotted Hoover King wobbling up the walkway.

"Sorry 'bout that." He was talking in between the huffs his hurried steps elicited.

Hoover had to be at least fifty to sixty pounds overweight and yet at six forty-five every night you could find him sitting in either The Silver Spoon or Charlie's Bar and Grille ready to order whatever dish was highest in fat and/or cholesterol on the menu. Lately, that could be partially due to the fact that his wife, Inez, had been arrested for money laundering and corruption. Hoover, however, based on his almost constant state of inebriation and home-town ties, had been cleared of any charges even though he and Inez were both members of the town council and for the most part acted as a couple. Mayor Fitzgerald and Sheriff Farraway figured it was just simpler to let Hoover continue on his own path to destruction.

Case in point, Hoover's round head with its balding center was presently dotted with beads of sweat as he began taking the steps that would lead him up to the front door, stumbling over the last two.

"That ol' clunker's got a hell of a kickback. Scared the little lady right good," Hoover finally huffed out, then stopped at the top step to catch his breath.

"I'm sorry," the female said immediately afterward, pushing herself away from Preston and looking more than a little embarrassed.

"Just wanted to apologize." Hoover kept right on talking, using the back of an arm, then the palm of his hand to wipe the sweat from his forehead.

"Why don't you come on inside and get a glass of water, Hoover?" Preston suggested. He was trying not to laugh at the scene before him but Hoover's car—the old station wagon he drove around town with its rust spots and broken fender, calling it the Sweetland taxi service—was comical. And Preston knew very well the sounds it made, almost like a dying animal coughing up its last meal.

"Don't mind if I do," Hoover answered, straightening up as much as his five-foot-one frame could and moving closer to the door.

The female gave a wavering smile and stepped to the side.

"Didn't mean to frighten you, miss," Hoover told her and reached for her hand.

Preston really wanted to laugh now because the female

clearly didn't want to touch Hoover's sweat-riddled palm, but took a deep breath and shook it anyway.

"It's all right." She spoke in a soft voice that Preston decided was the epitome of feminine, high and light like a breeze.

"Just go on through to the restaurant. Michelle's out there," Preston told him.

When Hoover was gone, Preston was able to return his attention to the person who had been knocking.

"Let's try this again," he said, giving her his smoothest smile—the one he and his twin, Parker, shared and the one that had been the cause of more broken hearts in Sweetland than he could remember. "How can I help you?"

Her smile came slowly, like she wasn't sure if that's what she should do or not. Preston was more than grateful that she had. The simple act lit up her entire face, her olive complexion brightening, eyes almost smiling as well. *Beautiful* came to mind, then sort of died in the seconds Preston continued to stare. She was more than beautiful, and that was dangerous.

"My name is Heaven," was her reply.

Of course. What else would her name be?

"Heaven Montgomery," she continued. "I'm looking for Preston Cantrell."

"And you've found him," Preston said, extending his hand happily.

She looked down and back up to him again.

"It's okay, I've known Hoover for years. His germs don't spread." Preston laughed and was rewarded by her light chuckle, then the touch of her hand in his. He held on for a couple of seconds too long then censored himself and let her go.

"That's good to know. I think," she said, then tried to inconspicuously wipe her hand on her pants.

Jeans, he corrected himself, that fit her slim frame perfectly. Her legs were long and he wanted to see more. She wore a white shirt, baggy, button-up, so he couldn't really get a good look at her other assets but he was willing to bet they were just as stellar as the rest of her. Hence the name Heaven.

Hence the step-back-and-look-away warning bell sounding in his head.

"You're here about Coco," he continued.

She nodded. "Yes. I saw your ad and I think she and I will be a great fit."

"Come on in and we can talk about that." Preston spoke as he closed the door because it was almost one hundred degrees outside on this late-June day and they had the air-conditioning running briskly inside the inn.

He watched her walk ahead of him, couldn't really help himself even though he knew better. That denim did a fantastic job cupping a perfectly round bottom that had his mouth watering. She was one nicely put-together female.

"We can sit right here in the parlor." Preston touched her elbow, guiding her through the French doors in the living room to the parlor. The room was bathed in bright sunlight that made the pink rosettes on the cream-colored wallpaper stand out and the dark carpet seem a little livelier.

He moved his papers off the high-backed Victorian chair and told her, "Have a seat."

She did, and he joined her by sitting on a love seat directly across from her.

"So as I was saying, I'd like to adopt Coco. That is, if she likes me," Heaven said, tucking a heavy dark brown curl behind her ear.

Her fingers were slim, like a piano player's hands. His younger sister Raine had learned to play the piano when she was ten and had grown really good at it until at seventeen she'd abruptly decided to give it up.

"I'm sure she will," Preston replied, sitting back in the chair. "Do you have other dogs?" His secretary had sent him a list of questions he should ask Ms. Montgomery, but Preston wasn't going into his room to dig them up. Instead he figured he'd use what worked best for him in the courtroom, his insight. He watched her every movement and decided she wasn't entirely comfortable in the body he thought was a brilliant creation. She fidgeted, slowly, methodically, like it was something she'd practiced. But her hands refused to keep still. They moved from the hair behind her ear, to her lap, to rub up and down her thighs; now they were clasped together, fingers drumming slowly against the backs of her hands.

She shook her head, and her hair moved slightly around her pretty face. "No. And I live alone. But I have a spacious apartment and there's a park right across the street from me. I know Labradors need a lot of exercise and love from their owners. I'm prepared to provide that."

And yet she'd said it all as if she were making a presentation. Her back had even straightened a bit.

"Do you work?"

She blinked, sat up straighter, unfolded her hands and brushed them down the front of her blouse, then cleared her throat before saying, "Why would you ask me that?"

She sounded defensive, a definite warning sound in Parker's book. He should have known she was too pretty to be true.

"Having a dog is not cheap. I wouldn't want you to take Coco and then neglect to feed her because you don't have money to buy food."

"I have money," she told him, lifting her chin a little higher. "Can I see the puppy?"

"How long are you staying in Sweetland?" he asked,

ignoring her request. There was more he wanted to know about her before he introduced her to Coco. Things he needed to know that would determine *if* he would introduce her to Coco.

He didn't want the dog, had already decided that fact. But that didn't mean he wanted this woman to have the dog, either. His gaze settled on her again, a lovely, leisurely look once more at this intriguing female. Intriguing because Preston was almost positive this pretty package was just like the ones that used to sit under the six-plus-foot-high and almost equally wide Christmas tree that used to grace the living room each year.

They were wrapped in the most festive holiday paper, a different cartoon character designating which boxes went to which Cantrell sibling. Some were small and some were larger; some rattled when they shook them, others remained deceptively quiet. Then there was always one, wrapped in the shiniest paper with glistening snowflakes or colorful Christmas trees. It never had a name on it so the siblings fought for weeks about who would get to open it on Christmas morning. Finally, when the box was ready to be opened—by each of them, as Gramma had proclaimed—it was a total shock to them all. One year it was a swing and monkey-bar set for the backyard; another, wood planks and cardboard that when summer came along the boys put together and the girls sold lemonade from. Each year they were all intrigued by the beautiful gift and anxiously anticipated the unknown.

That's what Ms. Heaven Montgomery was to Preston, the beautiful unknown.

She didn't like him.

That's the first impression Heaven had of Mr. Preston Cantrell. His loafers were expensive and his slacks were too long, almost an inch hanging on the floor as he walked.

His polo shirt was a nice shade of peach that comple-
mented his honey-gold complexion, but he stood as if he
knew he looked good and was just waiting for her to figure it out. He smiled like a player, to which she was deftly
immune. And he questioned her like he was the police, by
which she was extremely offended.

Not to mention the fact that she was tired of the police
questioning her, even though they had good reason to.
That he was doing it so he could tell if she was good enough
to adopt a puppy was a bit more than she could stand right
now. Her heart was just beginning to beat a regular rhythm
after that car had come up behind her making all kinds of
noise. She'd jumped so high and screamed so loud, She'd
thought everyone on the quiet little block had heard her.
Apparently not, since it took so long for someone to answer
the door at The Silver Spoon.

Now, looking at who had been the one to let her in,
Heaven wasn't surprised. He didn't look as if he rushed to
do anything. Probably didn't do anything all day long,
either, besides sit in this lovely parlor with its old-time feel
and drink iced tea.

"I'm financially stable enough to take care of a puppy,"
she finally replied to him.

His eyes never left her. He watched her as intently as if
she were a suspected burglar.

"They don't stay puppies. In the short time I've had her
she's gained about six pounds. They grow fast, chew on
everything, and play nonstop. Are you ready for that?"

"Were you ready when you bought her?" she asked. "Is
that why you're giving her up?"

He didn't look at all ruffled by her question. She'd
hoped he would be, and wanted to shrug off the mild dis-
appointment but didn't bother.

"I inherited her when my grandmother died a little more
than a month ago."

"Oh," she snapped quietly, feeling like an idiot for challenging him in the first place. Especially after catching the quick pained expression on his face as he'd said those words. Of course, he'd rebounded fast and was now back to looking like a smug cover model. One she could see clearly as the centerfold with his sculpted abs, powerful thighs, and a seductive look that made women weak in the knees—other women, certainly not her.

"Look," she continued, trying desperately to hold back her exasperation. "I know I'll be good to her. I'm not an angry person. I rarely yell and I spend more time daydreaming or itching to get outside than I probably should. That makes me a perfect candidate for Coco because at this point in my life there's nothing that would come before her welfare."

At this point in Heaven's life there was nothing at all.

"You want to see those noisy dogs?" A gorgeous female with long raven-black hair pulled into a ponytail that swung elegantly down her back entered the parlor and picked up Preston's glass to take a sip. "I'll take you out back even though I'm sure you can hear them all the way in here."

Preston looked like he wanted to say something but lifted his hands as if to tell Heaven to go right ahead and follow this other woman out of the room.

"Mmmm. She works my nerves but I swear that woman makes the best iced tea," the female said, putting the glass down and smacking her lips like she wanted more. Unfortunately she'd emptied the glass.

Heaven stood and extended her hand. "I'm Heaven Montgomery and I'm interested in adopting Coco."

"Oh," the woman said, looking from Heaven to Preston and back to Heaven again. "So I guess Preston should show you Coco since she was assigned to him. Let me know if you're looking for another puppy. For now I'm stuck with Micah but I'm sure he can be convinced to follow someone else around all day, biting off pieces of their shoes only to go to some godforsaken place to poop it all out again."

She sighed and with a dramatic roll of her eyes finally took Heaven's hand for a light shake.

"I'm Savannah, by the way."

"Savannah is my youngest sister," Preston told her as he stood to join in this new conversation. One he didn't look too pleased about, either. "Each of my five siblings inherited a puppy. Michelle, the illustrious cook here at The Silver Spoon, was lucky enough to inherit a mother–pup combination."

"Yeah, my grandmother's idea of a cruel joke," Savannah told Heaven. "And you'd better not let her hear you calling her a cook. She's liable to slap you with a spatula or something."

Heaven almost grinned at the exchange. How long had she hoped for a little brother or sister? And how many times had Opaline told her that was never going to happen? Staring at these two, she assumed they'd come from two exceptionally gorgeous people, who had raised them in a loving environment. Something else Opaline had denied Heaven.

"I can go out back. Is it through this way?" she asked, because the pang of jealousy poking at her was threatening to get worse.

"I'll take you out back to meet Coco," Preston announced. "You," he added, pointing to Savannah, "can get me another glass of iced tea."

Savannah frowned, which did nothing to mar her exceptionally pretty features. And Preston scowled, which, again, did nothing to mar his overtly handsome features. It should have been a sin, really, for both of them to have been blessed so abundantly in the looks department.

"It was nice meeting you," Heaven said honestly, admonishing herself for judging them solely on their appearance. She knew better than that, knew that things weren't always what they seemed. She was walking proof of that mantra.

"Likewise. And good luck," Savannah bid Heaven with a salute of her hand just before she picked up a magazine from an end table and plopped down onto the love seat. Not in any hurry to get Preston his glass of iced tea or, it seemed, to do anything else.

This time Heaven did smile because the frown on Preston's face was genuine, marked only by the obvious affection he had for his younger sister. In that instant Heaven thought maybe he wasn't so smug and arrogant as she'd originally thought.

Then he turned that heated brown-eyed gaze on her. He smiled, his lips parting slowly to show off gleaming white teeth. Thick eyebrows arched slightly in a you-know-you-like-it gesture, and heat rushed to her cheeks.

"This way, my dear," he said his voice as smooth and debonair as a Hollywood actor. Probably as fake and practiced as one, too.

"Thank you," she snapped, turning away from him quickly, refusing to think of him as handsome or sexy or cleverly enticing or anything other than a man selling a puppy, ever again.

Chapter 2

The backyard wasn't exactly what Heaven expected. It was huge, which she should have assumed since the inn with the restaurant neatly tucked onto its side would easily take up half the block of the street she lived on in Boston.

What surprised her was all the lush green grass. It went on for what seemed like miles and miles, only to drop suddenly into big gray rocks that formed a slope right down to water she assumed, from her minimal knowledge of Maryland, was the Chesapeake Bay.

"The Bay is really pretty from here," she said quietly. She hadn't meant for him to hear or to actually respond.

"That's the Miles River. It's a tributary to the Bay, so I guess it'll accept the compliment," was his bland reply.

A response that almost had the effect of cold water splashing onto the minute rise in her body temperature at his proximity. It was ridiculous, she knew, to feel any type of reaction to a man she'd just met, especially since their meeting was the farthest thing from a hookup. Admittedly, men and interacting with them were not Heaven's forte. She accepted that just as she accepted all the other ups and downs of her life, and normally it didn't bother her. But today, with this man . . .

She shook her head, closing her eyes momentarily, and reminded herself again that she didn't like this man. The decision came quickly and definitively, and all other thoughts of Preston Cantrell sifted slowly away as she opened her eyes and looked to her left. There she saw a large gated area containing six puppies and one adult Labrador retriever. Just beyond their outdoor playpen was a lovely white gazebo that was the exact image she'd seen in the pamphlet she'd flipped through on her ride into town. From the airport Heaven had to hire a car service to bring her the hour-and-ten-minute drive to Sweetland. The service was apparently familiar with the town because it had a lot of literature about it in the pouch behind the passenger-side seat.

"Which one is Coco?" she asked, stepping down from the two stairs and planting her feet solidly in the plush grass.

Today, for a change, she'd forgone the pantsuit or skirt and jacket she normally wore. This time, because this appointment was purely about her and her personal contentment, and since she was desperately trying to separate the Heaven who used to work twelve- to eighteen-hour days from the one who someday wanted a real life, and because the airline had lost her luggage so she could not change, she wore a more casual outfit. As of right now, her wardrobe didn't really consist of a lot of casual pieces, but she'd found this pair of jeans and shirt and figured they were sufficient. On her feet she'd decided on flats, leather, sensible. Now she wished she'd had something more feminine, more summer-like and open-toed so she could feel what she assumed was coolness from the soft-looking grass.

"How long are you staying in Sweetland?" he asked again because she hadn't replied to his first inquiry.

Heaven was walking toward the play pen and had forgotten he was there. Or at least she'd tried to. He wasn't making much effort to conceal the fact that he didn't really want her to take his dog. But if that was the case, why put the ad online? *Stop it! It's not your job to analyze him. Or anybody else for that matter.*

It had taken only two months of intense psychotherapy three times a week to get her to accept that point. And her trip to this small Eastern Shore town was part of her recovery. She had to keep reminding herself of that fact.

"Long enough to take care of all the remaining legalities of adopting Coco," she told him. She'd already filled out an adoption application, submitted it, had a telephone interview and a house visit by one of the LovingLabs liaisons. This was the next-to-final step, meeting the Lab she'd fallen in love with. After this, there was just the signing of the adoption contract and receiving temporary licensing and tags. Then she and Coco could be on their way. She hoped all that could be handled today, but was prepared to find a hotel and stay overnight if need be.

"We both have to sign the contract," he told her matter-of-factly.

"You're the one who listed her on the website as available. That was a foolish idea if you really don't want to give her up," she replied with a tinge of annoyance.

They'd stopped right at the gate, and reluctantly she looked up at him. He was too handsome, she told herself. That was another reason she didn't like him. Handsome men were trouble and for the most part ignored Heaven like the plague. And he looked dangerous. Well, not like he was going to turn around and choke her—that would be insane, and later she would admonish herself for being overly dramatic. Right now, though, she couldn't help but look at him, at his dreamy dark brown eyes and thick neat eyebrows. He had an easy smile—or he had when he'd answered the door and when his sister had first entered the room. His complexion was almost golden, as if he spent a lot of time in the sun, and his hair was raven black, cut short, waving a bit on the top.

She was in the process of gritting her teeth and trying to look away from him when he spoke again.

"I knew what I was doing when I listed her."

He didn't sound so much annoyed now as he did thoughtful. But Heaven didn't want to think too hard on the emotional state of Preston Cantrell. His physical state was already wreaking havoc with her senses. "That's good to know," she finally replied.

They were standing at the gate, side by side, when Preston leaned forward and flipped the latch. The minute the gate was open every one of the puppies bounded for the exit, big feet and floppy ears whizzing past Heaven so fast she couldn't help but let out a full-bodied laugh. Something she hadn't done in a very long time.

It took about two minutes for her to figure out that what had been an explosion of too-cute and adorably furry little feet running through the grass was not as hilarious as she'd first thought. Or at least, Preston didn't think so.

He ran after one puppy, stooping to scoop it up in his arms, then immediately bounding in the opposite direction for another. She figured she should help or meeting Coco might take even longer. After a couple of steps—she'd barely broken into a run—her hand was easily slipping beneath the collar of the adult Lab. Its pug nose and milk-chocolate-brown eyes stared up at Heaven, inciting another smile and a warmth that started a small swarm in the pit of her stomach.

Ushering the mother back to the pen, Heaven secured the gate, then took off to find another one of the runaway pups. In the midst of the hide-and-seek she played with the one pup that had found shelter behind a fat and cheer-ful azalea bush, she allowed herself to once again forget about her handsome host. Until she heard him curse loudly as he took off after another puppy. The curse didn't sound friendly or remotely cheerful, as she'd begun to feel during her merry little chase. Her smile had only fal-tered slightly as she decided to give Preston a hand.

He'd run all the way across the yard, down to where the border of rocks started the incline. It didn't take her long to catch up—she'd run track and field in high school, one of the only times she'd had a rebellious moment against her parents and won. By the time she hit the rocks Preston had already begun his trek down, taking slow steps, one in front of the other. The puppy, with its large feet and flopping ears, seemed to smile up at Preston. With each step the human took forward, the pup took one back.

"Come here, you little nightmare!" Preston yelled.

The puppy's ears flopped and one of her back feet slipped on a rock. Heaven gasped.

"Maybe you should talk nicely to her, coax her to come back up," she suggested.

"I know how to handle this," he snapped.

Heaven didn't bother gasping. It was no secret to her that men didn't like to be told what to do, especially by a woman—even though in her experience with them, men rarely knew what to do on their own. Still, that was fine and good for Mr.-Rude-Arrogant-And-Totally-Hot. She wouldn't tell him what to do again. She'd simply *show* him.

"Here, cutie-pie," she coaxed, taking her first step down onto the rocks. "Come on, girl, come on."

Her voice was soft as she moved slowly. The puppy had stopped her descent, flopping down onto her bottom and staring up at Heaven expectantly.

"That's a good girl. That's a good puppy. You're such a pretty little one." The puppy looked like she was lapping up every word, so Heaven continued until she was just an arm's reach from the puppy.

Now she would show Preston Cantrell that she knew what she was talking about, that she could certainly handle a puppy and that he . . . Heaven's words were lost somewhere on the rocks with her balance as she toppled into the chilly river.

Preston saw it coming about three seconds before it happened. He'd already cursed and taken another step to catch her when Coco stood abruptly and with her always playful and mischievous manner dived feetfirst, ears following, into the water. Heaven reached for her—and toppled over the last couple of rocks into the water right along with the puppy.

With a curse, Preston made it to the bank, reaching into the water to grab Coco before she could swim away. Beside him Heaven sputtered, wiping her long hair back out of her face. Her blouse was plastered to her chest . . . and what a delectable chest it was. Hell, he thought with a pang of lust so potent he almost fell back on his own butt gaping at her.

"If you laugh I'll punch you," she said, her eyes narrowing to mere slits as she glared at him.

Preston put Coco down on the rocks and pointed directly at her. "Stay," he said firmly, then turned back to Heaven.

"I wouldn't think of laughing," he told her with as straight a face as he could manage. Fifteen years ago he would have gaped and probably panted like Coco was presently doing. Now he remained stoic, or at least he hoped that's what he was doing.

"Let me help you," he offered, extending a hand to her.

"I don't need—" she began. Then her narrow gaze shifted and a small smile touched the edge of her mouth. "Thank you, Mr. Cantrell."

She reached for his hand, clasped the palm, and Preston instantly knew how this would end.

The splash of cold water wasn't a total shock. Still, his body gave a little jolt as he, too, was submerged in the river. She had some strength to her, this pretty, sexy wisp of a woman. He hadn't expected that. Nor had he really expected she would have the balls to pull him into the water. But she had, and Preston was mystified at his reaction to it all.

When she tried to make her way to the bank, standing because the water level at the entry of the river was only about three and a half feet, he got another glimpse of her extremely fine backside and had an idea of his own. He was just about to reach for her, about to take her by the waist and pull her back into the water with him. It had been a long time since he'd frolicked in the water with a wet and willing female—even though he admitted he might have to work on the willing part with her. But Coco had other plans. The hyperactive dog disobeyed Preston's direct order and bounded back into the river, waddling until she was splashing water all over Preston and giving Heaven the time she needed to get safely onto the rocks.

When he finally made his way out of the river, Coco tucked tightly under his left arm, Preston was no longer in a laughing mood. Heaven had just cleared the rocks when he grabbed her by the arm.

"Heaven Montgomery, meet Coco. Coco, meet Ms. Montgomery," he said, thrusting the puppy into Heaven's arms before stalking off.

Chapter 3

"The Bay Day celebration starts in two weeks. And I haven't been contacted yet about riding in the parade," Diana McCann complained in a nasal voice that every citizen of Sweetland was familiar with and hated just the same.

"We're not organizing the parade, Diana," Michelle Cantrell said with what felt like her last bit of patience.

It had been an extremely long day with preparing the restaurant's regular menu and baking the additional cakes and pies for the Sunday School's monthly bake sale tomorrow. She was tired and hot and just basically agitated. The very last thing she wanted to do at almost nine o'clock at night was sit in the living room listening to Diana's rant about what car she would be riding in during the Bay Day Parade. Especially when she really would rather see Diana riding *under* one of the parade cars.

Despite all that, Diana's rant continued.

"Liza told me to speak to you directly. She said the Cantrells were picking up where Janet left off and that you would be helping with the celebration. I tried to tell her how foolish that sounded, but of course there's no telling Liza Fitzgerald anything."

Michelle wanted desperately to roll her eyes but remembered Gramma telling her how un-lady-like that was.

"Well, she is the mayor, Diana," she said instead. "However, my sisters and I are only organizing the booths for all the businesses that will be lined along the parade route. That and decorating for the Bay Soiree are all we're responsible for. I think Louisa might be organizing the actual parade." Michelle just had to offer that last bit of information. The scowl that etched Diana's cold features almost made her laugh.

"That old hag doesn't know anything about a parade," Diana protested.

She stood with her arms folded across her chest, the black-and-white polka-dot slim-fitting sundress she wore matching the absolutely ridiculous wide-brimmed black hat with polka dots along the brim and a thick veil hanging down to cover her face. She looked like Morticia Addams revamped, except for the fact that she was wearing her long bone-straight hair in a strawberry-blond shade these days.

Michelle disagreed. "She should. She was on the original committee when the celebration started almost thirty-five years ago."

"Doesn't matter. She doesn't know what she's doing. At least with you three doing it I wouldn't have to explain everything I want three or four times," Diana said with another one of her dramatic huffs.

Raine sat in a chair near the window shaking her head. She wouldn't say anything, Michelle knew. Raine did not like confrontations, never had. Savannah, on the other hand . . .

"You don't have to explain a thing to us," Savannah quipped, unfolding her legs and rising to stand face-to-face with Diana. "If we were organizing the parade, I'd have you riding in the very last car, which as you well know is Hoover's prized taxi-wagon."

Diana dropped her arms, clenching and unclenching her fists at her sides so that her long acrylic nails clicked together.

"Look, you little wannabe," she began yelling at Savannah.

Savannah who was about four inches shorter than Diana and five years younger, took a step toward the woman pointing her finger—which had natural nails that weren't as long as Diana's but probably just as deadly—into Diana's face.

"Watch your mouth in my house," Savannah warned.

"Please!" Michelle raised her voice, the effort causing her temples to throb more intensely. She came to her feet because from the looks of things Savannah might slap Diana soon. And Diana was so dramatic, she would most likely fall onto the floor of the poor decrepit old inn she so despised.

"Diana, we are not in charge of the parade and that is a fact. Call Louisa in the morning, or stop by Java's to see her and Marabelle. I'm sure you can whine your way into one of the first cars in the parade."

"Even though you don't deserve a spot," Savannah added as Michelle stepped between her and Diana.

"A Beaumont has always ridden in the Bay Day Parade," Diana insisted.

"Technically you're no longer a Beaumont," Raine added quietly with a raise of her hand as if she were in a classroom and not the living room of her own house.

"You! Don't you even speak to me!" Diana yelled at Raine.

Raine clapped her mouth shut, but shook her head again. Michelle figured if Raine ever really stood up to somebody with all the repressed emotions that girl felt, the person she confronted was in big trouble.

"And on that note, you can now leave," Michelle told her. "You know your way out."

Diana made a series of sounds that ranked right up with screeching, growling, and overall annoying as she stomped out of the house.

"We need an alarm that senses when she steps up onto the porch," Raine suggested with a sigh.

"And dumps spoiled milk all over her head as she stands at the door," Savannah added.

Michelle laughed. There was nothing else her tired body and mind could do.

As her sisters joined in on the laughter, the front door opened and closed again.

"I'm sorry to interrupt," a soft female voice said about a second before her head poked around the corner so they could see her face and the long dripping tendrils of hair.

"Oh, hi, Heaven. I thought you'd be on your way by now. What the hell happened to you?" Savannah asked.

The female Michelle assumed was named Heaven came completely into the living room, a timid smile on her face, red splotches spreading rapidly at her cheeks, her clothes and everything else dripping water onto the Aubusson carpet.

"Ah, there was a little incident," she said slowly.

"I see," Savannah replied, then made the introductions. "My sisters Michelle and Raine. This is Heaven. She's here to adopt Coco."

"Oh, you're soaking wet and so is Coco," Michelle said, praying she didn't sound as disappointed as she felt that her brother was giving away part of his inheritance.

"Yes. The dogs sort of got away, and I tried to keep this little one from drowning, only to end up in the river myself." Her chuckle was slight and quickly replaced by a shiver.

Raine stood, extending her hand to Heaven. "Oh, this air-conditioning is so high you'll catch an awful cold if you don't hurry and dry off. I'll get you something to change into. And by the way, it's a pleasure to meet you."

Now, this was what Raine was good at, Michelle admitted—the pretense, the polite socialite. Her sister was everything prim and proper and perfectly trained, right down to the short haircut that didn't dare show disrespect by frizzing in the ninety-eight-degree humidity hanging around outside like an unwanted guest.

"Me too," Heaven said, looking down at the cell phone she'd just retrieved from her pocket. "And thank you. Oh, dear, I hope this still works," she was saying. Then she frowned and Michelle was instantly concerned.

"It's broke, isn't it? Those cell phones aren't worth all the money we pay for them, or the time it takes for us to figure out how they work," Michelle quipped.

"Mine is perfect. Works wherever I go no matter what the conditions," Savannah added brightly.

"Even being drenched in water?" Michelle asked her very mouthy younger sister. "That's usually a killer for all electronic devices."

"Oh, no," Heaven sighed. "It works, which is a good thing."

"Then what's the 'oh, no' for?" Raine asked, leaning over slightly to look at the window of the phone then taking a polite step back when Heaven's gaze met hers.

"The liaison from the agency tried to call me but ended up sending a text instead. Apparently some of the paperwork wasn't completed before they left for the day. I'll have to wait until Monday, and they'll fax everything so I can adopt Coco."

Heaven looked deflated. Michelle felt hopeful. She now had two days to change her brother's mind.

"Then you must stay right here until it's all worked out," she said instantly.

"No, that's quite okay. I couldn't impose like that," Heaven started.

"It's no imposition at all," Raine added. "We'd love to have you."

"The Sunshine Room is available. Savannah will get it all freshened up for you while Raine helps find you some dry clothes," Michelle continued happily. "I'll go into the kitchen and warm up some of the dinner leftovers."

"I don't know if it's a good idea that I stay here," Heaven tried once more.

"You're staying here?" Preston asked coming in from the parlor.

He was dripping wet, too, only he'd stopped off, probably in the first-floor powder room, and found himself a towel that he used to wipe his face.

"Yes, she is. And while you're at it you might want to work on your hospitality skills. Taking a guest swimming while fully clothed is just rude," Michelle stated before moving out of the room and heading into the kitchen.

"Hmmm, big brother, your skills with the females are definitely slipping," Savannah told him with a wink and a chuckle before heading up the stairs.

"You should get out of those wet clothes before you catch a cold, too," Raine scolded in her soft voice.

Heaven had the good sense not to even look at him before retreating. And the puppy, the one Heaven and Raine had conveniently left in the parlor with him, didn't have any decency at all. She rolled onto her back, mouth gaping open, eyes wide and pleading.

"The last thing I'm going to do is rub your belly, you

traitor," Preston told her with irritation that wasn't quite conveyed in his tone.

Coco was a traitor all right, and Heaven Montgomery was one hell of a woman. Too bad she was like all the rest of them. She wasn't telling him the truth. He should have expected it. Preston had been clued in to the female race at a very young age. First by his mother, who'd acted as if she loved her children to no end but ultimately up and left said children the day after her husband's funeral. Then there was his grandmother, who hadn't even told anyone she was sick and had died before they could get back to Sweetland to see and/or help her. Last, but certainly not least, was his doting and slightly overbearing older sister Michelle, with whom he was still very annoyed for not knowing their grandmother was sick since she'd been in this house with Gramma every day until her last.

And those were just the women closest to him. Others, Preston kept at arm's length all the time. He didn't trust any of them farther than the bed he had sex with them in.

And Heaven Montgomery was no different. She was certainly all woman, with her long legs and seductive curves. The quiet demeanor and nervous tendencies were probably an act. She had a sophistication about her; it wasn't overt or intense, but it was there. A fact that told him she wasn't as innocent as she'd tried to appear. And her eyes held secrets, loads of them, the kind only a female could keep stored. He should just give her the damned puppy and let her be on her merry way.

Except he couldn't quite dismiss what she wasn't telling him, whatever she was trying to hide. He couldn't quite dismiss *her*.

Half an hour later Preston was hungry and grumpy, part of which was the norm for him. The other part might have been an anomaly—but when he walked into the kitchen and glimpsed a certain female just finishing a glass of tea while sitting at the island, his grumpy mood resurged with a vengeance.

"We meet again," he said for lack of anything better to say—which coincidentally was another signal that he was a bit off.

Preston always knew what to say and when to say it. That was how he'd gained such renown as a litigator, and when it came to being back in Sweetland, it was how he had maintained his half of the Double Trouble Cantrells. Parker was the better-looking bad boy of the family, while Preston remained the still-good-looking smooth talker. Quinn was the American Dream, with his serious demeanor and eye on responsibility and commitment. It worked well for him since he was the oldest of the Cantrell bunch.

"I'm finished. I'll just get out of your way," Heaven was saying as she stood from the high-boy chair she'd been sitting in.

She grabbed her glass and the empty plate that had also been in front of her and was headed toward the sink before Preston could say another word.

He stopped where he stood, or else he would have run right into her on his way to the refrigerator. Instead, he watched her move. Long graceful steps, back straight and rigid, chin up as if all he needed to do was put a book on her head and make a bet to see if she'd drop it. That alone caused him to grit his teeth. She was too uptight, definitely not the type of female he was used to dealing with, or even wanted to deal with for that matter.

When she stood at the sink a second longer than he deemed necessary, Preston sighed and headed over toward the refrigerator. On the way, he kicked one of the huge containers Michelle used to brew iced tea. It fell, instigating a domino effect that ended with four containers sprawling across the floor. The racket was loud enough to wake up anyone who'd dare go to sleep before eleven o'clock, which to Preston—a perpetual night owl—was like a travesty.

A high-pitched yelp followed by the clanking of dishes in the stainless-steel sink added to the echo of noise and drew Preston's attention directly to the female he'd been trying to avoid. She stood with her back to him, almost perfectly still if he didn't catch the gentle shaking of her shoulders. He cursed, almost as loud as the other noise that had just subsided, and moved to put his hands on her shoulders. His thought was to still their shaking.

Instead she jumped at least a couple of inches off the floor and moved quickly out of his reach.

"Whoa, I'm not the bad guy," he said, holding both his hands up in the air and making eye contact with her.

It wasn't easy since she looked in the direction of the downed buckets, then toward the back door, all before finding him again. One hand was wrapped around her throat while the other arm had folded across her torso as if to protect herself from something, or someone.

Preston's sour mood worsened.

He took a step toward her. "Just me being clumsy," he started, his voice substantially calmer than it had been seconds ago. "No big deal. I'll restack them before Michelle gets back here at the crack of dawn. She'll never know I disturbed the perfect sanctity of her kitchen."

Heaven still wasn't speaking, but her fingers were no longer clenching her throat. They'd fluttered there a second longer while he spoke; then she'd slowly lowered her hand altogether so that her arm fell to her side.

She cleared her throat. "I'm so silly," she said with a shake of her head.

She pulled her long hair back. It still looked damp from their impromptu dip in the river, but the style gave her a youthful look, fresh and untouched, that was an instant kick in the gut for him.

"It's my fault, making enough noise to wake the dead at this hour," he told her, feeling the need to take the blame from her but not really knowing why.

She pulled her arms tightly around herself, still shaking her head. "Just a few buckets," she murmured. "I shouldn't have been frightened. New places make me nervous."

Her voice was low, and she was staring at something he thought might be just beyond his shoulders. It didn't seem as if she was talking to him. And he didn't like it. There was a spooked look on her face, her eyes just a bit brighter than they had been before. It probably wasn't the smartest thing to do, but Preston was doing it anyway. He stepped closer to her, close enough to extend his hands, placing one on each shoulder to hold her steady.

"No big deal," he said. "I'll clean up and you can go on to bed."

She looked up as if she was startled to see him. He was partially relieved when he realized she wasn't actually talking to him. She'd gone somewhere in those few seconds, somewhere that frightened her. Preston didn't like that revelation at all.

"No," she said with a heavy sigh. "I'm just being silly. Here, let me help you." This offer was her escape as she slipped quickly from his grasp and knelt down to pick up a bucket.

Preston wisely kept his mouth shut this time. He wanted to ask her what had happened to make her so jumpy, but he refrained. She wasn't liable to tell him, not right now anyway. But he would find out. In the meantime, he picked up the remaining buckets, and then stacked them beside the cabinets where they'd been before he disturbed them.

"Well, good night," she said. She was just about to turn away from him when Preston touched her once more.

This time there was a spurt of heat that started at his fingertips then settled in his palm as he wrapped his fingers around her arm and held tight. She felt it, too, because her eyes widened as she turned to look at him, about two seconds before she tried to pull away.

"I'll walk you upstairs," he told her solemnly, suddenly his hunger for food completely fleeing from his mind.

"I know the way," she argued.

"I insist," he told her, keeping her arm in his hold and moving toward the door.

"Really, this is silly. I can walk myself upstairs and you can continue to do whatever it was you wanted to do down here."

They'd gone through the swinging door and were walking past the parlor toward the foyer and the winding staircase with its original oak banister. That banister had held Preston and his brothers on many occasions as they'd slid down as a way of avoiding the numerous steps, or just to have fun, whichever excuse worked for the moment.

"Arguing is silly considering we're already at the steps and I'm not taking no for an answer," he told her firmly.

She opened her mouth to reply, then quickly snapped her lips shut. They took the rest of the stairs in silence, turning left at the top and heading to the end of the hall where the Sunshine Room was. It was bright there, hence the name. The walls were painted a canary yellow while the bedding and window arrangements were in a softer yellow, royal blue, and white paisley print. The bed, with its four brass posts that reached to within inches of the ceiling, was draped with sheer material. All the remaining furniture in the room was of a dark cherry oak, including the leather chest at the end of the bed. It was an extremely feminine room to Preston's way of thinking. And it was perfect for Heaven.

As she stepped inside the room and turned to him, he could almost swear she looked calmer. Of course that could also be attributed to the fact that he was no longer touching her and the noise from the kitchen had subsided.

"Now I'll bid you good night," he said, really intending to walk away and leave her in her room.

"Thank you," she said in that voice that should have been too soft to be sexy. She licked her lips and looked away from him.

"You're welcome," he replied and stood there like some high school kid on his first date. And just like that horny teenager, the sight of her tongue moving across lips kickstarted the arousal he'd been trying to hold at bay where this woman was concerned. Briefly he toyed with the idea of leaning in for a good-night kiss and maybe more. But from the way she was looking back into the room, then questioningly at him, he figured that was a bad idea.

On and on thoughts he might later qualify as ridiculous played in his mind, until she finally closed the door in his face.

"Right," he murmured and continued to talk to himself as he took the stairs again. "Note to self, she's a head case, so steer clear."

Chapter 4

"Steer clear of who or what?" his twin asked the moment he stepped into the foyer.

"Nobody," Preston replied quickly.

Parker chuckled. "For the record, 'nobody' is who you were talking to. I'm just asking who you were talking about."

Parker was walking with a slight limp after his motorcycle had taken a wrong turn on the interstate and ended up wrapped unattractively around a median strip. Since that thought still put a lump the size of a boulder in the center of Preston's chest, he looked away from his brother's injured leg and headed back toward the kitchen.

"Why are you up?" Preston asked, heading straight to the refrigerator.

"Michelle's gone home, which means my curfew has been lifted," Parker said with a chuckle. "Now your turn. What are you doing up and why were you upstairs?"

Preston had just resurfaced from his facefirst dive into the refrigerator. In one hand was a carton of orange juice; in the other, a plate of thick-sliced ham pieces wrapped in red cellophane—only Michelle Cantrell would find red cellophane in a grocery store, especially in Godfrey's, Sweetland's one and only stop for groceries. The place that carried absolutely no pre-packaged frozen meals sold multicolored plastic wrap. Amazing.

He went to the island and took the stool opposite his twin, opposite the one Heaven had been sitting in only minutes ago.

"Unlike you, who has always had a serious problem with following the rules, I do not have a curfew," he told him with a bland look.

Parker turned over two coffee mugs positioned toward the end of the island near the two-frogs-sitting-on-a-bench salt and pepper shakers and the ceramic apple with the worm centered atop that opened up to display a mountain of sugar. Gramma always had coffee in the morning when she came in to get breakfast started. Michelle was most likely keeping up the tradition. Preston opened the orange juice and poured his twin a cup first, then himself.

"I'll admit you were always a night owl, but you're looking particularly out of sorts at the moment." Parker talked while removing the wrapping from the plate of ham.

As competitive as the twins were in their youth, and as much as Preston was used to always coming out on top even if it was by the smallest margin, in the arena of eating Parker had always won hands down. Case in point: While it was Preston who had originally come into the kitchen for a snack, Parker was the first to stuff a huge slice of ham into his mouth, chewing heartily even as he continued to speak.

"Somebody pissed you off. Is it the case you just finished? I thought that pled out a couple of days ago, and that's why you came back to Sweetland."

Luckily Preston was accustomed to his brother's food-riddled talking and wasn't fazed by it. Had his sisters been in the kitchen they would have undoubtedly been screaming about manners and rudeness and common courtesies that men just didn't need from one day to the next.

"There's nothing I can do about the case now. The judge took the guilty plea even though it was for the lesser manslaughter charges. The defendant'll probably get a suspended sentence and a chunk of probation, and it'll cost the state thousands of dollars to monitor him. And he'll no doubt violate it, because he's a career criminal, and we'll repeat this asinine process all over again."

After that synopsis Preston drank from his own cup in big, thirst-quenching gulps. Parker simply nodded.

"I know that song. I'm sick of arresting the same guys over and over again. It's getting to feel like a reunion every time I show up at a crime scene," his brother said, taking another slice of ham.

Parker was a Baltimore City homicide detective. While Preston had headed to the University of Maryland to study criminal justice, Parker had gone to the police academy. And when Parker had begun patrolling the crime-riddled streets of Baltimore City as a beat cop, Preston had still had his head in the books at the University of Baltimore School of Law. They'd either seen or spoken to each other every day during those years, both of them keeping apartments in the downtown area of Baltimore where they could be close to work and school. When Preston joined the prosecutor's office, he frequently saw his brother as the arresting officer of the defendants he tried in court. If folk in Sweetland thought the twins had been inseparable during their teenage years, they should have seen them in their early adult years, but with ideals of ridding the world of bad people in the best way they knew how. Now, more than ten years later, it seemed they were both having second thoughts about those career choices.

"It's never going to change, you know," Preston said after chewing on his piece of meat. Michelle made the best brown-sugar-and-pineapple baked ham. That woman was simply a blessing in the kitchen, no doubt about that.

Parker shook his head. "We were crazy enough to believe it would. That we would be the ones to change it."

Preston nodded. "You're right. We were crazy." Still, Preston knew he wouldn't really change his career choice if he could. He'd always dreamed of being an attorney and knew he wouldn't be satisfied doing anything else. His main issue now was how to be an attorney with a thriving practice in Baltimore when his family was going through its own transition in Sweetland.

"And what are we now?" Parker asked contemplatively, which was a look that normally never crossed his twin's face. Parker was the impulsive twin, the act-now-think-later one who never backed down and rarely apologized for what he did if he thought it was right. And most times Parker thought he was right.

Preston was the thinker, the overanalyzer who once upon a time had a wild streak that he'd seemed to temper over the years.

"We're back where we started. In the small town that we were all born in. The town all but one of us hurried to get away from," he told his brother.

With a nod, Parker asked, "Yeah, but is that good or bad?"

Preston didn't answer because he was drinking more juice.

Parker continued, "I miss Gramma like I never thought I'd miss anybody in my life. I mean, when Dad died that was tough. We hadn't even been gone from Sweetland that long when he got sick. It hurt like hell that he was gone, but Quinn was there."

"Then Mom left," Preston added. It was a cold statement of fact that neither of them could dispute, yet it never failed to rattle him. Patricia Cantrell was not meant to be a mother and a wife. She hated the small town of Sweetland, despised the closeness of Mary Janet and her son Clifford, and blamed everyone in her life, including her six children, for all the unhappiness she'd endured. So the day after her husband of twenty-two years was buried, she'd packed up all her clothes and climbed into her car, driving herself right out of Sweetland and out of her children's lives forever.

Well, not necessarily forever. They'd all been invited to her wedding eight years later. She'd remarried on a private beach near Turks & Caicos, to a real estate mogul who had the money and the prestige to keep her entertained for the rest of her life.

That had been the last time Preston had seen or spoken to his mother. The last time he'd given Patricia any kind of thought or space in his life.

"And now Gramma's gone," Parker continued, snapping Preston out of his reverie. "It seems surreal that she had cancer and didn't tell anybody."

"Michelle had to know something was wrong. She saw her every day, how could she not know?" This was a question that Preston had been grappling with for weeks now.

Parker was already shaking his head. "Gramma didn't tell her, either. She only told Mr. Sylvester, and she swore him to secrecy. I can see her doing that. You know how Gramma was, and nobody dared go against what she said."

Yes, Preston knew his grandmother. He knew there was nothing he would not have done for her. Okay, yes, there was something he didn't do. She'd wanted him to come home more often, wanted him to be a part of the legacy that belonged to all of them. But hadn't he helped her with the legal aspects of opening the B&B, hadn't he gone over all her contracts as if they were documents of national security? He'd come back to survey the addition of the restaurant and had provided her and Michelle with a crash course in human resources and Maryland's employment laws. He'd taken all their calls whenever there was a legal question and had come home every Thanksgiving and Christmas. He knew his grandmother's ultimate wish was to have all of them living back in Sweetland, but that wasn't something Preston had ever considered.

As he'd grown up in the small town where everybody knew everybody and their family, he'd realized how stagnant the lifestyle could quickly become. In Sweetland, you were born, you went to school, then you got a job. After the job, you were married to someone else who'd been born in Sweetland and went to school there. Next came the house and the children. And the cycle continued. He knew that song and dance very well and had vowed to live his life differently.

So while he also knew his family had been brought up cherishing things like loyalty and responsibility, he felt that where his grandmother and this town were concerned, he'd done his part.

Funny thing was, the guilt sitting in his chest like another organ hadn't figured that out yet.

"We should have been here. She shouldn't have died in that room alone with all of us scattered across the United States," Preston declared.

"The world," Parker corrected. "Savannah was in Milan when she died."

"Thanks for the clarification," was Preston's stony retort.

Savannah was a model. She traveled more frequently than any of the other siblings, and she'd needed Gramma the most. Each day Preston was in Sweetland he paid close attention to his youngest sister, watching the way she grieved, the way she now lived, and wondered—as he tended to do with females—at the secret she was harboring.

"We've got to move on," Parker said, reaching for a napkin and wiping his fingers. "Onward, forward, keep your head up and your back straight. Cantrells never break."

Preston smiled at the mantra their grandmother had instilled in them from the time they'd learned to walk.

"You're right," he agreed with a smile. "That's exactly what she'd tell us."

"You're a great attorney," Parker told him as he stood up and took his cup to the sink.

Preston was a little startled by that compliment. "What makes you say that?"

He'd just rewrapped the plate of ham when his brother shut off the water and came back to clap a hand on his shoulder.

"You shifted my cross-examination of why you were upstairs, and who you were steering clear of, to another topic entirely. Lucky for you I'm a great detective and I never forget a single detail."

Parker laughed as he limped out of the kitchen, leaving Preston to smile at his retreat. Parker Cantrell was a great detective, and he did keep details in his mind as if a Rolodex or a small computer had been implanted there. But in this instance he was wrong: There was nothing to tell about the reason he'd been upstairs or the fact that he thought it might be best to steer clear of one pretty tempting female.

Heaven Montgomery was not for him. She was here for his puppy and that's all. No probing, no interrogating, no more thought was necessary. It was simple, she was simple.

She was, as he thought that night when he finally lay down to go to sleep, simply irresistible.

She was an idiot.

But thumping her head against the tile of the shower wasn't going to change that fact. It was going to give her a headache if she didn't call it quits. And so she did, because Heaven Montgomery was nothing if not a fighter.

Her therapist had told her that, and strangely enough she'd believed it. Still, months later her nerves were as frayed as they had been immediately following the accident. It probably would have been simpler if the explosion had left her with physical injuries instead of the emotional turmoil she'd been thrust into.

Warm water sluiced over her naked skin, relaxing tense muscles and conjuring images of one sexy-as-hell puppy owner who right about now probably thought she was a basket case. Closing her eyes, she imagined the lathered cloth moving sensuously over her body with his hands. Strong hands that didn't appear to be strangers to hard work even though he had a corporate-mogul look.

He would be firm and aggressive with his lovemaking, taking complete charge of the situation, of her. And she would let him. Of course that wasn't her nature, or at least she didn't want that to be her nature. She wanted to take charge, to be assertive. Maybe she would be the aggressor and put her hands on him first. Her fingers tingled at the thought of possibly moving over his naked body, feeling sculpted muscles, touching taut skin.

The vivid and tempestuous thoughts had her gasping. And that brilliant act had her swallowing water, as her head had been tilted back beneath the shower spray. Coughing,

Heaven inwardly cursed her stupidity again. By the time she stepped out of the shower she'd regained most of her composure and headed out into her room to figure out what she was going to do for clothes for the remainder of the weekend. It was no real surprise that the airline had yet to contact her about her misplaced luggage. But there was no way she could wear the same clothes for the duration of the weekend, especially since yesterday's outfit was probably still wet. She was just about to settle herself into thinking of a plan B when Savannah Cantrell gave a quick knock and entered her room with a picture-perfect smile and the kind of stunning beauty at the crack of dawn that made women like Heaven want to slap women like her.

"Good morning," Savannah said brightly. "I've come to help you with your dilemma."

Because this woman whom she'd only met yesterday knew the list of dilemmas Heaven kept in her mental Rolodex. Not!

"Ah, good morning, Savannah. What dilemma would you be referring to?"

A little self-conscious, especially when Savannah moved like a dancer, showing off her gorgeously toned body in very fitted capris and a halter top, Heaven pulled the towel tighter around her naked body.

"That one," she said with a nod toward said towel. "You need clothes, right? The airline lost your bags, which is a likely story. That just means one of their dim-witted staff members probably got sticky fingers and wanted to take a look-see before giving the bags back to you. That's happened to me more times than I can count. But I've given them so much hell over it, three airlines have upper management personally handle all my baggage from the time I arrive at the airport and then have it delivered to the hotel at my destination."

After all that Heaven could only nod. She was absolutely certain that Savannah could cause a great fuss over her missing luggage. Heaven, on the other hand, was patiently—well, not so patiently—waiting to hear back from them.

"I was just thinking I need to get to a store. Is there a mall close by?"

Savannah laughèd. Like the bend-over-and-hold-your-stomach type of laugh that Heaven usually only experienced when watching a Vince Vaughn movie.

When she could talk, her response was, "This is Sweetland, Heaven. There are one thousand, one hundred and five people in this town. It says so on the big sunflower-shaped sign that marks your entrance into this Mayberry-like patch of land. There's one grocery store and three cops, total. So the answer to your question is, hell no, there's no mall close by. If there was I'd spend the majority of my days there instead of walking around here like Michelle's kitchen slave."

Okay, that may have been way more than Heaven actually needed to hear. A yes or no would have sufficed. But something told Heaven that Savannah wasn't a simplistic, yes-or-no type of person.

"So there's nowhere in town I can get some jeans and T-shirts?" she asked. "I really do not want to wear the same outfit for the next two days."

Savannah waved a hand. "Believe me, that's not an option any of us wants to explore."

Heaven frowned. She didn't know whether or not to be offended.

But before she could say another word, Savannah had gone to the door and stepped out into the hallway. When she came back she had an overnight bag, which she promptly carried to the bed and set in its center.

"In here are all the necessities to get you out of the

house for the day, or at least for a couple of hours. Delia
Kincaid owns a nice little shop with some really unique
pieces. She used to be an actress and lived in LA until
her boyfriend thought it was okay to start slapping her
around. I met Delia while I was on a job in Europe and she
was shooting a movie about five years ago. Anyway, since
then I've been to her shop at least twice a week. She keeps
great stock and her prices won't raise your blood pressure.
Even though the diamond studs in your ears tell me that
you're not unable to spend money freely. So once you get
dressed, we'll head into town and get you all fixed up."

Somehow Heaven had managed to follow that entire
diatribe while watching Savannah take things out of the
duffel bag. A blow dryer, a flat-iron, jeans, a T-shirt, a
makeup bag that was so full it looked as if it would burst,
and high-heeled sandals that she tossed back into the bag
after a glance down at Heaven's feet.

Heaven frowned. She'd always had large feet; her
height sort of dictated they be large or else she might topple
over. Passing a discreet look at Savannah's, she raised a
brow; they didn't look so small. Which meant Savannah
must have just decided she didn't want to share her shoes
after all, which was fine, she could just wear . . . what?

"Michelle washed and dried all your clothes," Savannah said, pulling a plastic bag out of the duffel.

It appeared she didn't want her stuff to touch Heaven's.
She was a peculiar one, and Heaven wasn't quite sure how
to take her at the moment. Yet it seemed like she genuinely wanted to help, or maybe she just wanted an excuse
to make another shopping trip. Something told Heaven
that Savannah Cantrell didn't need an excuse to do anything she wanted to.

"Your shoes might be a total loss, but she wiped them
out pretty good with thick towels. I'm a size nine but
looking at your flats I guess you prefer not to wear heels

all day. Delia has some great Italian leather ballet shoes. I wish I could wear them but I think my feet would protest if they weren't elevated all the time."

"I'd think they'd protest to the contrary," Heaven said with a sigh. "When I was in sixth grade I had a growth spurt. From that point on I was at least five inches taller than everyone my age. So you're right, heels were never really my friend."

Savannah nodded. "Did you ever consider modeling? Your height and body build are perfect for the runway. And I know girls who would pay good money for your naturally smooth skin and those cheekbones."

Heaven was astonished. Nobody had ever asked her that question before. And no, she'd never considering becoming a model. But she didn't have time to answer Savannah, who was already on to the next subject.

"Michelle's going to want me to do something around here if I hang out too long. So I'll just wait here while you dress, then we can sneak out together."

"Ah, okay," Heaven said, still not sure she wanted to go shopping but recognizing that she didn't have a lot of choice. "Um, I'll just be a minute."

Grabbing the clothes off the bed, the ones Savannah had given her, not the ones she'd had on yesterday, Heaven went back into the bathroom. While she dressed, she smiled, thinking that this must be what it was like to have a sister. When she was finished dressing and about to open the bathroom door, she concluded that she liked Savannah. She liked her a lot.

Chapter 5

Sylvester Bynum sat at one of the patio tables at Jana's Java Shop. He'd wobbled a bit trying to sit in the chairs, which were iron but nothing short of dainty. After propping his cane up against the railing to his back, he'd flipped through the menu that was in the peculiar shape of a coffee cup. Normally he would have taken his coffee at The Silver Spoon with Michelle pouring and asking him about his day. That had been his routine, one he sorely needed to change.

Mary Janet had been gone for going on two months now. It was time for him to move on. But Sylvester didn't have anyplace else to go. Sweetland had become his home the minute Mary Janet had let him stay at her inn, and when he'd fallen in love with her, his roots had been planted. He was here to stay.

So it stood to reason he needed to get out and get to know more people around town. Or not, he thought with a glance to the inside table closest to the window where Marabelle Stanley and Louisa Kirk sat each and every day. They looked out at Main Street talking about everybody that passed—and even some people who weren't around, he figured. With a grumble he looked away from the two old biddies and focused on Boudoir, the new dress shop where he spotted Savannah escorting a pretty new face inside.

He'd heard there was a guest at the inn, a female, Michelle had told him this morning as he'd headed out. She hadn't said a pretty, young female. Of course she was too young for Sylvester; then again, he wasn't looking at her for himself.

After a few moments he'd ordered his coffee. It was brought to him in a steamy hot mug and smelled better than any cup of java he'd ever had. He sat back in his chair to think on the new arrival in town and just how she would play into the still-sticky situation at the Cantrell home.

"This is cute and it's sexy," Savannah said, holding up a yellow dress with a bikini-top bodice and enough straps in the back to make Heaven feel just a bit dizzy.

"I don't think so," Heaven replied, moving to another rack that held T-shirts in an array of colors. "I just need something casual for tomorrow and Monday, then I'll be on my way home."

Savannah grabbed her by the shoulders, turning her so that she now faced her again. "Nonsense, casual is boring. Yellow is sexy and flirtatious," she told her while pushing the dress up to Heaven's body.

Heaven was more than a little uncomfortable as Savannah continued to push the dress over her chest and waist. "I really can't tell like this but I think it'll look hot on you. Here, hold this while I look for something else."

"But I just want jeans and a T-shirt," Heaven said quietly. "Maybe a pair of shorts."

Of course she was talking to herself. Savannah had already disappeared to another part of the store, undoubtedly looking for something else she thought was sexy and flirtatious—even though Heaven didn't have any reason to be either one of those things.

"Can I help you, ma'am?" asked a pretty female who looked to be in her early twenties. She smiled and displayed deep dimples in both cheeks.

Heaven returned her smile, feeling warmed by the openly sincere question.

"This is only a weekend trip. But the airline lost my bag. I wanted to get a hotel but the Cantrells offered me a room. Still, I don't have any clothes, so I guess I need to buy a few things." And she had no idea why she'd told this woman whom she didn't even know all this.

Shaking her head, Heaven continued, hoping to sound a little more like an adult than a babbling teenager. "Basically, I need clothes for the weekend."

"No problem, we have plenty of clothes here," was the woman's response. "I'm Delia. I own this shop and for the record, when I came to town it was supposed to be for a weekend as well. I've been here almost four years now. So good luck with trying to leave on Monday."

Delia, the ex-movie-star—Heaven should have known. Actually, she should have remembered, since Savannah had told her not even an hour ago. Looking at her now, Heaven thought she might just recall her being in one of those Vince Vaughn movies she loved to watch. Delia was a couple of inches shorter than Heaven's five foot nine. He hair was cut short, almost to the scalp around the sides, and spiked with red frosted tips on top. She wore a tiny dress, much like the one Savannah had draped on Heaven, in a fire-engine-red color that only highlighted her daring hairstyle. Watching her move quickly through the racks, grabbing items and tossing them over her arm, all the while chatting about colors and fabrics in a happy little voice, made Heaven uncomfortable.

Actually, it caused an ache in the pit of her stomach. Something like longing overcame her, and she wondered what she should say or do next.

"Hey, Delia, I see you've met Heaven. She's our guest at The Silver Spoon, and we need to spice her up a bit," Savannah said when she almost collided with Delia in front of a rack full of bathing suits that Heaven was almost positive she did not need.

Especially since she and a tall handsome male she did not wish to name had already taken a dip in the river, fully dressed.

"She's gorgeous, Savannah. Thanks for bringing her into Boudoir. I'm sure we have lots of nice things that will suit her," Delia replied.

"She'll need a nice dinner dress, too. Not too fancy but something that maybe dips here, maybe a split there," Savannah was saying, dragging her fingers down the front of her chest, then up the back of her right leg.

Heaven's head swam as the two conversed about her as if she weren't even there. Until finally, she felt enough was enough.

She snatched two pairs of jeans off a rack and two T-shirts, then marched to the counter that was a pink-tinted glass confection with glitter evenly dispersed. Atop it was a gleaming silver bell, which Heaven unceremoniously smacked three times. "I'm ready to check out now," she called to Delia without even turning to face her.

Delia hurried over, still conversing with Savannah, whom Heaven suspected was coming over to survey her purchases.

"Okay." Savannah began picking up the items Heaven had placed on the counter. "These are fine. But she'll also take these."

With that she dumped lingerie, nightgowns, and that yellow dress onto the two outfits. And just when Heaven was about to object, Delia dropped a slinky little black dress atop.

"Perfect! I'll ring everything up. Cash, check, or credit?" she asked Heaven.

It was on the tip of her tongue to tell both of them to butt out and put all the things besides the two jean outfits back. Okay, well, she did need underwear so she'd keep that. And it probably made sense to have a nightgown so she wouldn't be forced to sleep in said underwear and nothing else. But she definitely did not need the two dresses, or the strappy sandals that Savannah had not-so-discreetly pushed under the pile of clothes. She just did not need all of this. She was only here to pick up a puppy and . . .

It's okay to live, Heaven. You were saved from that explosion for a reason.

Her therapist's words replayed in her head, and Heaven sighed heavily.

"Charge," was her begrudging reply.

"I thought you needed a ride back to the house," Preston said when he'd parked his SUV at the corner of Main and Maple Streets and stood talking to Sylvester Bynum, his late grandmother's boyfriend.

Sylvester shrugged his thin shoulders. He wore overalls even though it was inching toward ninety degrees. His shirt was bright orange with the number 33, which was partially hidden by the bib of the overalls. On his head was an Orioles hat, which matched the Eddie Murray shirt. His weathered skin looked shiny today, probably from the humidity, and he held tight to his cane in his right hand.

"Maybe I'll just walk. Decorations are starting to go up for the Bay Day celebration. I like to see the progress," he told Preston in an absent voice.

But Preston knew better. There was nothing absent about Mr. Sylvester. He was as spry and alert as any teenager walking these streets. He had an introspective type of personality and a wisdom that Preston figured only came with age.

"Mr. Sylvester, you called the house and asked me to come and pick you up. I can take you home, especially since it's getting pretty hot out here."

"Nah, I'm gonna walk and see the sights," Sylvester told him. "Might wanna do the same yourself."

Preston was the one to shake his head now, watching the traffic as Mr. Sylvester had stepped off the curb into the street. No cars were coming; traffic was as slow in Sweetland as the town itself. The cobblestones on Main were enough to slow any driver down, but even the side streets only saw a few cars per day. The people of Sweetland preferred to walk. Preston knew that. Hell, he'd walked these streets on many days himself. So he couldn't blame Mr. Sylvester. Still, he watched the old man as he passed Wicks & Wonders and then Boudoir, where he stopped to talk to . . .

Heaven had just walked out of the store with bags in hand. At that same moment Sylvester looked across the street, his smile as broad as the pink glittering BOUDOIR sign above the front door. Preston could only smile to himself as he realized just how spry and alert Mr. Sylvester actually was.

It took him just another minute to put aside the warnings to stay away from the woman before Preston was crossing the street himself. He was just going to offer to take her and Mr. Sylvester home, that's all. Innocent. Right?

"Shopping?" he asked the moment he stepped onto the curb and was face-to-face with Heaven once more.

She'd been smiling at something Mr. Sylvester said. It

was a pretty smile. A very pretty smile that did something even prettier to her eyes.

"Ah, yeah. I needed a few things," she replied before
clearing her throat.

She looked at the ground, then at the bags in her hand,
then nervously back up to him. Did he make her nervous?

"Let me take those," he offered and reached for her
bags.

Instantly she retreated, taking a step back almost too
quickly so that she stumbled a bit.

Before Preston could catch her, Mr. Sylvester had
stepped up, wrapping an arm around her waist and smiling at Preston. "This heat's something fierce today. The
lady looks a little thirsty."

"No, I'm fine," she said regaining her balance, her
cheeks flushed.

Preston couldn't tell if that was from the heat or if his
proximity made her more than nervous. He wanted to go
with the latter, but couldn't ignore the former.

"We can go down to the hot dog shop. They have a
great half lemonade, half iced tea. It'll cool you right
down," he told her. "I'll carry your bags for you."

He took the handle of the bag and she pulled her arm
back. "I can carry them. And I'm here with your sister, so
we'll just be going home now."

Nervous. Preston decided that he was definitely making her nervous. Which meant he should take a step back,
go back to his truck, go home, and work on his brief,
or . . . he could see just how nervous pretty Ms. Heaven
could get.

"Hey, gang's all here," Savannah said with her breezy
voice as she stepped out of the store. "Delia's going to
bring by some other things for you to try on, Heaven.
We're drinking and thinking tonight."

"Drinking and thinking?" Heaven asked with what looked like exasperation.

"Yeah, I'll explain later when the male species are gone. What's going on, Mr. Sylvester?" she asked, looping her arm in the older man's and dropping a kiss on his weathered cheek.

"Just hanging out, sweetie," Mr. Sylvester replied with a wink to Preston.

Preston shook his head, reminding himself to ask Mr. Sylvester not to call his baby sister "sweetie."

"Why don't you give an old man a ride home so I don't have to walk in all this heat?" he asked with a wiggle of his eyebrows.

"I told you I'd take you home," Preston told him once more. "I can give everyone a ride home and get Heaven a half and half. My truck's right across the street."

Savannah looked from Heaven to Preston, then smiled. "Ah, well, I was thinking about ice cream. How about you, Mr. Sylvester? Wouldn't you love an ice cream cone?"

"Orange sherbet in a cup with marshmallow on top," he replied. "Yes siree, that sounds nice and refreshing."

"Great, let's go," Savannah said, hooking her arm through his and turning away from Preston. Then she looked over her shoulder with her signature smile. "Preston, you take Heaven for her half and half and we'll catch up with you later."

Subtle, Preston thought to himself, undecided on whether to be ticked off or amused. They were both very subtle.

"Guess I'll need that ride now," Heaven said with a chuckle.

It almost sounded like a giggle, and she closed her mouth quickly as if it was a mistake. But Preston wanted her to do it again. It was ridiculous. He liked his women polished, sexy, submissive. Right?

"Can I carry your bags?" he asked this time and waited for her reply.

She looked down at the bags, then up at him, then shrugged. "Thanks," she said, handing the bags to him. "And I'd like to try that half and half, please?"

Chapter 6

In for a penny, in for a pound.

Heaven recited the words she'd heard her therapist say as she walked along what looked like a pier/shopping center with Preston.

She'd purchased almost three hundred dollars' worth of clothes she didn't need, after she'd come to this small town where she didn't know a soul to adopt a puppy to keep from dying a lonely old maid or having guilt simply eat away at her until she croaked—whichever came first. And she really wanted to dislike this man with the dreamy eyes and superstar swagger. But since he owned the bed-and-breakfast she was staying at, and owned the puppy she wanted to adopt, well, that wasn't going to work out, now, was it?

"How do you like it?" she heard him ask.

And she almost choked on the swallow she'd just taken. There were several answers to that question. How did she like the way he looked at her? She loved it, had always wanted a guy to look at her like he couldn't bear to turn away.

How did she like the way he smelled? It made her tingle

all over, and each time she inhaled she wanted to reach out and touch him.

"Heaven?"

"Hmmm?" she answered, still walking, still looking ahead at the way the brilliant sunlight fell onto the water.

"Am I really that boring?"

"What?" She looked at him then, saw the quizzical expression he was giving her. "I'm sorry, what did you say?"

"Which time?" he asked with a smile. "I asked if you liked your drink."

"Oh, yes. It's really refreshing."

He nodded. "Then I asked if I was boring you since you didn't seem to be paying attention to a word I said. I mean, it's okay if you want to be rude to the guy who's carrying your bags and just spent a whopping two dollars and twenty-five cents on the jumbo half and half to quench your thirst."

"Of course you're not boring me. I always talk while I'm drinking."

"And here I thought I was much more intriguing than a cup of juice."

"Good thing you don't get paid to think," she quipped. When he didn't immediately reply, she looked at him wondering if she'd gone too far.

She didn't have a lot of experience talking with men, outside of the lab that is. And when she did talk to them the mood was always so stuffy she hadn't dared crack a smile or a joke, for that matter.

"You're funny." He followed up with a chuckle that inspired her own smile.

"Thanks for the drink and for carrying my bags, and for giving me a ride back to the inn."

"Don't thank me for that yet, I'm still trying to decide if I'm taking you back there or if I'm going to find us a

nice cozy room with privacy so my siblings won't interrupt what I'm thinking of doing to you."

That stopped her instantly. People passed them on the
pier, two older women each with umbrellas in hand to
shield them from the sun and huge floral purses on their
arms.

"Hello, Preston, good to see you back in Sweetland,"
one of the ladies said.

"Hi, Ms. Daisy. Ms. Flora. It's nice to see you again,"
he replied and immediately turned back to Heaven. "Daisy
and Flora Huntington. They're also twins, the only other
set in Sweetland besides me and Parker. Isn't that something?"

Heaven nodded. "Right. Something." She cleared her
throat. "Can you go back to where you mentioned doing
something to me that required privacy."

Yeah, she really wanted to know what that "something"
was. Or did she?

"Here's the thing, Heaven. I don't normally mix business with pleasure, and I'm not into relationships. But—"

She shook her head. "But did I say I wanted to mix business with pleasure? I'm here to adopt your puppy, remember?"

Remember? Hadn't she just reminded herself of that
fact a couple of hours ago, before she bought all those
clothes and definitely before she accepted Preston's offer
of a drink and a ride home?

He didn't immediately respond—or maybe the step he
took until he was standing a breath away from her was his
response. Anyway, he reached up a hand to her face, and
Heaven instantly stepped back out of his reach.

He frowned, his brow wrinkling slightly. Then he moved
closer again and touched a wisp of hair, tucking it softly
behind her ear.

"It's what we're both being careful not to say that's

leading us in the direction of a nice comfortable bed Heaven," he told her in a soft voice.

"You are arrogant and presumptuous and way out o line, Mr. Cantrell."

"And I make you nervous, Ms. Montgomery."

"No," she replied, shaking her head.

"Yes, I do," he insisted. He lightly ran a finger over he cheek. "You feel the attraction between us but you don' know what to do about it."

"I don't plan on doing anything," Heaven retorted. Eve though her body was all but demanding she do *something* What, she wasn't quite sure.

"Fine. I like to be in control," were the last words sh heard him speak before he dipped his head and touche his lips to hers.

The first second or so she was in a daze, a luxurious cloud-filled abyss that cuddled and held her securely a his lips moved slowly over hers. Then instinct kicked i and she melted into the kiss, parting her lips and feelin the initial shock of heat that was his tongue scraping alon hers. That lovely heat swirled around in the pit of he stomach for what seemed like an endless amount of tim and then it was over.

Behind her there was a loud noise; something fell an broke and someone yelled. Then someone else yelled an the sounds echoed in Heaven's head, drowning out every thing else, including Preston's tasty kiss. Her heart ham mered in response, and she pushed away from him so fas her cup of half and half tumbled to the ground, liqui splashing onto her feet and the bottom half of her jeans Her hands and arms shook and the smell . . . smoke, acid fire . . . it was overwhelming this memory. Or was it he reality?

Chapter 7

Preston seethed. His back teeth clenched so hard he was either going to dislodge them or give himself a tremendous headache any moment now.

Walt Newsome who owned and managed The Crab Pot restaurant down at the pier had lost a very valuable shipment of lobster about ten minutes ago when one of his dockworkers slipped on the planks and upended eight very large crates. And being the brawny, cranky, sea-bred old bastard that only Walt could be, he'd cursed loud and long enough to have some of the locals shaking their heads, and the tourists pulling out their cell phones to record him.

Heaven, on the other hand, had startled again. She'd backed up so fast she almost ended up in the river, right alongside most of the lobsters that had escaped to safety. Of course he'd reached out to catch her, yet again. And whether by habit or simple instinct she pulled away from him, this time running away as if one of the remaining lobsters might be chasing her. Preston hadn't chased after her. She had no way back to the house but to ride with him—he suspected she didn't know her way to walk—so his guess was she'd end up at the truck waiting for him. He walked away, stopping briefly to make sure Walt didn' break the bones of his workers in his tirade.

When he'd arrived at the vehicle, just as he'd figured Heaven was there. The doors were locked so she stood against the passenger side, her forehead resting on the window. She looked deflated and his first instinct was to go and wrap his arms around her, to pull her close and assure her that all was well.

But that seemed awfully intimate, and Preston didn' know enough about her to assume that right. Sure, he' kissed her, a very delectable kiss, he might add. But even that lovely memory didn't override the sense that some thing bad had happened to her, something that had fright ened her and quite possibly hurt her physically. The thought that the particular "something" might have been a man made him angrier than he'd been in quite a long time. The fact that when he'd stepped up beside her, gently moving her to the side while he opened the door and watched her quietly slip into the seat, without once offering an explanation, pissed him the hell off. Because helpless ness was not a feeling Preston Cantrell was used to expe riencing.

"If you'd like, we could take Coco to the park for a while," he offered when the silence inside the truck wa threatening to drive him insane.

She shook her head and continued to stare out the window.

"Parker has one of those game systems. I don't know if you're the video game type, but there are a couple I'm pretty good at. You could join me or just watch me totally embarrass myself."

This time she inhaled deeply, only to let out a sigh that seemed pretty damned close to sounding depressed.

"Or we could sit by the water and talk about what has
you so frightened that the next time you hear a loud noise,
you might actually jump out of your skin," he said, trying
to hide his irritation.

"I just want to adopt a dog," she finally said. "Really,"
she added, grasping his arm, then pulling it back quickly.
She'd most likely realized that he was driving and pulling
on his arm when his hand was on the steering wheel probably wasn't the best idea.

"What I mean is that I came here to adopt a dog and
that's all I plan to do. On Monday I'd like to be on my way
home."

In other words, mind your damned business, Preston
surmised. Okay, that was fine with him. He didn't need to
know anything more about her. What he already knew—
that she was pretty and clearly a bundle of nerves, but
could kiss really well and felt like every bit of sunshine
in the sky as she'd been in his arms—was more than
enough.

"Right," he replied, pulling into the driveway beside
the restaurant. "I hope everything goes according to your
plan."

Turning off the ignition, Preston stepped out of the truck
and was about to walk around to the passenger side to open
her door when she'd already done so for herself.

"I'm going to my room. But I'd like to spend some
time with Coco later if that's all right with you?" she asked
and looked at him as if she fully expected him to say no.

"Sure. Michelle keeps them all kenneled in the basement. You remember the way?"

She nodded. He did the same and headed up the front
steps. He assumed she followed but didn't look back. Because looking back never solved anything. It wouldn't
bring his grandmother or his dad back, and it certainly

wouldn't make Heaven Montgomery answer questions she damned well didn't want to answer.

And who knew, that might be a good thing.

"Cordy said he kissed her. Right there in the middle of the dock they were kissing like the next step would be the bedroom," Nikki said, slapping her palms on the kitchen table before breaking into a nervous giggle that proved infectious. Mary Cordelia Brockington-Simmons—it was customary in Sweetland for the firstborn female in every family to carry the first name of Mary, after the wife of the town's founder, Buford Fitzgerald—was Nikki's older sister.

Savannah stomped her feet and let her head fall back as she laughed. Michelle clapped her hands and poured them each another glass of champagne.

"Preston kissing the pretty woman from Boston. Wow, what will happen in Sweetland next?" Michelle quipped and took another sip from her glass.

"It's kind of soon, don't you think? I mean, she just got here yesterday," Raine brought up with her sober and serious tone.

It didn't go over well because each of the three other females in the room looked at her like she'd grown another head.

"Love has no clock. It falls on top of you like a boulder whenever it damned well pleases," Nikki said, emptying her glass.

Six weeks ago Nikki had been named manager of The Silver Spoon. She'd also been accused of murder and swept off her feet by the solemn and studious Quinn Cantrell in the same time period. Now she was planning a Christmas wedding with her mother, sister, and soon-to-be in-laws.

"You are not allowed to rain on the drinking and

thinking night, no matter what your birth name is," Savannah slurred with a frown. She'd had more than her share of champagne but wasn't about to stop anytime soon.

They'd come up with the idea of drinking and thinking nights as a way for the females in the Cantrell house to get together and dump all their worries on one another. It had been Michelle's idea, one she'd been completely surprised that her sisters had agreed to. Having Nikki join them seemed only natural.

"I need to lie down," Savannah said and almost fell out of the chair as she struggled to stand, then sat again.

"You sure do," Nikki told her. "Let's move this party into the living room."

Minutes later they'd all found a spot in the living room, Michelle and Raine on the couch at opposite ends, feet up and tapping the other person on the thigh. Savannah had skipped the chairs altogether and stretched out on the rug-covered floor. Nikki sat in one of the high-backed Victorian chairs that added to the grandeur of the Queen Anne Victorian style of the inn.

"So he kissed her," Nikki continued. "We all know about Preston and Parker's reputation with the ladies. At thirty-three they've probably kissed millions of females by now. It might not mean a thing."

"And that's precisely why he shouldn't have done it," Raine added. "They should be tired of playing with females now and thinking more about settling down."

"The Double Trouble Cantrells settle down?" Nikki asked, then laughed. "That'll be the day."

Michelle shook her head. "No, I think Raine has a point. Kind of. I mean, they are older and we all have more responsibilities now. Wouldn't it be nice if Preston fell in love and got married like Quinn is doing?"

From the floor Savannah raised her arm as if she were

in class, but she didn't wait for the teacher to call on her to begin speaking.

"Wait a minute, Mary Michelle Cantrell Matchmaker." Her voice had begun to slur even more so her words sounded like mush and more mush. Nikki chuckled. Michelle frowned, as she'd probably managed to hear her name in the mix.

"Heaven doesn't even live in Sweetland. And your dream is for all of us to come home and stay home. You should know that might not happen," Savannah continued.

"But we're all still here," Raine added quietly. "The funeral was six weeks ago and all of us are still in Sweetland."

"But Savannah's right, Heaven doesn't live in Sweetland," Nikki added with a sad look to Michelle.

"When I was seventeen"—Michelle spoke softly—"I broke my leg ice-skating at Fitzgerald Park. The ice wasn't totally frozen, so not only did I fall—twisting my left leg in an unheard-of position—but I broke the ice and was stuck there for two hours while Mr. Brockington and his fire crew tried to get me out. I was in a hot pink cast up to my thigh and caught a terrible bout of pneumonia. I missed an entire month of school, and because I spent a lot of that time sleeping from Gramma's special hot tea concoction and the meds Dr. Stallings gave me, I couldn't do most of the makeup work they'd sent me. My third-quarter grades sucked big-time. So when I applied for the International Culinary College I thought for sure they'd never accept me. Sure, it wasn't an Ivy League school, but grades and attendance were still important. I worried from the moment I mailed that application off and every second afterward.

"And when my worry had finally turned into full-blown panic, complete with tears and hyperventilation, Gramma sat me down. We were out back, on that old bench, and she said, 'Anything is possible, Chelle. You have no idea what the good Lord's plan is so you just keep the faith and remember that anything is possible.'

The room was quiet as Michelle finished speaking.

"She always called you Chelle," Raine replied after a few seconds had passed.

"And she called you Sunshine because you were too bright to be considered a rainy day," Savannah added with a sniffle.

Nikki rubbed the edge of her wineglass, looking down at the movement of her hand. "She called you Vanna and used to laugh when *Wheel of Fortune* came on because you would parade around just like Vanna White."

"Oh yeah, I remember those days," Michelle quipped.

Soft laughter erupted then, a sort of connection lingering among the four women as they shared this memory. For the last ten minutes Heaven had been standing at the bottom of the stairs. Actually, she'd sat down, resting her head against the banister as she heard the ladies talking just beyond the foyer and didn't want to intrude.

They'd all known one another forever, and while it seemed each of them was vastly different, they were all connected by a familial bond that Heaven couldn't claim. Not only was she an only child, but her parents didn't seem to have a warm bone in their bodies. If they did she'd never seen it. Mary Janet Cantrell, or—as her grandchildren fondly called her—Gramma, must have been a very loving and caring woman. Everyone in this house had loved her and, as far as Heaven could tell, missed her intolerably.

There was no one in Heaven's life that she would ever miss like that, she was certain. As for the topic of their discussion, well, that made her nauseous. So much so she finally eased off the steps and tiptoed through the foyer and the front desk area of the inn to get to the kitchen, where she made her way out the back door.

The air was still thick with humidity as she walked down the steps, her bare feet touching the cool grass. After she'd come in from her shopping spree and yet another embarrassing moment in front of Preston, she'd showered and taken a nap. Dinner, thankfully, had been brought to her room by a smiling Michelle. She had no idea how the woman had known she wanted to be alone, but was thankful just the same.

Now she wanted air, she wanted to breathe, to rejuvenate herself. If she were at home in Boston she would have had a glass of wine and sat out on her balcony to a cooler evening and skyline filled with bright lights. Here, however, the gentle rustle of water in the distance, the steady creak of crickets, and the intermittent glow of lightning bugs offered another kind of solace.

Her heart was no longer racing as it had been earlier today on the pier, and again minutes ago when she heard her name mentioned with Preston's. His sisters had been talking about their kiss, no doubt, and if it were leading to some grand love affair. She'd almost wanted to run into that room screaming *Hell no!* She was not getting involved with Preston Cantrell.

Now she was calm as she walked toward the water's edge where just yesterday she'd taken an unplanned dip. Sitting on the rocks she pulled her knees up to her chest, wrapping her arms securely around them. Resting her chin on her knee, Heaven stared out to the water, thinking about her life and about her future.

Trying desperately not to think about the man with the great eyes, great body, mesmerizing scent, and killer lips

Until he spoke.

"I asked you if you wanted to sit out here and talk earlier," Preston said from behind her.

"I didn't want to talk then," was her instant reply. She didn't turn around, didn't have to.

He would be standing with his feet slightly parted, his muscled arms folded over an equally muscled chest. His face would be grim—not frowning, but just in that thoughtful look he liked to give. It didn't matter what he wore, she knew he would look good. Another reason she didn't bother to turn around.

"Do you want to talk now?"

"No."

"Then I'll just sit here with you and enjoy the scenery."

And without another word he did just that. There was maybe half a foot between them as Preston joined her on the rocks. He couldn't pull his long legs upward to match her position, so they stretched out in front of him, bare from the knee down because he'd changed into shorts and a T-shirt. Basketball-type shorts that hung baggy around his thighs, but did nothing to hide their sculpted form, or the light dusting of hair on his calves. Another quick side glance showed that his shirt fit him well—too well. Her mouth watered slightly at the sight of his biceps bulging from beneath the sleeve.

"Where's Coco?" she asked because she desperately needed her mind to be on something else besides how good this man looked without even trying.

"In her kennel," was his bland reply.

"Is that where you always keep her? I read that Labs need lots of exercise and love to play. It can't be good that you keep her kenneled up all the time."

He was quiet for a moment, looking straight ahead just as she was. Then he took a deep breath and released it.

"I took her to the park earlier and we played for almost two hours. I also walked her right after dinner so she could do her business and get a bit more exercise for the day. I know how to take care of my dog," he told her in no uncertain terms.

Really? Was she destined to embarrass herself in front

of this man? Maybe she could just get up and go back into the house, lock herself in her room until Monday morning when it was time for her to leave. No. That would be running, and Heaven was really tired of doing that.

"Sorry. I didn't know."

"It's okay. When you don't know, you ask. I answered. No big deal," he told her with a shrug.

"Must be nice to lead such a simple life," she quipped.

"My life's not simple."

That thought hadn't occurred to her. Probably because she shouldn't care; this wasn't a trip about meeting a man and getting to know him better. It was about her progress, her rebirth after the explosion that didn't kill her, but just might have killed the career she'd worked so hard to build.

"You have a great family. This inn is beautiful, and everyone in town seems to know and respect the Cantrells."

"That's not my life. I live in Baltimore City. I'm in court or at my office more than I'm in my apartment. I'm perfectly capable of taking care of my grandmother's puppy and giving him every bit of love and dedication that she did."

"But you don't want to?" He hadn't said that, but she could tell that's where he was going. She wondered why anyone would not want all this.

"I'm not cut out for small-town life. That's why I left. It's really simple, I don't want to come back. I don't want to do what everyone here does."

"So why are you here if it's not where you want to be?"

"Responsibilities. I've been raised not to ignore them," he told her then turned to look at her. "Why are you here, Heaven Montgomery?"

She'd also been raised not to ignore responsibilities, but that's exactly what she was doing by being in Sweetland. She wondered at the irony between them. "I'm here to adopt your puppy."

"Why? Aren't there puppies where you live?"

"I live in Boston. In a condo that overlooks the city. It's a great place to live, and it's only about thirty minutes from the lab where I work. Or worked," she corrected. "Sweetland is different."

"So you're unemployed now?"

Heaven shook her head, afraid she'd said too much. She didn't want to talk about her life in Boston, the life she was desperately trying to change.

"I just need to get a dog, that's all. I'll be just fine when this entire adoption process is complete."

He picked up a small stone and tossed it out to the river. It skipped along the top of the water three times before sinking down with a plop.

She couldn't help it, she smiled.

"Can you teach me how to do that?"

Looking at him then, she could almost ignore how his eyes glittered in the moonlight. Almost.

"You want me to teach you how to skip rocks?" he asked. "Because you don't want to talk about your life in Boston or why you're really here in Sweetland."

It was a starkly honest question, centered in a statement that she couldn't actually refute. She'd heard how good an attorney he was and figured this was just a glimpse of what it was like to be cross-examined by him in a court of law.

Whatever it was, Heaven was determined not to over-analyze it. She wanted to learn to skip rocks and that was all. If he could teach her, so be it. His assessment could be correct.

"You're absolutely right. Very smart of you to observe, counselor. Now," she said, standing and pulling at the shorts she'd just purchased this morning that were a little shorter than she'd expected. "Are you going to teach me or not?"

His eyes followed her every movement, up as she stood, down again as her hands moved to the hem of her shorts, settling there for long enough to make her nipples hard. Then he stood and smiled, and caused a reaction in her she didn't want to verbalize, not even in her own head.

Ignore it and it will go away, she warned herself.

"I'll teach you anything you want," he answered when he stood just a breath away from her. "Anything you want, Heaven."

How could she ignore his scent that permeated every crevice of her body, warming her as it filtered throughout? How could she ignore his gaze so intense her knees shook? How could she ever expect to ignore this man and go back to her previous life and the job that had almost killed her?

Chapter 8

"We're looking pretty good moneywise," Quinn said, not bothering to look up from his desk.

He'd moved the desk into Nikki's office, directly facing hers. Considering they'd be married in the next six months and both of them were managing the inn, Preston figured it made sense. Except the office was too small for two desks and two chairs and file cabinets and the kennel they had set up in there for Sweet Dixi, the Lab that Quinn had inherited.

"And all the bills are up to date?" Preston asked from his perch by the window where he looked out at the dogs running around in the yard.

"Everything is on time. Except Walt. Michelle just made a huge purchase from him two days ago for the crab feast that's booked for tonight," Quinn continued, his fingers tapping rhythmically over the keyboard to his laptop.

It was still kind of weird to see his older brother in this tiny office, sitting behind a desk, his attention focused on a computer instead of a patient. Quinn was a renowned oncologist who'd had a very successful career back in Seattle before their grandmother's passing. He'd given all that up for Nikki Brockington, whom Preston absolutely adored. Now his brother ran the local medical center since Doc Stallings was getting ready to retire and move to Florida with his longtime office assistant/girlfriend. On the surface Preston could see the logic of Quinn's decision. He was the older brother, the most responsible of them all, and from what Quinn had told them he'd been disenchanted with his job long before he'd come back to Sweetland. So the transition seemed to be a good one for him.

Preston, on the other hand, wondered if he would have been able to pull something like that off himself. His career was at its peak; he and his partner were making more money than Preston could have ever imagined. His life in Baltimore was exactly what he'd wanted all his life. It was a big city versus this small town, with its ideals of happily-ever-after and nosy-beyond-reason citizens. And for Preston, that was enough.

"I still can't believe Inez and Hoover King were swindling the townsfolk for extra taxes and fees," Parker brought up.

He was sitting in the chair behind Nikki's desk, playing with the fuzzy lime-green stress ball she kept next to her phone. He'd heard it was for when she talked to her mother or anyone from the women's auxiliary that Odell Brockington led. For Parker, it just seemed to be something to do.

"Inez was the brains behind the scam. Nikki's still trying to figure out how Inez got mixed up with her ex Randy and his money-laundering scheme as well," Quinn added.

Preston remembered Randy Davis's murder in Easton and the cops who had come to Sweetland accusing Nikki of killing him. As it turned out Randy had been murdered by some big-time loan shark from New York, but that was after he'd made a contact in Sweetland.

"I can't believe Hoover didn't get any jail time," Parker said.

"Not enough evidence to convict him of any crime," Preston added with a shrug.

"His only crime was loving the wrong woman and spending too much time with a bottle in his hand," Quinn added. "And speaking of loving women."

"Nobody was speaking of loving women but you, Quinn," Parker joked. "You're the only one of us crazy enough to take that kind of plunge."

"I'm the only one smart enough to know a good thing when I see it," Quinn replied. "And from what I hear another one of us might have a good thing staring right at him as well."

It was the instant silence that grabbed Preston's attention. He'd been staring at the dogs; then his attention had drifted to the water and the spot where he and Heaven had stood last night while he taught her to skip rocks. It had gone as well as teaching a female a generally male pastime could go. Actually he'd been thinking more about the sound of her laughter when she finally got it to work and the look of contentment as she continued on.

"Town's already abuzz with the news. What do you have to say about that, Preston?"

"What?" he turned asking Parker. "What do I have to say about what?"

Quinn chuckled. "First sign you're slipping is the memory loss."

"Second sign is gazing off and ignoring an important business meeting to daydream," Parker added, which only increased Quinn's laughter.

"I heard everything you jerks had to say. We're okay

on all the bills, even the property taxes that Inez tried to use to foreclose on the inn. Quinn and Nikki are doing a fine job managing the place, and business couldn't be better. See, I heard everything."

"You even heard the part about you kissing that pretty newcomer in the middle of town. Right?" Quinn asked, looking up at him from his keyboard.

Preston shrugged. "Pure impulse."

"Ha! That's my forte," Parker told him. "You mean to tell me you didn't ask her in that smooth and charming way of yours if you could have a kiss?"

Preston shook his head. "Didn't want to wait for her answer," he admitted, a small smile creeping up.

"That's my brother," Parker added, raising his hand for a high five.

Preston moved, albeit a bit reluctantly, to slap his brother's palm. He had thought about kissing Heaven before he'd actually done it. Actually, he'd been thinking of nothing else since he'd opened that door and she'd basically fallen into his arms. And the truth was he didn't want to ask her for the kiss, because he didn't want her to consider the option of saying no. Not because she didn't want it. Preston felt the attraction buzzing between them as if it were a live beehive. And he was almost positive Heaven felt it as well; she just didn't accept the inevitable as easily as he did.

"So you kissed her, now what?" Quinn asked.

"What's that supposed to mean?" Preston followed up, staring from one brother to the next.

Parker raised a hand. "Wait a minute, you telling me you don't know what comes after kissing a woman? You're killing our reputation, man, just killing it," he guffawed.

"Shut up," Preston joked. "Nobody's damaging our reputation. I just kissed her, that's all. She's not staying in Sweetland. She's going home tomorrow."

"After she adopts Coco," Quinn said slowly.

Preston sighed. It had been his original thought to keep her from adopting the puppy, or to stall the process at least. That way she would stay here longer. After last night he wasn't so sure about that plan. When she talked about why she'd come to Sweetland she'd sounded so sincere, like adopting Coco was definitely going to save her life in some way. He didn't have the heart to keep that from her.

"Right, after she adopts Coco," he said solemnly.

He didn't want the dog. Like he'd told her, it wasn't because he couldn't take care of it, because he could. There was nothing stopping him from buying a house outside of the city, but close enough that he could still commute to work. That would most likely be in one of the counties immediately surrounding Baltimore. His caseload was hectic and would no doubt continue to increase as long as he stayed in criminal law. So financially he was ripe to purchase a home. But that felt annoyingly like subscribing to the mandated life plan that came with living in Sweetland.

"Gramma wanted us to keep the puppies, and she wanted us all to stay in Sweetland," Quinn said with a sort of finality.

Because Quinn was the oldest, more often than not the siblings looked to him to make the tough family decisions. Michelle liked to believe she was the head of the family, and a lot of times Quinn would side with her, but ever since their father passed Quinn had been the man of the Cantrell clan.

"My job is in Baltimore," Preston said. "And so is yours," he added with a glance in Parker's direction so that it didn't seem like this portion of the conversation was all about him, even though he was certain that's the way it was leaning.

"Things change," was Quinn's simple response to both of them.

"We're so understaffed," Raine said in a huff.

"It's going to be fine," Nikki replied, reaching behind her back to tie the brand-new black apron with THE SILVER SPOON in script letters above an actual silver spoon on the front bib.

This was the new logo for the inn and restaurant that she and Michelle had discussed for the last four weeks. Quinn's approval had come after a candlelight dinner and night of lovemaking that had left both of them a little dreamy afterward. The new sign had been hung out front a week ago; new menus had been printed, and now the aprons. Mary Janet would certainly be proud.

"One hundred and ten people will be in the dining room of the restaurant in about twenty-five minutes. We have three people to serve while Michelle stays in the kitchen supervising the food. How is that going to be okay?" Raine continued with her mini tirade.

"Parker is here and he's volunteered to serve as the host. He'll direct everyone to tables, bathrooms, et cetera. Two Williams family members will be at the door to take tickets, and the rest of the Williams clan will file in afterward. Everything is buffet-style except for the crabs. Fifteen tables divided by the three of us gives each of us five tables to serve."

Raine gasped. "Five!"

Nikki simply rolled her eyes. Normally, Savannah was known as the emotional, temperamental Cantrell. Raine was the quiet, reserved one. Today, however, was not a good day for Raine to try to take Savannah's place.

"I can help," Heaven said in a low voice.

It wasn't that she hoped nobody would hear her; she

had really meant to volunteer. All morning she'd played with Coco, courtesy of someone knocking on her door around nine AM and leaving the puppy sitting there with an adorably innocent look on its face. Their time had gone uninterrupted, which she hadn't really anticipated since this house always seemed to be brewing with people.

Now Coco was happily enjoying the company of her mother and siblings and Heaven had nothing else to do. Sitting in her room alone only gave her time to think, which really was beginning to be a daunting pastime since the thoughts were starting to revolve entirely around Preston Cantrell.

"Great!" was Nikki's excited response. "Stay right here, I'll go get you an apron. Don't move and don't change your mind," she ordered Heaven.

The smaller woman with her head full of riotous curls and smiling face was really nice. In fact, all of the females in this household had been nothing but nice to her. The brothers, too, for that matter, with the exception of Preston. He ran hot and cold and somewhere in between, which was what he was last night by the water. He'd been patient with her, talking in a soothing, not condescending tone as he taught her, of all things, how to skip rocks. Never in Heaven's years at private schools, etiquette training, college, grad school, or working at the lab and mingling in her parents' society circles had she thought of skipping rocks in a river on a hot summer's night.

But it had been one of the most engaging moments of her life.

"Have you ever worked in a restaurant before?" asked Raine, who wore black slacks, a white shirt, and an adorable apron.

"No. I'm a biochemist. I normally stay cooped up in a lab for about twelve hours a day," she said, trying to ignore how dreadfully dull that sounded.

"Sounds intriguing," Raine added with a nod. "I'm a teacher. But for the last few weeks I've been a waitress, a maid, a hostess, a dog walker, and whatever else Michelle could find for me to do."

The words might have sounded like a complaint, but Heaven noted a light in Raine's eyes as she spoke that said she wasn't totally dissatisfied.

"All things you wanted to be in your next lifetime?" she asked jokingly.

Raine laughed. Her elegantly arched brows rose a little, her already high cheeks lifted a little higher, and her lips spread in a wide grin. She was astonishingly pretty even though you wouldn't notice it right away because she hardly ever smiled.

"Okay, I'm here," an exasperated voice sounded as Savannah entered the room.

This sister was more than used to smiling. Heaven had thought she'd recognized her the evening after they first met, and while she'd been online checking her emails the next morning she'd seen a perfume ad with none other than Savannah Cantrell gloriously draped over a suede sofa wearing a gorgeous black gown.

"Great, now there are six of us. Heaven's going to help out," Raine told a questioning Savannah.

"Wow, we're putting the guests to work now," Savannah quipped. "Welcome aboard, Heaven."

Heaven smiled and figured it wouldn't be so bad.

Three hours later every part of her body hurt—from her neck, which just seemed stiff, to the toes that screamed for mercy in the sandals she'd come downstairs in before she knew she'd be standing on her feet all day. She smelled like crab, which might not have been so bad if she'd had a chance to at least taste the spicy crustacean. A hot shower and her bed were what she was looking forward to after barely escaping the females in the kitchen, who were finished putting away food and cleaning but thought it was entertaining to sit around the island and share their sandwiches and coffee. Heaven felt as if she'd shared more than enough today. Besides, she needed to get up early tomorrow morning to head over to the adoption place and finalize all the paperwork. Then she'd be on her way home, to Boston.

On her way back to the memories—the inquisition, as she should probably call it. Investigators were still poring over her office and her private papers, she knew. The suspicion was still on her. She'd caused the explosion; she'd almost killed herself but had succeeded at killing the lab assistant and janitor who had been in the lab that fateful day six months ago. Ultimately, she'd cost Larengetics Pharmaceuticals millions of dollars in research and lost donations for their cure to Alzheimer's.

So why was she in a hurry to go back again?

Thoughts followed her like lost pets as she walked up the stairs. Entering her room, her shoulders slumped, not just from the strain of working manually for the last couple of hours, but from carrying all the guilt she thought she'd earned. After her shower she climbed into bed, ignoring the bologna-and-cheese sandwich she'd taken from Michelle and opting to bury her head beneath the covers instead. Denial had been her friend for so long, she didn't know how to abandon it.

And even more hours later Heaven was still awake and the covers over her head had been replaced by dried-up tears that made her cheeks feel stiff. Her mouth was dry and her head hurt, along with all the other aches and pains she was still experiencing. Still, she wondered why she wasn't asleep, almost berated herself for not at least being able to do that correctly.

From the nightstand her cell phone vibrated. It was late, just after midnight, so she was more than a little alarmed by the intrusion. Reaching for it she saw through the lighted screen that it was her mother, or her father, since it was the main number to their Beacon Street home.

"Hello?" she answered hastily.

"Heaven, dear, it's your mother."

Of course it was her. Opaline Montgomery, Boston's most elite and upstanding socialite.

"Hi, Mom. It's really late, is everything all right? Is Dad okay?" she asked, worry prickling against the pain in her temples.

"He's fine, and I know what time it is. We just came in from the Frostburgs' dinner party. You know they have this every year. Johanna was a bit perturbed by your absence. Her impending nuptials were announced."

Really? Heaven prayed this wasn't what her mother had called her in the middle of the night to tell her. Actually, if her father was all right, there really was no reason Opaline should be calling her at this time. Except that for Opaline, whatever she deemed important, at whatever time, came first, no questions asked.

"Great. I hope she and Daniel will be very happy together." Even though together they made the most boring couple Heaven had ever met.

"We should be planning a wedding of our own. A summer wedding would be best and just about a year to plan. Geoffrey's proposal still stands. I spoke to him last week, and he's willing to take you back."

Geoffrey Billingsley could barely stand himself. He was a forty-five-year-old financial wizard whose bank account tended to drown out the fact that he was an alcoholic with a pretty abusive nature when provoked, and when not. He'd proposed to Heaven at her parents' annual New Year's Eve party—it seemed everyone in Opaline's social circle had a specific time of year they hosted their signature parties. The explosion happened one week after that. She hadn't heard from or seen Geoffrey since.

"He can't take back what he never had," she replied drily.

"Nonsense. You know what I mean."

"Is this what you called for, Mom?" Because if it was, she was so tempted to hang the damned phone up in her ear.

"Don't be rude, Heaven. You know that will not be tolerated."

Don't be anything, Heaven—don't be yourself, don't be adventurous, don't be courageous or even independent for that matter—it will not be tolerated.

"Mother, it's late. I was asleep. Please tell me what this call is about?" See, not rude, just like the dutiful daughter was supposed to speak to her overbearing and controlling mother.

"I want you to come home. *We* want you to come home. Geoffrey has agreed to come to the house for dinner on Wednesday. Your father has canceled his meetings, and I've rearranged my foundation luncheon to get prepared. Now, I want you home by Tuesday night. We need to pick out your dress and get you ready to receive Geoffrey."

Like Geoffrey was the prize of the century she should be ecstatic to accept.

"No."

The word slipped from her lips before Heaven could reconsider it, or rephrase it, or simply not say it.

"Excuse me?"

Right. Wrong response.

"I'm in Maryland and I won't be home until the end of the week." Yes, it was a lie, but her mother didn't need to know that. And Heaven did not want to see Geoffrey or accept his dismal wedding proposal.

"What in God's name are you doing in Maryland? You're supposed to be resting at home. Isn't that what your doctor ordered?"

"No. It's not. I'm actually doing exactly what my doctor ordered." Not that her mother gave a damn about what anybody besides herself ordered Heaven to do.

"I'm not talking about that quack you insist on seeing. She does not have a medical degree."

"She's a licensed counselor and she's helping me."

"She's helping you spend your money. Which is in effect my money."

Right, Opal Montgomery never let anyone forget that she was a wealthy woman. Not even her daughter.

"I've never touched my trust fund. I am a successful biochemist and I make a good salary."

"Do not act offended when I state the obvious. Furthermore, we can have this discussion another time. Call me tomorrow with your flight information and I'll send Jiles to pick you up at the airport."

"There is no need. I will not be returning to Boston until Friday."

"Geoffrey is not available on Friday."

Great!

"That's when I'm returning, Mother. I'll talk to you later," Heaven said. "Good night."

But she didn't dare hang up yet.

"Heaven, this is not acceptable. Your insolence is causing a dreadful headache. I will call you in the morning, and we can take a look at available flights. Get some rest. Frown lines and circles beneath your eyes will not impress Geoffrey."

And with that Opal disconnected the call. Without a "good night," without a "how are you my only child who has endured a traumatic event," nothing.

Heaven wasn't surprised.

Chapter 9

"A preliminary hearing and two DUIs are all you have for the upcoming week. I can take them for you if you need to stay with your family. Of course, if we act on my idea of hiring a couple of associates to help balance out our workload, we'd both be able to have some semblance of a life."

Joseph Baskerville always had a solution. No matter what the problem, he could fix it, and if he couldn't he found someone who would—prime example, the not-so-subtle suggestion of hiring associates he'd been making to Preston for the last couple of months.

Joe had graduated first in his class at Harvard, under-grad and law school, and while he'd been born and raised in Boston, the gritty streets of Baltimore had called to him. That and the six-foot blonde with double-D-sized breasts whom he'd met in the Bahamas the weekend he'd passed the bar and followed back to the city with the mis-guided hope of marrying. Years later he turned out to be the best partner Preston could have ever hoped for.

"They all seem to be doing just fine," Preston said, thinking about his family. Michelle and the girls had pulled off a very successful crab feast while he and Quinn had visited The Marina Resort and the owners, the Redling brothers. Yates Passage, which was located about ten miles from Main Street and the center of Sweetland, was the roadway to acres and acres of unchartered land. Since the revitalization of the town under the guidance of Mayor Liza Fitzgerald and his very own grandmother, tourism had increased significantly in a short span of time. Which meant the town was making money, which of course would attract all types of vultures just like a dead carcass usually did. So he and Quinn had gone to check out what might very well become their biggest competition.

"Then why do you sound like you've just stepped on your Twinkie?" Joe inquired.

"Because a new resort has just opened on the other side of town. It's big and pretty and has golf," he said sourly. The golf course at The Marina was boss, he had to admit that himself. For any city-living golfer looking for a place to relax, visit a picturesque little town and all its quirky inhabitants, eat cultural food, and play a few holes, The Marina in Sweetland was the place to be.

"Really. Well, a little competition is good for the morale. It'll keep your family on their toes, especially since none of your siblings is really experienced in running a bed-and-breakfast. If they feel like it can all be taken away at any moment, maybe they'll try harder to keep it going."

Right, maybe they would. Without him?

"Quinn and I are going to meet with them tomorrow just to give everyone a heads-up about what we saw."

"How do you think they'll take it?"

Preston let out a wry laugh. "Michelle's going to flip. Raine will sulk quietly. Savannah will squawk, then pack her bags and head back overseas. Parker's not really vested

even though he's taken an extended leave from the force
to recover from his injury."

"And what about you?"

"What about me?"

"How are you reacting to the boss competition? You
feeling a little heat?" Joe asked seriously.

Man, was that a loaded question. Preston had definitely been feeling heat in the last three days. But that
heat wasn't coming from The Marina or any golf course
for that matter. It was from the slender beauty who had
answered his online ad. The one who was here to take his
puppy.

"I'm handling things. You know how I am."

"Uh-huh," Joe said. "I know when you're quietly con-
templating a big move. So why don't you give me a heads-
up about what exactly you're thinking of doing?"

Preston couldn't possibly do that because he had no idea.

"It's not totally my call. We're all equal owners of the
B and B, whatever we decide has to be unanimous. And
then there're the dogs."

"Right, the Labs. I told you my sister would love a
puppy. Her twins just turned five and they're taking turns
begging for a dog to be added to their family. They live in
the mountains of western Maryland, more land than they
can even use. They'd be perfect owners."

"They sound like it, and I'll let the others know about
the possibility. But my pup has already been adopted."

Joe crunched on ice cubes. He did that a lot, especially
in the summer when the heat in their city office was ex-
cruciating, despite running their air-conditioning at full
capacity.

"You gave your dog away already? To who?"

"Jamie told me about this online agency. I signed her
up and this lady showed up to adopt her."

"A lady, huh? An old lady?"

There was nothing old about Heaven Montgomery. "Nah, maybe in her late twenties."

"Really?" Joe asked. "Cute?"

"She's nice looking." It was a drastic understatement, but Joe was miles away and would most likely never set eyes on Heaven anyway.

"Single?"

"I believe so," he answered but wasn't 100 percent certain since he hadn't bothered to ask her. Hadn't really had a reason to ask.

"Body? Curvy? Manly? Boyish? Or centerfoldish?"

"What are you, fifteen?" Preston asked with a chuckle. "She's a nice-looking woman who was looking for a puppy. I met a need."

That had Joe laughing loudly. "I'll just bet you did."

"Mind out of the gutter, Baskerville. I simply signed the adoption papers this morning. Actually, she should be on her way back home."

"Home? She's not from Sweetland?"

"No. Actually, she's from your hometown of Boston."

"Really? Maybe I know her, what's her name?"

The last thing Preston wanted was for Joe to know Heaven. If he were totally truthful, he'd admit he didn't want any man knowing Heaven. But that was foolish. She wasn't his to be protective of, and that was, of course, by choice. *His* choice.

"Don't worry about her name. You don't know her. Now, are you taking over my cases this week or not?"

Joe laughed again. "While you stay in your little beachfront town and look at pretty, curvy women from Boston who want to own a puppy? Sure, I guess I can do that for a friend."

Preston shook his head and smiled at the ease of their relationship. He could depend on Joe and vice versa; that's what made their firm such a huge success. That's what made it so difficult to even entertain the thought of not practicing criminal law again.

"I didn't say she was curvy," was his final reply to Joe. He hung up before Joe could reply, smiling all the while as he knew his friend would now be racking his brain to try to figure out what female in her late twenties he remembered from Boston. A futile task, but one that would keep Joe occupied for a while.

It was a good thing Heaven was on her way back home. His resolve to stay away from her and to keep out the personal business she obviously did not want him to know wavered each time he stared into her very sad eyes. Now that she was gone, he could focus on the resort and what it meant for The Silver Spoon. He could focus on something other than touching her, tasting her, starting to need her like he needed air.

"Damn," he whispered to himself. "I'm glad she's gone."

"I was wondering if it would be okay if I stayed awhile longer?" Preston heard Heaven asking Michelle, who was standing at the inn's front desk.

"Of course it's okay. The Sunshine Room is still available, and we could sure use your help getting ready for Bay Day."

"What's that?" Heaven inquired.

"It's our yearly celebration of all things relating to the Chesapeake Bay and Sweetland. We have a great time with tons of food and vendors and parties. It's a blast. Maybe you could stay for the event as well. I mean, if you don't have to rush back to work."

She shook her head. "No. I'm sort of on leave from work."

Michelle nodded. "Oh, I see. Well, that's all the more reason for you to stay in Sweetland awhile longer. If it's relaxation you need, we've got it here by the handful."

"I'll pay," Heaven said, reaching into her purse. "Just swipe my credit card. And I'd be happy to help. You and your sisters have been so kind."

"Nonsense," Michelle said, taking the card Heaven extended to her and punching the keys of the computer register. "We love having you here. You kept all the dogs busy yesterday while we set up. I see you and Coco have really bonded."

"We have. I'm actually on my way into town now to sign the final paperwork. I hope Preston keeps up his end of the bargain."

"Well, Preston is a man of his word. If he said he was going to let you adopt Coco, that's what he's going to do. That's one thing you can rely on about my brother, he's brutally honest," Michelle added pointedly.

"That's a good way to be," Heaven said quietly then smiled as she accepted her card from Michelle. "I think I'll take Coco with me. And when I return I'll find you to see what I can do to help."

Michelle nodded. "You take your time. See some of the town while you're at it. I'm sure they've already begun putting up the sunflower decorations on Main Street."

"Really? I love sunflowers."

"Then you should definitely stop by Blossoms. It's our local florist. Drew Sidney owns it and she is absolutely amazing with flowers and stuff. She makes all the floats for the Bay Day parade, too. She'd love to sell you some sunflowers to put up in your room."

"Oh, that sounds lovely," Heaven replied.

Yeah, just lovely, Preston thought. Heaven Montgomery was staying in Sweetland.

His shoulders were broad, his back sculpted like those she'd seen only on fitness magazines. He wore basketball shorts again, tennis shoes, and ankle socks. Nothing else.

Back and forth he ran, throwing the ball to Coco, waiting for her to retrieve and return. Running farther away, he repeated the cycle. Coco enthusiastically followed.

And so did Heaven's gaze.

It was early evening. She'd been to town, picked up the signed adoption papers, stopped at Blossoms to buy flowers, and returned to the inn to help a very reluctant and somewhat moody Savannah build crepe paper balls. The silver-and-white decorations would adorn the booth The Silver Spoon would have at the parade and along Main Street to introduce townsfolk and tourists to their business. All of the businesses in town would have a booth to showcase everything they had to offer. And she'd been happy to help.

After that she had no plans and she'd come outside to spend time with Coco, except Coco was already being entertained.

His chest was hairless, smooth like fresh honey and sculpted, from perfect pectorals to scaled abs. Her mouth watered, and even though it was really humid outside, Heaven shivered.

Good ol' Geoffrey never made her feel like this.

The bright yellow ball tumbled about six inches away from where she stood, startling Heaven out of her thoughts. Just as she bent down to touch the ball, Coco intervened, happily scooping it between her teeth, long floppy ears flapping as she turned and bolted back toward where Preston stood.

He stared at her, even when he knelt down to accept the ball from Coco and rubbed adoringly behind the puppy's ears. His gaze never left hers. Heaven stood and so did he. Standing about seven feet from each other, it seemed like they were having some type of stand-off.

"Hi," she offered weakly with a tentative wave.

Preston nodded. "Hi, yourself."

"Ah, thanks for signing the papers. Everything looks good except for the final visit to the vet. I've scheduled that for Wednesday morning." It felt like she was babbling so she stopped abruptly.

"You're staying in Sweetland, then?"

It was a simple enough question, an obvious one since she'd planned to leave this morning and here it was after six in the evening and she was still here. Not to mention the appointment for the day after tomorrow.

"Yes." She cleared her throat. "I like it here and I have some time off work so I figured I'd make a vacation of it."

"An impromptu vacation. You must be self-employed to have that type of freedom."

"No. I'm not self-employed. I'm on leave from my job," she said, purposely being as vague as possible

Preston, however, didn't waver. "For how long?"

She shrugged. "For as long as I want." Because Larengetics probably didn't want her back considering how much money she'd cost them. They hadn't officially fired her, but Heaven figured that was just a formality. She'd already been locked out of her company email; her identification to get her into the building had been suspended, and her office was still blocked off by the police department's investigation tape. Yes, it had happened six months ago, but apparently there were more questions. And absolutely no answers, not that she could offer anyway.

"Are you in danger?" he asked.

Heaven didn't reply immediately, because again she wasn't sure of the answer. She was in danger of losing her control and possibly strangling her mother or Geoffrey Billingsley, or both of them if she had to see them right at this moment. But she didn't think that was what Preston meant.

"I'm on vacation, like I said," was her eventual reply. "How about you? When are you leaving?"

Savannah did not have a problem talking about her siblings, so this afternoon Heaven had learned that Parker was on sick leave pending his recovery from his motorcycle accident. Raine was on summer break from her teaching job, after taking vacation time for the first few weeks following their grandmother's death. Quinn had left his job in Seattle to manage the inn and marry Nikki—a cuter couple Heaven didn't think she'd ever seen. And Michelle had never left Sweetland for longer than it took to obtain her culinary degree.

Preston, whom she'd tried valiantly not to ask too many questions about, was a successful criminal attorney with a thriving practice in Baltimore City. He didn't live in Sweetland and had no real reason to stay here, especially since his inheritance had now been taken care of.

"I'm my own boss," was his tart reply.

Coco ran in circles between Preston's legs, jumping up as if to ask when he'd give the pup the ball once more. Probably catching the hint, Preston tossed the ball away and Coco took off.

"It's hot. I'm going for a swim. You're welcome to join me," he said, then walked away from her toward the river.

She was not joining him, of course. She had on shorts and one of those flimsy tops Savannah had thrown onto the counter for her to purchase. Reluctantly, Heaven had admitted the frothy soft pink off-the-shoulder blouse was cute. It made her feel relaxed and sexy at the same time. So no, she was not going for a swim with Preston, but she could certainly watch.

He needed the coolness of the river. Actually, he needed a freezing-cold shower to soften the edge of desire he felt whenever he was close to Heaven.

When Preston had learned she would be staying in town earlier today, he'd immediately gone back to his room.

To work, he told himself, but actually it was to regroup. Was he going to stay? He should leave, especially since she was staying. But they had business to take care of, business regarding the inn and its viability in the town. He wouldn't turn his back on his family, not ever again. He'd sworn that to himself and to his gramma as he'd stood over her closed casket letting warm tears fall freely down his cheeks.

He wouldn't go to the city and never look back. He'd keep his eye on his sisters and the inn and make sure they all kept in touch and stayed together. He'd visit more frequently and help preserve their heritage. He owed his grandmother that much. So no, he couldn't leave just yet.

But he also couldn't stay around Heaven without wanting to touch her.

This evening only proved his point. She'd stood there watching him, those shorts barely skimming her upper thigh and that shirt . . . who the hell designed shirts like that? Ones that showed one shoulder and teasingly hid the other. It melded against her breasts and was sheer enough that he could have probably seen the delectable mounds if not for the darker, formfitting piece of material beneath. It was the sickest kind of tease, the one that gave a man a headache and a hard-on at the same time, severely diminishing his mental capacity.

The minute he'd submerged himself in the coolness of the water, the pressure at his temples had slowly receded. He was still painfully aroused, but figured half relief was better than none.

"You should really invest in some swimming trunks," she called from her perch on the rocks.

He knew she was sitting there without even turning around to see her. In the same spot she'd been sitting the other night when he'd come to see her. Looking as pretty as a picture, as she did each time he saw her.

"I'm doing just fine. Don't complain if you're not planning to join me," he yelled back.

Oh, how he wished she would join him. Dipping his hands beneath the water, he allowed a brief touch of his erection to his palm and quietly moaned. Submerging himself once more was a cool relief, but he only resurfaced again to see her sitting in the same spot, Coco coming up to join her.

She played with the puppy, rubbing her ears and stomach as she rolled over. And Coco absorbed all the affection just as she did food, and socks, and whatever else might by lying around. She was a fun puppy, with loads of energy and a compassion she was readily willing to share with Preston or anybody else for that matter. He really had considered taking her back to the city with him, but in the end he'd decided his emotional state couldn' take any more upheaval. His grandmother was gone keeping this piece of her with him on a daily basis wasn' a good idea.

Besides, the way Heaven's eyes lit up each time she saw Coco, and the smile she could never seem to hold a bay when the puppy was near her, was enough to assure him he'd made the right decision.

He continued to swim until he heard Coco's increased barking. Looking back to the shore, he saw that Heaven had now stood and was talking on her cell phone. He was too far away to hear what she was saying, but the way Coco was reacting said there was some tension. The puppy was amazingly cognizant of emotions and made no secret of how she felt about them. Right now, Preston sensed Coco's uneasiness and moved toward the shore without taking his eyes off Heaven.

By the time he'd reached her she'd disconnected the call, but the hand holding the phone shook and she looked as if she needed a good stiff drink.

"Hey, everything okay?" he asked, reaching to grab the wrist that was shaking so hard he thought the phone might eventually hit the ground.

She licked her lips, an act that still managed to make his body tighten even though he was really more concerned with who she'd been talking to than with getting laid.

"I'm fine," she replied but wouldn't look at him.

"Your boyfriend mad that you're staying in Sweetland a little longer?" The minute the question was out Preston figured it probably wasn't his smoothest route to finding out who was on the phone—or if she had a boyfriend for that matter.

The immediate look of anger that she followed with was proof of that point.

"I can stay in Sweetland as long as I like. And I don't have a boyfriend that would tell me not to!"

She said all that in such an accusatory tone, or was it more defensive?

"And what's wrong with her?" she asked, stepping away from Coco who was still barking and looping around Heaven's legs expectantly.

"My guess is she senses you're upset. You've been spending a lot of time with her. Maybe there's an attachment and she wants you to calm down."

"Dogs don't form attachments that quickly and they don't know how a human is feeling?"

Preston looked down at Coco, and Coco looked up imploringly at Heaven, who finally sighed.

"It was just a stupid wrong number," she said finally.

"Are you sure?" Preston had eased the phone out of her hand, but hadn't tried to look at it. He was more concerned with the racing pulse he could feel through her wrist. Wrong numbers didn't make a person's pulse race.

"I'm positive." She took another deep breath, then knelt down to coax Coco. "I'm fine, girl. I'm just fine."

Coco ceased barking and went right into Heaven's arms. Preston watched as she held the dog close to her chest snuggling her against her chin, whispering soothing words into Coco's ears.

"We should go in for dinner," he told her, keeping her cell phone in his hand.

Heaven didn't respond but turned and walked in the direction of the house, still holding on to Coco as if her life actually depended on her.

Chapter 10

A week later, Heaven was still in Sweetland. She'd actually slipped into quite a comfortable routine with all the preparations for Bay Day going on, as well as the events Michelle catered at the inn. Her days were full of first-time experiences, such as stuffing fresh croissants early one morning when she'd made the mistake of getting up and coming downstairs because she couldn't sleep. Michelle had been in the kitchen working.

"You're always in this kitchen," she said casually. In her time here Heaven had found it easy to talk to all the Cantrell women, Michelle especially.

It was something about the way the woman watched her knowingly, but sort of waited for Heaven to say whatever it was that was on her mind.

"It's my job. Besides, I love it here. It's the only place I truly feel relaxed," Michelle had replied.

"I've been looking for a place like that," Heaven admitted without qualms. "I've always thought where I was in life was where I was meant to be. Well, I thought that until earlier this year. Now, I'm not so sure."

"Things change," Michelle said without looking up

from rolling out the dough and cutting it into perfect rectangles. "Wash your hands and come on over. I'll show you how to make scrumptious almond croissants."

Heaven didn't even question her, but did as she was told. In the next few minutes she was spreading a delicious-smelling almond filling onto the rectangles of dough, then rolling them the way Michelle had shown her and placing them on the lightly greased baking sheet.

"You see, Heaven, nobody's life is meant to stay the absolute same forever. Change is nothing to be afraid of, and it's healthy most times," Michelle began telling her.

"How old are you?" Heaven blurted out. "I'm sorry, I didn't mean to ask that."

Michelle chuckled. "Sure you did and don't worry, it's okay. I'm thirty-four but I have a very old soul. My grandmother used to tell me that. Actually, she'd told me that since I was about four years old."

"I never knew my grandmother," Heaven heard herself saying. She had no idea what was going on with her, but she was releasing all sorts of information about herself this morning. But maybe this was what she was meant to be doing at this moment in time—else why hadn't she remained asleep?

"That's too bad. I can't imagine how my life would have turned out without mine. She was such a blessing to all of us."

"I'm sure you're all missing her terribly now."

Michelle nodded and reached for another roll of dough. "Yes, we're all coping in our own way."

"Preston seems just fine," she said, then quickly snapped her lips shut. That was just going too far. She absolutely did not want Michelle to think there was anything going on between her and Preston.

In fact, after she'd watched him go for a swim and they'd all had dinner in the restaurant, Preston had disappeared for a while. Until he'd showed up again later that night knocking on her door to return her cell phone. Heaven was still shook up by the phone call she'd received so she hadn't even realized Preston still had her phone. She thanked him and he went about his business. And while she'd seen him in the days that followed, there was a careful kind of reservation between the two of them. One that both concerned and annoyed her.

"Preston has a contemplative soul, as Gramma would say. On the outside he seems like he knows everything—always has the answer and is usually right on the mark. But on the inside there's this quiet war going on, one only he can win in his own time. He and Parker are so different in that area because with Parker you know where you stand immediately, and usually wherever you stand with Parker you end up laughing."

"Preston doesn't laugh a lot."

"Sure he does. When he's happy," Michelle added with a shake of her head. "Right now he's pissed off with me because I didn't call and tell them sooner that Gramma was sick. But I couldn't tell him what I didn't know."

"And he doesn't understand that?"

"I think deep down inside he does. It's a part of that war inside of him I just told you about. Once he battles it out with himself, he'll see that it wasn't any more my fault that Gramma died than it was his. The key to dealing with Preston is patience," Michelle told her.

She said it as if she knew that's the advice Heaven had been aiming for all along. Which definitely was not true! Still, she'd thought about it for the duration of that day. Even now, two days later, she was still thinking about it.

Each evening after dinner, just when the sun was sinking deep into the sky, transforming the bright and humid day to a marginally cooler evening, Heaven would take Coco for a walk. She'd offered to take the other dogs as well, but Michelle was adamant that their owners needed to assume some responsibility for them.

So she and Coco had just set out about ten minutes ago, heading down Sycamore Lane down to Duncan, which she knew led to the pier where she and Preston had walked. This was the way they walked each night, and she was beginning to become accustomed to the scenery. Sweetland was a generally quiet town, except for the sounds of whatever night creatures were out, and she'd normally only see a car or two as she walked.

Tonight a black SUV passed them as they turned down Duncan Road. She noticed because it was driving really fast—so fast, she thought she felt a breeze when it passed. Which was absolutely crazy since it hadn't been below ninety degrees in the last seven days this week, and the humidity was above 80 percent. That thought had her feeling like she'd been in this town too long.

"But I'm starting to like it here, Coco," she said to the puppy, who was dutifully walking beside her—which for a sixteen-week-old Labrador puppy was almost extraordinary.

Coco barked in response and she smiled. Of course she was in love with this puppy. Who else could she communicate with this easily?

"Not Geoffrey, that's for sure."

That thought had her mind wandering to how ridiculously dysfunctional her life really was. A quick walk around the pier and they were headed back to the house. On the way Heaven decided that she was definitely not marrying Geoffrey Billingsley and her mother was going to have to figure out how to deal with that fact. Besides, Geoffrey didn't give a damn. She would be a trophy wife to him, some arm candy to take to all his business functions, to pose in magazines adoringly beside him, and to smile as he lied to her about business trips and all the mistresses he would undoubtedly meet up with on them. His reputation and three prior marriages preceded him, which had been the very first turn-off in her mind.

The second was that her mother had unabashedly approved of this older man even mentioning the idea of marrying her daughter. Then again, the fact that she'd always felt like an object or a possession of her parents, rather than a loved and cherished only child, shouldn't have made the previous fact a surprise.

Minutes later Coco chased a bright red ball that had been kicked out of a yard by playing children. Heaven laughed as she followed the puppy, then picked up the ball and tossed it back to the two little boys, who looked no more than four or five years old. They'd obviously been instructed not to leave the yard because neither of them made any attempt to go beyond the white picket fence to retrieve it, even though they were staring at it sorrowfully as it rolled away.

After a toothy thanks from both boys, she waved and continued walking. This time thinking of whether or not she'd ever have children of her own, whom she'd probably instruct to stay in the yard as well. In Boston she lived in a condo, no yard and no fence. No grass, either. Not very conducive to playing ball with little kids. Still, she could always move into a single-family home. Or she could move to another state, which she'd contemplated just after finishing college. The very lucrative offer from Larengetics—which she figured was courtesy of her parents' connections—had been too good to pass up, for any reason. So she'd stayed in Boston, just like her mother wanted.

Five years later she wasn't sure about that lucrative job, and she was certain she didn't want to be in such close proximity with her mother anymore. Her mother, who had been calling her . . .

That breeze came again, this time as she was being pushed to the ground with something heavy lying on top of her. Screeching tires sounded somewhere in the distance and Coco barked as if someone was chasing her.

"If you wanted to be on top of me all you had to do was ask," she said flippantly even though Preston could feel her heart beating wildly.

"When I'm ready to be on top of you, believe me, you'll be the first to know," was his response. Which didn't accurately depict how he was feeling at this moment, either.

Behind him he heard someone running toward them, his siblings no doubt. So despite how well their bodies seemed to fit, lying in the middle of the street with a puppy running loose wasn't his idea of a romantic evening.

"Here, let me help you," he said, moving off her, then reaching out a hand to her when he was standing.

She took his hand and got to her feet. As she brushed herself off, he noticed her trying to steady her breathing. Actually, Preston thought she may have been counting, but then his siblings converged and he looked away from Heaven.

"What the hell was that?" Quinn asked. He was the first to come up to them. "Are you all right, Heaven?"

"I'm fine," she answered quickly, nervously. "Where's Coco?"

"She's here," Raine answered.

Michelle had walked straight to Heaven, putting an arm around her shoulders. "We were all sitting on the porch having iced tea and talking about old times when we heard that truck speeding down the street."

Preston's teeth clenched as he thought of the moment he'd heard the truck's approach, then saw Heaven walk into the street. The feeling had been unexplainable.

"I got the tag number," Parker said when he made it to the curb where everyone else was standing. He'd been getting around a lot better on his crutches, but Preston knew his brother was getting sick of the hindrance.

To Parker's remark, Preston only nodded.

"Good," Michelle replied. "We can report it to the sheriff first thing in the morning. Probably a tourist who needs to be reminded this isn't the big city."

"I'm so glad I'm not in the city anymore," Raine replied quietly, her hand moving absently over Coco's head.

Savannah hadn't said a word, just looked from Heaven to the corner of Sycamore where the truck had come from, then subsequently made a U-turn and left.

"It was just an accident," Heaven spoke up. "And really, it was my fault. I wasn't paying attention. My head was somewhere else and I should have been looking before I stepped into the street."

And that damned SUV shouldn't have been speeding down this small quiet street. Unless it had a reason to.

"Let's get you and Coco inside. Michelle will make some hot tea and we'll all calm down a bit," Preston heard himself saying.

That was so not what he wanted to do.

The moment he'd seen the danger she was in, he'd run as fast as he could, getting to her just before the truck did. It seemed surreal, but he'd already been heading down the porch steps when they all heard the first screeching of tires. The truck had been at the corner then. So he hadn't run that far. Try telling that to his heart, which was running a pretty quick beat right now. All he remembered was seeing her step into the street and then everything had been a blur.

Everything until the moment he lay atop her and the truck was gone.

Now he just wanted to sit beside her on the couch, to

be able to look over and see that she was okay. Nothing else mattered at the moment.

This was all new to Heaven. Never had there been even one person who cared enough to earnestly fuss over her well-being, let alone six, but that's exactly what had taken place in The Silver Spoon.

Fifteen minutes after the accident Michelle had water boiling on the stove for tea. Raine had Coco settled on a huge puppy pillow situated on the floor in the living room right beside the end of the couch Heaven sat on. Across the room Parker sat in one of the matching high-backed wing chairs, his fingers moving quickly over the keyboard of his laptop. Every few seconds he would look up at her, a question in his eyes, but he remained quiet. She'd caught a few glances between him and Preston but didn't have a clue what they meant. Actually, she figured it might be some kind of twin thing.

In the past few days she'd noticed how they could complete each other's sentences or actually say the same thing, at the same time. And they looked a lot alike, except that Parker had more of an edge to his brown eyes and strong chin and Preston had a small mole by his right eye.

Savannah didn't say much, but she went to get a basin of warm water and two towels. She wet one and put it at the base of Heaven's neck; the other she gave Heaven to dabble over her face. Heaven wanted to tell them again that she was fine, but she feared none of them was really listening to her anyway.

Preston hadn't left her side since she'd come into the house. He hadn't asked any questions or really said more than a couple of words to her, but he'd stayed right there on the couch with her nonetheless.

"I'd really just like to get a hot shower and go to bed,"

she said quietly to Savannah when she stood over her with that wet towel again.

"I'll walk you upstairs," Preston said and almost immediately stood, grabbing her hands and pulling her up with him.

He moved so fast the towel from her neck fell onto the chair and Savannah had to take a quick step back to avoid being knocked down. Even Coco sat up on her pillow, her tail wagging wildly. Poor puppy looked as bewildered and bereft as Heaven felt.

"Come on, girl," she summoned, warming as Coco immediately took steps to get off the pillow and come stand beside her.

"Tell Michelle I'll come down to get the tea. How do you like it?" he asked Heaven.

Saying she didn't want tea would probably sound like a foreign language to him so she simply answered, "Three sugars, no cream."

Savannah nodded. "I'll tell her."

"We need to talk," Parker said as Preston escorted her out of the living room.

"Later," he replied sternly.

Heaven didn't complain when he practically pulled her up the steps behind him, and she kept her mouth closed when he walked her into her bedroom and followed her inside. But when he went into the bathroom, switched on the light, and began running the shower she panicked.

"What are you doing?" she asked from the doorway of the bathroom.

"You wanted to take a hot shower, right?" he asked as if her question had been the unusual situation they were approaching.

"Right. And I can do that myself," was her reply.

Preston shrugged. "I already did it."

As he passed her on his way out of the bathroom he said, "I'll wait for you out here."

She probably wanted to be alone, but Preston didn't. He wanted to be with her. Maybe it was something about almost losing her to a maniac driver. No, that wasn't it. At least it wasn't entirely.

Preston had wanted Heaven since the moment he first saw her. And for him, not going after a woman he wanted wasn't the norm. He'd had a good reason for keeping his distance, and still a part of him thought that's what he should continue to do. But that part was sorely overruled.

There was something primal going on at this moment, something that most likely would only be pushed away by Heaven herself. If she said no, he would go. That had forever been the rule with him and his brothers. The intense longing inside him that he swore was new—he'd never felt this way about another woman before—was no match for the teachings that had been embedded in the Cantrell men since birth.

While the water ran in the other room and to keep him from fidgeting like some hard-up teenager, Preston moved about the room looking for some piece of Heaven. On the dresser was a comb and brush and earrings. A few inches away was her purse, which he didn't even think about going in. His grandmother had been a stickler about a woman's privacy. Sure, he was in the room she was sleeping in, but Preston wasn't going to go into her purse, or any woman's purse, ever.

However, the frilly piece of material hanging from a partially closed dresser drawer quickly caught his attention. Pulling the drawer open enough to slip the garment free, he held it in front of him and groaned. It was almost nothing, in sheer pink, which he was beginning to think was the best color in the universe since it looked so damned good on Heaven. This would look spectacular on her, he knew. It was short, with lace here and there, and the softness against his fingers had the temperature in this room rising uncontrollably.

"Get it together, Cantrell, you're just torturing yourself," he mumbled.

About a second before the bathroom door opened and Heaven caught him red handed—or pink-handed if he were being absolutely specific.

"Looking for something to wear?" Heaven asked, surprise and just the barest hint of confusion on her face.

Preston paused a moment, then could only shrug. "Nothing I say is going to come out right," he admitted.

To that she smiled. "And here I was told you were the smooth one."

Chapter 11

Preston felt his own smile forming. The fact that she hadn't yelled at him to get his perverted hands off her clothes and out of her room was very inspiring.

Instead of trying to explain why he had her lingerie in his hand, he thrust said hand forward. "Here, you should put this on."

She was wearing a robe. It was short and green, a deep hunter green that made him think of Christmas trees and mistletoe. And kissing Heaven beneath the mistletoe. Actually, he was almost positive he wasn't going to be able to wait six months to kiss Heaven. Her taste still lingered in his mouth from the first time he'd touched his lips to hers. It was an addictive taste, one that called to him quite persistently right this moment. To be more precise, the memory of her taste was yelling at him to try again . . . once more.

"I should, huh?"

She didn't move so Preston crossed the room until he stood directly in front of her. "I think you look great in pink."

The smile that spread across her face was quick and

genuine and he couldn't resist, he touched a finger to her bottom lip. Just a gentle touch and her smile wavered. He watched his finger move over her lip, his body tightening instantly.

"What are you doing?" she asked.

"Making a memory," he said without thought. "My grandmother used to say that all actions could be recalled on some level, but when it was something really important you had to focus, to concentrate on keeping that memory intact."

"You want to remember standing in my room after you just tackled me in the street?"

Her voice had lowered to a whisper, a shiver taking over her body as his finger moved from her lips to her chin, tracing a slow line along her jaw.

"I want to remember that you weren't hit by that truck. I want to remember you standing here, your skin still moist from the shower so that this flimsy robe sticks to parts of your arm, your upper thigh. I want to remember how soft your lips feel against my finger, and against my mouth," he finished with his head lowered so close to hers, it would be a crime not to kiss her.

It was like sunshine on the cloudiest of days. Preston rarely ever compared his women, because he knew they were each different. He'd selected them with that fact in mind. Variety was a necessity.

But he hadn't selected Heaven. In fact, he'd had no idea this was where they'd end up.

Yet with his hands now cupping her face, lifting her just slightly so that her mouth was at the perfect angle, swiping his tongue just so and moaning when her taste filtered through him like a fresh summer's breeze, he couldn't really say he hated how things had turned out.

She lifted her hands to his shoulders, letting her fingers dig in as the kiss deepened.

"I don't know you very well," she whispered when he'd torn his mouth from hers to drop hungry kisses down the line of her neck.

"You know I'm a man," he said, kissed her again and moaned. "A single man."

His hands slid from her face down to her neck, then her arms, where they felt the softness of the robe a few seconds before they went to the belt at her front.

"How about you?" he asked, his mouth still loving the feel of her skin.

Her fingers dug into his shoulders as he sucked on a particularly tasty spot just beneath her ear. She moaned before replying.

"Ahhh, I'm single too," she said in a breathy whisper.

The sound was pure bliss, the way her body pressed closer to his at the stroke of his tongue along her earlobe, probably illegal in a few states.

"Crap!" he murmured.

The belt was in some kind of girlie knot that was wreaking havoc on his purely hormonal goals.

As if reading his mind, or possibly becoming just as impatient as he, Heaven let her hands fall from his shoulders and went to help him. Of course she had it undone quickly. When he moaned and pushed the robe aside to wrap his arms around her naked waist, she pressed closer to him. Then she did something he never—in his wildest and most imaginative dreams—would have pictured her doing. She wrapped a leg around his and mumbled something. He hadn't heard her because her leg had gone from around his leg to up and around his waist in like two seconds and all the blood had drained from his head, making any attempt at rational thought a complete loss.

"Huh?" he heard himself saying and thought for sure he was losing his "smooth" status.

"I said," she told him, this time cupping his face in hers. "That you're taking too long."

Well. Okay. That was . . . something to be told.

On that note he cupped her bottom and lifted her off the floor. Both her legs wrapped around his waist. "Good girl," he commended as he turned and led her to the bed.

By the time they got there she'd already pulled his shirt from the waistband of his pants. A nervous giggle escaped as her hands touched his bare skin. When his legs bumped the bed, Preston stopped. He thought about dropping her onto the bed, then setting a world record for how fast he could shuck his clothes, sheath his rock-hard erection, and sink inside her waiting warmth. Then the rational side of his mind took over. The hungry part of his body promised a big fight if mind and body didn't soon have a meeting of the minds.

He let her down slowly, grasping her wrists in his hands as he did. Now she knelt in front of him while he looked down into wide, excited eyes. She looked like the attractive woman who had come to his door a couple of weeks ago. Then again, she didn't. There was something wanton and intriguing about her now. Maybe it was her kiss-swollen lips, or possibly the reddening of her skin just beneath her ear where he'd suckled a little too hard.

She licked her lips, and he moaned.

It was definitely the way her tongue looked, brushing over her lips, and the way her gaze held his in impatient fervor.

"What's wrong?" she asked.

Preston closed his eyes and once again he groaned. "Nothing."

"Then—" she began and tried to pull her wrists from his.

"No," he said shaking his head. "This isn't how I work.

I mean, it's not usually how I am with women. I'm not normally this—"

"Slow?" she finished. "I should hope not. I've heard so much about the Double Trouble Cantrells, but the way you're acting does not add up."

No. It wouldn't. It shouldn't. This is not how Preston normally acted. It's not how he normally seduced a woman. Yes! That was it, precisely. Preston loved seduction. He loved the slow, sensual shift into sex, the touches and moans and exploration that ended with a bang to be harvested until the next time.

With Heaven, he'd seen the green light and heard the opening gunshot all in the span of the two seconds it had taken her to walk through that bathroom door. He could blame it on the lingerie that was now somewhere on the floor, but that wouldn't be true. The truth was he'd wanted her with this urgency since day one.

And for Preston, that was not normal.

"Okay, well if we're confessing, I never do this. Ever," she said, shaking her head as if that would make him believe her more.

It was really hard to keep his gaze focused on her face when her robe was open, her nakedness now summoning him, or at least a very specific part of him. And yes, that part was more than ready to respond as it pressed painfully against the zipper of his pants.

"Are you saying you're a . . . umm . . . ?"

He couldn't even say the word.

"Oh, no, I'm not. I just mean that it's been a really long time for me. Men aren't exactly knocking down my door, and even if they were, they'd have to knock down the door to the lab since I spend most of my time in there. But since they don't I'm not used to the fast or slow pace, really. And that's probably why I'm being so impatient." She stopped, inhaled quickly. "I'm babbling, aren't I?"

He could only nod.

"I have an idea," Preston offered. "Since we're both behaving a little out of the norm, let's try something different."

"Different how?" she asked skeptically.

"Not that kind of different. Wow, you really are impatient," he said with a chuckle so the seriously concerned look that had crossed her face would disappear.

"You close your robe and I'll take off my shoes. We can lie down and talk for a while." Maybe then he could regroup and get his old groove back. As it was now, he wasn't quite sure what was going on or who he was at the moment.

"Okay, that sounds like a plan," she said, already reaching for the belt of her robe. "But, um, could you take off your shirt, too?"

She looked up at him after the request, her gaze almost shy as it dropped to his chest. Almost. The moment she licked her lips, shyness jumped out the window and hunger took a seat in the front row.

"I can do that," he replied, his own hunger pulling up a seat to sit right beside hers.

Heaven hadn't lied. This was very unlike her. She didn't jump into men's arms and wrap her legs around them. And for the life of her she'd never remembered moaning as a man cupped her bottom and sucked her earlobe. If she tried really hard, she still wouldn't have recalled a man ever doing either of those things to her.

In her limited sexual experience, the two times she'd ventured into this realm, the episodes both ended with a few guttural groans and stilted thrusts. Her breasts were always squeezed almost to the point of tears welling in her eyes from pain, and the entire activity had never lasted more than five minutes.

Preston's sultry kiss had lasted five minutes.

And damn did that kiss have her thighs shaking, her center pulsating, and her mind abandoning all common sense telling her to let this man have his way with her quick, fast, and in a hurry.

She figured it was a good thing he'd been able to grasp rational thought. Or else she wouldn't have stopped him, she knew that for a fact. Heaven would have had sex with Preston Cantrell. Hell, she still wanted to have sex with Preston Cantrell.

He was unlike any man she'd ever met, and the most desirable thing she'd found about him was that he looked at her as if she were the only female in the world. Each time he stared at her it was as if he wanted to memorize everything there was about her. She remembered what he'd said his grandmother told him. Maybe he wanted to make a lot of memories of her. She didn't know why and didn't really feel up to questioning it.

For so long her life had gone according to plan. Then there was the explosion, and she was almost positive that wasn't on her agenda. Now she was in a small town, adopting a puppy and wanting desperately to have this man she'd just met put his hands all over her naked body.

If that weren't beyond Heaven's norm, she didn't know what was.

What Heaven also knew without a doubt was that her therapist would be so proud of her. Every step she'd taken in Sweetland was a step forward; it was a new direction in a life she'd desperately needed to change. So if she was ready to grab Preston Cantrell by those muscled arms and pull him down on top of her, begging until he made sweet passionate love to her, then there was absolutely nothing wrong with that!

But of course, she didn't do it.

She lay back on the bed lifting her legs so she could

slip them beneath the sheet and fluffy yellow comforter. Her heart did a little flutter as she watched Preston remove his shoes and his shirt, then slip into bed beside her. When she thought they would lie there staring at the ceiling in uncomfortable silence, Preston extended an arm and reached for her.

"Come on over," he offered cheerfully.

Heaven went willingly, albeit slowly into his embrace, letting her head rest on his bare chest, almost sighing in complete bliss as his arm closed over her shoulder, pulling her even closer. Nestled right there against his warm, hard body was the safest Heaven had ever felt in her life.

"So how are you enjoying your stay in Sweetland?" he asked.

That was an extremely dangerous question. She could tell him how much she was enjoying lying here with him, touching the taut skin of his perfectly toned chest and inhaling his scent that was all masculine, all enticing, all Preston. Or she could say something about how she liked being so close to the water. She couldn't figure out which one would make her seem more lame.

So she went with something else entirely.

"It was probably a nice place to grow up, I suspect. I've never lived in a small town before."

There was a brief hesitation before Preston spoke again.

"It had its good points and its bad points. I presume all places are like that, whether they're big cities or small towns."

"Tell me about the good points," she encouraged, realizing how much she really wanted to hear Preston's thoughts on this town he'd—in a roundabout way—brought her to.

"Fitzgerald Park is one of the perks to Sweetland. There's a great pond there, surrounded by lush green grass and rolling hills. Parker and I spent lots of time down there growing up. And the pier, that's another of my favorite spots. There's always something going on down there. Walt's shipments, like we saw the other day. Walt, he owns The Crab Pot, with the best steamed crabs on the Eastern Shore," he told her with an air of excitement in his tone.

"Some new spots have popped up down there in the years I've been gone. Quinn and Nikki like Amore, the little Italian restaurant down the far edge of the dock. And Parker favors Charlie's Bar. I think it's more like Parker favors Walt's niece, Drew, who hangs out at the bar, but that's another story all together."

"I met a woman named Drew the other day. I wonder if it's the same person."

"Sweetland is so small, I doubt there's two people with the same name here. Drewcilla Sidney owns the flower shop down off Main Street. She's not a native. Michelle said she and her mother moved here a couple of years ago. Her mother is Walt's sister."

"Yes, that's her! She sold me the prettiest sunflowers. I had them right over there on my dresser. I think Coco liked them, too, because she grabbed hold of the tablecloth one day and tugged until the vase tipped over. Water splashed in her face and the flowers landed on the floor. She wasn't apologetic, no matter how much I argued with her."

Preston laughed. "I'll just bet she wasn't. She can be a handful," he told her.

"I'm finding that out," she replied.

Her fingers moved slowly over his chest, just a small motion but one that sent delicious new tingles throughout her body.

"But you're ready for that, right? Being a pet owner is a big task, a huge responsibility."

"I'm ready," she said, thinking she had no choice but to be ready. It was either go out on a limb and try this ew thing, or sit in her apartment alone and continue to emember the explosion and the implications that made er look like an accomplice to some type of bioterrorism cheme.

"Sometimes you reach a point in your life where change s the only option," she finished, her gaze following her ingers that looked so small and inconsequential on his hest.

Or was it that his chest looked terribly imposing with ts size and feel? Could be that was the real problem.

"Depends how you feel about change."

"I don't think it's a bad thing. Do you?"

She could feel him shrug. "I guess it's necessary at imes."

"What about you? When you found out you'd inherited Coco and came back to the town where you were born, idn't the thought of moving back here and settling down vith that gorgeous puppy cross your mind?"

"No," he said quickly. Too quickly.

"No you don't want to move back to Sweetland or no ou never thought about it?" She suspected the answer was o to both, but wanted to hear it directly from him.

"My life is in Baltimore."

"I kind of thought your life traveled with you. I mean, ou could just as easily practice law here as you do in Baltimore."

He inhaled deeply, and she wondered if he was look- ng down at her in irritation for her questions. She didn't ook up to verify.

"I practice criminal law. The most criminal activity weetland's seen in the last ten years is Hoover running own one of the lampposts on Pinetree Way, then stum- ling his drunken self right into the creek down at Yates assage," he told her. "All while wearing only his white oxers and black dress socks."

She laughed. "Nikki said her ex was laundering money with one of the town council members. That sounds pretty criminal-like to me."

"Yeah, it was. But that kind of stuff doesn't happen often here."

"Well, I think at the very least there's a speeding problem going on. I saw that truck that almost ran me down earlier this evening, and he was going just as fast then as he headed for the pier."

Had she known her words were going to garner a particular reaction Heaven would have braced herself. As it was, the moment Preston heard her words he bolted up off the bed, sending her sprawling beneath him, her face hitting the mattress with a little more force than she appreciated.

"You saw that truck before he almost hit you?"

Adjusting herself, Heaven pushed back until she could lie back on the pillows and stare up at him. Damn, he was fine. His skin was that sun-kissed bronze all over, and she almost felt like she could simply lick him. Over and over and over again. Yeah, but he had just asked her a serious question.

"I always walk Coco the same way, to the end of Sycamore, down and straight down Duncan Road to the pier. We circle and come back the same way. That truck breezed past us on Duncan Road as we were heading down to the pier. I remember because he was driving so much faster than any of the other cars that passed us. So like I said, there's obviously someone in town who has problems with the posted speed limit."

"Or there's someone who has a problem with you," he replied through clenched teeth.

In addition to the change in his tone, Preston's brow furrowed, a muscle in his jaw twitching.

"Nobody knows me here," was her quiet response. She

wasn't sure, but Preston seemed to be thinking really
deeply about something as simple as a speeding vehicle.
A speeding vehicle that almost ran her down.

"Oh, no," she whispered. "How did they find me?"

Chapter 12

"And she didn't tell you who 'they' were?" Quinn asked, his voice tinged only slightly with the irritation Preston was feeling.

"She clammed up so tight I don't think a crowbar could've gotten a confession out of her," was Preston's reply.

The brothers were standing in the small sitting area of the caretaker's suite at the B&B. This was the room where their grandmother had stayed, an addition that had been built on when Mary Janet had decided to convert her family home into a bed-and-breakfast. At the moment Parker was living in this space, with Preston using the sofa bed whenever he was in town. Quinn had moved into the small apartment above Nikki's parents' garage until he and Nikki found what they were ominously calling "the perfect house."

"You're an attorney, man. You couldn't get a confession out of her?" Parker asked.

Normally it would have been in a joking tone, but as the three of them collectively were thinking that a speed ng truck in Sweetland was not the norm, it came off in a more accusatory tone.

A tone Preston had been giving himself all morning, but not only for the reasons Parker was.

"Whatever went on in her past, she's not willing to talk about. And really, it's none of my business," Preston said. "It's not like she came here asking for my help. She wanted my dog and now she has it."

"But she's still here," Quinn interjected quietly. "Don't you find it strange that she's still in Sweetland after the adoption went through more than a week ago?"

"And she's moving around here like she's our newest resident, waiting tables in the restaurant during lunch and dinner rush, helping Michelle prepare food, caring for all the dogs when any of us are tied up. She's even helping them make decorations for Bay Day." Parker added the last with an arch of his brows. "This woman is a professional, Preston. She did a double chemistry major at Yale and earned her PhD in two years. She works as a biochemist at a place called Larengetics Pharmaceuticals, where she helps to develop complicated medications for rare diseases. She's been in town for about two weeks now—wouldn't she need to return to work soon? And what about her family? Is she calling anyone? These are questions you should be asking."

"No, I shouldn't!" was Preston's overzealous retort. "She just adopted my dog. There's nothing else going on between us."

Neither of his brothers responded to that outburst. Preston ran a hand over his face trying to get himself together. They weren't the ones he was angry with.

"Look, I think something's going on as well, but I can't make her tell me her secrets." *Nobody can make a woman tell her secrets,* he thought to himself. And running phone number traces from her cell phone certainly wasn't going to help.

He'd stormed out of Heaven's room last night shortly after she'd made her comment about someone finding her. He'd asked her nicely, twice. And she'd refused to tell him, stating it was nothing and not a big deal. The last time he'd all but demanded she tell him what was going on.

The fact that he still knew nothing solidified his earlier statement that he couldn't make her tell him anything.

To be fair he admitted, sometime in the early-morning hours, that he shouldn't have left her the way he did. It seemed like he was doomed to do the wrong thing, or the out-of-the-ordinary thing where Heaven Montgomery was concerned.

"You asked Parker to run the tags on that truck and you asked him to look into Heaven Montgomery. You wouldn't do that unless you were personally invested in some way," Quinn said in his normal logical way.

Preston squeezed the bridge of his nose, in his abnormal not-in-control way.

"I'm not sleeping with her if that's what you're implying," he told them. "But yes, I did ask him to look into it because I think something's going on."

Parker nodded, shifting so that his leg, which was sporting a rather ugly black brace from mid-thigh to ankle, was now hanging off the side of the couch. He'd been lying on the couch when Preston entered and hadn't bothered to sit up until this point. Quinn sat in the recliner, which was normally Parker's spot.

"You think she's in danger," Parker stated. "And I agree with you. That's why it's probably best to keep her here where we can look out for her."

Preston shook his head. "We're not bodyguards."

Quinn stood. "But we're also not the type of men to let a woman be harmed if we can stop it."

"I can't stop what I don't know, Quinn. What do you want me to do?"

"For starters I'd like to know what you've done to my brother," Parker asked. "Look, the tags on that SUV came up stolen. But I can run some more in-depth reports see if there's anything on the police radar in Boston about her. If she filed any reports against stalkers or something like that, we'll know."

"You should probably look into her job as well. It sounds like she might be a pretty big deal to the company. Maybe they're the ones looking for her," Quinn added.

"And in the meantime she stays at the inn, around our family, around us, when we have no idea who she really is?" Preston asked sarcastically.

Quinn stood, his frown momentary, only to be replaced by a look that Preston thought was akin to pity. And that made him grit his teeth a little harder.

"You're absolutely right. Because as long as she's here with us, nothing's going to happen to her. And once you get your head out of the sand, you'll realize I'm right."

Preston left the room, then he left the house. He climbed into his own truck and drove without any real idea where he was going or what he was going to do once he got there. All he knew for sure was that he couldn't think straight in that house, with that woman in such close proximity. It just wasn't going to work.

"I wanted to find out if the investigation was still active." Heaven spoke on her cell phone with Detective Johansen of the Boston Police Department.

"We have a couple of leads we're following up on. I appreciate you calling in to let me know your location, just in case we have more questions," he told her in his ever-so-polite-even-if-intrusive voice.

And it hadn't really been her intention to call him and

report her location. She'd wanted to find out if they already knew where she was.

"So I'm no longer a suspect?" she asked tentatively.

"I never said you were a suspect, Heaven. But you were the only one with security access to that lab the morning of the explosion," he said slowly, as if he expected her to fill in all the blanks for him.

She'd tried that before, to no avail, because there was nothing she wanted more than to be finished with this entire ordeal. But once she'd told the truth there was nothing else she could have done. She did not plant the explosives in the lab, and she had no idea who would have done such a thing.

"No, you didn't. You simply questioned me like you didn't believe a word I said when I told you everything I knew."

"I'm sure you did tell me all you knew. Your boyfriend was pretty sure as well. And he was pretty upset when he waltzed in here to tell me to lay off you. Not in that polite of a way, but you get my drift."

Heaven was in her room standing near a window that boasted a side view of the water and surrounding land from the house.

"Wait a minute, did you say boyfriend? I don't have a boyfriend, Detective?" And the fact that someone would go to the police impersonating one made Heaven more than a little nervous.

"Geoffrey Billingsley came to see me about a week ago. He said you'd given your statement and that unless I planned to arrest you, I should back off. Before he had his lawyers get involved. You saying he's not your boyfriend?"

"That's exactly what I'm telling you," she said with irritation. "He has nothing to do with this case and nothing to do with me. I would appreciate it if you didn't talk to

him about this anymore. And if you didn't tell him where
I am."

She heard a chuckle on the other end of the phone and
was about to take offense, but then he continued.

"I'm happy to hear you say that. The whole time he
was in my office I was trying to figure out why a lovely
woman such as yourself would be involved with a pompous ass like Billingsley. He made sure I knew he had all
kinds of money, as if that would make a difference in a
criminal case like this. But don't you worry, now that I
know you're not attached to him I'll be delighted to kick
him out on his ass the next time he dares show his face."

"Thank you, Detective," she replied before hanging
up. She wasn't sure if that remark had given him implicit
permission to literally kick Geoffrey out of the office. Not
that it would be a bad thing.

With a loud sigh she sat on the bed and wondered what
the hell she was doing. She wasn't a suspect; the detective
had just confirmed that. It should be a relief to know they
were looking in a different direction, but it really wasn't.
Deep down Heaven had always known that if she hadn't
set the explosion, someone else had. What if that someone
was here in Sweetland? What if they were after her?

Her fingers moved over the cell phone. She held it in
one hand and then the other, all the while staring at the
window trying to figure out what her next move should
be. She should leave Sweetland. If someone was here
looking for her, trying to run her down, she should go
someplace else. But where? This hadn't been a running-
away trip; it was supposed to be a liberating one, a finally-
stand-up-and-take-charge-of-my-life one. But if she was
a danger . . .

The knock on her door had her almost jumping off the
bed. She hated being afraid, almost as much as she'd

hated being wrongfully accused. Coco, who had been dozing quietly on her pillow, immediately jumped up. Barking, she raced in circles at the door until Heaven opened it.

"Hello," Mr. Sylvester said, giving her a toothy grin.

"Hi, Mr. Sylvester." Heaven opened the door further and willed her heartbeat to slow.

She was safe here at the B&B, she told herself. Mr. Sylvester was a harmless old man with a friendly nature. In the days since she'd been here, he'd had breakfast with her a couple of times and she'd learned that he liked to talk. About sports most of the time, but then he always wound his way back to some lesson he'd learned in his long life. Heaven found him simply adorable and just like a grandfather, if she'd ever had the opportunity to meet her own.

"Didn't see you at breakfast this morning," he told her, lifting his baseball cap from his head to scratch before pulling it back into place.

"I wasn't very hungry," she replied.

Mr. Sylvester took a step back, then reached down to lift Coco into his arms. "This little lady acts like she wants to go outside."

"We did an early-morning walk today, before everyone else was up." She'd decided on that because she hadn't wanted to see anyone else.

Last night with Preston still weighed heavily on her mind, as heavily as the questions he'd raised just before storming out of her room.

"Gonna stay locked up in this room all day?" he asked.

"Probably. I have a lot on my mind today, Mr. Sylvester," she said, hoping she sounded polite but really wanting him to leave.

"Best thing for a full mind is to get out and let some fresh air in." He didn't wait for her to reply, just took Coco with him and turned away.

"There's a Read-to-Succeed fund-raiser picnic going on down at Fitzgerald Park. Lots of people there to take your mind off your troubles," he said as he continued down the hallway.

He hadn't turned back to speak directly to her, but Heaven knew the invite was meant solely for her. And with another sigh—she was really getting tired of sighing and feeling depressed over things she really couldn't change—she went back into her room to slip on some shoes and freshen up before heading down to Fitzgerald Park.

Preston had no idea where he was going when he'd left the house. He'd just climbed into his truck and started driving. He went all the way across town to Yates Passage, past The Marina Resort and the palatial homes where the Fitzgeralds and the Beaumonts lived. As the richest and most influential people in the town, their homes had always been the largest and grandest. However, there was a new house just down the road from the Beaumonts. Michelle had told them it was being built by a newcomer to Sweetland by the name of Drake Sheridan, the owner of a construction company. From what Preston could see on his drive-by, the completed house was going to be just as impressive as the Beaumonts' or the Fitzgeralds', if not more so.

He drove down the pier but didn't pay as much attention as he usually would have. His mind was elsewhere.

She was in trouble. Preston knew that as surely as he knew his own name. But he wanted to ignore that fact. He wanted to act like he didn't care and walk away. Only Quinn had been right—that wasn't the type of man he was. He couldn't walk away from a woman in trouble. Damn him.

No, damn her, for coming here with her secrets and

pretty smile and soft skin and heated kisses. Just damn
Heaven Montgomery!

He'd slapped his hands on the steering wheel in exasperation just as he was driving past Fitzgerald Park. Colorful balloons stretched skyward, blowing in the stiff humid
breeze. A large inflatable castle had children laughing and
playing inside and out, colored balls following them onto
the grassy ground. At the park's entrance stood a clown,
with his big red nose and huge black shoes, making balloon animals. Rivulets of smoke rose above the trees, sig-
naling a grill in action somewhere within the park's
depths. And parked just down the small path that led to a
parking area was an ice cream truck with the name SCOOP-
AHOLIC scrolled across its side. There was a line there that
stretched at least a mile—everyone wanted to taste Pia
Delaney's homemade creations.

And just as Preston figured the last thing he was in the
mood for was a town gathering complete with laughing
chattering children, music blaring from the ice cream truck
and a clown trying to make everyone laugh, he saw her.

Standing in the line to get ice cream was probably the
most attractive woman he'd ever seen in his life.

She wore white shorts that were a modest length at
mid-thigh and still hugged her bottom and hips alluringly. Her blouse wasn't pink—which was a color he was
thinking of banning from his eyesight forevermore—but
a bold lime green with something that sparkled right
across her breasts, breasts that made his mouth water
each time he saw them—especially since last night he'd
seen them partially bared.

He wasn't going to get out of the truck. Hell, he'd already parked the truck and had his hand on the handle by
the time he considered that option. Walking toward her
he swore he was just going to apologize for being a jerk
last night, and then he was going to leave. He had better

hings to do than spend the afternoon in the park with a
pretty woman.

"The peanut-butter-and-jelly flavor is fabulous! Mimi
orders that every time," Cordy Brockington-Simmons
said standing behind Heaven.

Mimi, her four-year-old daughter, looked like a little
replica of her mother, and from what Preston could tell the
few times he'd seen her she had the same spitfire personal-
ty as the rest of the women in the Brockington family.
Mimi stood next to her mother holding a bright red balloon
and looking at the line as if she wanted to run all the way
o the front and demand her ice cream right this minute.

Propped on Cordy's hip in a way that should have
been uncomfortable but actually seemed natural to her,
was her youngest daughter, Zyra, who had the plumpest
cheeks and prettiest bright gray eyes Preston had ever
seen on a child. Each time he saw her he wanted to hold
her, cuddle her, possibly keep her for his own. Then she
either began talking or said something like "I gotta go
potty," and his mind quickly switched into anti-baby mode
and he gave her back to her mother. As her father, Barry
Simmons, was still away serving their fine country in the
Marines, it was usually Cordy who had the kids.

"That, ah, sounds interesting" was Heaven's reply to
Cordy.

Then she looked over Cordy's shoulder to see Preston,
and the light that had been in her eyes as she, too, stared at
little Zyra vanished. Preston immediately felt like an ass
because there was no question that his presence was responsible for that quick change.

"Hey, Cordy. Hi, Heaven," Preston said cordially before giving in to the urge and holding his arms out for
Zyra. "And hello to you, beautiful princess," he said when
the little girl almost leapt out of her mother's arms to
come to him.

"Careful, Preston, she's still a bit young for you to be using your charms on her," Cordy said with a knowing smile. "Preston and Parker Cantrell are notorious for their way with women. When we were in high school every female with twenty/twenty vision and an ounce of sense was in love with them. You know Parker has that bad-boy swagger about him and Preston—"

"I know," Heaven continued for Cordy, "he's the smooth one."

The way she said that had Preston frowning, only to instantly smile as Zyra spotted her sister's balloon and happily reached for it. Mimi, being the older sister, of course pulled the balloon away, which almost made Zyra fall out of Preston's arms. Instead he held on to her tightly and kissed her chubby little cheek. "Want to go and get a balloon, Zyra?"

"Yes! Yes! Yes!" Zyra cheered then looked over at Cordy for permission.

"The clown's right over there, you'll be able to see me the whole time," Preston said, figuring Cordy was thinking whether she should let her daughter out of her sight with him.

"I know you're not going to steal her, Preston. Hell, I'd be surprised if either of the Double Trouble Cantrells wanted children at all," she said with a smile.

Walking away, Preston tried not to feel the sting of that comment. Cordy was only speaking from her prior knowledge of him. He was certain her words weren't meant with any animosity. Still, he acknowledged that this was precisely one of the reasons he didn't want to come back to Sweetland for good. Everybody knew everybody else, and if they didn't, they knew of them. Preston's reputation from years ago still followed him around as if he'd been caught just last week making out in the back of his car with Avonlea Grant . . . two days after he'd taken Marsha

Hindley to the sophomore dance. He wasn't that guy anymore, but he doubted anyone in this small backward town would care to know that.

By the time he returned with Zyra, a yellow balloon twisted into the shape of a flower and another festive-looking tie-dyed balloon tied with a blue string to her tiny wrist, Heaven and Cordy had both gotten ice cream cones. Mimi had a cup with a mountain-sized scoop of ice cream and whipped cream smoothed on top. She stuck a full spoon into her small mouth and sighed with glee at how good it tasted. Preston smiled right along with her, even though he doubted he would have liked peanut-butter-and-jelly-flavored ice cream.

"There's a dunking booth over near the pond," Cordy was telling Heaven. "That's where I'm headed with the girls. My brother Caleb volunteered to sit for an hour, and I don't want to miss my chance to see him fall into the well of ice-cold water."

"Poor Caleb," Preston said, setting Zyra down on her feet.

"Flowa," the little girl said to Cordy.

"Yes, a very pretty flower, honey. Thank Mr. Preston for being such a gentleman and getting the female flowers."

Preston did not miss the playful sarcasm in Cordy's tone. Nor did he miss the wink she gave Heaven before gathering her daughters and heading toward the pond.

"Buying flowers for two-year-olds is very smooth, Preston," Heaven said when they were alone.

She didn't look angry—her words had come across as lighthearted banter—but as always, he sensed so much more where she was concerned.

"I'm glad you like that because I brought you one also," he said, reaching around to his back pocket and pulling out the pink-flowered balloon he'd stuck there since he'd been holding Zyra in his arms.

She smiled, that very pretty, very genuine smile he found himself looking forward to on a daily basis.

"Thank you," she said, taking the balloon from him and holding it up to her nose as if it were a real flower and she could actually smell it.

"I wanted to apologize for last night. I was rude and out of line," he told her.

"And I was probably defensive and cranky. So I'll accept your apology if you accept mine," she said, looking as if she hadn't really planned to say all that to him.

Preston nodded his agreement. "Then we're even," he replied. "Wanna go check out the dunking booth?"

"Sure," she agreed and took the hand he'd extended to her.

Later, Preston would think that this was definitely not the way he'd planned to spend his day. But it hadn't been such a bad idea after all.

Chapter 13

Heaven had a stomachache.

A candy apple, a hot dog dripping with chili and cheese, and cotton candy all moved around inside her in their own private revolt. She'd been walking for hours, and her right baby toe rubbed painfully against one of the straps of her sandals.

Still, this had been the best day of her life.

Now she sat in the passenger seat of Preston's truck hating for it all to end. But they were back at the B&B and it was just a little past nine at night. The wonderful time she'd had walking along the park and talking to him was over. The games they played and all the food and snacks they ate would probably catch up with them later, but for a couple of hours she'd felt just like a teenager on her very first date.

"I like that you didn't go home as planned," he said, snapping her quickly out of her thoughts.

"When I thought about it, there really wasn't much to rush back for," she replied.

"Right, you told me no boyfriend."

And he remembered. A soft smile touched her lips as

the thought of Preston Cantrell remembering something she'd told him about her personal life touched her—even if that something was as dismal as the fact that she was thirty-two years old without any special person in her life.

"Right. How about you? I mean, I know it's a little late for us to be asking this considering what almost happened last night. But do you have someone special you have to get back to in Baltimore?"

"No. Just my job."

"And that's very special. Michelle told me how you're almost like a famous person with your reputation as a defense attorney in the city."

He'd shifted so that he was sitting sort of sideways in his seat, looking at her. A small smile appeared as he shook his head. "Michelle talks more like my grandmother every day."

"I wish I had met your grandmother."

He looked at her for long seconds after that. So long that Heaven moved uncomfortably in her own seat, unbuckling the seat belt as if she were getting ready to get out.

"She would have liked you," he said quietly. "She would have liked you a lot."

Heaven sat back in the seat then and simply stared at him. "I'm on leave from my job," she said from out of nowhere. "You wanted to know why I stayed in Sweetland, it's because I'm on leave. I don't have a boyfriend probably because I work so much. I don't know." She shrugged. "Anyway, I thought if I got a dog I'd finally have someone in my life, a companion, a friend. Sounds really lame, I know, but there it is."

The look he was now giving her could be classified as startled, stunned, amazed, or maybe disbelieving or unsure. Either way, it made her even more nervous than his silence had. She immediately reached for the door handle this time and was about to open it when he touched her arm.

Actually, he wrapped his fingers around her elbow to hold her still, she figured as she looked back up at him.

"I'm going to kiss you," he said seriously. "I'm telling you this so you won't try to get out of the truck until I'm done."

Well, okay, she thought hesitantly.

One thing she'd learned in the short time she'd known Preston Cantrell was that he was a man of his word. He said he would sign the adoption papers and he did. Last night he said they would take things slow and they had—so slow he'd ended up leaving. So when he'd said he was going to kiss her, guess what? He did!

His lips closed over hers about three seconds after he leaned over the console, one hand gripping the back of her neck to pull her closer. His other hand was still on her elbow as she leaned in. Her lips parted expectantly, as kissing Preston had become one of her favorite new hobbies.

This kiss was slow and explorative as his tongue mingled with hers, his fingers sifting through her hair. She leaned in closer, placing her hands on his shoulders loving the feel of his broadness beneath her fingertips. She clenched his shirt, pulling at the material as the kiss grew deeper and more urgent. When his hand moved from her elbow to her breast, she moaned and he tilted his head, his tongue dueling with hers.

His palm gripped her breast, his thumb grazing over her nipple, and she wrapped her arms around his neck, pressing herself further into his grip. He kissed her neck, mumbling her name or something that sounded like her name as he continued to knead her breast. His other hand joined its counterpart, so that now both her breasts were being fondled, her world being rocked, just a tiny bit.

He had this sort of hungry power about him, one that said *I take what I want* loud and clear. And yet, she felt like he was holding back. Maybe it was all she'd heard about the famous Double Trouble Cantrells and their infamous reputation with the females. Well, she didn't want him to hold back. For once in her life she wanted to go all the way, no questions asked, no recriminations.

With that thought in mind she repositioned her arms so that now, while he still massaged her breasts in that sinfully delicious manner, her hands were lifting the hem of his shirt until her fingers were greeted by the warmth of his skin. His mouth found hers again as he moaned and Heaven licked at his bottom lip, then sucked it deep inside while pushing her hands farther up his torso until the curve of his pectorals was beneath her palms. She flicked his nipples and was rewarded by a deep groan and a deepening of their kiss. She burned all over, wanting him with a desperation that was borderline scary.

His hands moved quickly, grasping her at the waist. She gasped as he pulled her over the console until she was straddling him. He pushed her blouse all the way up until her scantily covered breasts were revealed.

"Heavenly," he sighed before dipping his head to kiss one tender mound.

The touch of his tongue to her skin sent Heaven's mind and body to a place she didn't think she'd ever been before. She arched back, pressing her breasts further into his face while her bottom leveraged backward. Until it pressed right up against the car horn.

The blaring sound startled both Heaven and Preston. She jumped, hitting her head on the interior's roof while Preston tried to quickly shift her off the horn. She tumbled sideways, her thigh catching the gearshift—which wasn't good since his foot must have still been planted on the brake. The truck drifted forward, stopping only after the bumper had connected with Parker's motorcycle . . . which tumbled horrifically to the ground on contact.

Heaven was still pulling down her blouse when Nikki pulled open the passenger-side door. Preston watched from where he had just picked up Parker's bike as Nikki questioned Heaven. To her credit, Heaven looked more composed than Preston felt.

Or than Parker was acting.

"You wrecked my bike!" Parker yelled, stepping lopsidedly around to feel along the side of his bike.

He acted as if it were human and might possibly be bleeding from the collision.

"The bike's fine. Nothing broke," Preston replied tightly.

"You don't know that," was Parker's comeback. "What if she doesn't start? There might be some internal damage."

"To your bike or to Preston?" Quinn asked.

The oldest Cantrell stood on the curb, hands tucked in his pockets. He looked at Preston's face, then nodded down to his midsection, then back up to his face again with a knowing grin.

Thoroughly embarrassed and not liking one minute of it, Preston turned to the side and adjusted the telltale arousal.

"Were you making out? Is that how my bike got busted?" Parker, who was still inspecting his bike, had looked over his shoulder to ask the question.

Preston dragged his hands down his face, wishing a hole could magically appear on the ground and suck him completely under.

"Wait a minute, you mean to tell me that you two were—" Savannah stood about five feet away from Preston, which equated to about seven feet in the opposite direction from where Nikki and Heaven where now standing.

As if the proximity and Savannah's loud voice weren't

suggestive enough, she pointed from Heaven to Preston as she reiterated "you two."

"Hold it, I don't want to know what the two of them were doing in that truck," Michelle said, holding her hand up as if to stop all other talking. "I just need to know if all the humans involved are okay."

"I'm fine," Heaven said softly.

"It wasn't that big a deal," was Preston's contribution to the conversation.

"Not that big of a deal yet," Parker added. "But if something is wrong with my bike, you're buying me a new one. A better one!" he said, slapping the seat of his bike and simultaneously knocking his helmet—the one he'd just picked up—to the ground once more.

Heaven came forward and picked the helmet up, almost bumping into Preston as he'd been about to bend down and do the same thing. Their gazes locked and held for a second too long, because he heard a kissing sound from someone in the peanut gallery—what he was now dubbing his siblings who stood around gawking at them like they were the evening movie. Somebody else yelled, "Get a room," and he figured that was Savannah who had already begun walking back toward the house.

"Well, I don't think we're needed here, honey," Nikki, who had gone to stand beside Quinn, said with a smile.

Everybody seemed to be holding secretive or knowing smiles. Preston's teeth gritted. He wasn't a teenager and yet this was precisely how he'd felt when he was caught with Avonlea in the backseat of the car he and Parker had shared.

"Don't forget we're leaving early tomorrow morning for Queenstown, Heaven," Nikki said.

"I'll be ready," Heaven said. "I'm heading up to bed now."

She moved to walk away but Preston stopped her. He

should have let her go, he knew. Touching her again was a mistake, and in front of his brothers was even worse.

"Hold up, man. At least wait until we're all inside," Parker said with mock disgust.

"Be quiet," Preston said, finally fed up with the intrusion. "We're heading to bed as well."

He'd already laced his fingers through Heaven's by the time he said those words, which, again, was a mistake.

He opened his mouth to try to make it better, then closed it abruptly figuring that wasn't such a good idea.

"You're going to break my arm," Heaven said with a huff the minute they were in her room.

Preston was closing and locking the door, pushing her back up against it. His body was flush with hers, heat cocooning them. "I'm not going to break your arm, but I am going to make love to you," he said on a whisper just before he took her mouth hungrily.

He'd been trying like hell not to go this route with her again. Last night had shown him a side of himself he'd never thought he possessed. His control had slipped and he'd been about to take her like a horny teenager. And after twenty-four hours, a cold shower, a day at the park, and almost totaling his brother's motorcycle, Preston found himself right back in the same position.

Clearly this was something he needed to get out of his system. And that's exactly what he planned to do.

Heaven didn't resist, which was like music to his ears—he wasn't sure stopping was an option for him this time. He cupped her bottom, lifting her thighs until they wrapped securely around his waist. Her arms twined around his neck as she tilted her head to meet the demand of his kiss.

Nipping at her chin, he turned them around and headed straight for the bed. "This is going to be fast. I'll apologize for that right now," he told her as blood pounded through his body, landing in a heated pool at his groin.

"That's fine," she whispered, her breath coming in quick pants. "Just hurry up!"

Preston chuckled, loving the sound of her words. At the bed he set her down with as much care as he could considering he was ready to rip her clothes off and ravage her.

"I don't want you to get the wrong impression." He talked while hurrying to pull his shirt up and over his head.

Tossing it to the floor, he looked at her just as her eyes fell to his chest and she licked her lips. Preston groaned as his erection pressed persistently against the zipper of his pants. When she lifted tentative hands and planted her palms on his pectorals, Preston wanted to roar like something primal about to claim its territory.

"You're gorgeous," she said, coming so close her breath whispered over his bare skin.

Before he could reply, she'd lowered her head and captured his flattened nipple between her lips. Preston grabbed her shoulders, holding her tight as she kissed the width of his chest to find the other nipple. One hand went to the back of her head where he held her close, loving the feel of her tongue on his flesh.

When it was more than he could stand he pulled at her shirt, and since she was determined to keep her lips on him and Preston was determined to get her naked, he pulled until the material ripped.

Heaven, startled, pulled back to look down at her shirt, then up at him.

"I'll buy you a new one," he said as he gave another tug and the shirt was ripped all the way up the side.

She dropped her hands from his chest and lifted her arms. Preston pulled what was left of it up and over her head. He'd gotten a glimpse of what was supposed to be a bra, but looked more like a piece of lace pasted over the rounded mounds of her breasts. After a flick of his wrist to the front clasp, her breasts spilled free and his mouth watered.

He touched her nipples lightly before pushing the bra from her arms then reaching for the button on her shorts. When she was gloriously naked, Preston could only stare. Inch after inch of olive-toned skin was before him, generous curves in all the right places making his body harden further.

He was speechless.

She obviously realized that and reached out to undo the snap of his pants, pushing them down his legs until they were stopped by his shoes. Seconds later he was standing before her clad only in his boxer briefs.

Heaven cleared her throat. "It's been a while," she said in a soft tone, her fingers moving slowly over the band of his underwear.

Preston sucked in a breath, then pushed her hair back over her shoulder. She looked up at him then. "All you have to do is say stop," he told her, praying like hell she wouldn't take his advice.

She shook her head instantly. "Do you have a condom?" she asked, licking her lips.

If he didn't have one in his wallet, he'd run all the way to Godfrey's Market or Jen's General Store to find a box in record time!

"I'm prepared," was his response. He moved away from her only long enough to find his wallet, remove his boxers, and sheathe himself.

By the time he turned back, Heaven was lying on the bed. She'd pushed the comforter and the sheet down and lay on her side, her head propped on her arm, watching him.

"It should be illegal for one man to look like you. I'm certainly glad I didn't grow up in Sweetland."

Her words touched him in a way Preston had never considered. Despite his reputation he'd never been a conceited man. Confident in his abilities and intelligence, yes, but stuck on the way he looked, convinced that he was some sort of gift to females, never. The way Heaven was looking at him, the stark honesty in her words knocked him off balance. His steps toward her momentarily faltered.

"I'm not the only dangerous one in this room. I'm still trying to figure out why some man hasn't snatched you up and put a ring on your finger yet." He climbed into bed beside her as he spoke.

"Maybe I'm not their type."

Preston reached for her then, bringing her over so that she straddled him once more, because feeling her legs wrapped securely around him in the truck had not been enough. "Their loss," he said, cupping the back of her head and bringing her mouth down to his.

Even as their tongues dueled, his hands moved down her back and around to cup her bottom. She rotated her hips, her moist center rubbing seductively over his arousal.

"Every time I try to take my time with you, it doesn't work out," he said, nipping along her jaw and trying like hell not to thrust deep inside of her.

But apparently Heaven had other ideas.

"I thought we'd already decided this would be fast," she told him, arching her body upward to align her entrance with the engorged tip of his erection.

On a ragged curse Preston guided himself into her, gritting his teeth when with one quick motion she impaled herself on his length.

Yeah, he thought with a quick thrust of his hips, to hell with trying to go slow.

* * *

Heaven moved to some sultry melody in her mind. She'd never straddled a man before, never taken charge the way she'd been compelled to with Preston, but damn she was enjoying it.

Each thrust, each undulation of her hips brought new spikes of pleasure to prickle along her skin like goose-flesh. And when he pushed her upward so that she was sitting atop him while he held on to her hips, she thought she would die a sweet death. He guided her motions from there, lifting her upward then pulling her back to match the rhythm of his thrusts. Heaven panted and bit her lip until she thought she would draw blood.

"Come here, beautiful," he whispered when he shifted them until she now lay beneath him.

"I knew from day one you were going to be trouble," he told her before his lips touched hers again.

She loved the feel of his lips, his tongue. Closing her eyes she let herself go in that kiss. She also ignored the questions that would normally come with sleeping with a guy.

This isn't love, Heaven. It's sex. He's a hot guy. You're an aroused girl. End of story.

Over and over she said those words. Even when Preston looked at her as if he just might be thinking beyond the sex, she pushed that thought out of her head.

This was the here and now. It wasn't forever. And she was okay with that.

She was even more okay with the feeling of weightlessness that came with each stroke he delivered. Her legs had been wrapped around his waist, locked at the ankles, while he was leveraged above her, moving his hips in a circular motion that really should be illegal. Her thighs began to shake just as he whispered her name.

She loved how he said her name because it wasn't a reprimand, wasn't a directive. It was appreciative, endearing, and so not what she was used to.

He lifted her legs so that they rested on his shoulders, then worked his hips, and hers, until they were both struggling to breathe. His name tore from her lips in a voice she didn't recognize only seconds before her legs began to convulse and everything around her shattered into tiny pieces that fell in the air like confetti.

"I've never showered with a man before," she told him when he led her into the bathroom and closed the door.

"Then today will be a first for both of us," was his reply as he moved, naked and without an ounce of modesty, to the shower and turned on the water.

He turned to her startled expression. She was still standing by the door, arms folded over her breasts, legs as crossed as they could be considering she was still standing up. She wasn't used to being naked in front of men, either, he surmised.

"Really," he said, moving toward her slowly. "I've never showered with a female."

Preston didn't know why he felt the need to tell her that, but the little spark of relief he saw in her eyes was reward enough for him to not question it a moment further. Instead he reached for her wrists, pulling her arms slowly away from her chest. "You are a beautiful woman, Heaven. Every inch of you is spectacular." He almost told her she shouldn't be shy or ashamed, but wisely kept that to himself. He wanted her comfortable with him— relaxed and completely sated the way he was.

The water was just a breath away from steaming when they stepped inside the stall. Preston immediately positioned them so that Heaven's back was to the wall and his to the spray of water.

"I'll do the honors," he told her with a wicked smile.

"If you insist," was her timid but ready reply.

Lathering his hands, because he didn't want anything

to stand between him and the feel of her skin, he began with her breasts. Preston was sort of developing a fetish for them, which was weird since up until this point he'd proudly claimed to be a booty man. Yet each globe weighed heavily in his soapy palms, turgid nipples causing a heated friction.

"Heavenly," he whispered.

"You said that in the car," she said breathily.

He looked up to see that her eyes were focused on his hands as she once again licked her lips. God, he loved when she did that.

"Because that's what they are. A more heavenly sight I've never seen."

"They're just breasts."

"Spoken from the one who has had them at her command all her life," he replied with a chuckle. "I've had to wait for opportunities to get glimpses of these parts and for yours specifically. . . . Let's just say it feels like a once-in-a-lifetime opportunity. So," he finished with a sigh, "I have to take full advantage."

And that meant squeezing them softly, watching with intense arousal as soap suds slid through his fingers and her skin slipped out of his hand. With determination and a newly burning need, he continued to rub soap along her body. Down her slim torso, over the soft curve of her hips, between her legs where he had to suck in a breath to keep from groaning. Lifting one leg, he lathered her calves, ankle, and foot, then switched to do the next.

All the while she would sigh here and there or grip her shoulders for leverage. When he turned her so that her back faced him, he felt her body tighten.

"Trust me, Heaven. I'm only concerned with your pleasure right now."

She let her head rest against the wall as if in surrender. Preston couldn't resist: He pushed her hair, now damp and hanging limply, to the side and kissed the nape of her neck. Leaving a trail of kisses along the line of her shoulders, he let his soapy hands move up and down her arms. When he could finally stop kissing her delectable skin, he took a step back and lathered down her spine to the curve of her bottom, where he cupped both cheeks and let out his own strained breath.

He'd said she was beautiful, which should have been the highest praise. Still, with each time his eyes alit on her, each different part of her he saw, he realized she was so much more. And she was here, with him.

Of course Preston had enjoyed many females in his lifetime—not as many as his reputation might indicate, but still he was no virgin. But for him the norm was to have sex and go home. Females did not come to his place, he always went to theirs. He made the date plans, he decided when they would go to the next stage, and he decided when it would end. Preston always remained in control.

Always.

Then Heaven looked over her shoulder and whispered his name. Something shifted as he looked from her backside to her eyes and held her stare.

"I can do you now," she told him.

Preston swallowed, his erection thick and heavy, his mind just a little blurred.

If she was timid when they'd first come into the bathroom, that was gone now. Bold, soapy hands touched him, rubbing all over his chest. At his sides his fingers clenched and unclenched. She pressed herself closer, her breasts rubbing against him as her arms wrapped around and slid up and down his back.

"You're much taller than I am, so I may miss some spots."

He shook his head. "No. I think you're hitting all the right spots."

If she was alarmed at his obvious arousal, she didn't say, but continued to rub her body along his. Pulling back, she grabbed the soap once more and worked up a lather so thick Preston thought she might be aiming to clean the entire shower stall instead of just his body.

She came up on tiptoe and kissed him. A hot, open-mouthed kiss that had his hands tangling in her hair, his heart thumping in his chest.

"You do that really well," she told him when she pulled away, her chest heaving.

Preston had to shake his head to try to clear it. He was having a hard time remembering whose idea it was to climb into this shower together.

"You're not bad at it yourself," he told her, then cursed loud and long as she cupped both hands around his length and stroked.

First upward, all the way to the tip, where she let a thumb rub slowly, seductively. Then down, all the way to the base so that a couple of fingers actually rubbed against his scrotum. He swallowed once, then twice, then gasped her name. "Heaven."

He managed to say it twice, only to have her look up at him with a decidedly teasing smile.

"I think *heavenly* is the correct word," she teased.

It had taken a record five minutes to rinse both their bodies, do a spot-dry with the guest towels or the pretty ones that Michelle didn't like being touched, he couldn't remember. What Preston knew without a doubt was that had that condom ripped as his desperate fingers worked alongside her anxious ones to get it on, he might have yelled down the entire B&B.

As it was, fate was on his side. The condom was on tight, and so was Heaven as she sat on his lap working her hips and his arousal until they were both moaning and panting.

He sat on the edge of the bed, which was as far as they'd made it, holding her tightly in his arms as she rotated her hips and he thrust upward in a rhythm that was sure to lead them both to a blissful release. When he attempted to shift their positions so that he could lay her down, Heaven pushed back until he was the one who'd fallen onto the bed. She rose over him, their bodies still connected intimately, and rode him until that mutual goal of extreme pleasure was reached.

Later in the night or the early-morning hours, as Preston looked back on the events of the day, he would remember the idea of having control. He'd also remember Heaven and her hands, her mouth, her tongue, her breasts . . . and he'd agree that control was completely lost.

Chapter 14

"I don't think we have to ask how your night went." Savannah smiled brightly as she sipped from a cup of coffee while leaning against the kitchen counter.

Heaven hesitated. She'd known this would be uncomfortable, but there was no way to get out of the shopping trip she'd already agreed to. And actually, she didn't want to. Of course the Cantrell women would question her about the night spent with their brother. Wasn't that what sisters did? Seeing as she was an only child and had never been involved with a man with siblings before, this was all new to her. It was a good thing Heaven wasn't totally averse to trying new things.

"No," she replied with a smug smile as she reached for a blueberry muffin that was as big as her hand. "You don't have to ask if you don't want to know."

But of course they wanted to know. And strange as it might sound, Heaven wanted to tell.

Raine had been seated at the table, her muffin only half eaten, her coffee mug cupped in both her hands as she peered over the rim at Heaven. She didn't say anything

when Heaven sat down, but Heaven knew barely held re
straint when she saw it.

Savannah put forth no such effort.

"Okay, so Preston's been at this thing with seducing
women for a really long time so I'm not going to bother to
ask if it was good. But you can feel free to tell us just how
good it was." With a waggle of her eyebrows and a huge
grin, Savannah Cantrell earned herself a big spot in Heav
en's heart.

She was the lively sister, the one who had escaped the
small town to see the world and had come back with said
world on her shoulders. It was clear that Savannah was
a stunning beauty, but she was also compassionate and
loyal and as observant as the rest of her siblings. But spe
cifically, since the first day Heaven had walked into the
inn, Savannah had been in-your-face honest and more en
tertaining than any other female she'd had the pleasure of
meeting. She was refreshing in her liveliness and candor
and Heaven envied her that free spirit.

For those reasons and a few more of her own, Heaven
smiled.

"It was the best I've ever had," she said, then felt heat in
her cheeks and figured she'd better put something in her
mouth before she said too much.

"Hot damn! That's my brother," Savannah quipped with
a hoot of laughter.

"I'm assuming that means Preston and Heaven had a
hot steamy night," Nikki said, entering the kitchen with a
tray of dirty glasses and napkins.

A little after nine in the morning Michelle would al
ready be in the restaurant making sure the breakfast
crowd was handled, even though Tanya and Lisa Kramer,
residents of Sweetland who were home from college for
the summer and always worked part-time at The Silver
Spoon, were perfectly capable of handling it. Nikki, how

ver, came right in and checked on all the guests—which
ght now was a total of two elderly couples from Mis-
ouri. Best friends who had known each other all their
ves and had married their high school sweethearts. The
disons and Krandalls were celebrating thirty-five years
f love and laughter. That's what they'd told Heaven one
vening when all of them sat on the porch watching the
inset and drinking lemonade. She'd been touched
y their sincerity and their seemingly imperishable love
or one another.

Just one more thing in Sweetland that made her
nvious—a feeling she hadn't experienced much in her life.

"I hope you didn't deplete too much of his energy. The
uys are in charge of the inn while we're out today,"
ikki continued as she loaded the dishwasher.

Reaching over to snag a piece of Heaven's muffin,
avannah shook her head and popped the food into her
iouth. "Well, Heaven's looking a little tired so I'm not
ire how much energy Preston will have."

"I feel fine," Heaven replied.

"I'll just bet you do," Savannah fired back.

Raine shook her head, a small smile ghosting her lips.
All right, Savannah, give the girl a break. She's not used
> your raging hormones and candid exploration of every-
ie else's sex life."

"That's because I now have to live vicariously through
veryone else," Savannah replied drily. "It's not my fault
iere are only a handful of men in this hideously small
wn."

"There are more than a handful of men in Sweetland,"
ikki defended.

Savannah frowned. "I prefer men with all their hair,
eth, and other vital body parts. And I'd rather not have to
> down to Charlie's and scrape them off the floor just to
et a good bout of sex in each night."

"You prefer to have them fawning over you like you'r the queen of England, isn't that more accurate?"

The sizzle in the air and the tart words came whe Michelle entered the kitchen. As the oldest Cantrell sist and the youngest, these two went at it every time the were within three feet of each other. Some days it wa amusing and others it was tiring. If there was love betwee these two, it was really hard to see. And yet Savanna hadn't left to go home and Michelle seemed to look fo ward to seeing her youngest sister on a daily basis.

These family dynamics were intriguing to Heaven.

"What should we wear to the soiree?" Raine asked b way of keeping the peace and changing the subject.

She did that very well, but looked a little weary at ha ing to perform such a task so frequently. Heaven decide to help her out.

"I was going to ask the same question. I've never bee to a soiree before," she said.

"Really? I would have definitely pegged you for a so cialite. You have perfect posture and manners just lik those high-society ladies I've met on my travels. The one who look down their nose at the young model for fear she come to sleep with their husbands."

A few beats of almost intolerable silence followe Savannah's remark.

"I've been to dinner parties and business functions, a given by rich and uptight people who probably hadn laughed in ages," she said with her own wry chuckl "The Bay Soiree sounds like it'll be much more fun. D you wear ball gowns or will simple evening dresses su fice?"

Savannah had stood after her comments on societ wives and their husbands. She put her cup in the dishwash before Nikki closed it.

"There's nothing simple about evening dresses," sh

aid in an almost bereft tone. "I see I'm going to have my work cut out with all of you today. I'll meet you in the car." She left the three of them in the kitchen.

"She's hiding something," Raine said quietly.

"I think so, too," Nikki commented, still staring at the swinging door that Savannah had passed through.

Michelle pulled her apron off with such force it was a wonder the material didn't rip. "Vanna's been getting in trouble all her life. Nothing she does now would surprise me," she said with what was probably meant to be hostile disregard. But in her eyes Heaven saw concern and a pain that Heaven supposed could only exist among family.

"Then a day with the girls should make her feel a lot better," Heaven offered. She knew she could use a day with the girls, even if these girls were only temporarily hers.

"Being involved with a woman is like tending a garden," Mr. Sylvester said.

He'd been sitting at one of the tables on the patio side of the restaurant. The dinner rush had just died down, and now at a little after eight in the evening the only patrons left in The Silver Spoon's main dining room were Caleb Brockington and whatever female he was romancing this week, along with the town's mayor, Liza Fitzgerald, and her husband, Mike, who came in every week for dinner. The restaurant would be closing at nine, so right now their remaining guests were having coffee and drinks.

Preston and Quinn were cleaning off tables while Parker sat at another table rolling plastic silverware into paper napkins in preparation for tomorrow's Bay Day Parade. Michelle had left strict and detailed instructions on everything the guys were supposed to get done today. The list had been extensive and grueling, which they all figured Michelle had done on purpose. Still, they'd decided early on to divide and conquer because defeat was not a option.

"How do you figure that?" Parker asked Mr. Sylveste garnering irritated looks from both Preston and Quinn.

Mr. Sylvester was a nice old man. He was well mean ing and certainly cared about the progress of The Silve Spoon. He was also still mourning Gramma's loss ju like the rest of them. So Preston had decided he would cu the man some slack; besides, he wasn't that bad to talk t depending on what mood Preston was in. Tonight he wa tired and he couldn't stop thinking about Heaven, whom he hadn't seen since around nine thirty this morning whe he'd watched her climb into the back of Michelle's min van.

"You've got to tend to them daily. Not one day goes b that you don't have to water them, talk to them. That how they grow and flourish. And the one thing you wan with your woman is for the relationship to grow and t flourish. Standing still doesn't work for anybody," Mr. Sy vester continued.

He'd long since finished his dinner of smothered por chops and dirty rice. His glass of lemonade was half ful and the dish that had held his double-chocolate Smith I land cake was empty. For the most part his attention ha been focused on the game of solitaire he'd been playin for the last thirty minutes, slapping cards on the table i measured intervals as he surveyed his options like ther might be a cash prize if he won.

"What if moving into a relationship isn't what you wan I think a one-night stand should be legal in this day an age," Parker continued.

Preston wanted to go over and choke him. Quinn, c the other hand, only shook his head.

"One-night stands get old fast," Quinn added.

"Not when you're doing them right," was Parker's re-ort. "Or with the right person I should say."

"There comes a time in every man's life when he needs o stop dipping and diving and settle into something real," Mr. Sylvester told them.

Preston moved around the tables, taking one last look or dirty dishes and/or trash with a swiftness he hadn't ad in a couple of hours. He desperately wanted to get out f this room and away from this conversation before it ook a turn he didn't even want to entertain.

"Yeah, but you have to find the right female to have omething real with," Parker continued. "And I'm not onvinced there's a right female for every man. Some nen are meant to be just what they are, sexy and single."

"Or just stuck on stupid," Mr. Sylvester quipped before apping another card down. He hadn't even bothered to ook up at them as he talked.

Quinn chuckled.

"That Heaven girl seems like a nice one. A real one," Mr. Sylvester continued.

He knew it. Just as sure as he knew his name, Preston new this was the direction the conversation had been eading all along. Mr. Sylvester's bringing up Heaven had ll been a part of the plan. His frown wasn't going to make go away. So instead he headed for the entryway that ould take him back into the main dining room.

"A real one who just might be in some real trouble," arker added. "I meant to tell you that I ran a check arough the national database and her name was a hit in a ouple of reports coming out of Boston."

For as much as Preston didn't want to talk about him nd Heaven on a personal level, he definitely wanted to now what was going on regarding her safety.

"What kind of reports?" he asked, stopping in his tracks.

Parker folded another napkin, tying it off with strips of some kind of ribbon material that Michelle had pre-cut and stuffed into a Ziploc bag. "As a witness in some type of investigation. I didn't get a lot of details, just the name of the cop investigating."

"A criminal investigation?" Preston asked, his mind already entertaining scenarios.

What if she'd witnessed a murder and someone was looking for her to keep her from testifying? He'd seen plenty of those incidents go drastically wrong—or right for the wrong person.

Or she could have witnessed something a little tamer on the criminal scope, like embezzlement. She worked at a huge pharmaceutical company, so things like that weren't totally out of the question. Or maybe someone was stealing drugs from the lab and she was the sole witness? That would make someone angry enough to come after her. His teeth gritted so hard, his temples throbbed.

"Whoa, hold on there, don't go losing your temper," Parker said, standing up and walking over to where Preston stood. "She doesn't have a police record, so she's just a witness. I don't know the details yet but I'll get them."

"Fine," Preston said tightly.

Quinn had also approached him. "No. It's not fine. You look like you're ready to tear someone's head off. I'm thinking most likely whoever was driving that SUV that almost ran her down last night."

"That girl's got a lot of pain in her past," Mr. Sylvester put in from his spot at the table.

"Don't we all," Preston quipped, even though he really couldn't claim to have gone through a lot of pain. Yes, he'd lost his father and subsequently his mother, but his grandmother had always been the glue that held them together. So as long as she was still there for them each day

hey came home from school, all had seemed right in the
orld. Now was a different story.

"Whatever this is, we'll figure it out," Quinn told Preson, clapping a hand on his shoulder. "And if you're feeling
omething for her, that's okay, too."

"I don't like the idea of someone trying to hurt a female.
ou know that, Quinn," Preston argued, because that was
ll there was to feel where Heaven was concerned.

Quinn gave him a knowing look and shook his head.
None of us likes the idea of a female being hurt," he said,
tting his hand fall from Preston's shoulder.

"That's why we're going to take care of this situation.
ll put in a call to the Boston PD first thing tomorrow
orning to see what I can find out," Parker vowed.

"Thanks. I appreciate that," Preston replied and began
walk out of the room once more.

"Trying to convince yourself you're only worried about
r safety's like a dog chasing its tail. Just gonna keep go-
g in circles until you finally fall on your butt and face
e truth," Mr. Sylvester said, then scooped up his deck of
rds and stood from the table.

"You boys have a good night," he told them before mov-
g in his slow gait past Preston to exit through the front
staurant door.

llow, white, and black balloons and ribbons and bows
ecorated Main Street. Twined around each lamppost
ere thick satin yellow ribbons with sunflower-centered
ws. There was a yearly window-decorating contest so
at each of the stores along the street had gone all-out to
ecorate a window representing the town's theme: *Visit
veetland, MD—Life should be this sweet.*

There was no traffic on the street today as this was
e main route of the parade. Yesterday as they'd returned

from shopping at the outlet mall in Queenstown, Michelle
had driven along the parade route checking to make sure
that all of the booths had been assembled and were in
the spaces coordinating with the map she'd given to
Hoover and the band of barmates he'd assembled to help
him with the setup. Heaven had since learned that the
man whose vehicle had scared the crap out of her when
she'd first arrived in Sweetland was Hoover King, former
town-council member, who was still called on to do odd
jobs around town because most of the older citizens felt
sorry for him.

That's the way it was in this town, Heaven had surmised: Everybody looked out for one another. No matter
what. In the time she'd been here she'd watched as Nikki's
sister Cordy showed up at the restaurant to help out during the lunch-hour rush while her children played in the
backyard with the dogs. Nikki's father was the fire chief,
but he'd been right there helping shuck the corn and setting
up the steamers the day of the crab feast. And Michelle—
that woman cooked more than was humanly possible, it
seemed, on a daily basis. Heaven hadn't gone to school
for cooking and she didn't really do it all that well, but
she'd gotten into the habit of getting up early each morning to meet Michelle in the kitchen, helping to prepare
whatever she needed. This morning they'd been baking
cakes and pies to sell at The Silver Spoon booth during
and after the big parade.

That's probably why she'd missed seeing Preston.
While he and his brothers loved to eat whatever Michelle
cooked, being in the kitchen while she was cooking
was not one of their favorites. Heaven had almost expected to see him waiting for her in her room when she'd
finally gone back upstairs to get dressed for the day. But
he hadn't been there, either. Telling herself she was being
silly, she'd even walked into the backyard under the pre-

ense of checking on Coco but really hoping to see him. No such luck.

Sometime during their ride over to Boudoir—which was where The Silver Spoon's booth had been strategically placed, a block away from where the other food vendors and storefronts began—she'd decided that she wasn't going to let Preston Cantrell get to her. No matter how much her body craved his touch, or how much some mental part of her felt it needed to see him. She was going to be stronger. He was just a man, like she was just a woman. And they'd just had sex.

Terrific sex.

Mind-blowing, body-melting, terrific sex.

Dammit.

"The sun's really shining today," Raine said, looking up and shielding her eyes from the morning sunshine.

"That's why I wore a hat," said Savannah, who playfully tipped the wide brim of her wheat-colored floppy sun hat. Wrapped around the cap was a shimmering silver ribbon that tied and hung alluringly down to the center of her bare back. Her white halter-top one-piece romper looked equally cool and sexy, while wedge sandals completed the decidedly chic summer outfit. It didn't even matter that Michelle had given her sample duty, which meant she would spend the majority of her day slicing up pieces of pie and cake and walking up and down the street offering the free samples of The Silver Spoon's best.

Heaven secretly wished she could be that without-a-thought sexy. Maybe then Preston wouldn't have simply vanished.

That thought had her shaking her head, silently wishing for another therapy session. Even though she knew what her therapist would say. "You can be whatever you want to be, Heaven. Stop waiting for permission or validation."

It was good advice. Expensive-as-hell, three-times-a-week, $225-hour advice, but good nonetheless.

"You still thinking about that dress?" Michelle said as she nudged past Heaven to get behind the booth.

Heaven had just finished hanging the silver-and-white satin sash across the front of the booth that hung over the SILVER SPOON sign. She'd stood up and seen Savannah, then swiped her hands over the short sundress she wore. It was new; she'd bought it yesterday at the outlet. It was fuchsia, a really nice color on her, so Michelle had said. And it was short, coming only to mid-thigh in a swirling skirt while the bodice hugged her chest like a glove. It made her feel pretty and sexy and just a little self-conscious, all at the same time.

"It is okay, right?" she asked, commanding her arms to remain at her sides and not tug at the dress anymore.

"It looks fine," Michelle said. "Actually, I think it looks better than fine."

"And I happen to agree," Preston said, stepping up behind her.

She jumped and turned at his voice, her heart doing some crazy little flutter that made her feel like smiling. Instead she coughed to cover her silly schoolgirl reaction.

"I think I might be developing allergies," she continued, still covering up.

"I have some Claritin in my purse," Raine offered.

Savannah rolled her eyes. Michelle handed Raine a pie and indicated that she should start cutting instead.

"Have I told you how much I like you in the color pink?" Preston asked.

He wore shorts today, navy blue, with another polo shirt in a sky-blue color that made him look perfectly tanned and decadently handsome.

"It's fuchsia," was her reply. She wanted to bite a hole right through her lip for the silly response.

He smiled.

And that made her smile.

"It's a pretty dress for a pretty lady," he continued, reaching up to touch a soft curl that rested on her shoulder.

"You here to help?" she asked because he was too close. So close her breasts were already swelling with arousal, her pulse quickening.

"Michelle gave us a list yesterday. At the bottom it said to be here at ten fifteen and not a second later." He lifted his arm and looked at his wrist. "I've got ten minutes to spare."

She nodded. "She's a stickler and today's really important to her."

"Today's really important to all of us," he told her.

Us. The word had a special sort of ring and made her feel like smiling all over again. Standing here, today, beneath the sunshine on this beautiful summer's day in a town she never thought she'd be in, with people she'd never imagined meeting. She wanted to smile and to hold on to this moment forever. And to run at the same time because if something felt too good to be true that usually meant it wasn't true at all.

Except something else her therapist had told her replayed in her mind throughout the rest of the day.

"You can be happy if it's what you really want."

"See that up there?" Preston asked Heaven when they were alone walking along the riverbank behind the house.

"It's the moon," she replied, loving the feel of his hand wrapped securely around hers.

"It's the summer's moon," he continued. "When you see it hovering above the water, like it's ready to take a dip in the coolness, you close your eyes and make a wish."

She chuckled. She'd been doing a lot of that today—during the parade and afterward at the big dinner Michelle had cooked for them all, which they'd shared on the patio of the restaurant.

"You're making that up."

He shook his head and stopped walking to stand behind her. He reached around to put his hands over her eyes.

"Close them," he whispered in her ear.

She shivered at the warmth and took a deep breath. Then she did as he said and closed her eyes.

"Now think about what you want most in the world." His words brushed along her earlobe a second before his lips.

This time she shivered and didn't care if he noticed.

"Now wish for it," he finished, and his tongue stroked her lobe, then the tender skin beneath.

Heaven wished once. Then again for good measure.

Then Preston's arms wrapped around her waist. He pulled her back against him, holding her so tight that for a moment she almost couldn't breathe. That could also be attributed to the warmth that engulfed her at his touch. They'd been together all day long, in a roundabout sort of way. She'd stood at the booth passing out pamphlets and answering questions about the B&B and the restaurant alongside Michelle. Raine had taken more of a backseat to the festivities as she'd focused on cutting all the cake and pies—making Savannah's job easier, since at that point all she had to do was smile and hand out the free samples. Quinn and Nikki had been on foot patrol, walking throughout the crowd to get up close and personal with any tourists who hadn't managed to get to the booth. Parker, who wasn't as mobile as he wanted to be, opted to stay at the inn in case anyone decided they'd like to check in immediately. And Preston had appeared every now and then, each time talking to someone Heaven had nei-

her seen nor heard of before. Of course that really didn't
mean much to her since she didn't know a good portion of
the townsfolk. But at one point Michelle had even asked
about a particular man that Preston had been seen talking
to on more than one occasion.

"I hope your wish comes true," he said, reminding her
that she was standing in the almost-cool night air, looking out at the serenity of a calm river illuminated only by
the romance of the full moon.

"Did you make a wish?"

"Nah, haven't done that in forever," he replied.

She looked back at him with a mock frown. "Then why'd
you tell me to do it?"

He kissed the tip of her nose. "Because you looked like
you could use a wish come true."

Boy, could she, Heaven thought with a sigh. She turned
back to face the water, letting her head rest against his chest.
She'd folded her arms so that they were atop his at her midsection, and together they stood there for silent moments.

"I think I'm growing attached to this little town," she
admitted.

"It's a nice little town to grow attached to, if that's what
you're looking for."

And that was a very noncommittal response that only
surprised her minutely. Preston didn't seem like he really
wanted to be in Sweetland—and yet he hadn't left to go
back to the city, either.

"I don't really know what I'm looking for."

"Are you running from something?"

She shook her head immediately. "Running never solves
anything," was her quick reply, even though she was positive she'd done something akin to running all her life by
refusing to stand up to her parents and submerging herself in work instead of going after the things she really

wanted in life. Things that had been on her mind a lot in the weeks she'd been in Sweetland.

"You're right about that, but sometimes you need the escape."

"Escape can be dangerous. It's healthier to stay in the here and now."

"You sound like a shrink," he said with a chuckle.

She gave a wry laugh in return. "I've spent enough time with one." Heaven knew that admission was a mistake the moment it slipped from her mouth.

Behind her Preston tensed, but he didn't let her go.

"One's mental health is very important. If therapy is needed, it should be utilized."

"Are you giving me permission to be crazy?" It was meant to lighten the suddenly somber mood. Heaven decided to turn in his arms, lacing her arms around his neck.

He looked down at her, his brow furrowed. "I'm giving you permission to let yourself go, to be who and what you want to be honestly and freely."

Preston made that statement so seriously, she could almost visualize him in a courtroom leaning over a witness and telling her the same thing—he'd never use this tone with a male witness, she was sure.

The funny thing was, he couldn't possibly know how truly liberating those words were for her.

"You're giving me permission?" she asked with a smile, then pressed her body closer to his.

He nodded. "Let go and be who you want to be."

"You sure that's what you want?"

For a moment she thought he would say something like *Why not? Do you want to be a mass murderer or some thing?* Instead he stroked his hands up and down her back until they rested just above the curve of her bottom.

"There's only one thing I'm sure about right at this very moment," he whispered.

"I would ask what that one thing was, but it might jeopardize my taking your advice." She came up on tiptoe then, until her face was just inches away from his. "I want to let go, Preston. I want to totally let go with you."

Chapter 15

Preston had tried.

He really had.

Just ask the floor to his room where he'd paced back and forth for hours because he couldn't sleep. All night long he'd wanted to go to her, to slip beneath the covers and simply hold her. Hell, he'd even wished Coco was in his room; at least then the puppy would have kept him company in the wee hours of the night.

But Coco now resided with Heaven, upstairs in the Sunshine Room. Heaven walked Coco and fed Coco and played with Coco while Preston spent his time trying not to think of either of them. It was a battle he felt like he was losing.

He'd known she would be at the parade, had known he'd have to be near her all day long but keep his hands to himself. And after a quick run and a cool shower, he'd thought he could handle that.

Then he saw her.

And everything, even the sun, had paled in comparison. It was at that point Preston wondered if he should panic, if the casual attraction he thought he had to Heaven was turning into something a little more dangerous. He kept himself occupied with the politicians of Sweetland— town council members, the mayor and her family, and of course the Redling brothers, who were beginning their promotional efforts for their resort. Preston was a firm believer in keeping your enemies close, even the suit-and-tie, dangerously polite ones.

Still, he hadn't been able to keep his mind off her for more than a few minutes at a time. Eventually his don't-think-about-her mode shifted into gotta-get-close-to-her, and he'd hurried dinner with his family.

Now she was looking up at him, her pert lips parted slightly, eyes dim in the evening but still etched with passion. Her body was so soft and fit against his so perfectly. It was no wonder he grew hard instantly, no question that he would lower his head and touch his lips to hers.

Preston loved kissing Heaven. She was always so compliant, as if she'd been waiting just as long as he had for this moment. And when their tongues collided it was like a reunion, a sweet, intoxicating reunion that left him feeling aroused, a little bit weak, and a lot protective. The protection part came because he knew there was something she was holding back from him. He hoped that whatever Parker could find out from his cop friend would fill in all the gaps. But somehow Preston wasn't so sure. And he wanted to be sure, desperately. He wanted to know that Heaven was going to be all right when he returned to Baltimore. When she returned to Boston, or rather *if* she returned to Boston. He couldn't help but assume that since he didn't have all the facts.

For now, however, he was just content to feel her softness pressed willingly against him. She tasted sweet, like the homemade raspberry sorbet they'd had for dessert.

When she sighed into the kiss and let her fingers grip the back of his head, a wave of lust struck him so powerfully he almost couldn't breathe. His hands tightened at her waist, then of their own accord moved down to grasp her buttocks. She moaned, tilting her head so that he could deepen the kiss. His chest tingled where her breasts were pressed against him, his erection hard and desperate to be inside her.

But they were outside, exposed to any of his siblings who might wander out back. Or more likely Mr. Sylvester, who loved to sit out here on the old bench because that's what he and Gramma used to do on nice evenings like this.

Reluctantly Preston broke the kiss, but he couldn't pull completely away. Instead he rested his forehead on hers while they both struggled to catch their breath.

"This is unexpected," she whispered.

He pulled back to look at her, an act he knew would only heighten his desire.

"I agree."

"I don't really know what to do about it."

It was an admission he'd already made to himself.

"Right now I'd say we should take it inside. We don't need an audience." With that said, Preston reluctantly released his hold on her, but took her hand to keep the connection.

She threaded her fingers through his agreeably, and they walked toward the house.

"I've always wondered what it would be like to have siblings," she began when they were almost to the back steps.

"Crowded," was his light reply. "Especially if one is a twin."

"You two look almost exactly alike," she told him. "but you act so different."

"That's a good thing for you, believe me."

Preston let her take the steps ahead of him, but kept his

hand in hers. She reached out and opened the screen door, then the back door as if she'd been here much longer than two weeks. And when she moved through the house, it was with the ease of a resident and not a guest. He wondered how he felt about that.

"Are you saying Parker and I wouldn't be a nice fit?" she asked when they were heading past the powder room and entering the front foyer.

"I'm saying you're getting the better twin," he told her, refusing to even think of his brother with Heaven.

Preston and Parker had never fought over the same female; their tastes in that department were drastically different. Where Preston looked for the more intellectual and attractive females, Parker was driven completely by his hormones and followed wherever they led him regularly. The one thing they did share—aside from their obvious love for the opposite sex—was their aversion to commitment. Long-term entanglements were completely off-limits for both of them, and that was an undeniable fact, ask any of the females they'd ever been involved with.

"That sounds pretty conceited." She continued the conversation when they'd arrived at her room and she'd let them inside.

Closing the door behind him felt familiar in a good way, and when she headed directly to the bed, slipping off her sandals, a scene flashed across Preston's mind.

It was after a long day at the office for him, at work for her. Dinner had been meat loaf and mashed potatoes—Preston's favorite—from the restaurant, and now they were ready to settle in for the night. She would undress and slip into her nightgown, then go into the bathroom to do whatever it was women did before getting into bed. He would take off his clothes and put his cell phone on its charger on the table beside the bed. He slept on the left side and she the right, they'd agreed on that early on. Then they would lie in bed and talk about the events of the day, the plans for tomorrow. In the morning they would awake and start all over again. It was comfortable, fulfilling, stable.

And scary as hell.

"Preston?"

He jolted as if someone had shaken him awake from a dream. Clearing his throat to cover his unexplainable actions, Preston started to walk across the room.

"I don't want to talk about my brother anymore," he said, then placed his hands at her waist, pulling her up close to him.

"Okay." She looked momentarily confused.

"I don't want to talk at all." His words were rough, and so was the way he pulled her closer so that he could grind his burgeoning erection into her center.

She flattened her hands over his chest and looked up at him. "We don't have to talk anymore," she whispered.

"Good."

He kissed her then, dragging his lips over hers and thrusting his tongue inside to conquer. She sighed and leaned into him, and his mind was filled with her. The way she felt, sounded, tasted—everything about Heaven here and now was absorbed in that kiss.

She pulled at the hem of his shirt, pushing it up his chest until he tore his mouth from hers long enough for her to yank it over his head. The dress that had been taunting him all day long came off in a quick motion that he barely registered. All Preston knew was that he wanted her naked. Now!

His wish came true in a matter of minutes as they both tore at each other's clothes urgently. Cupping her face in his hands he kissed her again, loving the feel of her hands lacing around his waist, palms flattening on his buttocks as she pulled him closer.

He wasn't sure which one of them gave the safe-sex reminder, but he moved like time was of the essence to grab a foil packet from his wallet only to fumble trying to open it.

"Let me," she said with a nervous chuckle, taking the packet from his hands.

Any other time Preston might have argued but now he sensed it would only waste valuable moments. Moments he certainly did not want to lose as he wanted desperately to be inside her.

His entire body tightened as she gripped his length with one hand, then slid the latex over him with the other. A few quick gulps, and a second of entertaining thoughts of a baseball field with three men on base, and him up to bat, held his release at bay. The moment he was covered he grasped Heaven at the waist and lifted her off the floor. With her arms snaking around his neck, she instantly wrapped her legs around his waist. It was that little move that may have been the beginning of Preston's end.

He didn't hesitate but pulled back just enough so that his erection was perfectly positioned and thrust inside her waiting moistness with a fervor that had both of them crying out.

And that's how it proceeded. Fast and furious, a give-and-take, tit-for-tat, do-or-die type of lovemaking that both of them seemed to thoroughly enjoy.

When they finally fell onto the bed, it had been Preston's intention to rise above Heaven and enter her once more, taking them to the glorious release they so desired.

"I want you this way," she told him in a husky tone as she pushed him flat on his back.

"Your wish is my command," he told her after only a moment's dazed hesitation.

She straddled him, raised her hips, and guided his length deep inside her. Then she moved and he moved; she set the rhythm and he matched it. She let her head fall back as she moaned his name. His fingers clenched at her waist as he cried out hers. Through half-closed eyes Preston stared up at her, saw the generous swells of breasts moving with their gyrations, glimpsed the lovely curve of her torso as it stretched to the flaring of her hips. The line of her neck seemed softer as her head lolled to one side, hair cascading in dark contrast to the honey tone of her skin. When she cried out once more and stiffened atop him, Preston held her steady, waiting a beat to shift her so that she lay on her side. He kept them both in that position, his length still hard and deep inside her, and began to stroke.

Heaven lifted her leg to drape over his thighs, and he continued to thrust in and out of her, their breaths coming in quick pants, pleasure escalating.

And then there was nothing else. There was no bottom to hold him, no firmness to ground him as Preston slipped over the edge of desire into the gentle abyss of pleasure. He felt like he was falling and couldn't grasp onto anything to break that fall. As his body tensed, his release seeping quickly from him, Heaven wrapped her arms around him once more, holding him tightly against her.

She cocooned him—that's the only way Preston could describe it. Her inner walls had clenched so tightly around him he couldn't retreat even if he wanted to. And her arms held him with a certain totality he didn't know if he could explain. It was as if she didn't want to let go. And when his arms wrapped around her, it seemed to seal some type of unspoken deal, like maybe he wouldn't let her go, either.

The next day was the Summer Bake-Off. As reported by Michelle, the Summer Bake-Off was the second of Sweet-

and's annual baking competitions. This one was always held during the Bay Day celebrations, while the Winter Bake-Off was held Thanksgiving weekend. Of course Michelle was entered into the competition that she'd claimed honors at for the last three years. This year she'd vowed to use only recipes handed down to her from Mary Janet Cantrell, without any deviations, and if she won it would be in honor of her grandmother's memory.

Heaven had been touched by that declaration, and so it was no wonder she'd awakened just before dawn, showered, and headed down to the kitchen to help. What was a wonder, however, was that she'd left a sleeping Preston in her bed.

He'd held her all night long. In fact—she was going to admit it, even though it sounded funny to her own ears—Preston hadn't stopped touching her all night. Whether it was the soft intimate caresses that preceded sex so intense she'd almost shed a tear at one point, or to hold her close to him as they slept, the first moment she'd been without contact with him had been when she crept out of the bed.

Gazing down on him, she noted how even in sleep he looked intense, like something was running rampant through his mind that probably kept him from dreaming. Preston Cantrell did not strike her as a man who dreamed. He planned, yes; she had a sense that he'd planned his departure from Sweetland and his entire career before he'd actually graduated from high school. And to date he'd stuck to that plan perfectly. So there was no room for dreams.

That was a dismal thought, and she'd tried to push it from her mind as she'd dressed. But before leaving the room she'd been drawn to him once more. With a feather-light touch her fingers traced the strong outline of his jaw up to the lobe of his ear, and then stroked the softness of

his hair. He lay on his back, one arm resting on the pillow
atop his head, the other hidden beneath the sheet that lay
precariously at his waist. His chest was bare and magnificent, clean-shaven and magnificent. Had she already said
that?

A gentle tugging began in her center, and she backed
away quickly before that gentle nudge shifted to an immediate urge that she would have no choice but to act on. As
she closed the door behind her, Heaven smiled to herself,
wondering exactly when she'd become insatiable. Probably
the moment she walked into The Silver Spoon.

Heaven had gotten into the habit of not traveling every
step with her cell phone on her hip. It had happened right
after her mother's first call insisting that she return to
Boston to have dinner with Geoffrey. She'd looked at it every day, answering messages from the agency that wanted
to confirm everything was going okay with Coco after
the adoption had been finalized. Her therapist had called
for an update and she'd returned her call. Other than that,
Heaven had no contact with her world in Boston, which
seemed strange. For years she'd been dedicated to her
job; she'd hardly been able to think of anything but her
work and the progress she'd been making toward finding
a cure or at least a substantive treatment for Alzheimer's.
Until she'd arrived in Sweetland.

Now none of that seemed as important.

Sure, she was still interested in helping people through
her work. Her research had been groundbreaking, with
several universities asking her to lecture on the subject.
She'd even published a paper outlining some of the steps
she'd taken to finding what they thought might be a viable serum. She'd been flattered by the offers and had
actually entertained the idea of lecturing on a freelance
basis. But her parents had connections to Larengetics,

ey knew the founders of the company and had already
romised Heaven and her research to them. She'd gone
ong because earning a six-figure salary at the age of
venty-five didn't happen to people like her. She wasn't
1 actress or singer or superstar of any type, and doing
omething illegal had never crossed her mind. Accepting
1e job at Larengetics was a given.

And she hadn't heard from anyone there since the ex-
osion.

As she descended the last step and headed toward the
tchen, Heaven's cell phone vibrated. She almost cursed
 she thought maybe she should have left it upstairs after
1. Pulling it from the case at her hip, she looked at the
reen and saw the same number she'd seen before. She'd
issed the call, and they hadn't left a message. That was
hy she answered this time.

"Heaven Montgomery," she said in her professional
ice.

"You'll pay for what you did!"

Heaven was stunned, first by the deep gravelly voice,
en the instant silence as the call disconnected. She didn't
10w how long she'd stood there staring at her phone, but
at's exactly how Parker found her.

"Something wrong?" he asked coming to stand near her.

Heaven's head snapped in his direction, but she didn't
eak immediately. He touched her shoulder and she
mped, tripping over something—most likely her own
et—and tumbling back into the wall.

For all that his leg was in a brace that reached up to his
igh and on some days he used a cane to assist in his walk-
g, Parker was pretty fast. He grabbed hold of her before
e could slump to the floor. They both clumsily stayed
right, and she felt like a colossal idiot for almost mak-
g him fall.

"Oh, I'm sorry. I'm so sorry," she was saying, trying t
pull away from him.

"What's wrong? Did something happen?" he asked, fo
a second sounding just like Preston.

His eyes were the same shade as Preston's, like roo
beer, and his eyebrows were dark and thick like Preston'
too. He wore jeans and a T-shirt that looked as if it ha
been made specifically to fit him. Parker was more mus
cled than Preston, his arms roped with thick veins, shou
ders broad and intimidating.

"Nothing. I'm, ah, I'm fine," she stammered.

He shook his head. "No. You're not."

She clenched the phone in her hand, even as she wa
swallowing, preparing to tell him again that she was fin
when Michelle came into the room.

"What's going on out here? It's not even seven in th
morning and the two of you are out here making enoug
noise to wake the Smythe couple," she said in that no
nonsense way she had.

Her apron was already sprinkled with what Heave
figured was flour, her dark hair pulled back into a bun–
her cooking hairdo, as she'd told Heaven before. That wa
why Heaven had pulled her hair back into a ponytail be
fore she'd come down.

"It's my fault, I apologize," she said using this oppor
tunity to step away from Parker, who was watching he
like he knew for certain she wasn't telling the truth. "
won't happen again."

Then she was gone, moving quickly down the foye
and pushing through the swinging doors to the kitchen.

"What was that?" Michelle asked Parker. "What di
you do to her?"

Parker frowned. "I didn't do anything but walk in here
She was spooked even before I said a word to her."

"She's pale and she was shaking. Did you see that?

Michelle had folded her arms over her chest. She'd glanced in the direction where Heaven had gone, then back at her brother. "I don't like it."

"If you're feeling like that, how do you think Preston's going to feel when I tell him she's being stalked?"

Chapter 16

Mr. Sylvester watched her closely.

She'd been sitting in that same spot playing with tha puppy for the last half hour. Every now and then she'd looked up to the sky as if she was asking someone fo something; then her attention returned to the puppy. I made her smile, and Mr. Sylvester felt a softening in hi chest each time she did that.

Normally those pups would run wild and fast as soor as they were set free, but not this one. Nope, she—he knew it was one of the girls because Michelle had fittec them all with pink collars and the boys with dark blue since the siblings still had trouble telling them apart— stayed right up under Heaven. She climbed into Heaven' lap and put her front paws on her chest, licking at her face until Heaven giggled. Satisfied with her work, the pur would settle down, resting her chin on Heaven's thigh waiting with great expectation for her to rub behind he ears. Heaven did so without a second thought.

This girl was lonely. Mr. Sylvester had thought that the first time he'd seen her walking around the house alon the small hallway just outside the caretaker's suite. That's where Janet kept all her family photos. They lined the wall so that as soon as the door to the suite was opened each morning Janet could see them first thing. There were pictures of all the children through the various stages of their lives, as well as pictures of Janet's parents. Her father, Perry Davidson, had been the town's mayor for a time, and her late husband's great-grandfather Cyrus Cantrell had held that same office during his years.

The way Heaven had reached out and touched some of those photos, letting her fingers drift softly over the faces, saddened Mr. Sylvester. He knew then that she was brought here for a reason. Yes, part of that reason was obviously that little puppy she was holding. But there was something more. She needed to be here at this moment. And she needed somebody else to be here with her.

After a while he decided to go on over and talk to her. She'd been alone a lot in her life, he suspected, and he didn't want her to be alone much more.

"That little one sure is in love with you," Mr. Sylvester said when he'd finally approached Heaven.

"I'm in love with her, too," she said with a giggle.

It sounded genuine and it also sounded rusty, like laughing wasn't something she did often. "Love's like that sometimes. It comes on quick and bites you right in the butt so you can't run away."

"Oh I wouldn't run away from my Coco. She's my life now," Heaven told him. She continued to rub her fingers under the dog's ears and then over her stomach when she rolled over in Heaven's lap.

"A dog can be a really good friend. They can love you just as much as you love them, sometimes more I suspect. But they can't be your life. They can't give you everything you need," he told her seriously, leaning on his cane as he talked.

She reached up, tucking a lock of hair behind her ear,

then tilted her head to look up at him. Her eyes squinted in the afternoon sun, her hands still touching the puppy moving about in her lap.

"I know that she can't be my whole life. But she can be the beginning of my new life," she told him seriously.

Mr. Sylvester smiled. He couldn't help it. This was a smart girl. She'd been wounded, and pretty bad—she still looked shaken by whatever had happened in her past. But as she sat here right now she knew she had to start fresh, to rebuild and rejuvenate. That took guts, and it took a special person to achieve it. He had no doubt Heaven could start again. The only thing Mr. Sylvester wondered was if she knew that this time someone else would need to start over with her.

They talked for a little while longer, her sharing only that Sweetland was really beginning to grow on her. That, coincidentally, was just the thing Mr. Sylvester needed to hear. He whistled, something he realized he hadn't done since Janet's death, as he walked into the house.

"He's gonna fall hard. Yes indeed he is," Mr. Sylvester said to himself, chuckling as he headed down the foyer that led to his room. "That boy's gonna fight all the way, but she's gonna get him. He doesn't have a chance in hell of resisting a woman like that one."

"Mr. Cantrell, we weren't expecting you," Steven Redling said, sitting up straight in his chair.

That was obvious, Preston thought. He'd just stepped into Redling's office, only to see none other than Diana McCann draped over the man's lap. While Redling had been clearly startled and rushed to push Diana away, then straighten his tie and button the buttons on his shirt Diana had undoubtedly dislodged, she had sashayed from behind the desk glaring at Preston the entire time.

"Preston Cantrell never needs to be announced, do ou, Preston?" She'd come to a stop at the front of the desk esting her backside—her very shapely backside—on the dge while folding her arms over her chest—a generously ndowed chest.

There was no doubt that Diana McCann was an attrac- ive woman—that had been a given since she turned six- een and grew tits and ass that all the guys in town wanted o touch. But for Preston, there never had been much nore to Diana than the pretty smile, soft hair, irritating voice, and great body. As he stood looking at her today, ne thought not much had changed.

"Your secretary wasn't at her desk so I figured I'd just :ome on in. And the door wasn't closed," he added with an eye to Steven, who at thirty-two years old and the next n line to inherit the Redling millions obviously wasn't nearly as smart as his older brother.

Steven cleared his throat and stood. "She's probably down at the pool. There was a big celebration for its un- veiling today. You should head on down and get yourself some refreshments. Our cook is marvelous."

"Oh, no, Steven, Preston only eats his sister's cooking. And before that he would only eat his grandmother's. The Cantrells are like that, kind of narrow-minded, if attrac- tive, folk."

"*Loyal* is the word I think you were looking for," Preston corrected.

Diana had made it no secret that Parker was the pre- ferred member of the Double Trouble Cantrells for her. Preston didn't mind; in fact, he was glad she'd decided to cast her net in another direction. But that had only hap- pened after he'd rebuked her kiss and turned away when she'd lifted her shirt to show him that the snap had broken off on her bra. It had been one of those champion moments

Preston would later pride himself on. He couldn't say that he'd turned away from the sight of bare breasts—D cups he was almost positive—ever again.

His thoughts were interrupted by Diana's throaty laugh. Her head fell back, just enough so that her long hair fanned behind her, breasts poking out in front for all to see. Only "all" was just Preston, and he still wasn't interested.

"Was there something I could help you with?" Steven said, stepping around Diana and standing in front of her as if he was protecting what was his.

Preston thought about telling him there wasn't a chance in hell he'd ever reach out to touch Diana McCann, but figured that would be useless. Diana would no doubt take that as a sign he was interested—because her little mind couldn't comprehend anything beyond her own wants and needs. And Steven looked as if he was stupid enough to possibly take a swing at Preston under some misguided notion that he'd be fighting for his woman. Diana McCann was any man's woman—that was a known fact around Sweetland, and probably the one that had finally killed her uncle and guardian, George Bellmont.

"You said I could stop by whenever I wanted for complete tour." Preston held up his hands. "Here I am."

"Right. Right," Steven said, reaching over to the chair and snagging his suit jacket. "Let's start downstairs and work our way around. I'm sure you'll see what a smooth setup we have here at The Marina. Maybe you'll take some notes to see how you can improve over at your little B and B."

Preston stopped at those words. They were just about to go through the door when he turned back to Steven.

"Our little B and B is just fine the way it is," he said with an edge to his voice that he hoped didn't show the pinch of doubt he'd been harboring.

Steven smiled and clapped a hand on Preston's shoulder

er. "Sure it is. I've heard nothing but good things about
ne quaint yellow inn at the end of Sycamore. The towns-
olk love to talk about that place and its history. I figure
's going to take a while for them to get used a new fix-
are in town. But they will get used to us, Mr. Cantrell.
's only a matter of time."

The rest of the morning and the early hours of the af-
ernoon were spent in the company of that pompous, im-
nature ass. And the only thing that made it worse was
vhen they were finally joined by Phillip, the older pomp-
us ass who wore his millionaire status like a new hat that
e couldn't help flaunting.

By the time Preston arrived back at the B&B he was
eady to hit something. If he were home in the city, he
vould have headed straight to the gym and strapped on
is boxing gloves. When they had time, he and Parker
vould go a couple of rounds. When they didn't, Preston
pent a lot of time with the bag before swimming laps
ntil his muscles screamed. And that was how he dealt
vith his frustrations.

Today, however, the minute he walked into his room
nd saw Parker and Quinn sitting in front of the televi-
ion, both with dour expressions on their faces, he didn't
nink even a gym would help.

"I just spent the better part of my day with those
diculous Redling brothers. What they lack in common
ense, their money sure as hell makes up for. The Marina is
gorgeous resort with every amenity imaginable. If we're
oing to compete, we've got to think a little bigger than
ne restaurant and hosting family crab feasts," he said,
rossing the small room that was called the sitting area
nd taking a seat in the recliner opposite his brothers.

His brothers still remained sullenly quiet.

"I don't think we need to go for the big and fabulous
ngle because let's face it, The Marina has twice the space

we have. We should still look to be family-oriented, keepin
the original small-town feel. Some will want that above th
corporate and impersonal atmosphere. But I was thinkir
we could work with some of the local businesses to off
some one-of-a-kind perks. I could draft contracts once v
reach the agreements, but that spa that's about to ope
would be great to partner with. Females love spa day pac
ages," Parker continued, rubbing his eyes as he talked ar
trying to ignore the growling of his stomach that seeme
awfully loud in the way-too-quiet room.

Why was the room so quiet?

The television wasn't on—that was one reason. Th
other was that his brothers still hadn't said a word.

"What's going on?" Preston finally asked when he s
up in his chair and really looked at them.

Quinn had his elbows resting on his knees, his for
head knotted. Parker, who had for some reason remove
the brace from his leg, sat with it outstretched, a har
rubbing over his knee. His face was serious, stoic. It w
his police face, and that alarmed Preston.

"Where's Heaven?" was his next question, spoken wi
just a little more urgency.

"She was outside with Mr. Sylvester before I came
here. That was about fifteen minutes ago," Quinn said.

"Before that she spent the morning in the kitchen hel
ing Michelle bake. The bake-off starts in an hour a
Michelle expects all of us to show up for support," w
Parker's reply.

Preston nodded. "My previous question was—wha
up? Which one of you wants to answer that one?"

"Heaven has a stalker," Parker said seriously. "He
been calling her at least three times a day. It's the san
number from that first night you gave me the phone.
walked in on her this morning right after she'd taken
call. She looked like she was about to pass out, or run f

he hills, I'm not real sure which one. I asked her about it
nd she brushed it off. Michelle interrupted and agreed that
Ieaven looked frightened. So I pulled the record again."

"We've been waiting for you to return to talk to you
bout it," Quinn said.

"You should've called me on my cell!" Preston raged.
I would have come back immediately. Who is it? An
x? I asked her if she was seeing anyone and she told
ne no."

"The number is from a disposable phone. There's no
vay to track the owner. But newspapers say she's engaged
o be married," Parker offered.

"What? Married?" Preston's head throbbed.

Quinn shook his head. "I don't believe she came here
o cheat on a fiancé."

"Does anyone ever set out to cheat?" Preston asked,
ury soaring through him at the moment. She'd lied to
im. And he'd fallen for it. Now, more than ever, Preston
eeded that gym bag or possibly this fiancé of Heaven's
o punch on.

"She doesn't strike me as that type of woman," Quinn
ontinued. "I think there's more going on here. Have you
sked her anything about her personal life? I mean, be-
ore you slept with her did you at least try to find out the
asics?"

Preston didn't like the way Quinn had phrased that
uestion. "I'm not a kid, Quinn. I know how to talk to
emales before I take them to bed, and yes, I did ask about
er home and work life."

Quinn didn't look fazed by his outburst.

"And what did she say?"

Dragging a hand down his face, Preston reached for
he calm that seemed to be dodging him at the moment.

"She said she was on an extended leave of absence from
er job. There was no boyfriend at home for her to hurry

back to and she was thinking that maybe Sweetland was
better place for her. That's what she told me."

"That's *all* she told you?" Quinn asked.

Preston stood and paced, thinking the movement woul
better combat this urgency to go out and find Heave
Montgomery.

"I didn't do a background check, if that's what you mear
I asked questions and she answered them the way sh
wanted to. The same bull women pull all the time."

"Fear will make you hide things," Parker said. "Tha
and pride. Maybe she's ashamed of what happened i
her past. And maybe she didn't come here to jump int
bed with you. But I know you, Preston, maybe bette
than anybody else in this world. When you set out t
seduce a woman, she doesn't have a chance of turnin
you down."

"I don't seduce married or engaged women, Parker. You
of all people, should know that," was Preston's heated retor

Parker nodded. "I do know that. My instinct says w
still don't have the whole story. Besides, the fiancé i
some rich finance mogul. He's about fifteen years olde
than Heaven, and by the looks of the honey on his arm i
this picture snapped just two days ago, he's not missin
his so-called fiancée very much."

Parker had tossed a folder on the table as he talkec
Preston picked it up and opened it. The man did look ol
and that was a hell of a honey on his arm. So where di
Heaven fit into all this?

He couldn't think, didn't want to think about this. Fo
the past few weeks Preston had known he was off hi
game. He'd felt it each time he was around Heaven. An
still, somewhere in the back of his mind he'd continue
to remind himself that it was his motto not to trust an
female. Yet he'd fallen right into bed with her, and—
while this would remain his secret—he'd felt like sh

as seeping into a part of him he'd had locked off for all
is life.

"Dammit!" he cursed.

We need to talk."

Just like that, in a serious, don't-mess-with-me tone
nd a look that said *Try me*. Heaven was debating
hether to be offended or simply amused by the fact
at Preston thought this was all he had to do and she'd
me running.

"Well, hello. I was just about to take Coco into the base-
ent with the others. Then I'll be walking down to the
ke-off to help Michelle," she said, sparing him only a
ight glance over her shoulder as she walked toward the
sement door.

"I need to talk to you about something important," he
sisted.

"Then walk with me and I'll listen."

She'd seen him come from the house taking long steps
at spoke of determination. The furrow of his brows and
e thin set of his lips indicated he was angry about someing. Maybe because she'd left her room before he'd
vakened this morning. Heaven doubted very seriously
at was it. But whatever it was had put Preston in a
appy mood, a mood that was now being inflicted on her.

"I need your undivided attention," he said, reaching out
touch her arm.

Heaven shook her head as she moved out of his reach.
)kay, once I put Coco away you'll have it."

He didn't look happy with that, but it was the best she
as willing to do. Sitting in the yard most of the after-
)on playing with Coco had allowed her lots of time to
ink. She'd thought about her job and her parents,
eoffrey and her job again. At regular intervals thoughts
' Preston would interrupt. She wondered where their

relationship was going, or if it was a relationship at all. And while she'd come to some conclusions, the jury was definitely still out on the Preston situation.

He followed her down into the basement where Coco was escorted to her own kennel that was attached to her siblings' kennels. This way, Michelle had explained, they could all see one another and didn't feel separated even when they were inside. Ms. Cleo's kennel was on the other side so she could see her puppies. Behind her, as she secured Coco, Heaven heard Preston locking the door behind them. They could use the stairs to enter the house without having to go back outside.

"Parker thinks someone is stalking you," he said, his voice falling like lead in the dim basement.

She hesitated only momentarily, then continued to work the door to the kennel until it was closed and Coco was secured. Then she stood, wiping her hands down her thighs as she turned to face him.

"That's ridiculous. Nobody would want to stalk me," she said in as calm a tone as she could manage.

"How about the fiancé that you left in Boston? Did you try to run away from him by coming here? Is he the one who's calling you, or maybe he was the one who tried to run you down."

Heaven didn't like the way he was talking to her. She didn't like the underlying implication in his tone. Basically, she didn't like this entire exchange. But instead of yelling and possibly looking even more guilty than she presumed she already did, she took a steadying breath before speaking.

"Does your brother do a background check on every one who stays at the inn? You're going to lose a ton of customers that way." Her voice was perfectly calm. She wanted to give herself a pat on the back.

But Preston wasn't amused. He stepped closer to her.

"I asked you if there was someone back in Boston you needed to hurry back to," he said, accusing her with the way his eyes bore into her.

Heaven slipped her arms behind her back, clasping fingers she didn't have any other idea what to do with.

"And I told you no."

"Parker says you're engaged. He read it in the newspapers online when he searched your name."

She tilted her head, surveying him because she was trying to see what was really going on here. Was Preston pissed off at the thought that she might be engaged and had slept with him anyway? Or was he angry about some sort of betrayal he thought she'd inflicted? He had that hurt look, like somehow she may have disappointed him. But Heaven had no idea how that could be.

"You asked me a question and I gave you an honest answer. If you want to believe the newspapers that were undoubtedly written by someone other than myself, go right ahead."

"That doesn't really sound like a denial," he scoffed.

"Take it as you want." Then she realized she didn't really want to be here with him right now. He was in a pissy mood, and she had other things to do.

"I want to know about you and Geoffrey Billingsley, and I want to know how many times he's called to harass you," Preston told her.

"Have you ever not gotten what you wanted, Preston? I mean, your reputation with women precedes you, so it's no wonder I had to sleep with you even though I knew it was probably a mistake. Now you're talking to me as if you're giving me an ultimatum. 'Tell me the truth or else,' " she said, trying to mimic his tone.

"I'm not joking," was all he said.

She shook her head. "And neither am I. There's never been any reason to lie to you, Preston."

"So when you said there was no boyfriend to go back to that wasn't really a lie, since Billingsley is your fiancé?"

"Billingsley is a close friend of my mother's. He's the man my mother would like for me to marry because of his social status and bank account. I never agreed to marry him."

"Who called you this morning?"

"I don't know."

"What did they say that upset you?"

"Is Parker a reporter in his spare time?" she asked, crossing her arms over her chest. "The call was nothing. Someone telling me I'd be sorry for what I did. Considering I didn't do anything, I can't take the threat seriously. Case closed."

He was in front of her before she could take another breath, his hands on her shoulders as he pulled her close. "Case is not closed if there's some maniac out there trying to hurt you. First there was the speeding SUV, then the phone call. There's something going on, Heaven, and you cannot stand there and deny you're thinking the same thing."

Preston was absolutely right. She couldn't stand there and deny it. So she opted to walk away.

Chapter 17

"I'm not nervous at all," Michelle said.

It was the third time she'd said it in the last five minutes. Raine and Heaven cast each other knowing glances. The bake-off was being held in the basement of the city hall building because the forecast had called for late-afternoon showers. The place was packed, because each contestant had an individual booth—twelve in all, lined in a U shape around the room. The judges had tables spread across the front, just beneath the small stage-and-podium setup.

The walls were painted a cheery yellow with beige tiled flooring. Black and white satin had been draped all around. Big crystal vases bursting with sunflowers adorned each booth, with a framed number marking the contestant's identity in the contest. Michelle was number 5.

People milled about all throughout the center of the room, flipping through a program that listed the biographies of the contestants and the products each had entered. It was designed to look like a menu, which Heaven thought was a great idea. In fact, she thought this entire Bay Day celebration, or at least the parts she'd seen of it

so far, was turning out to be more fun than any of the so
cial parties she'd ever attended. Tomorrow the barbecu
cook-off would take place down at the pier, followed b
the seafood cook-off on Monday. Both these events too
place in the evening, allowing time for everyone to go
church on Sunday and then work the next day. Wedne:
day was all about the Fourth of July; restaurants woul
set up booths outside to serve customers as they explore
the town and searched for the best seats for the evenin
fireworks. On Thursday the boats arrived for the sailin
contest, which was slated for first thing Friday mor
ing. And Saturday night would cap off the week's celebra
tion with the Bay Soiree, one of Sweetland's most lavis
and formal affairs.

There never seemed to be a dull moment here, eve
though it was a small town and those were reported
boring and stale. Heaven wondered about whoever ha
come up with that description of a small town. That pers
must not have had the pleasure of staying in Sweetland.

"No, honey, you're not nervous at all," Raine sa
calmly. "But Heaven and I will take your entries over
the judges. You stay here just in case someone comes
with questions about the inn."

Michelle's hands were shaking as she closed the top
the container she'd slipped her double-chocolate-an
raspberry cake into. She had three entries: the cake,
apple pie, and strawberry tarts, each of which looked d
licious. As Heaven picked up one of the containers a
followed Raine across the crowded room, she felt a sp
of pride to be involved in such an event. These entri
not only represented Michelle Cantrell's cooking a
baking abilities, but they also spoke of the kind of trea
ment one would get at The Silver Spoon. The hospitab
way that Raine greeted each judge—showing Heaven ho

o duplicate the same—spoke of the gracious treatment
each guest would receive at the inn.

In this town, Heaven had learned, everything tied in
ogether to make a whole. All her life she'd felt like a loose
end. The child that Opaline had never planned to have,
the woman that no young, attractive, normal man was
good enough to date, the biochemist no company would
ever trust again.

"We need to finish our conversation later." She heard
his voice from behind, felt his hand as he touched her elbow. And she sighed.

She didn't want to talk to Preston again.

If he'd said they needed to go down by the river and lie
on the grass, holding hands as they watched the moonlight, she would have jumped at the opportunity. But talking, well, that wasn't going to end well and so she'd rather
avoid it altogether.

"I'm walking Coco later," was her sugary-sweet reply
as she turned away from the judges' table and found herself up close and personal with him.

"Heaven, this is serious. It's about your safety," he told
her adamantly, his brow drawn tight so that he looked like
he was in deep consternation.

She inhaled slowly and sighed. She totally got that he
was concerned and was actually touched by that senti-
ment. Nobody had ever been concerned about her welfare
before—concerned about her portfolio, maybe, and her
marriage of convenience to support the high-profile social
status her parents preferred, but never solely about her
welfare.

And really, she could see why he was feeling there
might be some danger. An SUV had almost run her down
in the street, and there was some crazy person calling her
cell phone and hanging up, but both of those things could

have been coincidence. Drunk drivers strike all the time and rarely do they know their victims. People dial the wrong number, cell phone numbers are recycled—there were numerous reasons she could be getting the crank calls.

Except the last one had told her she would regret what she did.

Heaven's answer for that was, she hadn't done any thing.

"I understand why you're worried, but really there's no one who would want to stalk me. Geoffrey is not in love with me, never has been. Nobody cares that I left Boston. Nobody has asked about my research or if I'm coming back to finish the serum. It's like I've dropped off the face of the earth for them. So I'm not worried about a few of things happening. I'm trying to start again," she said with an exasperated sigh.

Then, because the look on his face said she'd said too much, she moved back a step. And then another. Until she bumped into someone and heard a female screech that could burst an eardrum.

"Are you crazy? Don't you know how to watch where you're going?"

Those were the first words she heard before turning to stare into angry sea-green eyes.

"I apologize. I really didn't see you," Heaven began to say but Miss Stormy Eyes wasn't trying to hear it.

She'd stepped closer to Heaven, pointing a long-nailed finger in her face. "You should have seen me because you should have been paying attention. Don't you know who I am?"

And before Heaven could answer Preston had stepped up beside her.

"I know who you are, Diana. She apologized, now let it go."

"She destroyed my dress, Preston. I will not let it go!" Diana screamed.

It was then that Heaven looked down. Diana wore a white silk dress that danced in flirty ruffles at her knee. The bodice was smeared with what looked like hot pink and yellow frosting. On the floor at her feet was a platter of what used to be cupcakes.

"I'm so sorry," Heaven said.

"You already apologized and it's not enough," was Diana's retort before another sound erupted from her.

She seemed overly dramatic for a woman that Heaven doubted very seriously had baked those cupcakes herself. After staring at her for a few seconds, then Preston saying her name, she remembered the woman from the first day she'd been at The Silver Spoon. She'd been having a temper tantrum then as well.

"I'll buy you more cupcakes, Diana," Preston told her, grasping Heaven's hand as he spoke.

Diana's head tilted, and she looked from Preston to Heaven and back again. Heaven could feel it, the slow slithering down her back that signaled disaster. She'd felt it seconds before the explosion.

"So this is your new conquest? You Cantrell boys don't waste any time, do you?"

She looked at Preston as if he'd betrayed her in some way. Heaven felt compelled to say something, to stop the scene that was beginning to draw attention.

"No. It's not like that. Preston had nothing to do with it. I just wasn't watching where I was going and—"

Before Heaven could finish her sentence, Diana struck, pushing her with both hands on her shoulders. Heaven stumbled back. Preston reached out an arm to steady her. Diana bent down and popped up so quickly Heaven barely registered her next move. But the smashed cupcake appeared in her peripheral vision, and she reached up her hand to block Diana's. With her arm midair Heaven grasped Diana's wrist and turned. In the next seconds the cupcake collided with Diana's face and another scream erupted.

That was followed by some claps, some gasps of disapproval, and Preston putting himself quickly between her and a swinging Diana. Minutes later she was whisked through the crowd and pushed through a door, the early-evening breeze brushing against her face.

The door slammed behind her and she jumped, but Preston was right there putting his hands on her shoulders to hold her steady.

"I just closed the door," he whispered into her ear as he leaned close to her.

"I didn't mean to make a scene," Heaven said, her entire body shaking.

It had been a long time since she'd had to defend herself physically, but growing up a so-called privileged child, who was tall and lanky, quiet and unassuming, she'd turned out to be a beacon for bullies. And when pushed to her limits, Heaven had fought back. Then and now.

"Diana McCann is a scene, wherever she goes. It's in her nature to overdramatize and reach for any bit of attention she can. It wasn't your fault."

"I should have been watching where I was going," she continued, shaking her head.

Preston still held her, his arms moving to wrap completely around her, his front pressed into her back. "Do you have eyes in the back of your head? I'm standing back here but I don't see any."

"Not funny," she said when she felt his chest move and heard the slight ripple of laughter.

"I don't know, seeing Diana with chocolate cake and rainbow icing smeared over her face was pretty funny," he said, his laughter coming quicker now.

So quick and so infectious, Heaven found herself laugh-

ing with him. Diana had looked funny, stomping her feet
and screaming like a three-year-old with cake smeared
all over her.

"She's going to hate me forever now," Heaven said getting herself together.

"It's okay, she vowed to hate me forever about twelve
years ago. Your life will go on, believe me."

Heaven turned in his arms because the feel of his growing arousal pressing into her was fast becoming a distrac-
tion.

"What did you do to make her hate you? I thought you
were the smooth Cantrell, the one all the ladies wanted to
capture," she asked playfully.

Preston shook his head. "It's all talk. I'm just a regular
guy. One who on a hot summer's night had decided that
Diana's nasty attitude made even the sight of her bare
breasts unbearable."

"Oh, goodness, you saw her naked?"

"I saw her naked breasts, after she lifted her shirt and
bra to show me. I guess it was her attempt at seduction. But
we were both young and I definitely was not interested."
He shrugged. "She doesn't take rejection well."

Heaven smiled. "Rejection or cupcakes on her dress
and in her face. We're some pair, huh?" she asked and
chuckled.

Preston didn't even smile. Instead he traced a finger
along the line of her jaw, staring down to follow the path
of his finger until it lightly touched her bottom lip.

"We definitely make some pair, Heaven."

Her breath caught as his gaze locked with hers.

"Preston," she whispered.

"Don't think," he warned in a soft voice. "Don't think
about what we should do or shouldn't do, just feel. We'll
be the couple that just feels," he told her.

And then he kissed her.

And Heaven didn't think; she didn't even think she breathed. But damn, did she feel . . . like wrapping her legs around his waist and riding him until they both screamed.

"Really, you guys need to get a room," Savannah quipped as she came through the back door where Heaven and Preston stood. "Oh, I forgot, you have a room at the best bed-and-breakfast in town."

Heaven jerked away from Preston so fast she tumbled back a couple of steps. Preston didn't even reach for her this time. It seemed like the more he reached where she was concerned, the more she pulled back. At least in the area of her personal business, because as far as the desire between them went, she was right on board with him.

All he had to do was touch her and the heat was ignited. And damn, did he love touching her.

And yet that wasn't quite enough for him. He didn't like that realization.

"Is Diana okay?" Heaven asked Savannah.

"That drama queen is just fine. Somebody wiped her face but that dress is ruined. Pity." Savannah laughed to signify how insincere that last remark was.

"I didn't mean it," Heaven continued.

Savannah waved her words away. "She deserved it. She's a bitch and it's about time somebody told her so. Anyway, the judges are ready to make their decision and Michelle's about to lose her mind so you two need to stop making out and get in here."

With that message delivered Savannah went back inside. Heaven took a step to follow, but Preston wasn't finished with her yet. He didn't touch her physically because that would have led to other things. Instead he simply said, "I want to keep you safe. If that's a bad thing, sue me."

It was the truth and then again it wasn't the full truth.

There might have been more Preston wanted to say, but he refrained. Waiting to see how this settled with her was his excuse.

Heaven looked over her shoulder at him. "Thank you," she said in a soft voice. "I've never had anyone try to protect me before. It's kind of nice."

Well, all right, he thought, stepping forward until he was standing beside her. Preston took her hand in his, giving her what he thought was his best smile.

"I'm a nice guy, didn't you hear?"

"Right," she added with a smile of her own. "I think I did hear that somewhere."

Chapter 18

She was back at the lab, standing near the countertop a few feet away from her desk. Larengetics Pharmaceuticals was located at the Boston Marine Industrial Park. It was a three-story building that ran the expanse of three to four blocks with executive offices on the top floor and the laboratory on the bottom.

Heaven's formal office was on the second floor toward the end of the hallway that led directly downstairs to the lab and was officially used for a fire exit.

For more than a year she'd been working on a serum named LRG124. One two four was her apartment number, and she'd also assigned it to this serum because it had been late one night, approximately one twenty-four in the morning, when she'd completed the complex formula that would make LRG124—the answer to Alzheimer's.

Across the room Moira Lindsey, the lab assistant she'd just hired two months ago, worked on mixing the formula according to Heaven's notes. Near the door, emptying yesterday's materials into a biohazard bag, was Lewis Beam, the custodian. Heaven read over her notes on converting the serum into a dry formula that could be condensed into a pill form. It was nearing noon, she knew, because two food trucks had already pulled up and parked in their usual spots across the street. Billows of smoke came from the hamburger truck as they'd already begun preparing for the employees from the building who hadn't brought their lunches from home.

Moira liked to listen to music as she worked so one of her classical CDs was playing quietly, casting a sort of dreary mood in the lab. The rustle of things falling into the plastic bag Lewis held wasn't disruptive—until something fell onto the floor. It sounded like one of the beakers, as glass shattered. Heaven sighed and dropped her pen. She was just about to turn around to see what Lewis had knocked over, and if it was something of importance, when there was another noise, a louder noise that filled the lab with thick black smoke and bright orange sparks.

From a distance Moira screamed. More glass shattered, more things exploded. Heaven's chest hurt as she inhaled and coughed in response. Her eyes blurred and she fell to her knees, wondering if her next breath would be her last.

"Heaven! Heaven, wake up!"

She was jolted awake by the shaking and probably the yelling as well. Or was it the barking?

When she opened her eyes, it was to see Savannah sitting on the side of her bed, her own eyes wide with confusion. Then Savannah moved away, taking her hands from Heaven's shoulder. She lifted Coco and dropped the noisy puppy onto the bed, where she immediately jumped into Heaven's lap.

"I'm awake. I'm awake," Heaven said, absently rubbing Coco's head as the dog proceeded to lick her face.

She struggled to sit all the way up, Coco's rotation of barking and licking mixing comfort with the relief that Savannah had taken her hands off her.

When Heaven had awakened at the hospital hours

after the explosion, there had been police officers all around and one of them had his hands on her shoulders just as Savannah had. Telling Savannah to get off her would have been rude, but Heaven's heart was hammering and the feel of someone touching her right at this moment would have been just too much.

"Are you okay?" Savannah asked.

Heaven nodded, not really able to say the words because it wasn't totally true.

"The Smythes heard screaming and came downstairs where I'd just come in with Parker, but we heard you the minute we walked through the door," Savannah told her.

And for the first time Heaven noticed how genuinely pretty Savannah was. She wore no makeup and yet her elegantly arched eyebrows and high cheekbones highlighted a vintage beauty. Looking over her shoulder, she saw Parker leaning against the doorjamb. His T-shirt was tight, accentuating his muscled upper body—as was usually the case with him. Just the other day, she'd wondered if his entire wardrobe consisted of well-fitting jeans and even better-fitting T-shirts. If it did she was sure the female population wouldn't mind one bit. He didn't speak but raised an eyebrow at her as if to ask if she was okay.

Licking her dry lips, Heaven nodded in response.

"I must have had a bad dream," she said finally. "I'll just go down and get something to drink. Maybe some hot tea, that normally helps," she said more to herself than to the people staring at her.

"What's going on? I came as soon as—" Preston's words drifted as he pushed past Parker and entered the room.

"What happened?" he asked, kneeling onto the other side of the bed until he was right beside her.

Heaven was shaking her head as Coco bounced over to Preston, sniffing his hands, then resting her head on

he bed in front of him. She wanted him to rub behind her
ears. Without even looking down at her, Preston did just
that.

"Bad dream," Heaven said with a sigh. "Not the end of
the world."

"I could hear her downstairs and so did the guests,"
Savannah offered Preston by way of explanation.

Great, now more people thought she was crazy. "I'm
sorry, I didn't mean to disturb anyone," she said.

"Nonsense, what was the nightmare about?" Preston
pushed.

"Nothing. Not a nightmare, just a bad dream," she corrected him futilely.

"Same thing," Savannah tsked.

And here Heaven thought she was on her side.

"Come on, Savannah, let's go make sure the Smythes
are okay," Parker said from the doorway. "We'll talk later,
Pres," he said to his brother.

About her, Heaven figured. She knew Parker was a
detective. If Preston was so determined to make her believe she was being stalked, he probably had his brother
in on the case as well. Only there was no case. She was
not being stalked. Well, maybe she was, by these damned
dreams that just refused to leave her alone.

"I'm really sorry," she said when they were alone.

She looked down at her hands, her fingers clasping and
unclasping. By sheer will she stopped and looked up at
Preston. "I hope I didn't cost you customers."

"I wish you would tell me what's going on," was Preston's instant reply. "I went for a walk after dinner and
ended up at the pier. For the last two hours I've been
down there walking around, staring out at the water and
wondering what it was you could possibly be hiding."

And if that wasn't enough to make her want to tell him
everything, the sincere look in his brown eyes was. He

wore jogging pants and a baggy shirt. Not as enticing an outfit as his twin, but arousing to her just the same.

She lay back against the pillows, closing her eyes for another second, then inhaling deeply before opening them again.

"Six months ago there was an explosion at the lab. My lab assistant and the janitor were killed. I survived," she said simply. But the reality was anything but.

Preston looked at her like he wasn't surprised. Except for the twitch in his jaw, there was no reaction from him.

No turning back now, she told herself.

"The police investigated me for months because they believed I rigged the explosion since I was the only one to survive. But I didn't," she said adamantly. "I would never have done something like that."

Preston reached out a hand and cupped her cheek. "You didn't have to say that last part, Heaven. I know that's not something you would do."

She shook her head. "No. You don't know that. You couldn't possibly know because you've only known me a couple of weeks."

"It's been a great couple of weeks," he countered.

His hand felt so good on her skin—warm, solid, comforting.

"I haven't been back to work since that day."

"What were you working on?"

She didn't hesitate to reply. "A serum that would curb the effects of Alzheimer's. Larengetics wanted to go to the FDA the first of the year with a viable product. I'd already produced the serum; I just needed to figure out how to condense it into a pill form. I've been working on this for the last five years. I was almost there."

Her voice shook on those last words, her eyes watering against her will.

She took a deep breath, let it out slowly while counting backward from ten. Her heartbeat slowed only minutely.

"I wanted it to work. They wanted it to work. But I didn't want anybody to die trying to get to that point."

"Of course you didn't," Preston told her, his hand slipping from her cheek to her shoulder, where he kneaded slowly.

Heaven shook her head again, wisps of hair falling into her face. She tucked them back behind her ears with shaking fingers.

"It happened so fast. One minute we were working and the next"—she sighed—"everything went wrong."

"Do you know how it went wrong?"

"No. No. That's the worst part. I just don't know what happened. Nobody was working with anything combustible so it couldn't have been anything we did." She'd gone over the events of that day so many times in her head, every second had been memorized. Heaven knew exactly what Moira was working on and what she was mixing. She herself hadn't been mixing anything, but writing instead; Lewis had been emptying the trash. It just didn't make any sense.

"But it could be what someone else did?" Preston asked slowly as if he thought she hadn't considered that angle.

"I don't know why someone would blow up the lab. It's not like we were building a nuclear bomb. We were doing a good thing. Why destroy work that would save lives?"

"Maybe someone out there wants to be the first one to save those lives," Preston said thoughtfully. "Pharmaceuticals is a highly competitive industry. I'm sure you already know that."

Heaven shook her head. "Call me naive, but I've always thought it didn't matter who found the cure first, as long as the cure was found."

"Don't let Quinn hear you say that," Preston replie
with a shake of his head.

He was still petting Coco, who had apparently grow
tired of his touch and crossed over to stand her two fror
paws on Heaven's thigh. She looked up expectantly s
Heaven rubbed her fingers beneath her chin, giving her
small smile because she'd realized a week or so ago hov
much of an attention hog Coco could be.

"Does Quinn have an interest in finding the cure fo
Alzheimer's?" she asked a little absently.

"Before he came back to Sweetland, he was an oncolo
gist heading up a research clinic in Seattle. My dad die
of cancer, and we just found out a few weeks ago that m
grandmother died of cancer as well. For years he wa
obsessed with finding a cure, but finally realized that some
one else might stake that claim."

He'd sounded somber but obviously proud of his brothe
at the same time.

"He's still practicing medicine here in town, right?" sh
asked.

"He is, but it's not the same."

"Because he doesn't have access to the equipment, th
labs, and the staff like he did in Seattle," she stated with
nod of her head.

As crazy at it might sound to some, Heaven had bee
thinking about staying in Sweetland. There was so muc
she had grown to love about this town, but the main rea
son was that she felt like she belonged here. Still, this wa
a small town, with no lab or facilities vaguely resemblin
one. How would she continue her research?

"Because he's working at the inn and he's planning
wedding and he's tending to every sore throat and broke
arm in Sweetland. Which might not seem like ther
would be many, but you'd be surprised what people i
this town can get themselves into."

"Sounds like he made a smart career move then. I'm
ure he's still keeping tabs on the cancer research from a
istance."

Preston shook his head. "I don't know that he is. But
hat I'm trying to say to you is that there are alternatives.
 you don't find the cure, someone else will."

"I know that. It's not who will find the cure that I'm
orried about, it's when. I'd like to know that each time
m making strides toward something important, someing worthwhile."

Preston shook his head. "I know that feeling," he told
er then cleared his throat. "You said you wanted some
a. I'll go down and make it for you."

Coco let out a little yelp as Preston slipped off the bed.
he stood at the edge, wagging her little tail as she stared
 his retreat. Heaven sat forward, letting the sheets fall
vay, and reached for the puppy.

"Guess we said something he didn't like," she told Coco.

 want you to research her company, Larengetics Phar-
aceuticals, and find out what their financial situation
 and who their enemies are," Preston said into his cell
one.

"I thought your brother was looking into this," Ryan
elRio, another old college friend of Preston's said from
e other end.

Preston frowned. "He is, but he's on medical leave
ght now. I don't want him getting into trouble for doing
tside investigations. Besides, he said the Boston cop
dn't responded to his request for information yet."

"And you're tired of waiting?" Ryan asked with a
uckle.

"I'm damned tired of waiting. Something happened to
r in Boston and I want to know what it has to do with
hat's going on with her now."

"And then what?"

When Preston didn't reply right away, Ryan continued

"What are you going to do if you find out somebod really is after her? You're a lawyer, Preston. You know th repercussions of taking the law into your own hands."

Preston let out a breath. He did know the repercus sions, very well, in fact. He also knew that there was n way he was going to sit back and let anything happen Heaven. Clenching the fingers of his free hand, he mad a silent vow to do whatever was necessary to protect he even as he spoke.

"That's why I'm calling you. You're FBI, you can loc into this and get me faster answers."

"And I could also have my supervisor breathing dow my neck about why I'm working on something that doesn have to do with any open cases on our list."

"There might be some FDA violations, that's feder jurisdiction for you. You can act on a suspicion," Prestc suggested.

"I can, if I have a viable reason for suspicion. Do I hav that?" Ryan asked.

Ryan was a stickler for the rules. He'd come from hard life and swore that he'd make something of himsel something honest and good despite his upbringing. Pre ton respected that. He also knew for a fact that Rya loved women, above all else, including food. And if he ev thought one was in danger, he'd shoot first and ask que tions later.

"Someone tried to run her down. She's having nigh mares about an explosion that killed everyone in the la except her. And she was questioned by the police as suspect."

"Did she do it?"

"Don't ask me that," Preston replied quickly. "If

hought for a minute that she was guilty, I wouldn't be on his phone with you."

Ryan sighed. "I know, I'm just trying to make sure you now what you're getting into. I mean, you sound like this voman means an awful lot to you."

Offense came swiftly. Preston was getting damned tired f people discounting him when it came to women. "Is hat a problem? I can't care about a woman?"

"Whoa, whoa, calm down, counselor. That's not what 'm saying. But I will state a few facts for you just in case ou've forgotten."

Preston squeezed the bridge of his nose, knowing this vasn't something he wanted to hear.

"You are the love-'em-and-leave-'em type of guy. You ick the pretty and intelligent ones, wine and dine them, en bed and good-bye them without bothering to find out eir last name."

"And what's your point?" he asked bitterly.

Ryan chuckled. "You know what my point is. I'm uessing, though, that this is a serious situation, one you aven't quite figured out yet. So I'll leave all the serious-elationship stuff alone, because unlike you I'm not in enial about the type of man I am. And since I'm the FBI a this friendship, I'll do my thing and get back to you."

"Thank you. Can you do your thing in a speedy fash-on?" Preston asked just as the teakettle started to whistle.

"Anything for you, counselor."

He disconnected the call with a light smile on his lips. riends, good friends, had come few and far between for reston. Probably having something to do with his trust sues, even when it came to other guys. Maybe it was ore like a connection issue. Maybe he just didn't want to ake any more lasting connections.

Whatever the case, he was grateful for Ryan and knew

that if there was anything to be found out about this company and its dealings, Ryan would find it.

As he fixed the tea, Preston thought about somethin
else Ryan had said. He thought about it so hard he coul
feel his brow wrinkling in consternation.

All this time he'd thought the problem with Heave
was that she was a female with secrets. But tonight she'
opened up to him and told him what had happened i
Boston. So that was no longer an obstacle between then
He believed her story, and he believed she hadn't bee
engaged to Billingsley. In fact, each time he looked int
Heaven's eyes, Preston was amazed at how much trut
and honesty he saw there. Almost as if she were an ope
book. A pretty and compassionate woman who was a
passionate as she was stubborn, as smart as she was a littl
on the shy side.

With all that said, he should have been running u
stairs, unable to wait to see her again, to touch her agai
Yet Preston moved with slow steps, the hot cup in his han
the only reminder that he needed to get upstairs soon
rather than later. Because even with all the night's realiza
tions and observations, he was still in the same position.

His life was still in Baltimore and Heaven's was i
Boston. No amount of hot tea or honest eyes or passiona
kisses could change that.

Chapter 19

"It's bad practice, I tell you. I read it on the Internet," Lorrayna Sidney said, her legs crossed, hands resting still on her knee. "Walt tells me you're a big-city lawyer. Well, I want to press charges."

So this was Walt's sister. There was absolutely no resemblance, Preston thought as he looked at the woman now sitting in one of the dining room's cherrywood chairs. That was probably a good thing since Walt was over six feet tall and easily more than two hundred pounds. His face was a mask of defiance with his gruff, graying beard and intense dark eyes, with matching bushy eyebrows. Whereas Mrs. Sidney was of a shorter stature, no more than 125 pounds and with a face that was most likely pretty at some point but now held a gauntness Preston guessed was caused by stress.

Her daughter, on the other hand, Drew Sidney, sat at the other end of the dining room table flipping through a magazine, as if this conversation was the very last thing on her mind. Gossip around town—which Preston received from overhearing Louisa Kirk and Marabelle Stanley's conversations during their daily lunches at The Silver

Spoon—was that Parker had been eyeing her night afte
night down at Charlie's. From what Preston could see, sh
was a pretty young woman with long legs and encing
curves, the only prerequisite his twin had when it came t
the women in his life. But instead of looking sexy, toda
it seemed Drew was much more interested in ignoring he
mother, which made Preston wonder even more about thi
meeting.

Preston cleared his throat, giving himself another sec
ond to think about what he wanted to say. He could simpl
tell Mrs. Sidney that he was not a malpractice—or in he
words "bad practice"—attorney. But he had a feeling sh
wouldn't understand. Sweetland had one law office locate
in a small building right next to the police station for cor
venience. Considering there were only three police officer
in the whole town, it stood to reason that lawyers would b
another hot commodity.

Case in point, Edison Creed's name was engraved o
the wooden plaque swinging just beneath the ATTORNEY
AT-LAW sign on the old, almost dilapidated building. .
couple of weeks after Gramma's funeral and the readin
of her will, Mr. Creed had taken a vacation to Californi
to visit his daughter and her family. He hadn't been bac
since, and news from Lonnie, the mailman, was he'd pu
in for a change of address to have all his mail forwarde
out west. This news had come to the Cantrells via Lis
Kramer, one of their summer interns who was currentl
dating Sonny Creed, Edison's eldest grandson, now sta
tioned in Hawaii, much to Lisa's chagrin.

So there was possibly a good reason she'd been d
rected to Parker. Possibly, but not really.

"Mrs. Sidney, I'm very sorry for your loss. When di
your husband pass away?" he asked, trying to focus o
being as professional as possible.

"Five years ago, this Sunday. They said he wasn't going to live another six weeks. He believed them and he killed himself that next morning," she said stoically.

But her bottom lip quivered after she stopped speaking, her eyes watering. Preston reached out to take her hand.

"Like I said, I'm very sorry for your loss. However, in the state of Maryland there's a three-year statute of limitations on wrongful death claims. This means that you would have had to file your claim within three years of the time you first found out about the negligence. Now, when did you find out that the doctors told your husband he had inoperable lung cancer?"

She swallowed and took a deep breath. "He called me the moment he came home from the doctor's office. I left work early and we talked for several hours before Drew came home from work. She was working part-time at the library at the time. She'd just had a bad breakup and was trying to find something else to do with her time."

A sigh from the direction of where Drew was sitting said she didn't think that last bit of information had been necessary. Preston agreed but wasn't about to say anything.

"And he left a suicide note, I presume?" It was an awful question to ask anyone, but Preston was used to asking candid questions and expecting honest answers.

Mrs. Sidney nodded. "He emailed me and Drew. I rushed home and found a handwritten note on the kitchen table. We always used the back door to come into the house because the driveway had two parking spots in the back. He knew I'd see it as soon as I came in. Then I ran to our bedroom and there he was."

This time a tear slipped from her eyes, gliding slowly

down her cheek. Drew stood then and came to stand
behind her mother's chair, placing her hands on her
shoulders.

"I came home shortly after that," she said, giving her
mother time to gather herself. "Three days later we had the
funeral, a month later we found out more truth about my
dad, and six months later we moved from Havre de Grace
to Sweetland to stay with Uncle Walt."

That's why they were both new faces to Preston. Since
being back in Sweetland, he'd seen many familiar people and enjoyed catching up with some of them. The Sidneys weren't natives, but from what he'd heard, at least
Drew was making a home for herself here. Mrs. Sidney
looked as if she'd never be home anywhere as long as her
husband was gone. That was a sobering thought that had
Preston wondering once more about this falling-in-love-
and-living-happily-ever-after scheme.

"I'm so sorry. That must have been hard for the two
of you to deal with," he said, still holding Mrs. Sidney's
hand.

"They shouldn't have told him that! A month after his
death the doctor called me to say he'd made a mistake
and that Arthur wasn't sick at all. They'd mixed up the
X-rays. Arthur had COPD, not lung cancer."

Drew rolled her eyes, as if there was something about
her mother's words that she either didn't believe or was
tired of hearing. Disagreeing families were no mystery to
Preston. More often than not he'd have the mother and the
girlfriend of a client believing he was unabashedly innocent. Then there'd be a cousin or sometimes a father who
would hold firm to the fact that everything wasn't always
what it seemed. He got that impression here with the Sidneys but wasn't sure he wanted to delve deeper into it.

On the surface, Preston could admit he wasn't a doctor. Still, misdiagnosing something like inoperable lung

ancer and basically giving someone a false death sentence
was a huge mix-up, one that if Mrs. Sidney had hired a
lawyer two years ago would have cost that hospital plenty
of money. Unfortunately, it was just too late.

"That was a big mistake," he admitted to her. "And it
would probably have been worth litigating, two years ago.
Right now, there's nothing that can be done."

"I've tried to tell her that so many times," Drew said.

"But Walt told me you're from the city. I looked you up
and found out you win all your cases," Mrs. Sidney argued. "Surely there's something you can do."

Preston didn't win all his cases. Sometimes he'd been
forced to take plea bargains offered by the state because
either one of them had evidence that they were sure
would garner a win at trial. But over the years, Preston
had begun to admit—if only to himself—that it wasn't all
about winning. Defending people who were innocent until proven guilty, but more often than not guilty as sin, was
not turning out to be as rewarding as he'd first thought.

"Ma'am, I really wish I could help you. But I'm a criminal attorney. I don't handle malpractice cases. I know
generally about the law in these matters, but even if the
statute hadn't run, I still would not be able to help you."

"Do you know someone who can?" she asked.

Had she heard anything he'd said? A glance up at Drew,
who was shaking her head slowly, confirmed she probably
had but wasn't comprehending it. And as much as he
thought it was useless, Preston hated to see a female in
such obvious distress.

"How about this," he proposed. "I'll find you a malpractice attorney to speak to and in return you have to promise me that whatever he tells you, you'll accept."

There was silence.

"I know I can't bring Arthur back," she said, bottom
lip quivering.

"Why would you want to?" Drew quipped, then close her mouth tightly at her mother's sharp intake of breath.

Those words and Drew's reaction solidified Preston' theory that there was more going on here than just th wrongful death claim.

"No. Nothing will bring him back, Mrs. Sidney. But understand you need some closure. So I'll make that ca and get you a name and number. But if he tells you there' nothing that can be done, will you accept that and mov on?"

Because really, she needed to move on. It was clear t Preston that this woman had grieved every one of th days since her husband's death, and that was a shame. O course, he could relate to needing closure. He and hi siblings had found it somewhat, after they'd learned o their grandmother's cancer diagnosis and subsequentl grim prognosis. Still, there were some lingering after effects, and they all missed her just the same.

"I'll try," was what Mrs. Sidney ended up saying.

With a smile and a pat to her hand, Preston stood.

"I'll make the call and be back with the information, he told them.

On his way out of the parlor he ran into Parker. "Hey do me a favor and go in there and cheer up the Sidneys.'

"What? Are they guests?" Parker asked.

For a second Preston stared at Parker as if he wer crazy. Didn't he know who the Sidneys were? Then agai it wasn't unlike Parker to have no idea what the woma he was lusting after's last name was.

Preston shook his head. "No. They're not guests. The live in Sweetland. Walt sent them to me to talk about a me mal case. Seems the woman's husband committed suicid after learning he was dying of cancer, but turns out h wasn't dying after all."

"Damn," Parker said with a shake of his head.

"Yeah, tough. I don't think she can sue but I'm going to make a few calls and find her a med mal attorney to give her a more detailed answer. She's in there with her daughter and they're pretty shaken up."

"So you're sending me in to make that better?"

"Sure, you're used to talking to people about death."

"I'm used to telling mothers their sons have been shot dead on the streets, or wives that their kingpin husbands have finally met up with the other kingpins whose territory they invaded," Parker said with a frown.

Preston only nodded because he knew what the frown was for and could definitely relate. "Right. So go on in and work your magic."

"There's no law saying you can't take med mal cases, you know," Joe said into the phone.

Preston had gone into his room to make the call for Mrs. Sidney. This room was quickly beginning to feel like his office since he was making more and more calls regarding some form of case or law issue from there.

Down the hall he'd heard Michelle giving orders to whomever she'd wrangled into helping set up for the rehearsal dinner scheduled for late this afternoon. Tomorrow was the Fourth of July, a date Preston had no idea had become popular for hosting weddings. But at noon Tiffany Smythe would be married to Rockerfeller—Rock for short—Hanover at the Sweetland Presbyterian Church. Their reception would be held here at the inn, to the tune of seventy-five guests who'd begun to pour into Sweetland as early as Sunday night.

To say that having this big wedding in the middle of the Bay Day celebrations was a little stressful for Michelle would be an understatement. But Preston didn't doubt for one moment that his sister could handle it and that the events would go off without a hitch. However, he

felt the need to do his part. A successful wedding leading
into an evening of fireworks during Bay Day would only
emphasize The Silver Spoon's hometown connection
and tourist attractiveness. It was great publicity and gave
them a leg up on The Marina, which Preston knew for a
fact had nothing special planned for today or the remainder of the week. With that in mind he wanted to hurry up
and deal with the Sidneys so he could offer his help to make
everything go smoothly.

"I'm a criminal attorney," was Preston's ready retort.

"Really?" Joe asked. "I mean, I can't tell since you've
been gone more than you've been here."

"You offered to take over some of my cases. If that was
a problem, you should have let me know and I would've
come back," Preston said, slightly irritated at Joe's remark.

"But you need to be there with your family. On top of
that, Preston, you want to be there. Listen, man, I don't
blame you. If I had a family at home I could run back to
and get away from all the crap going on in this city, I
would. Hell, I'd have left years ago. You've got something
going there with the B and B and your family trying to
mend fences. I've already talked to an associate who wants
to leave Brindle Rachette. He can start the first of August."

Preston sighed. "Okay, so we hire an associate. That's
fine. We'll both have more free time. How does that help
me with this med mal issue?"

"For a man who graduated at the top of his class I spend
a lot of time spelling things out for you," Joe said with a
chuckle. "You're licensed to practice law in Maryland;
Washington, DC; Delaware; and New York. I think Sweetland's somewhere in between there."

"I'm not moving to Sweetland to practice law, Joe.
They already have an attorney." Even if he was on his last

leg and possibly about to announce his retirement. "I just need a referral," he said adamantly.

"You can handle a med mal case, all you have to do is read up on the law," Joe persisted.

"The statute has already run. There's no case to litigate. Look, just text me a name and a number. I want to try to help this woman before she drives herself insane."

Joe sighed with defeat. "I'll find someone and I'll call them first to give them the heads-up that this woman will be calling. Give me the name."

Preston told him the name and ended the call before Joe had the opportunity to say anything more about him moving to Sweetland. It was not a possibility. Preston loved his job in the city. Okay, maybe *love* was too strong a word to use. But it was his job, his identity, his life. The only thing here in Sweetland was the B&B, his family, and Heaven.

For two nights Preston had slept in the bed beside her. This morning as she'd dressed, Heaven wondered how her two-day trip to Sweetland to pick up a puppy had turned into weeks in this picturesque small town, with a man in her bed.

It seemed surreal.

One day she was alone in a city that should have been her home, with parents who treated her more like an employee than a relative and a job that was fulfilling in its own way, but most likely lost regardless. And the next she was here baking almond croissants and smashing rude females in the face with frosted cupcakes. She was staying in a pretty room, getting to know her adoring puppy, and falling for a man who would undoubtedly break her heart.

The upside was that Heaven was smart, educated, and

trained in biochemistry. She could go anywhere she
wanted to go and find a job doing research or lab work, or
simply writing papers if she wanted to. And if she didn't
she had a multimillion-dollar trust fund that had reverted
completely to her on her thirtieth birthday. She hadn't
touched any of it, determined to make her own way. But it
was there if she ever needed it. If Preston did break her
heart and she found herself needing to leave Sweetland,
she had options.

Unfortunately, those options didn't really appeal to her.

Especially as she carried folding chairs outside to set
at the four nine-foot-long tables already assembled. During
the morning briefing—which she secretly called the breakfast hour in the Cantrell kitchen—Michelle had told them
all that today's rehearsal dinner would consist of thirty
people: the bride, the groom, the wedding party, and their
parents. The menu was Chesapeake crab cakes, with a
choice of two salads and two veggies: coleslaw or potato
salad, steamed broccoli with cheese or snap peas. The
dough for the yeast rolls was already rising, pitchers of
iced tea and lemonade chilling. Dessert was pecan pie
and lemon poppy seed cupcakes—favorites of the bride and
groom.

Drew Sidney had been here earlier with her mother.
Heaven had no idea what that was about. But when she'd
seen Drew leaving, she'd stopped to speak.

"Hi, Heaven, it's good to see you," Drew had said.

Heaven had shrugged. "Yes, I'm still here."

"How long are you planning to stay? When I saw you
last, you were leaving when everything was settled with
the puppy."

"Right. And then I just stayed. I can't really say why."

To that Drew had only smiled. A pretty smile that
reached her eyes and made her makeup-free face look
just a little angelic.

"I saw you and Preston at the bake-off. I'd say that's as good a reason as any to stick around," she told her.

"We're just friends," Heaven said, sounding a little off even to her own ears.

Drew had touched her shoulder then and gave her a knowing nod. "Friends with benefits are the best kind."

Heaven didn't respond immediately. She wasn't quite sure how to.

"I'll be back later with the flowers Michelle ordered," Drew had told her before continuing out the door.

Now, hours later, Heaven sighed as she put down the chairs. Each table had been covered with a white tablecloth. In the center were floral arrangements in pretty pastel colors—baby roses and lavender were the first flowers Heaven identified. The rest she wasn't totally sure of. She loved how the festive arrangements looked at any rate.

The scent from the flowers and the light breeze filtering through the air put a pep in her step and she heard herself humming as she moved along, unfolding chairs and pushing them under the tables.

Savannah came out with plates and napkins and silverware. Heaven began setting each place.

"I'm never getting married," Savannah said, slamming a plate down.

It was a good thing it wasn't one of Michelle's famed Haviland china plates, but rather a sturdier china set in a basic white color she used for crab feasts and outdoor functions.

"Okay, did somebody say you had to?"

Savannah was very moody. Yeah, Heaven had heard men at the lab talking about women and their mood swings happening according to the calendar, but Savannah was the exception to the rule. Her moods could change in the blink of an eye. Heaven was sort of getting used to the frequent fluctuations and tended to simply go with the flow. Today's flow was obviously agitated.

"It's wedding season—that's what Michelle said first thing this morning. Nikki has bridal magazines all over the place, like guests want to come in, have a seat in the parlor, and read about the latest wedding styles." She huffed as she worked, slamming down plates and silverware, leaving the napkins alone completely.

That was probably a good thing. Michelle had gone through great pains to show them how to fold napkins; it wouldn't go over well if Savannah messed them up.

"I guess it's an exciting time," Heaven offered, following behind each place setting Savannah left. She carefully folded each napkin and straightened the silverware beside it. "Getting married is starting a new life, leaving everything in your past behind and deciding to create new memories with the man of your dreams. I think it's kind of romantic."

Silverware clinked against the next plate. Heaven looked up slowly to where Savannah stood across the table from her. Obviously she'd said the wrong thing.

"Really? Are you thinking about marrying Preston? Because if you are, let me just stop you right there," Savannah said, dragging a hand across her throat like she was ending more than this conversation.

"That's not what I said," Heaven tried to open, but Savannah was already shaking her head.

"Look, Preston's not the marrying type. He and Parker wrote out their life goal list when they turned thirteen, and it did not include marriage. I know because Nikki and I stole the list and tacked it to the tree in Fitzgerald Park."

More than a little confused by the jolt in conversation, Heaven asked, "Why would you do something like that?"

"Because the list also doubled as a sort of hit list for all the girls in Sweetland they planned to conquer before they were eighteen. We thought it would be pretty embarrassing. Instead the goofy girls whose names were on the list lined up at the house hoping to hurry along their slot in line." She rolled her eyes after that, sighing heavily before picking up another plate.

"So all I'm saying is that he hasn't changed a bit since then. The last time I was in Baltimore and stopped by his office to see him, there was a half-dressed woman sitting in his chair obviously waiting for him to return. Of course I kicked her skanky ass out, but that wasn't the point."

Heaven was almost positive Savannah wasn't trying to upset her; she really wasn't that type of person. Savannah's emotions, good or bad, revolved solely around her; whatever anyone else felt or did as a result she had no clue of. So as Heaven had paused, her fingers going perfectly still with the napkin she held, the thought of Preston having sex with some—as Savannah put it—"skanky" woman in his office filtered through her mind. Something sharp pierced her chest, and she wondered if it was jealousy or anger that he'd do something so obviously juvenile and unprofessional.

"The point is that men mean what they say and they say what they mean. Women who don't believe when they say they don't want a commitment and definitely do not want kids are idiots!"

Savannah's rant continued and Heaven struggled slightly to keep up.

"Not all men are like that, Savannah," Heaven added when she'd snapped out of her own jealous trance and resumed folding the napkin.

"Men are idiots! All of them! And I wouldn't marry any of them if I were offered a million dollars!"

Those were her parting words as she dropped the remaining silverware in a heap on the end of the table and stalked back into the inn. When Savannah opened the back door, the puppies came streaking out in a wail of barking, running down the steps before anyone could catch them. This brought another shriek from Savannah, who made no attempt to capture them, stomping into the house instead.

Heaven saw them coming and thought about chasing them but figured it made more sense to let them run loose for a while. At least until she finished setting the table.

To her surprise Coco ran straight to her, stopping at her feet and looking up expectantly.

"You're not supposed to be out here," she told her.

Coco fell back on her bottom, her tongue hanging out as she panted.

"And I'm not rubbing your ears, no matter how nicely you ask," she continued while she worked.

Coco followed dutifully until Heaven was finished, and she finally sat cross-legged on the grass, laughing when the puppy plopped her head on her thigh.

"He's a womanizer," she said with a frown and rubbed Coco's ears despite her previous statement. "He acts like he's not, at least sometimes with me he acts like that. But his own sister knows what he is and she's known him a lot longer."

Coco jumped into her lap, planting her front paws on Heaven's chest. Heaven obliged her by lowering her face for the puppy to lick her cheeks. Coco wasn't the only one who enjoyed that.

"You're such a good listener," she said between chuckles.

"If you'd needed someone to listen, all you had to do was ask," Preston said, kneeling down beside her.

"Will you do whatever I ask?"

Heaven didn't know why she'd said that, especially since she wasn't totally sure she believed anything Preston said to her at this point. No, he hadn't lied to her about anything, and he hadn't tried to deceive her, but wasn't that what he would end up doing eventually?

"If it's something I can do," was his reply.

He reached out a hand to pat Coco, who had taken a defensive stance against Heaven's chest.

"She really loves you now," Preston continued. "You two make a good pair."

"I think we're kindred spirits, both of us trying to find our way and ending up together."

"So you think you've found where you belong? You think you're going to stay in Sweetland?"

Heaven shook her head. She had been thinking that, but she hadn't told anyone.

"Ever since I graduated I've received offers from professors to help with their research or to cowrite papers with them. It's a more solitary kind of work but I could live anywhere and still make a living," she said, looking down at Coco's pretty dark brown eyes.

Everything on this puppy was a chocolate-brown color. At first it had amazed Heaven; now she was used to it and could tell her puppy from all the others.

"You can work here in Sweetland," he said.

"I can. And Coco wouldn't have to leave the town she's used to. There's so much grass and running room for her here."

"You planning to permanently rent a room at the inn like Mr. Sylvester?" he asked with a little chuckle.

Heaven looked up at him and shook her head. "No. Actually, I don't really have a plan. I'm just going with the flow for right now. And that's something I never used to do."

"What did you used to do? How did you come to this point in your life?"

She shrugged. "I did what was expected of me. I went to school, got good grades. I went to college and set my eye on a career. I came home and got a good job. That's what they wanted me to do so I did it. No thinking required," she admitted, feeling more than a little foolish for knowing what she'd done all those years was wrong.

"And what do you want to do now?" he asked, his gaze locked with hers.

Heaven tilted her head, watching as his eyes remained riveted on her. He always looked at her that way, as if there was nothing anywhere on this earth more important than her. And normally that look would leave her breathless, stunned that a man such as Preston Cantrell would even consider her that important. And in this instant, ignoring Savannah's "Preston will never get married" warning, Heaven leaned a little closer to him.

Her heart thumped wildly in her chest, Coco shifting slightly in her arms. She couldn't put into words what she was feeling and figured it may have some pretty bad repercussions, but try as she might she couldn't stop. And didn't really want to.

"I want to kiss you right now," she said in the barest whisper as her face drew closer to his.

He didn't speak. She hadn't really thought he would. Certainly he wasn't going to turn her down. No, Preston was too damned smooth for that.

He cupped her face, letting his thumbs rub along her cheekbones, his palms warm against the bottom half of her cheek. Tilting his head in the opposite direction he lowered his face to hers.

"Then kiss me," he finally whispered, so close to her now that his breath fanned across her face.

If she blinked the moment would be lost; hesitation would settle over what was a blissfully lovely idea. So Heaven didn't blink. Later she would realize she probably hadn't even breathed. She moved just another inch and let her lips touch his. Soft, slow, then disregarding that idea, she took the dive. She opened her mouth over his, her tongue danced along his lips, pressing along the seam until he parted them and let her taste his tongue instead. It was a brilliant taste, all man, all sex, all day long. She suckled hungrily, anxiously until he moaned.

He pulled her closer until Coco got the message and scrambled off her lap and Heaven fell into his arms. For his part Preston fell backward, lying on the soft grass, Heaven now on top of him. They both took a reassuring breath before resuming the kiss that would take the temperature up about ten or twenty degrees.

She straddled him, rubbing her center over his thick arousal. He cupped her bottom, gripping her cheeks hungrily in his hands. They panted, trying hard to breathe and not break the connection of their mouths.

Heaven ached all over. She wanted his hands on her skin, wanted the direct contact of this man as soon as possible. His mouth on hers made her nipples tingle, her center throb. No matter how much she moved the burgeoning desire spun more out of control, with only one reprieve in sight. She nibbled on his bottom lip. He moved one hand to slip beneath the hem of her shirt, upward until he cupped her breasts. She gasped.

"Well, is this the type of entertainment The Silver Spoon offers its guests?" a shrill voice asked.

Heaven and Preston grew perfectly still. Turning her head slightly, Heaven caught a glimpse first of five-inch black patent-leather pumps, then smooth-shaven legs. Upward her gaze traveled until the full length of Diana

McCann's black-and-white full-skirted strapless dress came into sight.

This time her gasp was not of pure pleasure, but pure embarrassment.

Chapter 20

"I'm telling everyone I know to go to The Marina from now on!" Diana screamed when Preston and Heaven had finally gotten up off the ground.

"This disgraceful behavior is not what we want tourists to see when they come to Sweetland," she continued.

"And it's not what they'll see when they come to The Silver Spoon," Preston assured her.

Of all the people to be caught necking by, Diana McCann was the absolute worst.

"I certainly can't tell from what I've just seen. And with her! Why, you don't even know anything about this woman. She's nothing but a tourist," Diana continued, waving a dismissive hand in Heaven's direction. "And she'll probably be arrested by the end of the day since I've already signed a formal complaint for her assault against me at the bake-off. The sheriff is probably swearing out the warrant as we speak."

Preston sincerely doubted that. Kyle Farraway knew exactly what type of woman Diana was as a result of the vicious games she'd played with his son Carl when she first returned to town. For his part, Carl had been swept away by an older woman, an older, much more experienced woman with a reputation that should have preceded her.

"You're making way too much of this, Diana," he said, taking another step toward her, being careful to keep Heaven behind him.

He couldn't see Heaven's face, but he didn't have to in order to know she was made very uncomfortable by this scene. It wasn't something he would have looked forward to, either, but Diana had to be dealt with.

"I'm only stating the facts. And when I have dinner with Steve tonight I'm going to make sure I recount this whole sordid tale for him. I'm sure there won't be any issues like this at The Marina." She folded her arms over her chest, tapping one foot in front of her as if she were waiting for him to say something else, or offer money for her silence. Preston wasn't quite sure.

"Ms. McCann." Heaven stood beside Preston. "We apologize for any embarrassment our . . . situation may have caused you. But this is not a reflection of the services The Silver Spoon offers."

"Oh, I wasn't embarrassed. I've seen this one in action before."

Beside him Heaven stiffened at Diana's words.

"Oh, didn't he tell you?" Diana continued.

"That's enough," Preston interjected. "What are you doing here anyway, Diana? This afternoon's function is private."

Diana only nodded. "Right, just like that night we shared was private."

To his dismay Heaven laughed.

Preston looked over at her as if he needed to confirm. Yes, she was laughing.

By this time Parker had joined them, barely using his cane as he walked in an almost normal manner.

"What's going on?" he asked. "Diana?"

Diana surprisingly didn't speak.

Heaven continued laughing. "Ms. McCann was just about to tell us how she and Preston spent the night together, some time ago I presume."

"Oh, really?" Parker asked with an arched eyebrow. "You were with my brother?" he asked Diana.

Diana's mouth opened, then shut quickly.

"Sure she was," Heaven continued. "I think the story goes something like this: She wanted you, Parker. But since you weren't paying her any attention, she set her sights temporarily on Preston. To convince him she was worth his while she did an impromptu flashing in the woods, I believe. Apparently her, ah, girlfriends weren't as appealing to Preston as she anticipated and he left her standing there. Embarrassed to no end she decided Preston wasn't the right Cantrell man for her, either. Is that what you wanted to tell me about you and Preston, Diana?"

She looked mad enough to spit fire. Really, Diana's cheeks were so red Preston would bet he'd burn his fingers if he touched her. Her arms quickly fell from her chest and she clenched her fists at her sides.

"I don't like you!" she spat. "And I don't see what he sees in you. But the day you came to Sweetland was the day The Silver Spoon lost any credibility it might have had in my eyes. As I stated before, I'll be telling anyone who'll listen not to waste their time or money on this place!"

Preston grabbed her by the arm before she could stalk past him. "Be careful, Diana. Before you start this verbal war, think about all the things in your past and how they could come back to bite you and the hooks you've managed to sink into Steven Redling in the ass."

"Don't threaten me, Preston. I'm not afraid of you," she told him.

"You should be, Diana. You see, I know the terms of your uncle Hugh's will. I know you're about to be kicked off that estate and that your ex-husband left you penniless. So if you don't want me to cause trouble for you and your new sugar daddy, I suggest you keep any bad words about the B and B and my family out of your mouth."

"Is that a threat?" she asked, elegantly arched eyebrows lifting with the question.

"It's a promise," he said in his most lethal defense attorney tone.

"One of you want to tell me what happened?" Parker asked. "And I'd suggest you make it quick because Michelle's on her way out here to check on our progress."

"She caught us kissing and threatened to tell the world this place is no good and not to spend any money here," Heaven volunteered. "I would have apologized if it were anyone else, but I really don't like her."

Parker chuckled. "You're not alone in that area. But maybe you should keep the kissing in your room, especially tonight. We already have a bride and groom for that."

Heaven smiled at Parker. "Good idea. Another good idea is to go offer more help to Michelle before she comes out here giving out assignments."

And with that she was gone. Preston couldn't help it he turned, watching her walk into the house, ass twitching in the tight capri jeans she wore. His mouth watered and he almost cursed Diana McCann for the millionth time since he'd had the fortune of meeting her. Not that he had any intention of making love to Heaven outside in broad daylight when they should have been preparing for a bridal shower. But he could have easily convinced her to join him upstairs for an hour or two.

"She's fine as hell," Parker said from behind him. "But

he police in Boston think she was set up by someone at
Larengetics."

"What?" Preston asked, turning quickly to face his
rother.

"I spoke to a Detective Johansen. He says all the evi-
ence pointed to Heaven orchestrating the explosion. But
vhy would she have stayed in the lab if she knew it was
oing to blow up? They've been digging deeper and found
ut a lot was riding on Heaven creating this medication, a
ot of Larengetics money and a lot of animosity growing
rom their competitors."

"So one of the competitors could be gunning for her?"
e asked.

Parker shook his head. "If they planned the explosion,
hat would make sense. But there's no reason for them to
e after her now."

"But there's plenty of reason for Larengetics to be pissed
ff with her," he finished.

"Ryan tried your cell but didn't get an answer. He
alled the main number and since you were otherwise
ccupied I took the call. He has all of Larengetics's fi-
ancial information and he's going to fax that along with
rofiles of each board member over later today. In the
neantime—"

Preston nodded. "I know, I'll keep her close."

he Smythe wedding and reception went off without a
itch the next day. Preston and his brothers had donned
lack suits and silver bow ties and served champagne on
ilver trays as the guests mingled throughout the inn and
utside.

The forecast had called for late showers and possibly
hunderstorms in the evening, so an emergency tent rental
ad been necessary. This consisted of Preston and Quinn
aking the hour-and-a-half ride to Easton to the party

store, whose owner charged them an additional thre
hundred dollars to open on a holiday and pack the ter
into the back of Michelle's mini van. Another hou
tacked onto the three-hour travel time, was consume
with him and Quinn fussing over the instructions and f
nally getting the tent up. Parker, the lucky bastard wit
his leg injury, had been responsible for coordinating th
flower and cake deliveries, which meant he'd spent th
entire morning flirting with Drew Sidney and whateve
female had been assigned to deliver the cake.

The final dance at the reception had been punctuate
by the fireworks that could be seen clearly from the back
yard, since the boat that they were based on was docke
in the middle of the river right behind their land.

"Here, you deserve this," Preston said to Heaven, wh
had come from the kitchen where she'd been helpin
Michelle fix plates and wash dishes.

She startled, jumping as he came up behind her offerin
her the glass of champagne.

"You don't have to be afraid here, Heaven. I'm not go
ing to let anything happen to you," he told her, hatin
every time she jumped or looked over her shoulder.

"I just thought I was alone," she replied, taking the glas
from him and giving him a small smile.

She also wore black, skintight pants and a ruffled blous
that matched the one Raine and Savannah wore—he fig
ured that was most likely a result of their recent shoppin
spree. Michelle wore an apron over her black pants an
white top so he hadn't noticed any ruffles, but she prob
bly had the same top as well. Her shoes were flat wit
some sort of silver buckle at the toe, and when she looke
up at him Preston thought of a high school girl. A ver
lovely high school girl he would have tried his damnde
to date if she'd gone to his school.

"I'm here with you now," he said. "So we'll toast to ou

ountry's independence and see what they've prepared
or us tonight." With a nod toward the sky and a tap of his
lass to hers, he looked forward to the first burst of fireworks.

She touched her glass to his. Out of the corner of his
ye he watched her take a tentative sip.

"I've never watched a fireworks display before," she
aid softly after the first two or three minutes of the show.

"Don't they celebrate the Fourth in Boston?"

"Yes. But I never attended any of those celebrations.
Usually I worked late in the lab to ignore the fact that I had
obody to celebrate with."

"What about your family?"

"I'm an only child whose parents are more concerned
vith their social status than with me." She took a deep
reath, then emptied her glass. "I sound like a whining
hild, instead of a thirty-two-year-old adult."

"Nonsense, you sound like a woman whose endured
ome disappointments. It's nothing to be ashamed of. We've
ll either been let down or let someone down in our lives.
's the natural course of things."

He looked away from the lights then because she moved
o stand in front of him.

"Who disappointed you, Preston? What happened that
nade you turn into such a cynic?" she asked.

Suddenly uncomfortable with the shift of the conver-
ation, Preston emptied his glass, too.

"I'm not a cynic. I just know what works for me and
vhat doesn't."

"And what happened to make you feel that way?"

"Nothing."

She nodded as if she agreed or understood, but her eyes
efinitely said differently. "You were just born with all the
nswers, huh?"

"No," he said, then snapped his mouth shut. He had the

feeling that this was another one of those times whe
whatever he said would come out wrong. She'd never ur
derstand how he came to be the man he was, so what wa
the point in telling her?

Preston shrugged. "I'm just who I am, Heaven. Can yo
accept that?"

She took a step closer to him. "That depends," she saic

"On what?"

"On how fast you can take me upstairs and convinc
me that I should accept who you are, without any mor
questions."

He thought about that a moment, twirling the stem o
the champagne glass between his fingers. Then he too
her glass from her hand and stuck both glasses in h
jacket pocket. She yelped when he scooped her up int
his arms.

"About two minutes should do it," he said, and turne
toward the house.

Preston was naked and it was a glorious sight.

With fingers that shook only slightly, Heaven touche
the back of his shoulders. His muscles bunched and sh
rubbed slowly, kneading against the tightness. He sighe
as if she were giving him the best massage ever. She wa
kneeling on the bed behind him, her clothes having bee
just about ripped off two seconds after they entered th
room.

"You need to relax," she said to him in a soft voic
"You're worrying too much."

"That might be easier said than done," was his ligl
reply.

"No." Heaven continued letting her palms splay dow
the length of his back. "Stress is a silent killer. To comb
it you should come up with ways to purge yourself dail
from the burdens that weigh you down."

She leaned in a little bit, kissing his side before kneading there.

He sucked in a breath. "You sound like an expert on stress relief."

Heaven laughed softly. "I read a lot. And I spent a small fortune on a therapist this year. I've learned a few things."

"Really? I'd be interested in finding out just how much you know," Preston said.

He'd reached back for her. Heaven rubbed her cheek along his arm, kissed the inside of his wrist, then slipped off the bed. When she was standing in front of him, she once again put her hands on his shoulders.

"One way to relieve stress is to find a hobby. Do you have a hobby, Preston?"

He'd already reached out, had his hands on her hips as he pulled her close, between his legs.

"I think I do now," was his reply.

His thumbs circled across her hip bone, his fingers splaying over the top swell of her bottom. Heat spiraled through her in enticing tendrils.

"You are beautiful," he whispered, his gaze meeting her eyes, then sliding over her body in a slow, appreciative perusal.

She let her fingers roam down his arms, over taut muscle and roped veins. His skin was smoothed tight almost to the point of straining, and she couldn't help touching it. There was so much strength in his arms, so much man as she looked into his eyes. He was beautiful with his strong jaw and thick eyebrows. His dark eyes made him seem more intense than he really was, and the thin mustache he kept neat and close-cut gave him a kind of movie-star quality.

"I could touch you all day, every day," he told her, reaching behind her so that his hands cupped her bottom completely.

"I don't think either of us would worry much if you di
that," she said, trying to keep her voice light.

With each grip of his hands her heart skipped a bea
her knees trembled. And when one hand slipped slowl
between her legs, pressing persistently on the place tha
was quickly growing damp with arousal, her eyes close
involuntarily.

"No, we wouldn't worry," he told her when his finger
parted her plump folds.

His hands were moving from the back, so her front wa
pushed even closer to him. So close that when he shifte
his head slightly, his breath brushed over her clean
shaven mound as he spoke. A tingle of pleasure delve
straight down her spine.

"We'd be too busy to worry about anything," he whis
pered. Her center throbbed.

"Right," she sighed. "Nothing."

He dropped a kiss on her mound and Heaven gasped
one knee buckling completely. As if to help her out—bu
really it just made matters worse—Preston lifted that leg
planting her foot on the mattress beside his thigh. His
fingers returned to slip seductively between her tender
folds once more. And then his tongue followed.

She grasped his shoulders so hard, her thankfully
blunt-tipped nails slipped slowly into his skin. He lifted
her closer to his face as if she were a chocolate sundae
and he was in search of the cherry on top. With slow and
purposeful strokes his tongue talked to her in an entirely
different language, one she'd never before experienced
but felt like she'd missed anyway. Something akin to
pleasure but way more intense rippled through her and
she shifted. So did Preston. He lifted the leg that had
been propped on the bed so that it now draped over his
shoulder, and he kissed her again, deeper, wetter, more
intimate than he ever had. She moaned.

Moaned really loud and really long.

When she thought she was going to melt into a puddle on the floor, Preston lifted her once more, this time turning her so that she was lying flat on the bed. Again he propped her legs up onto his shoulders and thrust into her with a quick urgency that had her gasping.

Then he stilled.

Preston didn't move and he didn't blink, just stared down at her as if this were the first time he'd ever seen her. Heaven blinked, licked her lips, and looked into his eyes. It wasn't the first time he'd ever seen her, but it was definitely his first time for something.

"Preston," she whispered, and he shook his head.

She cupped his cheeks to keep him still.

"This thing between us," she began, and he closed his eyes.

"No, look at me, Preston." Heaven waited until his eyes were once again open.

"It's good, right. I know," he said through gritted teeth and began stroking inside her long and deep and oh so slow she almost screamed in agony.

Instead Heaven tried to speak again; she tried to tell him what had been nagging at her all day. But as Preston picked up the pace, their bodies making a slapping sound each contact, she couldn't think. Words wouldn't form, only moans and gasps and occasionally his name as if to signify that he was the one making her feel this way, he was the one bringing her this insatiable pleasure.

"It's never been this good," she thought she heard him whisper.

But when she tried to get her eyes to focus on him once more, he'd turned his face away. His hands were planted in the bed, one on either side of her face, and her legs were still thrown over his shoulders. He pulled out and stroked a particularly sensitive spot that made her entire

body quiver. In that moment everything shifted, eve
movement, every thought she'd ever had about man ar
women, this man and herself, everything changed.

And when he'd stiffened above her, and they shared
a blissful release, Heaven felt like crying. She didn't e
actly know why, but tears welled in her eyes. To kee
from looking like a total idiot in front of Preston, sl
quickly pushed him off her and ran to the bathroom.

Chapter 21

reston cursed, long, low, fluent.

He'd messed up. No, he thought dismally shaking his
ead, he'd *fucked* up, royally!

Despite what people thought they knew about him,
reston was no fool when it came to emotions. They weren't
s favorite things to deal with, but he had them and he
new when it was time to face them. The moment he'd
ipped inside Heaven had signified the exact second that
olted door to his heart burst open. For weeks she'd been
using her way inside, whether it was with the dogs or
lping his sisters, or looking at him with that stubborn-
-a-little-naive glare. She was smart enough to obtain a
aster's degree and work as a biochemist in one of the
rgest pharmaceutical companies in the country, and yet
e was just timid enough to let her parents intimidate her
to a job and a life she didn't really want. She had enough
ass not to stoop to Diana McCann's baiting and enough
umption not to let herself be walked on by the imperti-
nt wannabe socialite.

She was nothing he ever expected to fall for.

And everything he'd ever wanted in a female, on th
rare occasion he'd allowed himself to want.

And at this very moment she was in the bathroom cry
ing because he was a jackass. He could take this momer
to get dressed and leave, to go into his own bedroom an
fall into a deep sleep in the hope that tomorrow th
would have all been a bad dream. With his luck he
wake up with a huge *J* tattooed to his forehead, lettir
everyone know just how big a jackass he really was.

No, he wasn't going to leave. He hadn't left her in th
four nights since her nightmare, choosing to hold h
while she slept just in case she awoke screaming agai
She hadn't, and Preston had allowed himself to feel th
was partly due to his presence.

So he would stay with her again tonight, there was r
question about that. Unless she threw him out.

Hoping that would not happen, Preston got up fro
the bed and picked up the clothes they'd discarded whe
they'd come in. He was at the bathroom door waitir
when she came out.

"I'm sorry," he said the moment she looked up at hir
"I'd let you kick my butt but I'm so tired I don't think e
ther one of us would last longer than another five mi
utes."

The corner of her mouth lifted in a smile, and Prest
felt that clinching in his chest that had developed the m
ment she slammed the bathroom door—even though he
tried to dismiss it—dissipate.

"I'm tired, too. Whose idea was it to do this instead
taking a shower and heading right to bed?" she asked wi
a lift of an eyebrow.

"Never mind that," he said, taking a step toward her an
pushing her back into the bathroom. "He doesn't have a l
of common sense these days."

"Oh, really? I think he has lots of common sense, just
[no]t enough courage."

Her words stopped Preston, and he stared down into
[he]r face. She was right. He was a coward because he
[wo]uldn't ask her what she meant by that statement.
[H]e wouldn't give her the opportunity to tell him that
[sh]e'd fallen in love with him, or to insinuate that he might
[be] in love with her. He was a big jackass coward, and he
[w]asn't ashamed to admit those were his shortcomings.

"We'll shower and then we'll go to bed and maybe
[co]mmon sense will return in the morning."

He moved around her and switched on the water. Step-
[pi]ng inside, he reached out a hand to her. "Join me?" he
[as]ked.

She'd turned to look at him, one hand on a gloriously
[na]ked hip.

"Maybe courage will also," she said as she stepped
[in]side.

Preston didn't reply, but he wasn't betting on it.

[F]amily meeting in the dining room. Quinn and Nikki
[pi]cked up steamed crabs from Walt as a thank-you pres-
[en]t to Preston for helping his sister with her legal prob-
[le]ms. Michelle's timing everyone and you've got exactly
[te]n minutes," Savannah said to Heaven as she came down
[th]e stairs, Coco tucked in the crock of her arm.

"I'm not family," Heaven replied instantly.

[S]avannah stopped, sending her a look over her
[sh]oulder—a look Heaven now knew was translated to
you've got to be kidding me.

"You're kidding, right?" she asked. Heaven almost
[sm]iled at how on point she'd been.

"No. I'm not related to the Cantrells, although I've
[be]en working with all of you for the past few weeks like I

am. I've really enjoyed my stay here at the inn, but I w.
thinking it might be time for me to move on."

That had Savannah turning around completely. Sl
eyed Heaven suspiciously. "So you're going back to Bo
ton?"

Heaven looked down at Coco to pet her head. "I didr
say that."

"Oh? So you're going to stay in Sweetland but you dor
want to stay here?"

She looked over at Savannah, who now stood right
front of her.

"I like Sweetland. I feel like I was brought here for
reason. So yes, I want to stay here, and I want to find n
own place, to figure out how I can make my own life he
Can you understand that?" she asked, not sure what sl
was hoping Savannah would say.

"I understand you're just as confused as the rest of n
family so you might as well come on into the dining roo
and have some crabs with us."

Without another word Savannah came around to hoc
her arm in Heaven's, talking as they walked. "We ca
ask, who sells real estate around here. If you're gonı
stay we might as well find you a great place. One with
guest bedroom for when Michelle plucks my nerves anc
need to run away."

Heaven smiled and was laughing when she walke
into the dining room. Until she saw Preston.

Of the two of them she was definitely the early bird,
she'd been up and downstairs long before him. Arouı
midday she'd seen him in passing. He was carrying box
into the restaurant and she was heading outside to wa
the dogs. There was a shared smile that went along wi
the companionable silence. They weren't going to ta
about her running off last night, or what she'd almost a
mitted to him. Or what she'd seen in his eyes.

Now wasn't going to be much different, she could tell. Besides, they weren't alone; discussing their feelings for each other or how far they planned to take this relationship wasn't an option.

"You sit here," Michelle told her happily. "Have you ever had steamed crabs before, Heaven?"

"No," Heaven answered as she took her seat. "I've had crab cakes, but not actual crabs. I noticed how good they smelled at the other crab feast."

"Well, these are hot out of the pot. Walt caught us as we were walking down the pier and asked us to deliver them," Nikki said.

Quinn held the crate and dumped the contents in the center of the table, which had been covered with layers of newspaper. Steam rose from a mountain of crabs much bigger than her hand and caked with what she knew was a Old Bay–based seasoning mixture. Her mouth actually watered at the sight and she lifted her glass to allow Preston to fill it with lemonade.

"They're better with ice-cold water, or a beer," he said. "But I figured you'd prefer lemonade."

"You figured correctly," was her reply.

Ten minutes later all the Cantrells were around the table and Preston was showing her how to crack open a crab, clean out its guts, and get to the succulent meat. She'd closed her eyes in a state of complete bliss at her first taste and happily went about cracking and cleaning another crab for herself.

"So what's the deal with The Marina?" Michelle asked, looking directly at Preston.

He, like the rest of them, was chewing, and he looked up from his crabs to reply when he finished.

"It's almost completed. They've already started taking limited reservations," he told her.

"What he's not saying is that they're big competition,"

Savannah added, and earned a quick glare from bo[th]
Preston and Quinn.

"They're bigger, Savannah," Quinn said slowly. "N[ot]
better."

"He's right, they are bigger," Nikki chimed in. "Hug[e]
if I quote my mother and her friends. The women's auxi[l]
iary was invited out yesterday morning for a tour. Sh[e]
said the gardens are lovely, but the food was a litt[le]
bland."

"See, the food's not good," Parker spoke up. "Every[-]
one in town knows where to find the best food."

"Yeah, but we only have seven rooms to rent. On[e]
that can accommodate four people, the others only two[.]
Savannah continued to make her point. "We don't have [a]
pool or a spa on the premises and we're all the way dow[n]
here tucked in a corner."

"Are you trying to get us to sell? Because I thought w[e]
went over this before. We're not selling the B and B[,"]
Michelle said adamantly.

"She already knows we're not selling," Quinn said i[n]
an equally determined tone.

"I think she's just pointing out the obvious. Isn't tha[t]
right, Savannah?" Preston asked.

Heaven paused because as she'd been listening to th[e]
discussion she'd wondered what Preston's position was i[n]
all this. For as much as he claimed his life was in Balt[i]
more, Preston was still here in Sweetland, and he was a[l]
ways going around the B&B talking about improvemen[ts]
or marketing strategies. While he hadn't shared any [of]
this with her personally—which earned another strike i[n]
their relationship column—Heaven had overheard him [a]
few times talking to his brothers. In his voice at tho[se]
times she'd heard pride and determination. He wanted th[e]
B&B to succeed; he wanted his family to do well. Tha[t]
alone told her a lot about the man he was.

"Right," Savannah agreed with a nod. "If we're going compete, then we've got to get in the game."

Preston winked at his younger sister. "I completely ree."

"What did you have in mind?" Michelle asked Preston if Savannah's words still didn't count.

"I think we should add a spa," Savannah offered, be- use she really loved pushing Michelle's buttons. "Women ınt to come someplace where they can relax. Waking and walking down the stairs to enjoy a luxurious spa y would be the ultimate."

"There's a guy from New York who just moved down re about a month ago. Nobody knows why. Anyway, he st signed a lease for that old building down on Elm, ed to be the fish market," Michelle told them all with a d like they should remember the place. "He's opening lay spa there."

"A man's opening a day spa?" Raine asked after choos- g not to participate in the conversation up until this int.

Heaven noted that Raine did that a lot. She listened ıch more than she talked, observed more than she con- buted, and longed to do more all around. Heaven saw r as kindred spirit; she'd had that feeling herself for ars.

"He went to one of those schools where they teach you w to rub on people," Mr. Sylvester said, entering the om. "Y'all think just 'cause a man's asleep he can't smell amed crabs."

Without a word Quinn got up and pulled a chair over the table for Mr. Sylvester. Michelle poured him a glass water and leaned forward to kiss him on the forehead.

"You need your rest, Mr. Sylvester. Savannah says u've been walking the floors in the middle of the night," ichelle said as she moved back to her seat.

"A man should walk the floors as long as his legs s[a] he can," he told them, reaching for a crab at the sam[e] time. "Now, that other man, his name's Rice or Price [or] something like that. He went to one of them fancy schoo[ls] and was making a lot of money on Wall Street. Then h[e] caught his pretty little wife in their big expensive be[d] with his coworker who'd happened to go to that sam[e] fancy school with him. That's why he's in Sweetland," h[e] told them while he opened his crab and yanked at the gu[ts] like they were irritating him somehow.

"Wow, Sweetland's becoming a refuge of sorts," Heave[n] couldn't help but add.

"It's the sun," Mr. Sylvester said to her. He was poin[t]ing the half of his crab he'd broken, and seasonings we[re] flying in Quinn's direction. "The sun and the water an[d] the sea air, all that cleanses your mind, makes you se[e] what's important. You can't see none of that in the b[ig] city with all those tall buildings and loudness. Can't eve[n] hear yourself think in those places."

Heaven nodded because she remembered those fee[l]ings.

"So I've been talking to Parker and Quinn about mayb[e] visiting some of the local vendors and striking up som[e] type of agreement with them. Like a partnership of sort[s]. Say, for instance, I talk to this Rice or Price person an[d] work out a package that can be linked to our Relax and Pla[y] Getaway package. We get the room booking and anoth[er] local business gets a booking as well. Gramma was a[ll] about the community. I think it makes sense that we kee[p] that going, keep that part of her alive."

Michelle sat back in her chair and stared at Preston. "[I] think that's a wonderful idea, Preston. A wonderful wa[y] to keep Gramma alive."

Preston looked at his sister, then quickly looked awa[y]

his grandmother's passing, as well as his sister not telling him sooner about her condition, was still a very sore point with him. They had broached this subject briefly, at which time he'd made it perfectly clear to Heaven that it wasn't something he liked talking about.

"Drew suggested designing centerpieces for the restaurant on a weekly basis. Each one could have a Blossoms card on it, and each time someone sits down to eat they'll think they might need some fresh flowers or at the very least be notified of where they can go should the need arise," Raine added.

"That's a good idea, right, Parker?" Quinn asked.

Parker looked over to him with a frown, then at Preston who tried to hide his own smile. Heaven had no idea what that exchange meant but considered Drew a really nice woman. She'd definitely visit her shop again, as the thought of keeping fresh flowers in her own home seemed like an excellent idea.

"I think we should do this," Michelle said, adding her own smile. "We should work on partnering with the local businesses. We'll need to make it legal, though, so everybody's liabilities and rights are covered. You can do that, right?" she asked Preston.

He nodded. "I can do that."

"How soon?" Raine asked.

"Well, Nikki and I want to take a look at our marketing budget before Preston solidifies any contracts. Whatever we decide to do will have to be properly publicized," Quinn added.

"We need a website," Parker said. "Preston's good with computers. He can do that."

"I thought you were good with computers?" Heaven asked, remembering Parker working on his laptop.

Parker shook his head. "I'm good at keying stuff into a

database to find the info I need. And ordering from Ne
flix," he told her with a wicked grin. "Preston designe
his firm's site."

"Really? I didn't know that, Preston. You have a gre
site. Professional and informative," Raine said.

Heaven remained quiet because she hadn't known tha
either. Funny, there seemed to be a lot she didn't kno
about Preston Cantrell.

"Then he'll make one up for the inn," Mr. Sylvest
said before licking seasonings off his fingers. "Everyboc
needs to pitch in around here. It's a family business ar
we want to attract more families to come down and shar
with us. You can do something, too," he said to Heaven.

"Me? No, I'm into chemistry, not marketing or runnir
a B and B," she insisted.

"But you know people, don't you?" Mr. Sylvester co
tinued. "You could get some of your friends to take the
vacations down here, instead of spending gobs of mon
on those fancy-schmancy islands and stuff. And you lil
to travel or you wouldn't have ended up here. Seems
me you could take the advertising right to some of thos
big business folk."

Preston was shaking his head as if this entire line
conversation was out of the question. "She's not an adve
tising executive. She works in a lab making medications

Mr. Sylvester looked at Preston pointedly. "As I hear
she makes medications for sick people. Well, she has to se
those medications once she makes them, right? So sk
knows how to sell stuff."

"Actually," Heaven put in, "Larengetics has an adve
tising department. I only have to sell my ideas and re
search to the board of directors to secure funding." Sk
hoped that clarified her position a little better, even thoug
she wasn't really sure why she wanted to clarify it since sk
wasn't sure she still had a job with the company.

"Bingo! She can sell stuff," Mr. Sylvester said triumphantly, then cracked open another crab.

"It doesn't matter what she can sell. She lives in Boston," Preston stated firmly.

Too firmly to Heaven's way of thinking.

"Not for long she doesn't," Savannah added with her own little smile.

When Preston looked at Heaven in surprise, then to his sister, then back to Heaven again, she didn't know what to say. Which really didn't matter, because Savannah took it upon herself to fill in the blanks for everyone.

"Oh, yeah, Michelle, we need to know who sells real estate in Sweetland. Heaven's going to stay, so she needs to find her own house. You know she and Coco can't stay at the Sunshine Room forever. Can they, Preston?"

The day of the Bay Soiree came a lot sooner than Heaven had anticipated. All day Friday had been spent with Savannah, Michelle, and Ethel Dansbury, the real estate agent Michelle had called as soon as they'd finished eating crabs Thursday evening. She'd looked at several properties but had determined that the majority of them had been too big.

Sweetland consisted of mainly Victorian-style houses with sprawling lawns and dramatic turrets and stained-glass windows. They were lovely, even the one at the very end of Duncan Road just before it turned off onto Route 3. That house had looked a little run-down with its peeling pea-green paint and mud-colored shutters hanging from most of the windows. The landscape needed lots of work, as witnessed by the overgrown shrubs and too-high grass. The front gate of rusted iron stood locked. When Heaven inquired about the house's less-than-stellar presentation, Ethel had informed her that it was known as the old Gallagher place and had been on the market for

more than three years. She'd driven past the house so fa
Heaven wouldn't have been able to see any more of
even if she wanted to. Still she'd looked through the bac
window of the car trying to get another glance at th
property that for some reason she'd been intrigued by.

When the house was completely out of view Ethel ha
pulled the car over to the side of the road. She'd looke
back at Heaven and said, "You don't want that house, it
H-A-U-N-T-E-D."

And she had spelled *haunted* as if there had been som
one in the car she didn't want to overhear, or as if it wou
have more impact on Heaven that way.

Savannah had laughed and Michelle only shook h
head, which meant there probably wasn't a whole lot
truth to the old haunted-house cliché. Then again, Heave
hadn't turned back around to get another view of the plac
either.

When they'd returned to the inn it was late, so late th
after Michelle had dropped them off at the inn, Savann
and Heaven had only gone into the kitchen for a drin
then both retired to their rooms.

Last night after the crabs and the meeting when Sava
nah had told her little secret, she'd seen the look of abs
lute surprise on Preston's face and had wanted to sa
something. He'd looked around the room as if to say,
didn't know, either; then when his gaze fell back to her
was replaced by a slight look of agitation. After the cra
Preston had washed up and said he was going into tow
to start hustling those deals. When she'd asked to g
along, he quickly told her no. Friday morning she'd awa
ened in her bed alone.

Friday night had been a repeat of the same.

So this evening as she'd showered and slipped into t
ivory-colored gown she'd purchased on their shopping tri
she'd tried valiantly not to think of him at all. Glitteri

ewel-encrusted cap sleeves were the highlight of this fitted gown to Heaven, and after she was completely dressed
she stood in the bathroom continuously looking at them.

Sure, she'd worn gowns before, and more expensive
ones at that. In her closet at home there were dresses from
Vera Wang, Calvin Klein, Dolce & Gabbana, and more.
Shoes that had cost hundreds of dollars as well as diamond necklaces, ruby earrings, sapphire bracelets—she
had more baubles than one woman she be allowed. And
the really sad part was that she'd never worn any of it
more than the one event it was purchased for. On so many
occasions she'd looked into that closet and sighed with
the waste. Selling everything inside would go a long way
for a nonprofit foundation such as LovingLabs, the adoption firm she'd used to obtain Coco.

Smoothing her hands down her dress once more, she
thought that might be an idea she would have to work on,
once she found a house in Sweetland. Because she was
staying here, whether or not her parents, or Preston, for that
matter, agreed with her.

There had been a last-minute change of plans. A very
last-minute one that still had Preston's temples throbbing.
The location of the Bay Soiree had been changed from
the city hall to The Marina. Sweetland's most reliable—
and sorely outdated—method of quick communication, the
infamous phone tree, had been activated to let everyone
know.

Michelle had come into the dining room to tell him.

"You know you should think about renting some office
space here in town," she'd said upon entering.

"I have an office," had been his reply. To say he was in
a sour mood might have been an understatement.

"You have an office in Baltimore, a place you haven't
been back to in just about a month now."

"I went back for the trial," he said without looking up from his computer.

"Which was in the beginning of June for just about two weeks. Today is July seventh and you're still here. And every time I come into this dining room lately, you're in here with papers spread all over the table and that computer opened. So forgive me for stating the obvious—you should get an office here in Sweetland."

She'd taken a seat across the table from him, folding her arms so they rested in front of her. Preston stopped what he was doing to sit back and look at her. She looked like Gramma. Not like their mother or their father, but just like Mary Janet Cantrell, at a younger age of course. But Michelle's milk-chocolate complexion, ebony hair, and high cheekbones were a mirror image of the woman who'd raised them. Hell, she even sat like Gramma, staring across the table at him with that I'm-right-and-you're-wrong-all-the-time look.

"I don't need an office in Sweetland because I don't live in Sweetland."

"I can't tell," was her quick reply.

"You obviously can't tell a lot of things. For starters, that our grandmother was sick and possibly dying," he told her with anger still bitter in his throat.

Michelle sat back with a little sigh.

"When are you going to let that go? I did not hide anything from you and the others. If I had known she was sick, I would have flown to every state to bring all of you back here for her, but she didn't tell me. And I'm sorry if I was too busy running this inn to follow her around town visiting her doctors and ask what was going on," she stated evenly.

That wasn't the answer Preston wanted. It didn't make him feel any better about not knowing his grandmothe had been sick, and it sure as hell wasn't doing anything for the mood he was currently nursing. "You were here with her, you should have taken care of her," he spat.

Michelle only nodded. "Right. I should have stopped my life, the life I'd already dedicated to my family, to make her tell me something she didn't want to reveal. Or better yet, I should have stuck to her side waiting on her hand and foot so that the moment she coughed I would have been there to offer her a glass of water."

"You should have done more to help save her!" he yelled, standing up and slamming his palms on the table.

She startled only slightly, and Preston admitted he felt like an ass. He didn't yell and he didn't slam things, but today he was so on edge about everything he felt like exploding. Michelle hadn't known it but she'd just walked into a hornet's nest.

"I am not a miracle worker!" Michelle yelled right back. "I helped her start this place. I made beds and cleaned toilets, I cooked cakes and fried chicken on blistering-hot summer days even after the grease had splattered my hands so much I looked like I had chicken pox! I had coffee with her every morning and sat with her in church on Sundays while all of you gallivanted around the country doing whatever the hell you wanted. Don't you dare stand here and tell me what I should have done, Preston Cantrell! You should have done more!"

She hadn't stood up to meet him eye-to-eye or changed her position at all. Her eyes had followed him and blazed with anger as only a Cantrell's could. And as Preston looked at her, heard the words she'd said, he didn't know how to respond.

Everything she'd said had been correct. She had been the only one to stay in Sweetland with their grandmother. She had been with her every day, doing whatever was

needed. And she'd worked at the inn making it every
thing it was today. She'd done more than her share, and
he'd known that all along.

"I came back to help," he said even though it sounded
pitiful to his own ears.

"I never said you didn't," she told him. "I never faulted
you or the others for following your dreams or for the fact
that your dreams led you away from here. And neither did
Gramma."

"But she wanted us to come back here to stay. We all
know that's what she wanted."

Michelle nodded. "You were born and raised here so
yes, Gramma thought no other place in this world was
good enough for you to settle down and live in. I believe
her."

"How can you say that when you just said you didn't
begrudge any of us for leaving?"

"I don't because I believe everyone should have the
chance to follow their dreams. I managed to follow my
dreams, but the love of family and of my family home
brought me right back here. Now I'm doing both."

She made it sound so damned easy. Like there weren't
other options, other considerations. "We should have that
same love, is that what you're saying?"

"We were brought up in the same home, by the same
person. It stands to reason that would be correct."

He sighed with frustration. "That's not correct, Mi
chelle. What's good for you is not good for everybody
else. What works for Savannah doesn't work for Raine.
We're all different people with different roads to walk."

"Savannah's road leads in a circle right back to here
every time. If she would sit still long enough, she'd real
ize that all that attention she's been looking for all her
life, she's already received right here in Sweetland. But

outside of that, I could understand if all of you had gone away and found happiness and contentment someplace else, but you haven't. And at the same time you won't give Sweetland a chance. You won't give our legacy a chance."

"I've always supported The Silver Spoon. Nothing would stop me from continuing to do that. I just don't want to live here."

"Just like Mama didn't want to live here."

"She stayed for all the wrong reasons," Preston admitted reluctantly. "And first opportunity she had to break free she did. She never looked back and Savannah suffered for that, Raine suffered."

Michelle shook her head. "You suffered," she said quietly.

Preston didn't respond.

"She left all of us, Preston. Not just you. She walked out on her family because she could only think about herself. You were raised differently than that. The fact that you came back even temporarily and did everything you could for Gramma to get this place up and running is proof of that. If you're still holding a grudge against Patricia for leaving, you need to let that go. It wasn't your fault."

"I know it wasn't my fault. It was nobody's fault but Dad's."

Now Michelle did look stunned.

"He should have never asked her to stay where she didn't want to, should have never forced her to be here and have his children. She was a runner; he should have known that."

Michelle had been shaking her head while he talked. "She was a selfish and inconsiderate woman who is still selfish and inconsiderate to this day. And the only thing our father did was love her!"

Michelle's eyes brimmed with tears. Preston sighed, feeling like crap once more. Women and tears weren't a good thing, on a normal day. Michelle who was always the strongest of them all, the toughest and the most resilient, couldn't cry. She should never cry because it ripped at something so raw in Preston he almost cursed with the pain.

"I had a goal. I worked really hard to achieve that goal. And now, now—" He couldn't finish the sentence.

"Now you don't know what to do. Well, Preston, I can't find that answer for you. It's your life and you have a right to live it any way you please. Just don't forget that you weren't dropped out of the sky onto this earth. You were born into a family, and within a family there are ties and emotions and responsibilities that bind us all together. Whatever one person does will affect those ties and emotions, just like Patricia's leaving affected us even though it was her decision and her life."

She'd stood from the table then and took a deep breath, as if willing those tears that still brimmed in her eyes to stay away. "And let me tell you something else. If you don't know what you're doing with your own life, you probably shouldn't be messing with Heaven's. That girl is trying to get herself together after that traumatic event in her life. If you can't commit to her, or at the very least try to give her everything she wants, you should leave her alone. Because I don't care what your reputation is, playing with a woman's feelings is wrong, and Gramma would not be pleased."

Somewhere between that statement and the time she vanished completely from the room she'd told him about the soiree's change in venue. He'd cursed so loud and so fluently he almost thought she might turn back to come and continue to put him in his place. Since she'd already started she might as well finish it off. Instead she'd left him alone with even more to think about than had already been plaguing him.

At the window now, with papers and laptop long forgotten, Preston wondered if this day, this week, this year, could possibly get any worse.

Chapter 22

Tiny white lights danced in the moonlight. They'd been strung from the awning on the wraparound deck in back of The Marina to the edge of the three large white tents in straight rows. The lush green grass was an uncommon but comfortable flooring for such an elegant event. High-boy tables were strategically placed about twelve feet from the front entrance and every six or so feet in a zig-zag pattern upto the opening of each tent. Tuxedo-wearing wait staff walked around greeting everyone with trays full of champagne glasses. Instrumental music played lightly in the background while the low murmur of voices created a festive atmosphere.

And for about five minutes as Heaven stood in the center of it all she felt like Cinderella. Like all the hard work and goals she'd continually met had paid off big-time be-cause now she was at the infamous ball. She was alone—meaning no date in sight—but at least she was here.

That entire line of thought was crazy since this was not the first black-tie event Heaven had ever attended. As Mortimer and Opaline's only child, she'd been obligated to attend all of their events from the time she was five years old. And the moment she turned sixteen the invitations to more dress-up-and-act-like-royalty events came to her attention. She'd been working the socialite network for more years than she could count.

Yet tonight was drastically different. She could feel it. All around her people mulled about. Women were dressed in gowns like she was, but they moved differently. Their backs weren't stiff, necks straight, heads held high. That's because Heaven doubted very seriously any of them had ever attended Mrs. Everly's Etiquette Establishment, which was kind of a coup for them since Mrs. Everly was perhaps one of the rudest people Heaven had ever had the opportunity to meet.

"You look stunning," Delia said, walking up to Heaven. "That is a great dress."

Heaven liked Delia because she felt like the woman was 100 percent; what you saw was exactly what you got with her. What Heaven and everyone else at the soiree tonight saw was Delia dressed in a red satin gown that looked like it may have been red ink poured over her slim, but curvy body. Her spiked hair gave the dress an even more vixen-like look. The deep plunge in the front that almost exposed her belly button definitely said *Too hot too handle*. The men of Sweetland were in for it tonight.

"Thanks, Delia. Your dress is . . . it's . . ."

"It's freakin' hot!" she said with a deep chuckle and a toss of her head so that the diamonds at her ears glistened beneath the twinkle lights. "I haven't worn it in over a year," she continued with a shrug. "I actually wasn't sure I could still fit in it."

Hmmm, well, Heaven thought, the jury was still out on whether or not she was fitting the dress or the dress was simply fitting her.

"You look fantastic. All the guys in Sweetland are going to follow you around all night long."

A waiter passed them, and Delia grabbed him by the arm. "Hold on there, cutie. I need one of those in a bad way." She snagged a glass, then took another and extended it to Heaven.

"My sentiments exactly," Heaven said, graciously taking the glass and an immediate sip.

"Wow, this is high-quality stuff," Delia said, looking at her glass after the first taste, then putting it up to her lips for another.

Heaven did the same, the second sip going down smoother and sweeter than the last. "You're right. This is the good stuff."

"So they're serving top-of-the-line champagne. Nice touch," Quinn said as he and Nikki joined Heaven and Delia.

"They also have a couture dress shop. I've already planned to send in a spy to see what type of merchandise they're hauling," Delia said with a frown.

"But you have high-end things at your shop," Nikki added. "And the women of the town already know you, they know your merchandise is good. A little competition in a town this small might be a good thing."

Delia shook her head, then finished off her champagne. "There's no such thing as good competition, whether it's big or little. The Marina has one purpose in mind for Sweetland, conquer."

"Don't you mean divide and conquer?" Heaven asked. "I really think there'll be a portion of the town that will remain dedicated to what they know. The older generations do not do change well." She knew, her parents were of an older generation—one that was probably started by some crazy cult, but that was another story altogether.

When the champagne tray came by again, Quinn picked

p another glass for Delia and one for his fiancée. He
didn't take one for himself but looked intently at Heaven.
"I think you've got a point. Maybe we need to focus on that
generation. They all have relatives that have left Sweetland.
They could easily get them to come back, at least for a
visit."

"Not if they're family members are anything like the
Cantrells," Nikki said quietly.

With the mention of the Cantrells and coming back to
Sweetland, Heaven looked around. She wasn't looking for
Preston, had already told herself she wouldn't look for
him. She hadn't seen him since early this morning and
he'd overheard Michelle and Savannah talking about
him wanting to go back to Baltimore. Still, she'd gotten
dressed and planned to have a good time at the soiree tonight. Especially since this was her first official outing as
a soon-to-be resident of the town. She wanted to meet
people, and begin settling in as soon as possible.

The absence of Preston Cantrell wasn't going to stop her.
At least that was the plan.

Preston straightened his tie. He took two steps and straightened the vest. Another step and he checked his cuff links.
He stepped again and . . .

"If you don't stop fidgeting, I'm going to have to kill
you," Parker said in a cool tone.

"What are you talking about?" he asked his brother,
who had been behaving a little off himself in the last two
or three days.

"You're acting like a nervous ninny. You'd think you've
never worn a tuxedo before," he told him as they made
their way through the entrance.

"I've worn a tuxedo plenty of times. I just want to make
sure I don't look like I've never worn one."

"You just want to make sure Heaven sees how good

you look in one," Parker said, moving a step ahead of Preston.

Tonight Parker had donned a tuxedo as well. Every man in Sweetland had probably headed up to Easton to rent a tux if he didn't already own one. And even with his cane—probably *because of* his cane—Parker looked like a movie star dressed in his Calvin Klein tuxedo. All three of the Cantrell men had taken a couple of hours and driven to Easton to rent their tuxedos. Quinn figured it made sense to go ahead and try out the outfits they'd be wearing in the wedding in a couple of months.

Preston and Parker had the same tux while Quinn's had tails. Each of them looked debonair in his own way. None of their ways could compare to how Parker looked. Nothing about him said *city homicide detective*—he looked so polished and clean cut. Preston looked down at himself again and silently admitted to being a little nervous. Not only would this be the first time Heaven would see him all dressed up, it would probably seem like the first time they'd seen each other in two days. Since the announcement that she was staying in Sweetland.

Preston had purposely stayed away from her, unsure of how to act around her at that point. Even though he recalled asking her if she was going to stay, the reality of the situation hadn't really hit until Thursday's announcement. She was going to make a home for herself here in Sweetland. She wasn't going back to Boston. What that meant for Preston was that his easy way out of the fling they'd started had now grown extremely complicated.

"And you're walking so fast so that Drew Sidney won't get a chance to see you in your tux," Preston said, elbowing Parker when he finally caught up to him.

Parker stopped and grabbed a glass of champagne from one of the traveling trays. He emptied the glass.

"I don't hide from women," was his eventual retort.

"And neither do I," Preston said, looking around.

"So now you've decided to look for her." Parker chuck-
ed. "You are so gone over this one. And that's a pretty
amazing feat since you don't normally give a female enough
of your time to become this involved with her."

"I'm not gone. And I'm thirty-three years old, I know
how to be in a relationship with a woman."

Parker gave a full-out laugh at that one. "I'm the same
age and neither of us has ever been in a 'relationship.' We've
had women, lots of women, but never one we wanted to
keep. It doesn't look so bad on Quinn. If you get your head
together in time, you and Heaven might even make a go
of it."

"She lives in Boston," was Preston's instant reply. Then
he closed his mouth tightly.

Parker was already shaking his head. "Not anymore."

"Yeah, right. Did she find a house yesterday?" he
asked as they'd begun walking again, this time toward
the second tent where they'd seen Savannah and Raine
walk in.

"I don't think so. Savannah was rumbling about all the
houses in Sweetland looking the same last night, and Michelle said it might take Heaven a little time to find something she's comfortable with."

"She's used to condos and drivers picking her up,"
Preston said.

"How do you know?"

"Her family's pretty rich. Joe talked to his mother and
mentioned I was dating a woman named Heaven from
Boston. She remembered a pretty prestigious couple with
a daughter by that name."

"Damn, bro, how many people do you have looking into
this woman's background?"

"Just enough to find out what I need to know. Don't
you think it's strange that the black SUV was never seen

in town again and Heaven hasn't received a call from that
number you traced since then?"

"You mean the untraceable number since it belonged
to a disposable cell phone. I do find that a little strange,"
Parker added.

"The calm before the storm," Preston said, then felt a
clench in his gut. His mouth was suddenly very dry as he
stopped just a few steps into the tent.

"And there she is," Parker said. He clapped Preston on
the back and took another sip from his glass. "Yeah, you
might as well give up the fight, buddy. She's got you."

She did not have him, Preston convinced himself,
leaving his brother behind. He was walking toward the
table where Heaven stood with Delia, Savannah, and
Raine.

She stepped away from the table and moved around to
the other side to pull out a chair. Preston drank in every
inch of her. She looked taller, which meant she must have
been wearing high heels beneath the floor-length gown.
The gown that didn't have much color, but sparkled each
time she moved. Her curves, the line of her back as it extended outward toward her delectable bottom, her torso
as voluptuous breasts sat high showing a tremendous
amount of skin above the sparkling neckline. He swallowed again, his groin tightening with desire. Her hair was
pulled up in a stack of curls that were both elegant and
sexy as hell.

"If we pull over two more chairs all of us can sit together," Savannah was saying.

"This is not the type of event where you simply pull
over a few more chairs," Raine interjected.

"I was thinking the guys could sit at one table and all
the females at another," Delia added. "Your brothers are
fine, but they're all taken, which is completely killing my
plans to find me a hot sex partner to go with this hot dress."

Heaven laughed. "Are you really looking for a sex partner at the Bay Soiree?"

"Honey, you just stay in Sweetland awhile longer. You'll learn there's no better place to find a sex partner. Unless you're down at Charlie's drinking a beer. Then you don't know what you might end up with. At least here you get to pick one that's all dressed up and ready to party."

"I don't know about all that," Heaven was saying as Preston came to stand behind her.

"Oh, really. Well, I guess you wouldn't since you've already set your sights on Preston Cantrell," Delia said with a knowing smile as she took her seat.

"Have you set your eyes on Preston?" Savannah asked, taking a seat right beside Delia.

"Be careful," Preston leaned forward and whispered in her ear. "I think they're setting you up."

Heaven turned quickly to look up at him. She blushed and Preston couldn't resist rubbing a finger over the pretty pink tinge to her cheek.

"Hello," she said in a soft whisper.

"Hello to you," he replied letting his fingers whisper down her arms.

"Hello, Heaven." Another voice entered the conversation. A cold and stern one that had Heaven stiffening in his arms.

"Mother?" Heaven whispered as she looked over Preston's shoulder.

Preston turned and found himself face-to-face with someone he could only assume was Opaline Montgomery. A very angry, but elegantly polished, Opaline Montgomery.

"Look who pulled up at the inn just as soon as I was about to leave," Michelle said, moving from around the

Montgomerys and coming to stand beside Preston. "Thes
are Heaven's parents, Opaline and Mortimer Montgomery

"Mr. and Mrs. Montgomery, these are my brother
Quinn, Parker, and Preston," Michelle continued. It seeme
the entire Cantrell clan had come together in the last fi
teen seconds as if there were power in numbers.

"And these are my sisters, Savannah and Raine," M
chelle finished.

"I'm Delia and I need another drink," Delia said, con
ing from where she'd taken a seat to saunter right past th
Montgomerys.

Opaline did not take her eyes off Heaven, not even
acknowledge the people who had just been introduced
her. Mortimer, however, followed Delia's retreat until th
act had turned him completely around.

"It's time to go, Heaven," Opaline said solemnly.

"It's a pleasure to meet you, Mr. and Mrs. Montgon
ery," Preston said, stepping just a little in front of Heave
to extend his hand.

To Heaven's horror, her mother looked down at Pre
ton's outstretched hand, then back up at him in utter di
gust. She wouldn't shake his hand, and she wouldn't spea
to him or the rest of the Cantrells. She'd seen this look i
her mother's eyes before. She obviously thought she wa
better than the Cantrells, that Heaven was better tha
them. From here it would only get worse.

"Of course. We can find another place to have dinner
Heaven said, moving so that Preston was now standi
behind her.

"We will not be having dinner in this place. Our driv
is right outside waiting to take us back to the airport
Opaline told her.

She'd known this moment would come. Hadn't in he
wildest dreams thought her parents would come all the wa

Sweetland, Maryland, to find her, but she'd known she would have to tell them about her plans.

"Okay, well, we can step outside and talk on our way to the airport," Heaven said. She went to take a step and felt Preston's hand at her elbow.

"I'll come with you," he said into her ear.

"That's not necessary," she whispered over her shoulder.

"Really, Heaven, I cannot believe that you have been hiding here for weeks. You left your job without any notice and you have not returned my calls. Geoffrey is simply beside himself," Opaline finished with a flourish of the handkerchief that had mysteriously appeared.

Actually, it wasn't mysterious at all. Her mother always carried a handkerchief. It was the one thing that kept Heaven believing that her mother really was human versus being some computer-generated warden who ran her household with more of an iron hand than the real thing at the penitentiary. Opaline wore a dove-gray pantsuit with a frost-colored camisole beneath the single-button jacket. In the pocket was no doubt where the handkerchief, which her mother had told her once before reminded her of her father, would have been. The fact that Opaline had despised her father was the only strange thing about this keepsake.

"You should have brought good ol' Geoffrey along with you, Mrs. Montgomery. I would have loved to meet him," Preston said with a smile that looked good on the outside but Heaven suspected was 100 percent lethal.

From behind, Heaven heard a snicker.

"Look, Mother, they have a band." Mortimer finally spoke up.

He'd come to stand beside Opaline again. He was five inches shorter than her, dressed in his favorite tweed jacket and black slacks. "Nobody uses a real live band

anymore," he said staring toward the front of the tent no
talgically.

"Quiet, Mortimer. Young man, I would ask you to tak
your hands off my daughter. She is an engaged woman
Opaline said to Preston.

"No. I'm not," Heaven told her mother.

"What did you just say?" Opaline asked.

Mortimer snapped his fingers to the tune the band ha
just begun to play. "I said nobody uses a real live band an
more," he repeated.

"Not you, Mortimer," Opaline scorned, giving her hu
band a look that stopped him just before he could snap h
fingers or shake his bottom once more.

Heaven cleared her throat. The last thing she'd wante
was to create a scene—and at the Bay Soiree at that. A
ready out of her peripheral vision she could see peop
stopping and pointing in their direction.

"Let's just go outside, Mother," she said, and reached f
her mother's arm.

Opaline looked like she might actually make Heave
stand right there and talk, but with a huff she clamped h
lips tight, so tight it looked like someone had drawn
straight line across her face. With some relief Heave
watched as her mother turned, her perfectly coiffed sa
and-pepper hair pulled into a neat bun. Mortimer ga
another bounce and smiled at Heaven before followi
his wife.

Preston touched the small of her back, guiding her
the entrance.

"So these are your parents?" he whispered from besi
her.

"Not by choice," was her reply.

She was shaking, she was so nervous. Whenever h
mother didn't get her way things could get really bad. T

ght, with Heaven planning to tell her she was moving to
weetland, she was bound to explode like those fireworks
e town had enjoyed a few days ago.

The moment they were outside the tent, Opaline whirled
ound to once again face Heaven. Her mother was usu-
ly a shade or so darker than Heaven, her skin carrying a
aturally tanned tone. But the foundation she'd used for-
er made her look lighter, much lighter, almost dead,
eaven thought with a start. There wasn't a wrinkle in
ght on Opaline's face, and her hazel eyes were as sharp
ever. But for one quick second her mother had seemed
d and maybe tired. She was fifty-six years old, but re-
orted herself as being forty-eight. Her father was short
d a bit stout, much to Opaline's dismay. His jovial
nile had turned to a confused frown as they both stood
oking at her.

"I'm not returning to Boston," Heaven said immedi-
ely, figuring prolonging the inevitable would only make
ings worse.

"You're not returning tonight, you mean?" Opaline
ked with a frostiness to her tone as she folded her arms
er her chest.

Heaven shook her head. "I'm going to move to Sweet-
nd," she said, then added, "For good." Just in case her
other wanted to misconstrue those words as well.

"You are doing no such thing. You have a job at Laren-
tics and a fiancé to return to."

Rigid and *unyielding* had always been words she'd used
describe her mother, in private. Right now those traits
ere coming through loud and clear, and she was embar-
ssed that Preston was seeing it firsthand.

"With all due respect, Mrs. Montgomery, Sweetland is
very nice town," Preston chimed in. "It's one of the saf-
t places to live in Maryland, and it's made up of folks

who would do anything for one another. Heaven would
a welcome addition to the community that's already er
braced her."

Really? Heaven thought. Was this really how Prest
felt about her moving to Sweetland? If so, why hadn't
just said so two days ago?

If it was said simply for her mother's benefit, he mig
as well have recited the Bill of Rights in Portuguese for
coldly as her mother was regarding him.

"Young man, I have no idea who you are or who y
would like to be in my daughter's life, but I assure you
is all a mistake. She should never have come here, and t
thought of staying here forever is preposterous. Now le
get your things so we can leave," her mother told her, a
turned to walk away as if the conversation was finished

"I'm not going anywhere with you," Heaven said, l
spine stiffening as she talked. In all her years she'd ne
spoken in such a tone to her mother, had never stood
front of her prepared for battle the way she was.

But that had been her fault. She should have stood
to Opaline much sooner.

"Heaven." Opaline said her name in that warning to
that Heaven had only had to hear around three times
her life.

Hearing it while Preston was standing right next to l
was more than a little demeaning and gave her yet a
other reason to take a stand.

"Everything you say I have in Boston is for you
didn't want to work at Larengetics. I wanted to teacl
Heaven had to pause and let out a whoosh of breath,
that was the first time she'd ever said it out loud. "You
ranged for the job offer and probably made it so I could
resist accepting it. You invited Geoffrey to that first d
ner party, introduced us, and courted that relationship

we were the prince and princess of Boston. My entire
fe has revolved around the things you wanted me to
o."

Behind her she could feel Preston's hand going to the
mall of her back. A soft touch, a comforting and reassur-
g touch, a touch that only added to the inner strength
he'd learned in the last couple of months to rely on.

"So, no, I will not be returning to Boston, to the life
at you want me to have. I'm going to stay here in Sweet-
nd and rebuild a new life, *my* life," she said pointedly.

There was only a moment of silence between them.
eaven hadn't really expected it to last that long. But when
e outburst came, as frosty and chilling as it was, it in-
antly drew a crowd.

"You are not in your right mind! What have these
eople done to you? Have they hurt you? Threatened you?
will see the entire Cantrell family jailed for the assault of
y daughter!" Opaline said, her gaze searing right past
id daughter to land on Preston.

"Someone, quick, call the sheriff, this woman needs
e police!" a loud female voice yelled from just behind
eaven to her right.

A glance over her shoulder, and Heaven's blood boiled.
iana McCann stood with her arms folded over her chest,
smirk as big as the magnolia flower she had tucked into
er hair above her left ear on her face.

In the next moments chaos seemed to break loose. A
an in a tuxedo came pushing through the small crowd
at had assembled, right behind him a younger man in a
olice uniform. Heaven gritted her teeth at the sight.

"All right, all right, what's going on here?" asked the
ortly man who actually did sort of look like a penguin in
s tuxedo.

His hair had been slicked back with what Heaven was

sure had to be a half can of mousse or some other ha
product, while his bushy eyebrows had been allowed
roam free in a gray-streaked mess across his face. Th
mustache that was too long and as bushy as the eyebrow
didn't help the overall image, but Heaven recalled seein
him before. The last time he'd had a jovial laugh and
lemon meringue pie in front of him. She doubted tonigl
was going to end on a sweet or happy note.

"The Montgomerys were just leaving," Preston sai
keeping Heaven close to his side.

"But not without their daughter, whom the Cantrells a
holding against her will," Diana added.

"Shut up, Diana!" Preston yelled. "She's not going an
where with them."

"Are you an officer?" Opaline asked.

Beside her, Mortimer tapped her on the shoulder like
petulant child waiting for his turn to speak.

"Not now, Mortimer," Opaline replied to him with cle
exasperation.

"Yes, ma'am. I'm Sheriff Farraway. What seems to l
the problem here?"

"The problem is that my daughter would like to lea
this godforsaken town and these people won't let her
Opaline said.

Heaven rubbed her temples, her stomach lurching
revolt at the sudden turn of events. "That's not true," sl
said to the sheriff. "I'm staying in Sweetland because it
where I want to be."

"You're being brainwashed by these people. There's 1
other explanation," Opaline continued.

"Sounds like a controlling mother to me," a male voi
yelled from the crowd to be followed quickly by guffav
and murmurs.

"She doesn't belong here." Diana spoke up again. "Lo
at her, wearing her diamonds and glittering all over th

lace. She's trying to make us look bad, like she's so much
etter than us."

Was this really happening? Heaven couldn't believe it.
er mother was causing a scene—which normally would
ever do for Opaline. And Diana was thoroughly enjoy-
ig the scene, which made perfect sense for the self-
entered wannabe. And the townsfolk, well, they seemed
 be taking the night's entertainment in stride.

"Can't make grown folk do what they don't want,"
heriff Farraway finally told Opaline. "Take my son Carl
ere. I want him to find a good woman, settle down, and
ive me some grandkids. But he's hell-bent on gallivant-
ig around town with every pretty tourist he can dig up.
or all I know, with his track record, I might have some
randkids on the other side of the country."

Laugher erupted, with some men patting Deputy Carl
arraway, who was dressed in uniform standing right be-
ind his father, on the back good-naturedly.

"I don't care what goes on in this rock-bottom town.
 came to bring my daughter home," Opaline told them
ernly.

Mortimer touched her shoulder once more, this time
aying, "Maybe we should just get a room for the night
nd talk about this in the morning."

"I'm not staying in this town, in one of those houses,"
paline continued with disgust.

"Good, because The Silver Spoon is completely booked."

Heaven hadn't seen Savannah arrive, but she wasn't
irprised to hear her smart retort.

"Let's get out of here," Preston said, taking her hand.

"All right, all right, back to the party," the sheriff told
l who had gathered. "Nothing to see here. Just a little
isunderstanding."

Yeah, right. Opaline didn't misunderstand, she just
dn't listen. Especially not to Heaven, she never had.

* * *

They arrived back at the B&B in what Heaven though
was record time. As Preston pulled up in front of the in
she finally let the emotions that had been whirling aroun
inside her go. Covering her face, she breathed in and ov
heavily to keep from crying. When Preston reached ove
to pull her close for a hug, she couldn't hold back.

She cried.

She sounded like a blubbering idiot, but damn did th
release feel good. In truth, it felt more than good, it fe
cleansing. She'd stood up to her mother and she'd walke
away with the last word. Whether or not her parents wer
still in Sweetland at this moment Heaven didn't know an
she didn't really care.

"It's not your fault, you know," Preston told her as h
hands moved over her back.

Warmth spread wherever he touched. Not the sexu
kind, just the reassuring kind. It was so comforting si
ting here with him, knowing she could fall apart and h
wouldn't be appalled and he wouldn't criticize. N
Preston would soothe and he would coax, he would c
whatever was in his power to make her mood better. Sh
knew because he'd been doing it since she came
Sweetland. And on some unconscious level, Heave
thought with a start, it had been exactly what she wa
looking for.

"I know. I didn't think they would come here. They'v
never done anything like that before," she told him ho
estly.

Preston pulled back, a slight chuckle escaping. "I'
guessing that's because you've never run away before."

She couldn't help but smile in return. "No, I guess
haven't."

Heaven sighed then, and sat back against her seat.
told her I was staying here. I said it and I meant it," sh

whispered, mostly to herself. She hadn't expected a reply from Preston.

"You sounded pretty certain of your decision," he said quietly.

She looked at him. "I am."

He nodded. "So you're looking for a house. What are your other plans? Are you going to find a job here as well?"

"No one from Larengetics has contacted me since the explosion. I have to assume since that was six months ago that I no longer have a job there."

"Have you still been getting paid?" he asked, looking at her strangely.

"Yes," she said with a nod. "I was on a monthly pay schedule, and each month since the explosion the deposit has been made into my account." She hadn't thought of before, but that certainly seemed strange since she hadn't been allowed back into her office, nor had she spoken to any of the board members.

"So they've been paying you for not being there?"

"I guess so."

"How long do you think they'll continue that?"

Heaven shook her head. "Not much longer. I'm going to contact them so that I can officially resign."

There was silence.

"I wish you all the best," were his next words.

Heaven didn't know what she'd expected to hear. This conversation had come so quickly on the heels of another emotional event that she was a little off when it came to comprehending and letting all this register. Preston hadn't spoken to her in two days. Tonight the conversation about her staying had sort of forced itself upon them, all things considered. So she wasn't prepared for his questions and subsequently did not have all the answers.

Even with all that, his cool well wishes were not what she'd expected. In fact, they made her feel a certain way.

"The best only comes to those who seek it," was he
somber reply. "At this point I'm only seeking happines
If that means I'll live in a cabin near the water with onl
Coco for company, then that's precisely what I plan to d
I'm not asking for anyone's permission or approval in thi
regard. It's my life and I plan to make all the decisior
from now on. I plan to be happy regardless what anyon
else says or does."

With that she reached for the door handle and let he
self out of the vehicle. She walked quickly up the path t
the inn, praying Preston didn't follow her, that he didn
try to stop her, to talk to her, to hold her . . .

Michelle had told her once, "Heaven, don't ever b
afraid to pray. Prayers are always answered. They're n
always answered when we want and the answer is some
times not what we want to hear. But they're answere
always."

Preston's non-action was an answer she didn't want. B
it was still an answer.

He sat in the car for what seemed like endless moment
replaying tonight's scenes over and over in his mind.

Heaven had been beautiful. There was simply no othe
word. That dress had been made for her, and for him a
the sight of her in it turned him on inexplicably. Whe
he'd approached her at the table, she'd looked up at hi
with eyes so bright with life and laughter, and somethin
softer that reached out and grabbed hold of his heart ii
staneously. He'd allowed it to grab hold, to settle with
warmth in his chest, because he didn't want that look t
be given to any other man. He'd wanted Heaven all t
himself.

Until her parents had arrived and he'd been reminde
of her decision to live in Sweetland. She was going to sta
in the town where he was born, where his family live

ere he'd sworn he'd never reside again. That should be
ood thing and probably would have been to another man,
t not to Preston.

There had been way too many changes in his life these
st few months to even consider another one like relo-
ing. His grandmother was gone; he was now part
ner of a B&B and restaurant that was now in competi-
n with a big coastal resort that could easily put them
t of business. And to top all that off, his partner was
adily crying about hiring more help so that they could
th have more free time. What the hell was Preston go-
 to do with free time, besides work more?

And what would he do with a woman and a dog and a
use in Sweetland? How did that play into his ultimate
ns for life? The plans he'd made when he was younger,
 ones he'd been so steadfastly living out, the ones
t . . . had been so quickly interrupted.

She sounded so sure of herself, so strong and intent on
 goals, and for that Preston was supremely thankful.
ere was a difference in the Heaven he'd seen tonight
sus the one he'd met almost a month ago. She was
onger, more self-assured, more beautiful than ever.
d he thought he might just be in love with her.

Love. That was another thing that hadn't been in his
n. He didn't want to fall in love, didn't want to dedicate
 time, his heart, his life to a woman whom he couldn't
st to stay with him forever. Because for Preston that's
v he thought of love. He loved his grandmother forever
l knew without a doubt that she'd loved him that way,
. He loved his siblings and their legacy with the same
cceness and loyalty. Loving a woman this way, Preston
sn't so sure.

Her parents, he could deal with. Even though they
re rich and thought that made them entitled and/or
vileged, whichever—he really didn't care. They were

just people, people who needed desperately to learn the place in their child's life and be careful not to cross th line again. He had a sense that if pushed, Heaven wou cut herself off totally from her parents. Just as he su pected Opaline Montgomery would be the one doing th pushing. It was only a matter of time.

"There's a chair up here on the porch if you just wa to sit," Mr. Sylvester yelled from the porch.

Preston hadn't seen the older man up there. In fact, hadn't even looked in that direction since Heaven h gotten out of the car. If he'd watched her go into the hous he would have been tempted to follow her, to catch with her and say . . . say . . . what? What could he say her to make this better? Heaven had a life plan set in h mind, and while they hadn't discussed it, Preston was most positive it didn't include shacking up with him the days he was in town. She was looking for happine for contentment and stability, a place that she could b long to and it to her. If he was perfectly honest with hi self, he'd allow that Sweetland was most likely the perfe place for Heaven. He was the one who had the problem

He opened the door and stepped out of the car. If M Sylvester knew he was sitting in there and he'd invit him up onto the porch, staying in the car wasn't going help. Mr. Sylvester would eventually get up and make way down to the vehicle with him. That's just the way t old man was.

Stepping onto the darkened porch, Preston sat in t Adirondack chair beside the one Mr. Sylvester w sitting in.

"Nice night," Preston said, loosening the bow tie fr his neck.

"Good night for folk to get all dressed up and have fur Mr. Sylvester said. "You two are back early. I guess y had all the fun you could stand."

"The plans changed," Preston said, leaning back in the chair, closing his eyes so that the sounds of crickets and rustling water filled his senses.

"Yep, they do that sometimes," Mr. Sylvester replied with a laugh. "My daddy used to say this quote but he never could remember who originally said it. Something about the best-laid plans."

"'The best-made plans of mice and men often go astray.' That was from Robert Burns," Preston offered.

"Right, that's it. Smart man, that Burns fella," Mr. Sylvester said.

"Why did she want us all to come back here?" Preston asked. He knew that if anyone would have the answer to that question—anyone besides Mary Janet Cantrell herself—it would be Mr. Sylvester.

"She believed that family should be together. Always. Think about it, remember how it felt growing up in this house with your sisters and brothers. The good times you had, the memories you made. Wouldn't you want that same life for your children? They could grow up with their cousins and others who'd grown up with their parents. It's a connection, a link that strings all of you together, that makes you whole. That's what she wanted."

He dragged his hands down his face.

"I learned early in life that you don't always get what you want," Preston said leaning forward. "I only know how to be the man I planned to become. It's too late to change that now."

Mr. Sylvester sighed. "Way I see it, becoming the man you're meant to be takes a lot of time, a lot of ups and downs, potholes in the road and storms in the night. But you get there finally and when you do, you know, it's because there's a good woman standing right beside you." He coughed a little, then finished with, "I said that myself. Maybe you can quote me one day."

Then Mr. Sylvester stood from his chair. It took him
couple of tries and Preston had even stood ready to he
him at any moment. But Mr. Sylvester swatted his har
away and reached for his cane when he was finally up
right.

When he was gone, Preston stood on the porch alon
in the dark, staring out at what he wasn't quite sure. If h
mind hadn't been so diluted with women and houses ar
jobs and responsibilities he might have seen the black SU
at the end of the street.

Chapter 23

The dogs were barking. Loudly, incessantly barking. To the point Heaven couldn't stand it another moment. Tossing back the sheets, she reached for her robe. The room was still dark, not even dawn yet. And of course, she was the only one in her bed. Preston had not returned to her room. Then again, she hadn't expected him to.

Her robe was at the bottom of the bed, and she pushed her arms quickly into it. One particularly loud, deep bark, which she assumed was from Ms. Cleo, scared her, and she stumped her toe on the edge of the bed just as she was searching for her slippers. Biting her lip against the pain, she made her way to the door and out into the hallway finally. She had to find out what was wrong with the dogs and get them calmed before their one remaining guest was disturbed. After the Smythes and all their wedding guests had checked out on Thursday, only Abigail Mulroney remained, in the Chesapeake Room at the far end of the hallway. She was a gentle older woman who kept to herself, said she needed some R & R, and was from Maine. Heaven was sure a bunch of rowdy dogs barking in the middle of the night was not the woman's idea of R & R.

Mr. Sylvester and Parker and Preston's rooms were o
the first floor of the inn, past the kitchen, down the hal
way, and to the right. The restaurant entrance was in th
opposite direction. She knew the layout of the entir
place and moved quickly to the door of the basemer
where the dogs were kept at night. As she turned on th
basement light, Heaven thought she heard some move
ment, probably from Parker and Preston's rooms. Surel
they would have heard all this racket by now. Still, sh
kept moving down the stairs.

The moment she stepped off the final riser Heave
knew something was wrong. Each dog had his or her ow
kennel, the puppies lined along one wall with Ms. Cle
about three feet away from them so she could see the
all. The door to Coco's kennel was open.

Normally, Coco slept on her pillow by the window i
Heaven's room. But tonight when she'd come in, Heave
had been so irritated by her parents' surprise appearanc
and Preston's pigheaded ignorance that she'd gone straig
upstairs without stopping to pick up her puppy. Now he
heart thumped at the possibility that something had hap
pened to her. She immediately walked to the middle c
the floor, checking each kennel to see if Coco was insic
with one of the other dogs. Instinct told her that was
waste of time. And instinct proved correct when she stoc
from the last kennel and saw that the back door leadin
out into the yard was also open.

She gasped.

"What's going on down here?" Parker asked when h
cleared the last step and stood in the basement with her.

"Coco got out," she said, looking at him over he
shoulder.

She was already in the doorway about to go outside. "
don't know how she could have gotten out and who le

his door open?" she asked, but didn't wait for Parker's
answer.

"Wait, Heaven, Preston's coming now. He'll go out and
look for her," Parker said.

But Heaven didn't listen. She wasn't waiting for Preston to come and find her dog.

Outside she'd already started calling for Coco, moving
steadily toward the water and praying Coco hadn't decided to go down on the rocks. Tears pricked her eyes at
the thought. She loved sitting out here with Coco in the
afternoons. Sometimes they would sit right on the rocks
where they'd all taken their first impromptu dip into the
river. Breaking into a run, she continued to call for her
puppy, heart heavy with the thought that she might have
fallen in and drowned.

She was almost to the water, her mouth open as she
yelled once more, when strong arms wrapped around her
waist. Her words were about to turn into a scream when a
hand clapped over her mouth with stinging pain. In the
next instant she was being lifted off the ground and carried. Fear had her fighting back, kicking and attempting
to flail her arms. It was all to no avail as they rounded the
house and were now heading down Sycamore.

It was dark and basically still, no sounds except for the
feet of the person carrying her. In the distance she could
still hear the dogs barking. Now the tears streamed from
her eyes. She had no idea where Coco was and no idea
where she was about to be taken. And then she saw it.

The black SUV.

Her heart pounded, adrenaline kicking up a notch. She
squirmed and kicked, then grabbed at the hand holding
her mouth, scratching with her nail.

"Keep still, bitch!" a deep male voice growled in her
ear. "Or I'll make it so you can't move again . . . ever!"

Yeah, that was a death threat. Just like the one he'd is
sued that night he'd almost run her down. Dammit, some
body had been after her all along!

Heaven continued to fight, even when the lights on th
SUV turned on and even more so when the back doo
opened as they came closer. He threw her inside, and sh
tumbled off the seat onto the floor. She was moving in
stantly, trying to wiggle her way out.

"I wouldn't do that if I were you," said another mal
sitting on the far end of the backseat with a ski mask ove
his head, a knife in one hand and Coco in the other.

Everything stopped, her movements, her screams, eve
the tears seemed to freeze on her face.

"That's what I thought," the man with the knife said.

Behind her Heaven heard the door close. Then sh
heard another and then the start of an engine.

And then Coco barked.

And Heaven's frozen tears once against fell in warn
rivulets down her cheeks.

"Why the hell did you let her go out there alone?" Presto
yelled at Parker as they stood on the front porch of th
inn.

"Whoa, don't go blaming this on me. If you weren'
acting like such an ass about her moving here, you woul
have been in her room with her and we wouldn't be stand
ing here right now" was Parker's quick retort.

Savannah groaned. "And you two standing here bick
ering is making things so much better."

"When are you going to get your own place?" Parke
asked her with a frown.

"I don't live in Sweetland," Savannah replied instantly

"I can't tell," Parker quipped. "Look, we've alread
called the sheriff. They'll be here any minute now."

"And Sweetland's not that big, so they couldn't have gone far," Savannah offered.

Raine was staying with Michelle at her house down the road. They'd been called, and when Preston looked up the street in search of the sheriff's car, he'd seen the two of them pulling up instead.

"That little pup's gone, too," Mr. Sylvester said, scratching his head.

"Which one?" Raine asked the moment she walked up onto the porch.

"Heaven's puppy is gone," Savannah announced.

She looked tired and on edge, Preston noted. He wasn't totally sure that look was based solely on the events of the night, since they'd all noticed her having severe mood swings lately. And just as Parker had pointed out, she was still in Sweetland, even though she was quick to state she didn't live here. Preston didn't think too much on that last part considering he was doing the same thing.

"Use the dog to lure her out," he said quietly. The thought had been floating around in his mind since he'd first gone into the basement to find Coco missing and then run outside just in time to hear Heaven scream.

It was a sound he would never forget, one that he knew would haunt him for years to come. Only to be rivaled by the completely impotent feeling he'd had as he ran around to the front of the house just in time to hear car tires pealing off down the street. He'd seen only the headlights of the black SUV but knew instinctively it was the same one from before.

"But why?" Michelle asked. "She's not from around here and she hasn't been here long enough to make enemies. Diana and her melodramatics don't count."

Parker frowned. "The enemies Heaven has aren't from Sweetland."

Preston cursed, gritting his teeth and clenching his fist so tight he thought his knuckles might break through the skin.

Quinn and two Sweetland police cars pulled up at the same time. Everyone hurried out of their vehicles, moving quickly up the pathway to where they'd all assembled on the porch.

"What's going on? Where's Heaven?" Raine asked, going straight to Preston and touching a hand to his shoulder.

"The dogs were barking. They knew something was wrong," Preston said slowly. "Dammit, they knew!"

Sheriff Farraway and both his deputies pulled out notepads and pens.

"We heard the dogs, too. Around midnight they just went wild," Parker added. "By the time I got dressed and went into the basement, Heaven was already there."

"Any of the dogs missing?" Carl Farraway asked.

"Just Coco," Savannah said in a small voice.

Michelle had gone straight to her, standing close but not touching her. Not yet, anyway.

"Maybe Heaven Montgomery stole the dog and took off," said Jonah Lincoln, the other deputy. He had dated Nikki for about fifteen minutes after Quinn had foolishly returned to Seattle.

Only the fact that he wore a gun and Preston's huge respect for the law kept him from punching the guy in the mouth. "Heaven doesn't need to steal anything. Besides Coco is legally hers. She adopted her from me."

"So maybe she just ran off with her fiancé. Her parents did say she was engaged," Carl continued.

This time Preston did move: He walked until he had closed up on each of the deputies, Raine keeping a tight hold on his arm as he did. Parker also took a couple of steps forward so that he was now between Preston and the officers.

"I said Heaven doesn't have to steal and she's not engaged to any pompous-assed money counter!" he yelled.

Sheriff Farraway pushed both his deputies back and stood in front of Preston.

"All right. We know Ms. Montgomery's not the stealing type, Preston. We also know she's not from around here and that her hoity-toity parents are holed up at The Marina waiting to take her home. So there's a good possibility she just up and left."

Parker shook his head. "No. She was in her robe and slippers. This was no slip-away in the night."

"And the truck she drove away in tried to run her down just a couple of weeks ago," Preston told them.

"Wait, a truck tried to run her down in my town and nobody thought to alert the authorities?" the sheriff asked, obviously annoyed by that fact.

"We didn't think anything of it at first," Quinn lied. "She wasn't hurt so we just took it as someone speeding."

"Nobody speeds in Sweetland," Carl said. "Hoover tries to, but his cab always cuts off when he goes above fifty. If someone was speeding, you guys should have called the police."

"I traced the tags, registered to a rental company in New York. The rental guy was dragging his feet on the records of his renters since I didn't I have a warrant," Parker told them.

The sheriff turned to Parker. "You doing cop work in my town behind my back again, Parker?"

"Just because you're some big-shot detective in the city doesn't mean you have to come down here to help the country folk out," Carl said, moving closer to Parker.

They'd had run-ins before, Parker and Carl, stemming from their teenage years. And then again when Preston and Parker had helped clear Nikki's name for murder. It was no secret the two guys didn't like each other. The fact that both of them were now licensed to carry guns didn't make matters any better.

"Why don't we take this inside," Michelle suggested. "Last thing we need is for the neighbors to come outside like we're late-night special programming."

She wrapped an arm around Savannah, and they both walked inside first. Quinn clapped Parker on the back and nodded for him to go inside. Nikki followed with Mr. Sylvester limping behind her.

"After you, Sheriff," Preston said.

The sheriff and the deputies went inside.

"Thanks," he whispered to Raine and kissed her forehead.

"Can't have our star attorney getting arrested for punching a cop," she said with a smile and went inside with him.

An hour later the Cantrell men rode in Quinn's car behind the two police cruisers down to Yates Passage.

Only seven hours earlier, they'd all come to The Marina dressed in tuxedos ready to eat food, dance, and endure what was easily Sweetland's biggest party of the year. They'd entered through the rear where tents and tables had been set up for the event and the band played music so boring Preston had immediately wanted to find someplace to lay down and take a nap.

This time, as he walked with his brothers beside him, the Sweetland police in front of him, past the fountain in the center courtyard and the intricately designed topiaries, through the freshly painted front doors, he was pushed by an even deeper need. It burned in the pit of his stomach like a freshly lit fire. Each time he swallowed it burned faster, brighter. His temples throbbed, the pressure so intense he could easily fall to his knees in pain. But he wouldn't. Just like he hadn't slugged that idiot

leputy. Preston knew how to control his temper and his
actions. He'd been doing it for years. If there was one thing
a good defense attorney needed, it was control.

But even Preston had to admit, if only to himself, that
f whoever had taken Heaven harmed her in any way—that
control would be shattered. He would kill, without blink-
ng an eye.

The Redling brothers were already waiting and led
hem into a conference room down the gorgeously deco-
ated lobby. They were dressed in suits and ties despite
he late hour, standing with backs ramrod-straight as they
howed them to a table where the Montgomerys were al-
eady seated.

Opaline was up out of her seat the moment Preston
walked in.

"What have you done to my daughter? What kind of
ness have you gotten her involved in?" she asked, stand-
ng in Preston's face like she wanted to slap him.

"Come, Opal. Have a seat and we can hear what's go-
ng on," Mortimer said, trying to get his wife back into her
eat.

"Mr. and Mrs. Montgomery, your daughter was ab-
lucted from The Silver Spoon about an hour ago. I've al-
eady talked to the state police and we've shut down the
oads in and out of Sweetland. Witnesses saw a black
SUV pulling off. This vehicle has been traced to a rental
company in New York, but as of right now we do not have
ny further information on it. Now, I understand your
laughter's been in town for just about three weeks. In that
ime she's made some friends and seemed to enjoy her-
elf. You come into town tonight and try to take her home
until she states her plans to stay here permanently. And
ow she's gone."

"What on earth are you accusing us of?" Opaline asked,
a hand going to her neck.

She sounded appalled, but that alone wouldn't have convinced Preston. It was the way her hands shook that proved what he'd been thinking earlier. Opaline Montgomery loved her daughter, but she had no idea how to show it.

"When Heaven first came here, a truck tried to run her down. She was receiving prank calls that unnerved her. I asked her if anyone was after her, and she said no. She asked why they would be. I think you know," Preston said to her, his intent gaze holding her's.

"My daughter is a world-renowned biochemist. She's written publishable papers and is responsible for what may be the biggest medical discovery since penicillin. She's intelligent and she's worth millions. How dare you and these inept officers suggest I would know anything about her disappearance," Opaline told him in that frigid voice of hers.

"Heaven is very important to us," Mortimer put in. "She's our only child."

"Which means you want to get to the bottom of this as quickly as the rest of us," Sheriff Farraway suggested.

Nobody seemed to look at Opaline anymore. They certainly didn't ask her anything after her little tirade. But Preston sat right across the table from her, watching her carefully, waiting.

"How do you plan on finding her, Sheriff Farraway? Will you and your little friends go around knocking on everyone's door asking if they have my daughter tied up in their basement? It's apparent that you are not equipped to handle this situation. I will be calling our attorneys just as soon as I leave this room. What I suggest you do is look into this man's financial background. There's no doubt in my mind he's after my daughter's money. I wouldn't be at all surprised if he has her tied up someplace himself," Opaline said, pointing her shaking finger at Preston.

"Now, wait one minute, Mrs. Montgomery," Quinn began, but Preston held up a hand to stop him.

"I don't need your daughter's money, Mrs. Montgomery. I have my own. But I am beginning to wonder about your financial status."

Chapter 24

The room wasn't dark and dirty. It didn't stink and she wasn't bound and gagged the way she would have pictured in a kidnapping. But as Heaven lay on the twin-sized bed, Coco curled in her arms, she thought, a tear rolling down her cheek, that's exactly what had happened

Why? Who? And how would it end?

All questions that had filtered through her mind in the last minutes, hours, that she'd lain here. It was a waiting game now, she supposed. For her kidnappers to get whatever they wanted, or do whatever they needed. There was nothing she and Coco could do but wait.

Or try to get away.

That was a fleeting thought, one she wasn't so sure she would carry through. One of the men had a gun, the other a knife. So far she'd only seen the two of them with their black ski masks, turtlenecks, pants, and shoes. They looked like the proverbial kidnappers, or bank robbers, or murderers, or whichever unsavory character one could imagine.

Fear still engulfed her, anger resting subtly inside as she racked her brain trying to figure out who would want

kidnap her and what they might get out of it. Money
as the easy answer, the likeliest. She was rich. They could
quest a hefty ransom for her safe return. But would her
rents pay it?

Opaline was more than a little upset at Heaven's ac-
ns. She'd expected the same unquestioning agreement
eaven had always given her. What she hadn't expected
as that her daughter had finally grown a backbone.
nny, surviving an explosion could do that to a person.

Now she needed to survive a kidnapping. The differ-
ce this time was that Heaven felt she had so much to
e for. She'd found a place where she belonged and that
ade her feel like her whole life was ahead of her.

Then there was Preston. She thought of him intermit-
ntly—well, *every few minutes* was more like it. What
as he doing? Was he worried about her? Did he care
ough to try to find her? Did he love her?

The last question was by far the most important be-
use Heaven was certain that she was in love with him.
e was the man she'd always wanted, even though she'd
st realized it. It sounded a lot more complicated than it
tually was. She'd come to this small town in search of a
mpanion and she'd found a puppy, a man, and his family.
e didn't want to lose any of it, certainly not at the hands
a kidnapper.

"Preston." She sighed quietly. Coco moved upward so
at her head was now tucked right beneath Heaven's
in. "You love him, too, don't you?"

Coco's answer was to lick her chin, then resume her
uggling position.

"We'll get back to him, don't worry," she whispered and
her eyes close once more.

could smell her as he buried his face in the pillow on
r bed. Her nightgown, that pink one she'd never had

a chance to wear for him, was clutched in Prestor
hand.

He lay on her bed, staring up at the ceiling. Michel
had forced everyone to bed. She and Raine had bo
agreed to stay in the room with Savannah, who was st
acting strange. Quinn and Nikki had taken one of tl
guest rooms, and Michelle had given a room to Depu
Jonah. Deputy Carl wouldn't have stayed because I
and Parker were only seconds away from a physic
altercation. The sheriff said he would be back in tl
morning.

They'd left the Montgomerys at The Marina, the arr
gant and woefully ignorant couple whom Preston st
could not understand. They had a wonderful daughter, b
they thought of her as an object, one they could control
their whim. It was a shame, not for them, but for Heave
because she deserved so much better.

She deserved the best, he thought with a sigh. A ma
who loved her above all else, who cherished and respect
her and who would take care of her for all time. Tha
what Preston wanted for her. For himself, he wanted h
to live, needed her to come out of this situation safe a
sound. There was no way he could live through any oth
outcome.

This was the exact moment he hated. The one whe
the love you had for a person just wasn't enough. F
could go to the roof of the house right now and shout th
he was in love with Heaven Montgomery, but it would
persuade the kidnappers to let her go, it wouldn't ma
her magically appear in this bed beside him. So he w
helpless, once again, to change the circumstances su
rounding him. Or was he?

"Thomas Riordan holds the controlling shares in Lare
getics Pharmaceuticals. He's sixty-one years old, divorce

th two grown children. His sister went to school with paline Montgomery." Ryan DelRio sat at the dining room ble, a half-eaten slice of apple pie beside the folder he'd ened and was now looking through.

It was almost noon on Sunday when he'd arrived at e Silver Spoon.

"So she got Heaven the job at Larengetics," Preston id.

Heaven had said that the offer was too good to turn wn and that her parents had expected her to take it. Of urse they did if they orchestrated it.

Ryan drummed his fingers on the table. "Not only did e get Heaven the job, but she was collecting a very ndsome chunk of change from the company herself."

"How was she being paid?" Parker asked. "She doesn't ork for them. She's from a long line of her own money, why would she need more?"

Ryan shook his head and looked up at them. "She was m a long line of money. Seems the rest of the Mont- mery fortune—the part Opaline hasn't spent on her travagant lifestyle—is locked tight in a trust fund. Give u one guess who holds the trust?"

"So Heaven's rich?" Quinn asked. "Even without work- g at this company, she's rich."

Ryan nodded. "She's what some might call filthy rich. e account came fully into her name the day she turned rty. She's never touched it. Ever."

"Larengetics is still paying her," Preston said, his head ly mildly pounding with the information Ryan had just ven him.

He wasn't going to think about Heaven's money, be- use just as he'd told her mother, he didn't give a damn out it. Besides, he'd known she had money, thanks to e's mother. His bigger concern was how Heaven's trust nd played into her kidnapping.

"Even though she hasn't worked there in six months
Quinn asked.

Preston nodded. "She wasn't sure why, either, since
one from the company has tried to contact her since t
explosion."

"The explosion that cost Larengetics more than thr
million dollars. Riordan was not happy about that. :
while Heaven has remained on payroll, Opaline has no
Ryan said as he reached for his fork, cut himself anoth
piece of pie, and stuffed it into his mouth.

"And that's why she showed up wanting to take Heav
back to Boston," Parker added. "The investigator in B
ton said Heaven was no longer a suspect in the explosic
They had another lead."

"Right," Ryan said, brushing crumbs off his hands th
flipping through the papers in his folder. "Johnny Tu
caverdi, or rather one of his men."

"Wait, I know that name," Quinn said. "He's some bi
time loan shark from New York, right? I remember hi
because he's the one they think killed Randy Davis, Ni
ki's ex."

All eyes rested on Quinn at that moment, then shift
slowly back to Ryan as he continued.

"Tuscaverdi works for a huge crime family out of Ne
York. If he's involved in the explosion, there's a much bi
ger problem than just Heaven's kidnapping," Ryan said

"No!" Preston said adamantly. "There's nothing mo
important than getting Heaven back. Absolutely nothing

The room was quiet.

And that made the ringing phone all the louder.

Preston was standing closest to the stand that held t
cordless phone, so he picked it up.

"Thank you for calling The Silver Spoon. How car
help you?" he asked out of habit since he'd been here f
weeks now.

"You can help me by delivering three million dollars
the back of that church, the one down Route 33. There's
Dumpster in the back. Put the money in black trash bags
d leave it there. Once I get it, I'll drop her off somewhere
this hillbilly town of yours. Five o'clock this afternoon.
ot a minute after."

Then the line went dead.

Preston stood there for a moment. He'd sat at the trial
ble with murderers and drug dealers only inches away
om him. He'd walked into penitentiaries to visit with
aximum-security prisoners and sat right across the
ble from them. And never, not in all the years that he'd
acticed law, had he felt such stark, white-hot fear ripple
rough his body.

It wasn't a feeling he relished.

"He wants money. Three million. The exact amount
arengetics lost because of the explosion," he told every-
ne in the room.

"So Riordan had her kidnapped to get his money
ack?" Parker asked.

"Or her crazy-ass mother had her kidnapped so she
ould resume getting her paycheck?" was Quinn's thought.

"Or," Ryan suggested, rubbing a hand over his goatee,
Tuscaverdi was paid to set up the explosion at the behest
f a rival pharmaceutical company with an Alzheimer's
rug of their own ready to hit the market, all the while
aming Heaven for the job. After the success of the ex-
losion, he caught wind of Riordan's loss. Now he figures
e can cash in a second time, and frame Riordan."

"Son of a bitch!" Preston yelled.

"Calm down. We'll get her back," Ryan said, way too
almly for Preston's way of thinking. "The minute Tus-
averdi's name came up I was given carte blanche by my
irector to do whatever's necessary to bring him in. I put
gents at The Marina and inserted some around the town.

Your sheriff did good by closing down the road in and o
of town. It was hell getting in, so our kidnapper is st
here. After hearing about Parker's cell phone trace, I f
ured it couldn't hurt to put one on Preston and Heave
phone as well as the business phone here, since it's ob
ous that somebody already knew she was here."

"So you traced that call? He wasn't on it that lon
Parker said.

"It's been recorded. We'll at least get a phone numb
and if it's a cell phone—we're almost positive it w
be—we can get a location from the device's GPS," Ry
said.

"Wow, and I've been wasting all my time dating m
lionaires and princes. I should have been looking for
FBI agent all along," Savannah said as she entered t
room, a smile on her face directed solely at Ryan.

Savannah's entrance—while she took full advantage
meeting Ryan—was actually to announce that the Mo
gomerys had arrived.

They weren't invited but Preston stood to greet the
anyway.

"Any news, son?" Mortimer Montgomery asked t
moment he walked into the dining room.

"There's been a ransom call," Preston said, his ga
shifting from Mortimer to Opaline searching for t
woman's reaction.

She was dressed in a black skirt and a pale pink blou
Preston immediately noted that the color did nothi
for her sallow complexion and dark, assessing eyes. H
hair was pulled back tightly, so tightly her face look
pinched—perfectly made up, but pinched nonetheless.
her right hand was her purse, a big black patent-leather b
that looked more like a portfolio. In her left hand we

ack gloves, as if she expected to put them on to keep the
rms at bay.

"I suspected there would be one. How much?" she asked
a drab tone.

"Mrs. Montgomery, I'm Agent Ryan DelRio from the
deral Bureau of Investigation. Please know that the
BI will be using all of our resources to ensure that your
ughter is returned safely."

Ryan, dressed in black suit pants, a white shirt, and an
e-blue tie that he'd straightened only moments before
rs. Montgomery's entrance, stood to extend his hand.

Opaline reached out immediately to accept it—probably
inking he was safe because he couldn't be from Sweet-
nd.

"Finally, some real law enforcement to handle this
uation. I swear I don't know what those others were talk-
g about last night. They're probably not even real officers."

"I take offense at that statement," Sheriff Farraway
id, making his entrance into the dining room with Mi-
elle right behind him.

"Well, I'll get some lemonade and cookies," Michelle
id, looking around the room. "Everyone just have a seat
d make yourselves comfortable."

She left the room as quickly as she'd come while Ryan
owed Mrs. Montgomery to her seat—passing Preston a
owing look as he did.

"The ransom request is for three million," Ryan said,
oking directly at Mrs. Montgomery.

She didn't flinch, barely batted an eye. Mr. Montgom-
y, on the other hand, clutched at his chest as if a heart
ack was imminent.

"Dear God," he whispered. "She's my baby. My little
rl."

Savannah stood and went to him, placing a hand on his

shoulder. Preston watched his younger sister, and fel[
surge of pride at her selflessness at this moment.

"They won't hurt her," Mrs. Montgomery said. "Sh[
worth more to them alive."

"Really? What makes you so sure?" Preston asked h[
"How would you know what the kidnappers want w[
Heaven?"

She wouldn't even look in his direction.

"Can you get the money?" Ryan asked.

Mrs. Montgomery hesitated. "Not all of it. Not witho[
Heaven," she finally admitted.

Ryan nodded. Preston sat back in his chair. It wasn'[
surprise to them, since Ryan had already told them s[
was running out of money. She needed Heaven to wi[
draw anything from her trust fund. Preston had a feeli[
that request had been made before and Heaven had d[
clined.

"Do you know who has your daughter?" Ryan ask[
point-blank.

He'd leaned over in his chair, letting his elbows rest [
his knees as he stared directly at her.

"No. I do not," was her reply.

"I don't like her," Raine said standing in the kitchen w[
Nikki and Michelle. "What kind of mother uses her ch[
for money?"

"I guess the same kind who leaves her kids high and d[
when her husband dies," Michelle quipped as she plac[
glasses on the tray alongside a pitcher of lemonade.

"Mom was nothing like this woman. Opaline Mo[
gomery is a witch," Raine continued.

Nikki shook her head. "No wonder Heaven left B[
ton."

"Women are funny folk," Mr. Sylvester said, comi[

ough the back door and taking a minute to make sure
screen door didn't slam behind him.

"Take your grandmother, for instance. She let me come
d stay here and didn't know a thing about me. My ex,
ra, I lived with her for near two years before I found
t she was already married," he finished.

The women looked at one another not bothering to
sk their confusion, then back to Mr. Sylvester, who to-
y wore seersucker shorts that touched his bony knee-
s, a white button-down shirt with small yellow birds
it, and a baseball cap, ragged around the brim.

"A woman can either hold a secret or she can trust a
n with her heart. They usually don't do both. And
en they have children they change altogether. Like an-
er species. Sometimes they love the child uncondition-
y, other times there's a bit of jealousy that taints that
e. Again, it's one or the other, they can't do both."

"So you're saying that Heaven's mother is jealous of
and that's why she treats Heaven the way she does?"
ine asked.

Mr. Sylvester had moved to the counter where Michelle
s standing. He took one of the glasses off the tray and
ited while Michelle filled it with lemonade. He took one
g sip before looking over to Raine in response.

"I'm saying she made a choice a long time ago of what
ir relationship would be. Now it's Heaven's turn to
ose."

"But she's being held against her will now. She can't
anything if she's in danger," Nikki said.

"Your brother and that FBI guy came in this morning
l get her. She'll be safe, and then the real work will
gin."

Raine opened her mouth to say something else but
chelle interrupted.

"I'm sure you're right, Mr. Sylvester," she said, a
crossed the room with the tray in hand. "Raine, you a
Nikki come on out and help me. The guys will need
support while they deal with this situation."

Raine and Nikki took the hint and followed Miche
into the dining room.

"All of you need support," Mr. Sylvester whisper
when he was alone. He took another sip of lemona
"You need one another."

Chapter 25

hey had no intention of paying the ransom. Three hun-
ed thousand flash money via the FBI was spread out in
ash bags lined with stacks of newspaper. Ryan had
ttled on Tuscaverdi being the culprit in this elaborate
heme. He'd also verified through his confidential in-
rmants in the New York and New Jersey area that
uscaverdi was not in Sweetland. This meant he'd hired
meone to do his dirty work, which fit his reputation
erfectly.

Opaline had been right about one thing: Heaven was
orth much more to the kidnappers alive. If the Mont-
omerys didn't pay the ransom, Larengetics just might to
rotect the trade secrets she held. But Ryan was positive
uscaverdi just wanted the money. He'd been researching
hnny Tuscaverdi and the families he worked with for
oing on three years now. He knew them very well—too
ell for a man who'd always wanted to lead a normal life.

Today, normal would be leading his team of ten agents
 the location where Heaven was being held and bring-
g the woman home. Without bloodshed, he prayed.

Sweetland, Maryland, was a quaint little town. A

shootout on the streets definitely would not go over we
His director had said as much in their communicati
because he'd already heard from the governor, who h
heard from authorities in the surrounding counties, wl
had heard from Sheriff Farraway's desperate call to sh
down all the roads in and out of town about the kidna
ping.

He checked his gun, holstered it, and put a foot on t
chair to check the backup he kept there. Then he smell
perfume and smiled.

"I could do that for you," Savannah said.

When Ryan straightened, he saw Savannah Cantre
sitting on the table, legs crossed—long caramel-ton
legs, glistening with either a fresh tan or oil. Either o
was damned sexy and had his body reacting instant
She wore high heels, very, very high heels that made hi
think of a stripper pole . . . and a naked stripper. B
when he looked into her face all he saw was Preston.

Yeah, not cool.

Her eyes were so much like those of the man he'd go
to college with and had hit a few strip clubs with over t
years. For that reason, Ryan laughed in an attempt to bru
her off, again.

"I've got it," he said instead and walked past her.

"It's not going to work, you know," she told him.

He should have kept right on walking. Instead Ry
turned back, looking at her over his shoulder. "What's n
going to work?"

She hopped down off the table, her breasts bounci
with the motion. He inwardly groaned.

"You can't ignore me. It's just not possible."

And as she sashayed her fine ass—yes, her ass with
small handfuls of cheeks—out of the room, he want
nothing more than to run after her.

But Preston arrived. Disaster definitely averted.

"Parker's got some dumb-ass notion that I'm not going
th you," Preston said. "And before you say a word . . .
d after you pick your jaw up off the floor and get imes of my little sister out of your mind . . . I am going
th you. Try to stop me and I'll shoot you."

Those words were punctuated by the gun Preston pulled
m his back waistband.

"Whoa," Ryan said, taking a step back and holding his
nds up. "I was with you when you purchased that gun,
n't point it at me."

"I just wanted you to know how serious I am."

Preston checked the gun and put it back, pulling his
rt out of his pants to cover it.

"She's your woman, I get it. If it were my woman, I
uld want to go as well," Ryan began.

"I'm going, Ryan," Preston insisted.

It was quarter after four. Debating with Preston was
ing to waste more time than they had. Ryan finally
hed and wiped a hand down his face. "Fine. But you do
t get to shoot, do you hear me? There's no way I can
olain that in a report."

"If I see that bastard, I'm shooting," was Preston's re-
onse.

"Look, I'm going to take Tuscaverdi down, you can
int on that. But today isn't about him, it's about getting
aven back safely. Now, my guys have an idea of which
e of Tuscaverdi's boys are on this job. They're not all that
ght, and definitely not the killers Tuscaverdi normally
es. He probably didn't want to waste too much money
 this and figured what could go wrong in this small
vn."

"Everybody's always underestimating this town," Pres-
 said sullenly. "Do you know where they're holding
 ?"

"We think it's an old house near the interstate—that's

why the drop-off was named behind the church. T
guys will make the drop and wait for the pickup; anotl
pair will hit the house simultaneously. In and out, dc
deal," Ryan said, snapping his fingers.

"I'm going to the house with you," Preston said. "Parl
can go with the money since he knows the town."

Ryan sighed, then shook his head. "Who's runni
this operation, you or me?"

Preston didn't reply, just turned to walk out of the roo

The Gallagher house was definitely not haunted, Heav
surmised when she'd awakened on the small bed a
looked out the window. She remembered the yard tl
needed a tremendous amount of work from Friday's c
of house hunting. The floors squeaked—she'd heard th
throughout the time she'd tried to sleep. There was
electricity, which meant no air-conditioning. That u
mately meant she'd stripped out of her robe when s
scooped Coco up in her arms and headed for the do
Her puppy needed to pee and so did she.

She touched the knob with great care because it look
as if it was ready to fall off the dirt-stained door. It v
locked. It made a clicking sound but didn't move, remii
ing her quickly that she was being held against her wil

"Okay, what now?" she asked out loud to the emj
room, then quickly clapped her lips shut.

Coco barked and licked her chin. "Right, I was aski
you for suggestions."

With a frown she moved back to the window and look
through the glass, which was covered in a few more lay
of dirt than the door had been. She saw the yard or
more, thick with overgrowth and a broken-down wo
fence.

A cold breeze blew across her neck, and she jumj
with surprise. Turning quickly, she looked around

om, only to see the same thing she'd seen before. Noth-
g. The only furniture was the bed she'd slept in. Her
ghtgown was stuck to her body, heat and humidity just
out suffocating her.

But the breeze had been cool.

Coco whimpered, and she hugged her closer.

Heaven didn't know why, but she moved toward the
or once again. Her hands were sweating profusely, her
art beating so loud it echoed in her ears. She reached
t and touched the knob. It turned.

Elated, she pulled the door open and let out one hell of
cream as she stared into the face of a masked man.

"Shut up!" he yelled in her face before grabbing her by
e neck and pulling her out of the room.

Coco barked, almost falling out of her arms as she
umbled into the hallway.

"You're never going to get away with this," she said
en she'd regained her balance and saw they were headed
ward the staircase.

"Don't tell me how to do my job," he spat, all but drag-
g her down the steps.

"I won't tell you about my research. You can't black-
il them with that information," she said.

When she hadn't been thinking about Preston, which
sn't very often, Heaven had been trying to figure out
y someone would want to kidnap her. She thought
out the explosion and the phone calls, and of course the
ck SUV. It all made sense now. It probably would have
fore if she hadn't been so hell-bent on not wanting to
:ept it. Preston had asked repeatedly if she was in dan-
r, and she'd denied it. Now she couldn't deny it any
iger.

This had to be connected to the explosion. Whoever
the explosion was now gunning for her. But if she
re the original target, why not just kill her? No, they

needed her; that's why they were keeping her ali
They needed her, but the only thing she had was her
search.

And money.

The thought hit her as she stopped on the last step.
pulled on her arm, but she wouldn't move.

"How much do they want?" she asked.

"Come on!"

"No!" She said again, "Tell me how much they ask
for me." This time she glared right into the dark eyes s
could see through the slits in the mask. "How much
they think will be paid?"

She had money, she could easily pay her own ranso
But she wanted to know who they'd asked and how mu
because that made all the difference in the world.

He got up in her face, pulling her body close to h
Then she heard a click. It was the knife positioned ri
against her neck. Coco went wild in her arms, and s
almost dropped her again as she tried to rub her ears
keep her calm, all the while swallowing against the ra
beating of her heart.

"We're gonna make three million off you. Now shut
before I decide to go against his order and cut your pre
little neck."

He wouldn't, she thought with an inward sigh. H
been told not to kill her, and three million dollars was
the line. She was safe, sort of.

"Is Larengetics paying you?"

"No more questions!" he yelled, the knife pricking h
skin. "Shut up and move!"

Okay, she would do as he said. She walked fast behi
him as he dragged her toward the back of the house. T
layout was similar to The Silver Spoon's—the same la
rooms and French doors, only these had the glass brok

. When they reached the kitchen, he stopped and pushed
into a chair.

"Stay," he warned her as he moved to a corner of the
om.

Heaven looked around for something, anything. If she
ld knock him out she could run. But he came back too
ckly. With a swipe of his arm he knocked Coco off her
. The puppy whimpered and cried for a second, then
to all fours and barked with as much rage as her little
dy could manage.

"It's all right, baby. I'm all right," she tried to coax.
co wasn't worth millions of dollars, and the last thing
wanted was for this lunatic to turn that knife on her.
m right here, girl."

Heaven patted her knee just before he jerked her hands
ind the chair and began to tie them with rope.

Coco came to sit right at Heaven's feet, looking up at
with concerned eyes, her little chest heaving. Heaven
t eye contact with her to keep them both focused on
viving, and for the first time since this ordeal had be-
n she prayed that someone cared enough about her to
e her.

's the old haunted house," Preston said the moment the
they'd ridden in came to a stop across the street.

"Haunted?" Ryan asked.

Preston shrugged. "That was always the rumor. Never
lly confirmed except by a few kids who swore they felt
reeze or heard the wind whistling while they were in-
e."

Ryan chuckled. "Good. Just what we need, a ghost to
tend with."

"There's no such thing as ghosts," Preston said. "And I
n't care, I'm going in."

"No," Ryan warned, putting a hand to his arm. "We in first. You stay behind until I call for you. Got it?"

He was shaking his head, not wanting to go throu this with his friend again. "Ryan?"

"Or I'll cuff you to this seat, Preston. This is serio business. While I don't think these guys are smart enou to shoot us all, I'm not taking any chances. We'll go in fi and secure the scene. Once we have her safe I'll call you Now, are we cool on this?" Ryan asked in all seriousnes

He was reluctant, but Preston knew that arguing w only wasting more time. He was a logical man, reacti in an illogical situation. But Heaven's safety came fir The thought of her being hurt was not something he w willing to risk. With his lips closed tightly he nodded, h ing every minute that Heaven was with the kidnappers.

Moments later Ryan and his men filed out of the va They were all dressed in black Kevlar vests with FBI bold white letters on the back. He watched as they su rounded the house, his heart hammering in his chest. few minutes later they disappeared into the house. Pr ton counted. He reached into his pocket, held his c phone in his hand waiting for it to ring. And when t took too damned long, he did something he hadn't do in years. He prayed.

And then heard the gunshots.

Hoover King's cab broke down.

Sweetland Presbyterian was within walking distan but the sun was so blasted hot he hated to get out of the a conditioned car. Well, it wasn't going to be air-condition for long since it wasn't running.

"Blasted, no-good piece of crap!" he yelled, kicking one of the tires after he'd slammed the door getting ou

Something rumbled and fell to the ground with a lo clack. He was about to walk away when he forgot son

ing and turned back. Reaching right through the win-
w, he lifted his bottle off the passenger seat and put it
his mouth immediately.

"Freakin' hotter than hell out here," he murmured af-
r swallowing. "Somebody's probably in the church."

It was late, and the church was the very last place Hoover
anted to be, but he didn't have a lot of other choices at the
oment. He walked, tripped a couple of times, wiped
vay, the sweat that dripped from his straggly hair onto
s forehead and stumbled some more.

Finally, he made it to the back parking lot of the church
ith a guttural burp and a silent prayer because he had to
e the bathroom something terrible. At one point he fell
his knees, his bottle almost tipping over. He kept it
pright even though he was having a hell of a time keep-
g himself in the same position. Struggling to get to his
et, he took a couple more steps then saw a man climb-
g into the Dumpster.

"Hey! Hey! What you doing in there?" he asked.

The man had just leaned into the Dumpster but turned
ack to look directly at Hoover.

"What's that on your head, boy? It's mighty hot out
ere to be wearing a hat," he said, blinking once, then
vice to make sure that's what he was seeing.

The man didn't answer but leaned back into the Dump-
er and pulled out a bag. He dropped it onto the ground
en reached inside again.

"You stealing trash?" Hoover asked, moving even
loser.

He kicked the bag that was on the ground when he was
tanding right in front of the Dumpster. "What's in here
nyway? You gonna recycle this trash or something?"

"Mind your own business, old man," the man said,
mping down from the Dumpster with one more bag in
is hand.

"This here's my town. What happens here's my bu
ness," Hoover told him and reached down to grab one
the bags.

The man pushed him back so he stumbled and fell
the ground. Hoover dropped his bottle, liquor spilli
onto the ground. "Goddammit all to hell!" Hoover yell
at the sight of the luscious brown liquid going to waste.

"I said to mind your freakin' business!" the man yelle
this time pointing a gun directly at Hoover.

"Put your hands in the air!" someone screamed from
distance.

"Drop the gun!" another person yelled.

Hoover put his hands up quickly, his heart beati
so hard and so loud he thought it might burst rig
through his chest. The man in front of him dropped h
gun, and Hoover looked around to see men running t
ward him. He tried to get up, tried to say something, b
at that moment the most pressing thought was that he
finally used the bathroom.

Chapter 26

eston couldn't let her go.

He'd stopped breathing the moment he heard the shots.
Then there was shouting and he must have began running
because the next thing he knew, he was inside the house.
More shouting ensued as he made his way through the
rooms, then something moved in his pocket. It was his cell
phone.

He didn't bother to answer it but followed the noise to
the back of the house. An agent was on his knees in front
of her untying ropes. Preston pushed him out of the way
and finished the job. When she was completely untied,
Heaven threw her arms around his neck. Preston caught
her and held on tight, so tight he was afraid he might actually hurt her.

She held on to him, breathing heavily, crying he thought,
which made his chest ache more. At his feet, Coco barked
and jumped, pressing her paws to his leg. But he didn't let
Heaven go.

"Pres, man, you can bring her out to the van," Ryan
said from behind him.

"In a minute," he said, his face still burrowed down the crook of her neck. "In a minute."

"You're crushing me," she said in a weak voice a fe moments later when they were alone.

Preston shook his head. "I'm remembering you," was h reply.

"I'm in love with you," was hers.

The initial reunion was put on hold as Preston broug Heaven and Coco in through the back basement entranc They came up the steps and headed straight to her roo without having to face the Montgomerys—or anyone el for that matter, thanks to Ryan and his team, who ha taken on the task of informing the family and the loc authorities what had happened.

Hot water from the shower had poured over their ski their hands on each other as if they were magnets inev ably bound to connect. There weren't many words, on sighs and embraces that seemed more emotional than ther of them had ever imagined.

And when he lay her on the bed, slipping the tow from her body, Heaven reached out to him. She wrapp her arms around his neck as he lowered himself ov her.

"I hoped that you would come for me," she admitte "I wasn't sure, but I prayed."

He kissed her temples. "I knew," he whispered. "I kne I couldn't sit back and do nothing."

"Why?" she asked, because she really needed to kno

For weeks she'd been here in this town, in this in owned by his family, and often in this bed with him. was time she knew how he felt about it all. Original she'd thought this thing between them would play out ar they'd go their separate ways. Then she realized her wa was right here in Sweetland. That decision had chang

ne expectations for Heaven. She wanted things and she
owed to have them.

One of the things she wanted was Preston Cantrell.

"Why did I come for you?" he asked.

"Yes."

He waited a beat, staring down at her as if the words
.e needed to say would suddenly appear on her face.

"I had to make sure you were safe," he told her.

"Why?"

A muscle twitched in his jaw.

"Because you mean a lot to me." He paused, but before
.he could ask another question he kissed her. Just a light
orushing of lips, a quick touch of his tongue to her bot-
.om lip, and then he was pulling back to look at her once
more.

"Because before I met you I never thought I could feel
his way about a woman."

Heaven waited a beat. Actually she waited through a
couple of really loud and intense heartbeats before prompt-
ng him once more.

She was going to ask him how he felt when she caught
he faint twinkle in his eyes.

"You're doing this on purpose, aren't you?"

He feigned innocence, of course. "Doing what?"

Okay, she figured, if he wanted to play games. She
reached between them, cupping his thick length in the
oalm of her hand. "You're trying to tease me. Trying to
make me ask you if you love me."

He swallowed hard—she could see his Adam's apple
move with the action. His eyes glazed as she stroked him
from the base of his arousal to the tip.

"But I'm not going to ask," she said, her voice a little
deeper as she moved beneath him, spreading her legs wider.

"You're not?" he managed even though she knew it
was difficult.

She massaged him slowly, loving the feel of his heate
flesh in her hands. Then she moved a little faster, enjoy
ing the hitch in his breath with her motions.

"No. I'm going to make you tell me," she said, lickin
her lips.

His eyes lowered, that muscle in his jaw twitchin
again as he watched her tongue tracing her lips. She did
again and he groaned.

"I'm going to make you tell me how it feels when I d
this." She rubbed her thumb over his tip, feeling th
moistness from his arousal. At the same time she licke
her lips once more.

He hissed. "You know that feels good."

"I know," she replied with mild triumph.

She lifted her hips, guiding him to her center, and whe
she touched the tip of him along the crevice of her mois
ness, he cursed. She smiled.

"How do you feel about that?" she taunted him.

His initial answer was a thrust of his hips so that h
tip slid inside her center seamlessly. It was her turn t
gasp. She undulated her hips to keep him only partiall
impaled, then flattened her hands on his chest, her thumb
whispering over his nipples.

"I feel like sinking deeper, taking us both to a place w
desperately need to be."

"And?" she said, twisting her hips so that another inc
of his length was inside her. "What else, Preston? Tell m
how this makes you feel."

Then she lifted her face to his, touched her lips to hi
her tongue to his, and kissed him with all the love an
desire she had.

Preston moaned, wrapping his arms around her so th.
she was now pressed against his naked body. She lifte
her legs and locked her ankles around his waist while h
slid all the way inside her. He pulled out, then sank bac

. Repeated that motion until Heaven had forgotten what
he was asking him and why. He kissed her hungrily, then
softly, with a longing she'd never felt from him before.
He pulled his lips away from hers, their breathing erratic,
his hips still moving, hers still meeting each of his greedy
thrusts.

"I love you, Heaven Montgomery," he whispered. "I
love being inside you. I love talking to you. I love looking
you. I just love you."

Her heart soared because those were the exact words
she'd wanted to hear. Well, she hadn't anticipated all of
them, but the *I love you* part was the best. The way the
words sounded in his silky-smooth voice, the way he
looked down at her as he said them, all the while driving
her mad with his tender thrusts. She wanted to scream
and shout with joy. Instead she undulated her hips, pushing them into a faster pace, loving the feel of him, just
simply loving him.

reston had fallen. He felt it in his chest, the sense of being filled completely, like there was someone else sharing
that space with him. There was no fear, the way his family would have thought. He embraced this newness, this
next level they seemed to travel to. He embraced it totally,
specially when she shifted so that he rolled over on his
ack.

She straddled him—a position that seemed to be her
favorite. He reached up and palmed her breasts as
he settled herself over him and began steady motions
that almost made his eyes cross. Her eyes were closed as
he moved.

"Heavenly," he whispered over and over again, until
they were both panting and riding that lustful high to-
ether.

Their release came simultaneously, her body slumping

over his. They remained quiet for endless moments, tr
ing to catch their breath.

Then Coco barked.

And barked some more as she scratched against th
door sending the message that she was ready to go out.

By eight o'clock Sunday evening, just about everyone i
Sweetland knew about Heaven's kidnapping, the shoo
out at the old haunted house, and Hoover's close brus
with death from the criminal element—the last was a d
rect quote from Marabelle Stanley and Louisa Kirk, oth
erwise known as Sweetland's Action News Hotlin
According to the pair there was a seedy criminal eleme
lurking around Sweetland, and they were already callin
for a town council meeting to see what they could d
about it. So far, Mayor Fitzgerald hadn't taken any of th
gossip to heart.

But Preston was beginning to wonder about the sudde
influx of crime in Sweetland himself. The fact that th
Johnny Tuscaverdi's name had come up in two separat
incidents could not be just a coincidence. Ryan had agree
and told Preston he would keep in touch with his invest
gation. He'd needed to get on the road immediately, thougl
with the two suspects they'd captured.

He'd come down from Heaven's room to find the in
full of people and Michelle ready to serve them all.

"What's going on?" he asked when he stopped her ju
before she could get into the kitchen.

"Everybody wants to make sure Heaven's all right.
told them she was taking a nap, but they wanted to wai
Savannah thinks it's good for business to have them at th
inn looking around at our new additions and the restaurar
menu. She's even out there talking about new package
that we plan to offer."

"What? We haven't even solidified any of those pack

ges yet. I still have meetings to schedule and contracts to raw up," Preston protested.

Michelle held up a hand. "Don't worry, she's not taking reservations, just putting out feelers. And I'll tell you, rom the whispers I heard, people think it's a great idea. I now Drew is already on board, she's just waiting for you o make everything legal."

He ran a hand over his face. "Does anybody realize hat Heaven's just gone through a traumatic ordeal here? he house is full of people and Savannah's the new sales-erson."

"Have you forgotten where we are? You know people n this town are as nosy as they come. And this is exciting ews for Sweetland. They need to see Heaven to believe ll they've been told so far. And believe me, Marabelle nd Louisa are out on the front porch telling one whop-ing story after another."

It was Preston's turn to shake his head. "I'd better go p and warn Heaven. She was worried about coming down o face her parents, but she has no idea about these other uests."

"I'll send Raine up to tell her. I need you to get some nore folding chairs from out of the basement."

Michelle seemed calm and resigned to the fact that hey were entertaining half the town and their gossip bout Heaven.

"What are you feeding them? I know you weren't pre-ared for a crowd like this," he asked her before heading oward the basement door.

"Now, you know me better than that. Gramma taught ne to always be prepared for company. Quinn's out there n the grill with some hot dogs and hamburgers I had own in the deep freeze. I'd already made a batch of potato alad for tomorrow's menu, so I'll just have to come in ven earlier in the morning to replace it. Mrs. Brockington brought pecan pies, and Walt's already set up a table out back where he's shucking the oysters he caught this morning."

He nodded, not wanting to accept any of this, but knowing it was futile. This was how it was in Sweetland. Whenever something happened, they all showed up. Death, birth, marriage, divorce—it was all reason to get together and eat. With a shake of his head, he moved down the basement. Because what else was he going to do but help out?

By the time he'd come back upstairs and put the chairs in whatever open spaces he could find around the house, Heaven was on her way down the steps. The first person to spot her was Mayor Fitzgerald, who immediately moved to get closer to her. Preston moved, too, figuring Heaven would need all the help she could get dealing with them.

She wore a flowing white skirt and a yellow tank top. Her hair was loose, hanging to her shoulders. She looked fresh and pretty and not at all like a woman who had been kidnapped.

"Ms. Montgomery, I'm Mayor Liza Fitzgerald. I wanted to personally meet you and to apologize for all the trouble since you've been in town. I assure you, things aren't always this tumultuous here in Sweetland."

Liza Fitzgerald was a pretty woman, pale blue eyes and honey-blond hair that she'd pulled back with some type of headband. She'd married into the Fitzgerald family almost five years ago and was just recently elected mayor. Quinn had known her previously so she was a pretty good friend to the Cantrells.

Heaven smiled. One of the prettiest smiles Preston had ever seen, he thought when he came to stand next to her.

"Nonsense, Mayor Fitzgerald. It seems I brought this trouble here to your town. So actually, I should be the one pologizing," Heaven told her as she shook the mayor's and.

"Well, we're just happy you're safe and that the Cantrell oys are so quick and so connected in the law enforcement community that they could get help here so fast. I eally can't believe the FBI had to be called in," Liza ontinued.

"I'm very lucky to know such great men," Heaven said, ooking over the Preston.

"Do your parents get a moment?"

Both Heaven and Liza turned to the shrill voice. Preson immediately stepped closer to Heaven. But she moved way, going to her father to wrap her arms around him. Iortimer hugged his daughter, relief apparent on his face. Opaline watched from the side.

She wanted to talk to Heaven, no doubt about her going back to Boston again. Preston now knew why it was o important to Opaline to have her daughter back in soston and once again working for Larengetics. Heaven vas now her meal ticket.

"Why don't we go into the kitchen so you can have some rivacy," Preston offered. "You'll excuse us, Liza. I'm ure the Montgomerys would like a moment alone with Ieaven."

"Of course, of course," Liza said apologetically. "I ompletely understand and I didn't mean to monopolize our time. I'm sure all of the townsfolk would like to neet you and make sure you're okay. Especially since I ear you're going to make Sweetland your home."

"Yes, I am," was Heaven's reply. "I need to find a place o live, but I don't think that'll be too difficult. And I'd ove to meet everyone."

Then she looked over to her mother. "But there's someing I need to take care of first."

Heaven reached for Preston's hand as she turned t
head toward the kitchen. He took it and could feel the bur
of Opaline's eyes on them as they walked ahead of ther
out of the room.

The moment they were in the kitchen Opaline pounced.

"I fail to see why you are continuing with this silly no
tion of living in this place. You were meant for bigger an
better things, Heaven."

This was the voice, the one Heaven heard even in he
dreams, directing her, coercing her, driving her absolutel
crazy.

"Now, wait a minute, Opal. I've been giving this som
thought," her father interrupted. "If this is where she'
happy, this is probably where she should be."

He didn't do that often—speak up on Heaven'
behalf—but Heaven found it comforting nonetheles
She'd been so happy to see him a few moments ago, no
realizing how the thought of actually never seeing some
one again could affect her. In the hours that she'd bee
held she'd thought a lot about Preston and the possibility o
never seeing him again. A little less thought had gone int
her parents, and when she did think of them it had bee
Mortimer who had garnered most of Heaven's concern.

The look her mother cast him after his remarks woul
have made anyone else cringe. But by now, both Mor
timer and Heaven were used to Opalne's expressions
Nothing either of them did seemed to please her, so a
some point they should both cease trying.

"Why do you want me in Boston so badly, Mother?
Heaven asked finally.

If she was surprised at the question, Opaline didn'
show it, but folded her arms carefully in front of her a
she replied, "It is where you belong."

"Or is it because if I leave Larengetics you'll have t

nd another way to finance your lifestyle?" Heaven asked
1 a cool tone of her own. Seems she'd learned something
rom her mother after all.

"My lifestyle is your legacy," was Opaline's irritated
esponse.

Heaven shook her head. "Not exactly. Two years ago I
onsidered buying a house. I scheduled an appointment
vith our accountant to figure out my financial options.
ven though I didn't intend to use any of the trust fund
noney, I knew I would have to disclose all of my finan-
ial information to any lending institution. He told me
aat my trust fund was the bulk of the fortune your father
ad left. When I asked how you were surviving since
aere was no way you could access the trust fund without
ay permission, he informed me of your monthly stipend
rom Larengetics. A stipend that was conditional upon my
ontinued work and progress there."

"That fool! As soon as I get home he's fired. That is no
usiness of yours," she stuttered.

Yes, her mother stuttered, which gave Heaven a sec-
nd's pause.

"If I no longer work for Larengetics, the stipend stops,"
he said clearly.

The heated flush on her mother's face only confirmed
vhat she knew to be true.

"I want you at Larengetics because you're too smart to
vaste your life in this backward town. What are you go-
ag to do here, Heaven? Learn to knit or start a farm or
ome other such foolishness. You want to pretend my mo-
ves are self-serving, but I'm thinking about your future,
bout your well-being," Opaline argued.

"No, Mother," Heaven told her, shaking her head. "I
on't think you've ever truly given my well-being any
nought. If you had you would have told me the truth about
ne explosion long before now."

"The explosion? What are you talking about?"

"I'm talking about the meeting you had with Riorda after the explosion. The one where he told you he though I'd double-crossed him and planned the explosion so could sell my serum to the highest bidder."

Opaline was shaking her head.

"There's no use denying it. I talked to Riordan's secre tary before I came downstairs. I wanted to know wh they continued to pay me when I was no longer workin there. She told me it was because they didn't have proo of my duplicity, but your stipend had been put on hold a a sort of punishment for not keeping me in line."

Now Opaline's face paled.

"So really, Mother, I should not have another kin word to say to you. After all, you've done nothing but us me my entire life. You controlled my every move, an tried to control my thoughts as well. As long as I contin ued to do what you wanted, you would stay rich and im portant."

Heaven took a deep breath. She looked toward the bac door, out the paned windows to where the dogs were i their pen, yipping and playing. Then she looked in the op posite direction to where Preston was standing beside he watching her with curiosity, ready to support whateve she said or did, she supposed. And nothing, not Opaline Larengetics, or even her trust fund, meant a damned thing

"I resigned from Larengetics today. It's official. I don' know where that leaves you, and I don't really care. In th coming weeks I will be traveling back and forth from Boston in an attempt to get all my things moved here. will always be your daughter, but I will no longer be un der your control," she said with more strength than eve she thought she'd had.

Preston's hand was on her shoulder instantly, pulling he closer to him.

"Well said," Mortimer told her.

"Mortimer?" Opaline began until he held up a hand to
op her.

"She knows, Opal, so you can give up the pretense.
rankly, I'm glad she knows. I told you not to accept that
eal with Riordan anyway. But you didn't want to live off
y money. It's never been enough for you. Well, I'm
appy for Heaven, happy she's found something for her-
lf. And I'm certainly not going to let you stand in her
ay anymore."

"I will not stand here and be treated this way," Opaline
id, turning to leave.

Mortimer shocked Heaven by reaching out to grab his
ife by the arm. "You will say good-bye to our daughter
operly. And you'd better get used to this backward town
ecause we're going to come visit her the first chance we
t."

Heaven smiled at that proclamation. "I'll need to find a
ouse first, Dad. Then you can come visit."

The good-byes were stiff and cool on the part of Heaven
nd Opaline—she hadn't expected anything different. As
r her father, Heaven hugged him tightly once more, feel-
g the blossom of new beginnings prickle.

She was safe, Coco was safe. Preston loved her and
e'd stood up to her mother. All was well in her world.

Chapter 27

One Week Later

"It's perfect! Absolutely perfect!" Heaven squealed as sh
came bursting into the kitchen.

It was a cheery place, the Cantrell kitchen, with i
yellow-painted walls and white eyelet curtains. The co
stant scent of something delicious being prepared made
homey and welcoming, a feeling that grasped Heaven in
mediately upon entering each and every time.

"I know I am," Savannah said with a flourish and a mo
curtsy.

She wore a long peach-colored sundress today wi
wedge heels and a large floppy-brimmed hat.

"I'm going into town today to have lunch with Del
and then to take that god-awful puppy of mine to the ve
I think he swallowed something, again," she said with a
exasperated sigh.

"A bit overdressed for a lunch date and a vet appoin
ment, aren't you?" Michelle asked.

"Nonsense, overdressed has never been an issue for me
Savannah said.

"Um, I wasn't talking about you or your dress, eve
though I think it's very pretty," was Heaven's quiet repl

Michelle laughed. Savannah pouted. Heaven nodded happily and went to take a seat at the table.

"I found a house. An absolutely perfect house for me and Coco," she started.

"Really? Where?"

"It's off Elm Road, a little way back, close to the water. I mean, I can literally walk about twenty feet from my back door and I'm at the water's edge. It's so perfect!" she said with elation.

"Elm Road," Michelle said. "I'm trying to picture it."

"Oh, don't bother. I have pictures." And Heaven happily pulled them out of the folder she'd slapped down onto the table.

"It's blue," Savannah squealed. "You want to live in a blue house?"

Heaven didn't even bother to sigh, she was too used to Savannah's mood swings and somewhat irritating candor.

"If you haven't noticed, most of the houses in Sweetland have been painted some pastel tone, as if the town wanted to resemble Oz rather than a Chesapeake Bay resort town. Anyway, I like this house. It's the perfect size, three bedrooms, one and a half baths. And look at those lovely trellises."

"Three bedrooms. You plan on having roommates?" Savannah asked with a lift of an eyebrow.

"Well, I don't know," was Heaven's reply.

Of course she'd thought of Preston the moment she'd seen the house. She'd thought of his truck parked in front, Coco's pillow sitting in the living room, another one upstairs where she would undoubtedly sleep. She'd also thought of the back room on the first floor where she and Preston could share office space. But she wouldn't mention that right now, not to his sisters.

"Come on, you're hoping Preston will decide to stay in

Sweetland and play house with you," Savannah said wi
a smile.

"That's none of your business, Savannah," Michel
reprimanded.

"Right, like you aren't hoping the same thing," Sava
nah quipped, rolling her eyes at Michelle. "Look, Heave
I like you. And I love my brother. So if this thing work
for the two of you, I'll be first in line to congratulate yo
But if it doesn't, if Preston's not game for the happil
ever-after, don't say I didn't try to warn you."

With those parting words Savannah left and Heave
sat back in her chair, feeling more than a little deflated.

"She's a barrel of sunshine," she replied in what sl
hoped was a casual tone.

But Michelle was smarter than that. She came over
the table and sat across from Heaven. Picking up the pi
tures, she looked at the house.

"I've seen this house before. It's pretty. Nice yard. Yo
should check with Drew to see what she can design f
you. That girl's a genius with flowers. And you're righ
it's by the water, Coco will love it there," Michelle to
her as she flipped through one picture after another.

"Do you think he'll stay?" she asked quietly.

Michelle's hands stilled on the table. "I would like hi
to stay. And if anybody can convince him to, it's you."

They walked along the water's edge after dinner, Coc
running in front of them. Preston held her hand as the
walked in silence. Heaven's heart beat rapidly as sl
planned what to say next.

All day long she'd been thinking of how to broach th
subject with Preston. They'd never had the talk abo
their future beyond the fact that they were in love. For da
that had been enough, but Heaven knew eventually th
moment would come. The moment where she would ha

assert herself, her wants, her needs, once more. With a
ep breath she stopped walking, thinking she might just
getting better at this confrontation thing.

"I found a house today. Ethel's putting in an offer, but it
ouldn't be a problem since it's been empty for almost a
ar and the owners have already moved to another state."

Preston let her hand go. He stooped to pick up a yellow
ll Coco had just dropped at his feet. When he stood up
ain and tossed the ball, he looked at her but still did not
eak.

"It has three bedrooms and is right up against the water,
st like here. I love walking by the water after dinner. And
s a nice nightcap for Coco, too."

He nodded. "Yeah, Coco loves the water. Crazy dog."

"So I was thinking that there's a room in the back on
e first floor. We could share the space for our offices,
h separate phone lines and things like that. It isn't huge,
t I think it'll work, especially since I only need space for
lesk. There are lovely built-in bookshelves in the dining
om where I can store my research texts so you could
e the majority of the space."

"You're going to work from Sweetland?" he asked with
omber look on his face.

There was a light breeze, an almost cool one tonight.
r. Sylvester had warned at dinner that a thunderstorm
as coming. Her hair blew with the breeze, and she
cked it back behind her ears.

"I'm going to do some freelance writing. I've already
oken to an agent who can coordinate speaking engage-
nts for me. So yes, I'll continue with research and
iting about my findings, and when there's a speaking
gagement, I'll travel and come back."

He nodded as if he agreed with that idea.

"You have everything all planned. Your life, I mean,"
said.

Tonight he wore gray slacks and a white dress shi͏
He'd removed his tie and rolled up his sleeves when ͏
came into the dining room for dinner. He'd talked abc͏
his meetings with Price Griffin, the owner of the spa, a͏
Drew. He'd also mentioned something about a wom͏
named Pia who wanted to host an ice cream social for t͏
regional Girl Scouts meeting next month. Michel͏
Nikki, Raine, and Quinn had been very excited by ͏
progress. And for him, Preston had even looked please͏
Heaven had taken that as a sign he was really getting in͏
the business of marketing the inn, hence contemplati͏
staying in Sweetland.

"For too long I've let others plan my life for me. I͏
time I took charge of that." She shrugged. "So the hou͏
is down on Elm. It's blue, and Savannah almost had a cc͏
about that fact. I mean she really flipped like she'd nev͏
lived in a colored house before. Or like that was a fa͏
that should even matter."

"You sound really happy about this."

She *was* happy about it. Until she looked up into h͏
eyes. Heaven knew what was coming before he took t͏
deep breath and said her name. Thoroughly disgust͏
with herself for believing, for wanting so desperately ͏
believe that everything would fall smoothly into pla͏
with him, with her life, she held up a hand.

"Let me save you the trouble. You're not staying ͏
Sweetland. You have a job in Baltimore that you love, a͏
practicing law here in Sweetland, or even helping yo͏
family keep this inn alive and thriving by continuing t͏
marketing ventures you've started, isn't an option."

"Heaven," he started.

"I know, you love me but this won't work becau͏
we'll be a distance apart. You never meant for this to g͏
so serious and you wish you had been able to stop befo͏

went this far. You're very sorry but happily-ever-after is not in your life's plan. Did I cover everything?"

Her heart was racing but Heaven wouldn't show it. Her eyes stung from the tears she was trying desperately to hold back. Coco came back with the yellow ball, dropping on the ground and sitting back on her bottom, looking at the both of them expectantly.

"I usually like to speak for myself," he said finally.

She shrugged. "Why waste time? I knew what was coming so I saved you the trouble."

"I don't consider talking to you trouble. Heaven, you've got me all wrong. You may think you know all there is to know about me, about how I think, but you don't."

"Really? Then tell me what part of what I said was incorrect?"

He was quiet.

"That's what I thought." She sighed. "Look, Preston, it's fine. I'm a big girl, I can take it. We had fun, we fell in love, but that wasn't the plan. These things happen but we're both adults and have the capacity to move on."

She stopped talking to bend down and scoop Coco into her arms. She needed that comfort, needed to feel her warmth against her as she threatened to break down completely.

"Heaven, I need for you to understand," he started.

"Understand what, Preston? That you don't want to live in the small town you were born in because you want a bigger, better life. You need me to understand that while I feel at home here, you don't. It's okay, you have a right to your feelings. You were living with them long before I came along. I shouldn't have thought that I'd be able to change you or how you feel."

"Stop putting words in my mouth!" he yelled. "Dammit! This is not how I wanted to do this. I wanted to explain

things so that you would understand. I even decided th
maybe I could commute a couple of days out of the we
so we wouldn't be apart for so long. I've been thinking t
days about how we could make this work because I lo
you. That might be the only thing you had correct, I
love you, Heaven, very much."

"Just not enough," she said shakily.

"Why does it have to be all or nothing? We could t
the commuting thing and see how that works."

She shook her head. "No. Not this time," she told h
adamantly. "I need more than a couple of days or a tr
relationship. I need to know that I'm moving forward a
working toward something. I know you probably can't u
derstand that, but it's where I am. I . . . I love you, too, t
this is what I need."

The next steps Heaven took were so much harder th
getting on that plane and coming to Sweetland to ge
puppy. They were harder than picking up the phone a
calling Larengetics to quit the job she'd spent years wo
ing at and would truly miss. Every lift of her leg, eve
touch her feet made to the ground, was like movi
mountains, and with each movement a tear escaped, h
chest constricted, and her heart broke.

Late August

Preston stepped off the elevator on the second floor of t
Circuit Court for Baltimore City. He'd just come from t
judge's chambers where he'd had a meeting with the pr
ecutor in one of his cases. As it turned out, his cli
might be a material witness in a federal drug case, whi
put them in a great position to negotiate the state charg

With his briefcase in one hand, his stomach growli
from hunger after being in court all day long, and a sli

adache threatening to morph into a huge one, he moved
wly on his way to the lockup where the inmates were
ld until they were called into the courtroom.

He spoke to a few colleagues, then nodded to the cor-
ctional officers that he knew from seeing on a daily
sis. It was at that point he realized how much time he
tually spent in this courthouse. As he stood at the
ckup entrance, the call was made for everyone to stop
d move to the side. Officers were bringing inmates
om some other part of the courthouse, and the hallway
eded to be cleared. Since he was an attorney they let
m through the lockup doors, but he still had to stand
ainst the wall while the officers with the inmates
ssed.

The familiar clanking of chains at the feet and hands
the inmates seemed to perfectly coordinate with the
robbing of his temples. One of the inmates tripped and
rsed. The correctional officer pushed him forward, which
ly brought on more cursing. On another day Preston
ight make a comment warning about brutality. Today
remained silent.

"Can I help you?" one of the female officers dressed in
all-black uniform asked him.

"Yes. I need to see Perry Bradbury."

"Wait over there," she directed with a sour look on her
ce.

As Preston crossed the room to set his briefcase on top
the scarred wooden table, he took a seat thinking of
w tired and irritated the majority of the correctional
ficers looked. It was quite possible they weren't enjoy-
g their jobs as much as they used to, either. For the past
w weeks, that thought had been nagging at Preston.
ith as much success as he'd achieved one would think
had it all. Today, however, he would beg to differ with
yone making that claim.

A cell door opened and closed in the not-too-far di
tance, jerking Preston out of his personal thoughts. Whe
he looked up an officer was leading Perry Bradbury to
table. This was a young man Preston had seen on seve
occasions. He'd been his client for going on four yea
now. His first charge when he was seventeen years old h
been assault with a deadly weapon. He'd been tried as
adult and received a not-guilty verdict largely based
Preston's stellar defense strategy. Over the next yea
Perry had incurred an array of new charges: drug poss
sion, handgun violations, assault, and now his new
charge, attempted murder.

One of the things the judge had said to Perry at the e
of that first trial was, "Don't let this acquittal be the b
ginning of your professional criminal career."

It was apparent that Perry hadn't listened.

"Hey, Preston, you fix things to get me outta here ye
Perry asked the moment he was seated in the chair acro
from Preston.

"We have a few things to iron out first," Preston sa
This was his job, time to do the work; he'd deal with t
doubts and recriminations later.

He pulled his file out of his briefcase and opened it
the page where he'd taken notes of the meeting with t
judge and the prosecutor.

"The state's attorney thinks you have information
another case. A federal one. She said you witnessed a
drug buy in New Jersey a couple of months ago."

"I don't know what she's talking about. Just get me
of here, man. I gotta get to work to take care of my kid
Perry told him.

Preston wasn't fazed by Perry's work statement. He
ways used his children—six, if Preston wasn't mistaken
as an excuse when he was incarcerated. When he w

me, Preston doubted Perry had time to see said chil-
en since he was usually in the street breaking the law.

"If you agree to testify in the federal case, they'll re-
ce the attempted-murder charge to assault and offer
u a suspended sentence," Preston told him. A sentence
at would make him a free man once more.

"I don't know about no drug deal in Jersey," Perry said
amantly.

Beneath his sheet of notes there was a charging docu-
ent that the state's attorney had given him. It was for the
w Jersey case. Preston hadn't read it in the judge's cham-
rs because he wasn't concerned with that charge—it
sn't against his client. Still, while Perry was going
rough his mini tirade, Preston skimmed the report.

The name Johnny Tuscaverdi all but leapt off the page.

"How do you know Johnny Tuscaverdi?" he asked,
oking up at Perry.

"I don't know nobody," Perry said.

"It says here that you rode in an SUV, two men in the
ont and three men in the back. One of those men in the
ck was identified as Johnny Tuscaverdi. He's accused
orchestrating the drug deal. You watched from the
ckseat as the money was exchanged for drugs."

Perry was shaking his head slowly. "I told you I don't
ow nobody. You gotta go back and get me another
al."

Preston sat back in his chair. He closed the file and
red at this twenty-one-year-old. On the outside he
ked like a clean-cut young man, high school educa-
n, medium build, from a two-parent home with sib-
gs. Some would say he'd just gotten mixed up with the
ong friends in his later high school years. Others would
 he was predestined to a life of crime given his inner-
y address. Preston said Perry had made a choice. And

for years Preston had ignored Perry's choice. He'd tak
his money and defended him, and watched him go back c
onto the streets.

Today, he wasn't so sure he could do that again.

"From what I hear Tuscaverdi is into a lot of bad stu
The feds are really after this guy, which means they'
gunning for anybody associated with him as well. You'
saying you weren't in that SUV and you don't know hi
Eyewitnesses say differently."

"I'm not testifying," Perry said adamantly.

Preston closed his file. "Then there's no deal on t
table and your attempted-murder trial will proceed
Monday."

"You can get me out, Preston. You've done it befor
That's why I pay you all that money," Perry insisted.

Stuffing the file back into his bag, Preston stood fro
the table. "And you will receive representation for yo
retainer. Be ready for trial next week, Mr. Bradbury."

He'd already walked away from the table but sti
heard Perry calling after him. Preston didn't care, l
wasn't talking to this young man anymore, and he wasi
representing him next week.

"So what now?" Joe Baskerville asked when Preston ha
returned to the office.

Joe sat across from Preston in his modern-fit suit. F
had one ankle propped on his knee, the sleeves of h
shirt rolled up. Preston sat behind his big cherrywoo
desk in a high-backed leather chair, his arms on the arn
rest. He leaned back in the chair and turned so that h
was sideways next to the desk.

"I don't want to practice criminal law anymore," l
said thoughtfully.

The room grew quiet.

"You've been leaning in that direction awhile now," e said. "Remember, we talked about it earlier this year. hat's when I started mentioning the firm branching out."

"I remember," Preston said. "It was my dream," he con- nued. "I'd always wanted to do some good in the world d law seemed the right way to go. Maybe I should have ayed on the prosecution side."

Joe waved a hand. "They're getting burned out, too. s not a personal issue as much as I think it's a commu- ty one. We see the same things over and over again, the ily change is that they seem to be getting younger and unger. The prosecutors' dockets are as full as our cal- ndars. Everybody in the criminal system is overworked, erybody except maybe the criminals."

"That's a pretty cynical thing to say seeing as you're a fense attorney," Preston countered.

"Right," Joe said with a chuckle. "That's why I've been orking so hard to hire associates. Look, Pres, our firm is nown for its criminal defense work. We can still capital- e off that reputation and give ourselves a break."

"I've been doing some contract work for the inn," he id. "Trying to get some partnerships going that might ring in more customers."

Joe nodded. "You've been heading back to that town nce the moment they called about your grandmother's assing. Frankly, I don't know why you're still sitting ere."

"My life is here," Preston countered.

"No. It used to be. But over the last few weeks I've en that change. You want to be there more than you ant to be here. And when that happens there's nothing ft to fight. If you stay here and continue to work, you're oing to grow angrier and angrier at the job you're doing. ventually that'll affect your representation of the clients.

And no matter how guilty they might be, or how much 〉 get an attack of morals, the job of a defense attorney is defend."

"I would never not do my job," Preston countered.

"But you wouldn't like it and it would eventually beg to show. Look, I can't tell you what to do. The decision yours. But as your partner, I think it'll be in both our in terests if you opened another branch of the firm an started some civil work where you could focus on yo contract writing and still practice some litigation."

"Another branch of the firm?" Preston asked. "Let n guess, in Sweetland."

Joe smiled. "Now, that's a fabulous idea!"

"Summer's almost over," Drew said, kneeling down i Heaven's front yard. "But all around the perimeter he are wildflowers that will drop seeds and regrow prett much on their own. Dawber does the landscaping work s he can come over weekly or monthly to do your weedin and keep everything nice and neat. That is, if you're n the type to come out and do it yourself. I planted mult colored tulip bulbs in the front beds so they'll come u nice and pretty in the spring. That's about all we can d for now."

Heaven stood in the yard, looking around at the beau tiful array of colors still offered by the spray of wildflov ers. Her move-in date had been approximately one wee ago. Two truckloads of stuff had arrived from Boston tw days after that. She'd had no idea she'd accumulated s much in a life that had yielded her so little. At any rat she and Coco were just beginning to settle into their littl blue house, and she was loving every minute of it.

"It's so pretty, so calming," she told Drew.

In the two months Heaven had been in Sweetland she' gotten to know lots of the townsfolk. A few she'd grow

oser to—the Cantrells, of course, Michelle, Raine, and
vannah becoming the sisters she'd never had. Delia and
rdy had also shown themselves to be friends. And defi-
tely Drew, who with her sandy brown hair that had a
ndency to frizz in the heat, but otherwise had the nicest
een, always showed up when Heaven really needed
meone to talk to. And they talked about flowers instead
men, which for both of them seemed to be working out
st fine. Heaven had sensed a bad relationship in Drew's
.st, but she hadn't asked, hadn't wanted to pry.

"That's how I got hooked," Drew said, coming to a
.nd, brushing her hands on the thighs of her faded jeans.
'he colors suck you in, then the petals soothe some inner
.ge, and next thing you know you're head over heels in
.ve with everything from bulbs to blossoms to things
.at are called weeds but still have a whimsical appear-
.ce."

"You're absolutely right," Heaven said. Coco ran freely
the yard loving all the open space and the time Heaven
.lowed her to go free.

"So what's on tap for this evening?" Drew asked Heaven.

"Probably get some reading done. Unpack some more
these boxes."

"What about pizza?" Drew asked pushing flyaway
.sps of hair from her face. "I was feeling a little off this
.orning so I didn't get breakfast. Then I've been going
.ost of the day. I don't think I've eaten at all. I'm starv-
.g." She rubbed her stomach.

Heaven chuckled. "Pizza sounds great. I was probably
.ing to throw some lunch meat on a couple of slices of
.ead and call it a day. But I could certainly go for a nice
.t slice. Vito's has great pizza! I was so glad when Nikki
.ok me there. She loves the Hawaiian pizza and now I'm
.oked on it, too. Parker and Quinn are bigger fans of the
.eat lover's with anchovies and mushrooms."

Heaven kept right on talking, suggesting they cou
maybe stop for ice cream and then walk the dock to co
vince themselves that they were working off most of t
calories consumed. Drew was silent.

Heaven turned to be sure her friend was still there a
she wasn't walking throughout her yard talking to he
self. Developing a reputation as the crazy lady in the bl
house wasn't her goal. Drew was standing in the san
spot Heaven had left her. She was even still holding h
stomach as she had been when she'd first brought up t
subject of food. But she didn't look good at all. And whe
Heaven came to stand beside her she wobbled a bit un
Heaven wrapped her arms around her.

"You all right?" she asked.

Drew lifted a hand to her head, her eyes closing th
opening slowly. "I don't know. Just felt dizzy for a mome
Really dizzy," she told her.

"That's not good. Let's get you inside. I'll call Quir
to come over and have a look at you."

"No," Drew said as they headed for the door. "It mig
just be the heat, and I haven't eaten anything. I'll just
in and sit for a while. Do you have something to drink?

"I do," Heaven said. "But I'd feel better if we c
Quinn. He's just a few blocks away and he won't mind
all."

Drew tried to protest but Heaven insisted. Quinn a
rived in less than ten minutes as he had already left t
medical center and was on his way back to the inn. F
took one look at Drew and said she needed rest an
maybe to have some blood work drawn to see if she mig
be anemic. He also ordered her to eat three meals a da
The remainder of the doctor's orders meant their night
pizza and ice cream was out of the question.

So after everyone had left, Heaven called Coco into t
house, fixed herself a ham-and-cheese sandwich, and s

er cute little kitchen table with her book and notepad
ront of her. That's where she was when there came a
ck at the door.

ston had no idea what he was going to say.

He'd come back just last night, and since then so much
ice and a good measure of I-told-you-so looks had
n tossed his way.

"Good to see you come to your senses. I told you be-
e she was a good one," Mr. Sylvester had said when
d watched Preston walk up onto the porch carrying his
cases.

Preston had only smiled. The old man saw and knew
olutely everything, he deduced. There was never any
nt in arguing with him; it made more sense to just lis-
to what he had to say. Especially since Mr. Sylvester's
rds inevitably came back to mind, and when they did
y made all the sense in the world.

"I know she's good. That's why I came back to get her,"
d said as he approached the door.

"Janet always said you were a smart one," Mr. Sylves-
had added with a chuckle.

His brothers had given similar responses. Quinn
pped him on his shoulder and shook his hand while
ker looked playfully devastated, declaring this the end
the Double Trouble Cantrells. Savannah had been in a
od so he hadn't seen her that night or the next morning
ore he'd left the house. Raine had been quietly happy.
chelle wasn't there. Preston was told that his older sis-
had a meeting with a couple about catering their wed-
g. Before he did anything else, Preston needed to see
.

He drove down the street. It was only about a block, but
had plans to go someplace else after speaking to Mi-
elle so he'd opted not to walk. His sister lived in a nice

little two-bedroom town house surrounded by trees a
shrubs that she gave great care. Her van was parked
front so he was relieved that this conversation woul
have to wait any longer.

He knocked and waited. She opened the door and j
stared for a few moments. Then with a partial smile
moved to the side to let him in.

"Go ahead and say it," he told her the moment he step
into her living room.

It was decorated in girlie colors, beige and pink a
light green, that somehow managed to flow together wi
out making him nauseous. Everything was in its place,
cluding the two dog pillows that were neatly positioned
the corner just beneath the window. She'd been slowly
ing to get Ms. Cleo and Lily, the two Labs she'd inheri
used to being in her house. It was a little harder for Ms. C
to adjust since she'd been at The Silver Spoon the longe

"What would you like me to say, Preston?" she ask
propping one hand on her hip.

He took a deep breath. "I know I was wrong to be n
at you about Gramma. I guess I just needed somebody
blame."

Michelle nodded. "I guess I was an easy target."

"I'm sorry," he said, looking into eyes that remind
him more and more of their grandmother.

She smiled, and Preston instantly felt better.

"I accept your apology."

"Now you can say it," he said with a slight grin of
own.

Michelle laughed. "You want me to reaffirm my sta
that you should stay in Sweetland? Or do you want m
tell you how foolish you were for walking away fr
Heaven the way you did? Take your pick."

"I've sort of come to both those conclusions on
own," he told her sheepishly.

"And they called you the smartest of the bunch." She
[c]ntinued to laugh.

Preston shook his head. "No, I thought that was Quinn."

"And you see what type of role model he turned out to
 That's probably why you thought it was okay to run
[bac]k to Baltimore, instead of staying here and fighting for
[wh]at you wanted."

"The fight was within me. I thought I needed to get
[aw]ay from here to win the battle. But leaving made me
[fee]l like mom. It made me feel like I was running away
[fro]m every day that mattered," he admitted. "Still, I think
[it w]as something I had to do. A lesson I had to learn on
[my] own."

She shrugged. "I guess you have a point there. Another
[poi]nt you may have missed, however, is that you've been
[go]ne for weeks. Heaven's moved on."

At her words he went perfectly still. Preston remem-
[be]red when Quinn had gone back to Seattle after break-
[ing] things off with Nikki. Deputy Jonah had asked Nikki
[ou]t and she'd accepted, a couple of times. Quinn had not
[be]en happy about that when he'd returned.

"If you tell me she's seeing someone in town, there's
[go]ing to be a lot of trouble. You might want to get the
[sh]eriff on the phone right now."

"More trouble than the FBI shooting at bad guys behind
[Sw]eetland Presbyterian?" She laughed again. "I sure hope
[no]t."

"Michelle, tell me what's going on."

She waved a hand and walked into the kitchen, the
[roo]m Preston would swear was her favorite in any house.
[He] followed her.

"She's all moved into her little house with Coco and
[th]ey're doing great. She's researching and writing and she
[rea]ds for an hour each day to the preschoolers who visit the
[lib]rary. That's in between working at The Silver Spoon

as if her name were on the deed as well. She's really fitt
in here."

He sighed. "I never doubted she would."

"So you only doubted that you'd fit here with her?"

"I doubted that happily-ever-after was what I want
Our family doesn't exactly have a good track record w
relationships."

"Then I think it's about time this generation shak
things up a bit. You can have happily-ever-after if tha
really what you want, Preston. We've all been through a l
We deserve it."

He nodded. "You're right. So I'm heading over to s
Heaven. Any words of advice for me."

Michelle smiled. "Beg," she told him. Then she left t
room and came back with a small black bag in her han
which she extended to him. "And give her this. It w
Gramma's. She would have loved Heaven the moment s
met her."

Preston loved Heaven now. He had for each moment sin
he'd met her two months ago.

That's why he was standing in front of her very bl
house, knocking on the door and trying unsuccessfully r
to focus on the color too much.

When she opened the door he had stepped back to g
a full view of the house. She looked breathtaking and s
only wore cutoff jean shorts and a button-down shirt th
she'd tied above her belly button. Her hair was braid
and hanging over one shoulder, and her eyes glistened wi
flecks of gold as she looked up at him in surprise.

"I don't know if I can live in a blue house," Prest
said.

He stood in front of the little riverside cottage, han
in his pockets, looking the place up and down. He look

the white trellis on both sides of the porch—rungs
ere missing and would need to be repaired, and they
uld use a coat of paint. Two brand-new cedar-planked
nches sat beneath the windows on both sides of the
or. She'd just bought them from Duke Cramden. He'd
en crafting handmade furniture since Preston was a
tle boy. And from the looks of it, still doing a damned
od job.

The house really was blue, like the water in the Carib-
an islands. He looked around to the huge oak tree on
e left side, its base covered in a thick brush of hostas.
ere was no fence like the ones around most of the
uses in Sweetland, but a brick wall about three feet
gh instead. On the inside, up against the wall, were
wers—tall ones, shorter ones in bright yellow and or-
ge and soft pinks and blues. They hugged the wall like
ey were related, stopping only for the walkway with its
bblestoned path inviting visitors inside.

That had invited Preston inside because the owner of
e little blue house was standing in the doorway, arms
ded across her chest, eyes fixed on him in a serious
are.

"You don't live here," was her curt reply.

Okay, so he knew this wasn't going to be easy. In fact,
an, Quinn, and Parker had warned him she wasn't go-
g to run to him with open arms. Michelle had told him
beg. He was prepared to do that and then some.

"We could build an extension over here," he said, walk-
g through the front yard to the left side of the house.
ffices, for both of us, with a separate entrance over here
clients wouldn't have to trek through the house."

She came out to follow him. He'd hoped she would.

"I already have an office inside," she stated from bend.

"I hope not upstairs because we'll need those roo[m] for the kids. Besides, it's better to have our offices do[wn] here so when we're finished with work we can just go [to] the other side of the house. Yours can go in the back [so] you can see the water while you write."

"It's research writing, not creative. I can do that just [as] easily upstairs."

"But you love the water, and this way you can see in[to] the yard where Coco will be. I know you like to keep yo[ur] eye on her."

Speak of the devil, Coco barked from her spot on t[he] back porch the moment Preston rounded the corner.

"Hey, girl, you miss me?" he asked, stepping up o[n] the porch and instantly rubbing behind her ears.

The way she jumped into his lap, licking all over [his] chin was answer enough, and Preston chuckled. He f[ell] backward against the wall letting Coco have her way w[ith] him, inhaling deeply of the crisp late-summer air, t[he] scent of the river and a faint tinge of the flowers t[hat] seemed to be everywhere. Out of the corner of his eye [he] glimpsed Heaven.

She leaned against the side of the house, not at all faz[ed] by his reunion with Coco.

"Come here," he said to her when he was sitting u[p] right on the step.

She didn't move.

"Please, Heaven. Sit next to me for a minute," he i[m]plored.

She moved, albeit reluctantly, to sit on the step next [to] him, being very careful not to let their bodies touch.

"You know I love you."

"What I know, Preston Cantrell, is that you are o[ne] stubborn, hardheaded man. No matter what anybody sa[ys] to you, it has to be your way, all the time. I can't live w[ith]

man like that. I won't live under those stringent circum-
ances ever again."

He leaned over and touched his fingers to her lips,
osing them.

"I love you. I've never loved anyone in this world the
ay I love you."

She tried to say something but he kept his fingers in
lace and shook his head.

"I thought I wanted to live in the city defending the
lsely accused—or the accurately accused, either or—for
ie rest of my life. I thought I never wanted a family and
home in Sweetland because my father had thought he'd
ad all that. My mother was a selfish woman, but I figure
ie had to love my father an awful lot to stay in Sweetland
s long as she did when she'd been itching to get away. I
ever wanted that type of life.

"But my apartment in Baltimore seems so small now,
o quiet. Coco could never live there. And when I'm at
ie office I feel like the walls are closing in around me.
fter imagining that bastard felon with his grimy hands
n you, I can't imagine looking at another jail cell or pos-
ible criminal client again. I still love the law, but I think
iy criminal days are over.

"The bottom line is nothing I did before, nothing I had
efore that day you stumbled into The Silver Spoon, is
nough anymore. It's just not enough, Heaven. And I'm
ot happy."

Preston sighed, searching for the smoothness he'd once
ad a reputation for. He racked his brain for words that
vould make her melt in his arms, beg to be with him. But
one came.

"A very smart woman once told me that she planned to
ind her own happiness. Well, it took me a while to figure
his out—I can tell you anything about the law, but this

love thing has really got me stumped," he said with a ne
vous chuckle that died quickly as he looked once mo
into her soft hazel eyes.

"I'm not happy without you. I can practice civil la
from a home office and go into the city for court case
I can help rebuild the trellis and have Drake Sheridan g
started on the addition. I can take care of Coco when yo
have to go away to lecture and be waiting for you whe
you return. I don't want to say I can make you happ
Heaven. But what I will say, what I know without a dou
is that you're the only woman who can make me happ
You're the only woman I've ever wanted to spend my li
with, to have children with, to start a family with. To eve
live in a little blue house with."

Her eyes were brimming with tears, but Preston didr
know if they were the good or bad kind. He hurried
moved his fingers from her lips and apologized. Then I
looked down at Coco, at her rich brown fur and eyes, ar
nuzzled the dog as close to him as he could.

Preston didn't know what else to say, and she was b
ing too damned quiet. Coco's back paws moved with h
as she licked at his face and the bag Michelle had give
him pressed into his thigh. He readjusted Coco and reache
into his pocket. Taking Michelle's advice, he gave it
Heaven without even opening it.

Her hands were shaking as she opened it and pulle
out a sterling-silver ring with one huge pearl in its cente
She ran her fingers over it for a second as Preston remen
bered seeing this ring on his grandmother's finger whe
he was a young boy. In her later years she hadn't worn
but it was something he would never forget.

When Heaven looked up at him again, it was with tea
in her eyes. "I don't see why you have a problem with
little blue house. You lived in a big yellow one all yo
life," she said quietly.

He looked at her then, a smile spreading quickly across his face as tears streamed down hers.

"It will be just like heaven living here with you," he told her, then leaned forward to kiss her lips. "Just like heaven."

The Silver Spoon Recipes

Adorable Almond Croissants

Ingredients

4	teaspoons instant dried yeast
½	cup lukewarm water
3½	cups bread flour
½	cup milk
⅓	cup granulated sugar
3	tablespoons butter, melted and cooled
1½	teaspoons salt
1	cup butter, softened
½	cup Sweet Almond Filling (recipe follows)
1	egg
2	tablespoons milk
¼	cup sliced almonds

Preparation

1. Dissolve the yeast in the warm water for 5 minute Add the bread flour, milk, sugar, melted butter, an salt to the dissolved yeast and water. Mix the doug on medium speed for about 2 minutes. If the dough i sticky, add extra flour ½ tablespoon at a time until it is firm enough to fold.

2. Shape the dough into a ball and cover loosely wit plastic wrap. Rest at room temperature for 30 minute Roll dough into a 10-inch by 15-inch rectangle, an then cover it loosely. Let it rise for up to 40 minutes.

3. Brush the rectangle with the softened butter and the fold the dough into thirds. Roll the long, thin rectangl back into the original 10-inch by 15-inch shape. Fol it into thirds again, and then cover the dough wit plastic wrap. Rest in the refrigerator for 1 hour and 1 minutes. Repeat this process once.

4. Cut the dough diagonally with a sharp knife to make 20 triangles. Pull the tip of each triangle taut, spread small spoonful of Sweet Almond Filling across it, and then roll the croissant up from the base, curving the ends slightly to make a crescent shape. Arrange on a lightly greased baking sheet at least 1½ inches apart Cover them loosely with plastic wrap. Let rise for 4 minutes to 1 hour, or until they are nearly doubled i size.

5. Preheat the oven to 375°F. Whisk the egg and 2 table spoons milk together to make an egg wash. Brush thi across the surface of each pastry and sprinkle with sliced almonds. Bake for 14 to 16 minutes, until the croissants are puffed and golden brown and the almonds are toasted.

Makes 20 servings

Sweet Almond Filling

Ingredients

½	cup ground almond meal
½	cup granulated sugar
1	egg
3	tablespoons butter, softened
¾	teaspoon almond extract
1	tablespoon all-purpose flour

Preparation:

1. Using a food processor, combine all the ingredients until a smooth, creamy paste is formed.

Smith Island Cakes

Effective October 1, 2008, the Smith Island Cake became the state dessert of Maryland (chapters 164 & 165, Acts of 2008, Code State Government Article, sec. 13-320). Traditionally, the cake consists of eight to ten layers of yellow cake with chocolate frosting between each layer and slathered over the whole. However, many variations have evolved, both in the flavors for frosting and the cake itself.

Smith Island Cake, Smith Island, Somerset County, Maryland, 2008

Read on for an excerpt from Lacey Baker's next novel

Summer's Moon

Coming soon from St. Martin's Paperbacks

He'd waited months to get his hands on her again. Damn if those months hadn't seemed like years. And even if the touch was as simple as his hand on her waist, it was enough to send blood soaring through Parker's body, resting soundly in his groin where an erection was inevitable.

His attraction to Drewcilla Sidney had hit him hard one night, and he'd presumed it was the result of the trio of rum and Cokes Charlie had served him. But the next day, when he was completely sober and he'd been on his way to the bar, he'd seen her going into The Crab Pot. Of course he'd followed, he'd had no other choice. Watching her work that night, bringing drinks to tables, leaning over said tables to roll out paper for the customers having crabs, laughing so that her eyes were alight with joy, her hair hanging in lazy curls down her back, had proven one point. His desire for her was not alcohol-induced and it wasn't going away easily.

This evening her hair was pulled back from her face, giving Parker an unfettered view of pretty brown eyes and elegantly arched brows. She licked her lips, then nibbled on the bottom one for a split second before squaring

her shoulders and looking directly at him. If he wasn't
man, a decorated homicide detective at that, he might hav
said her actions made him just a bit dizzy with desire.

Instead of actually admitting to that, Parker cleare
his throat. "You look really pretty tonight" were the word
that tumbled from his mouth.

They sounded so juvenile, so spontaneous, and possi
bly contrived. He mentally kicked himself for not coming
up with something better. For weeks he'd been waiting
for the moment, to not only get his hands on her again
but to have the chance to speak to her. And now that the
moment seemed to have arrived, this was what he'd said

"Thank you," she said about a second before she took
a step back so that his hand fell from her waist.

"You act like you two have never met," Louisa said to
Drew, "which I know can't be true since I specifically re
member seeing you climb onto the back of that noisy
monstrosity he drives around here like he owns the town."

Parker was used to Louisa's abrupt candor, or at leas
he'd become reacquainted with it in the weeks he'd been
back. Louisa and Marabelle frequented The Silver Spoon
restaurant at least twice a week. He suspected it was
equally for the food as it was to fuel more of their gossip
In the times he'd seen them there he'd also overheard
some of their conversations, where no one was exempt.
His family was one of their hot topics, so Louisa's comment was no shock to him.

As for Drew, well, the completely mortified look on her
face said she was feeling differently.

"I'm always available to give a young lady a ride home
when needed, Mrs. Kirk. You wouldn't have wanted me
to leave Drew to walk home alone would you?" he asked,
tearing his eyes away from Drew only long enough to lock
gazes with Louisa. If not, the woman would most definitely believe she had the upper hand.

Louisa shook her head. "She has a car. A very bright
le thing looks like a buggy. She keeps it parked in her
:k yard all the time, but I see it whenever she zips up
in Street on her way down here to help her uncle out at
e Crab Pot."

And Parker needed to know all that information. It
s a good thing he already knew the details Louisa had
t divulged about Drew's personal life and an even bet-
thing he wasn't some deranged stalker. If he were, that
ormation could have put Drew in danger. Of course that
s his cop's mind thinking but that didn't make it any less
e.

"I think it's good that a couple have a practical car and
:n something completely whimsical and a little danger-
s," Marabelle said with a smile to Parker. "Besides that
:e of yours is kind of hot."

She whispered the word "hot" as if it might have actu-
y been a sin to say it and if heard she would burn in the
ry pits of hell.

"We're not a couple," Drew stated adamantly, her eyes
dening as she looked from Marabelle to Parker plead-
;ly.

Parker cleared his throat. "She's right, we're not a couple,
rs. Stanley. But I think my bike's kind of hot, too."

Marabelle smiled at that. Louisa frowned, and Drew,
:ll, she looked like she might actually faint. A hand went
her neck, fingers shaking, and another brushed past her
>mach, then fell to her side. But it was the clammy look
her skin that really concerned Parker and spurred him
to action.

"Ladies, it's been lovely visiting with you, but I really
:ed to get Drew alone for just a second." He thought
out how that comment would be perceived by these two
omen and decided to add, "Michelle's looking for her to
lk about purchasing more flowers for the inn."

"Oh yes, the bouquets in the church sanctuary ¦
beautiful, dear," Marabelle told Drew. "You two run alo¦
I can't wait to see what you come up with for the inn. T¦
Michelle we'll be there tomorrow night for dinner ¦
usual."

"I will," Parker said with a nod. He stepped toward Dr¦
then because she hadn't moved.

"You look sick, Drewcilla," Louisa spoke up from b¦
hind Parker. "Maybe you should call your brother ov¦
here, Parker. Instead of trying to drag the girl off son¦
where."

Drew shook her head then. "No. I'm fine, really I an¦
she said, attempting to pull away from Parker's gra¦
once more.

This time Parker leaned in to whisper in her ear. "E¦
ther go along with me and make an easy escape fro¦
these two, or stand here and try to fight whatever is bo¦
ering you and them at the same time. It's your choice."

She clapped her lips shut and swallowed deeply.

"Let's go, Parker. I don't want to keep Michelle wa¦
ing," Drew said finally.

With an arm resting around her waist once more¦
a position that felt oddly comfortable to Parker—th¦
walked down the pier away from the town gossips. T¦
wind blew, and he inhaled the sweet scent of her perfun¦
a scent he remembered well from their night togeth¦
The night he'd dreamt of for the past few months, wo¦
dering, hoping, and quite possibly needing a repeat.

Obviously that was not Drew's intention as she'd be¦
dedicated to keeping her distance from him since th¦
fateful night.

"I'm fine," she said in a soft voice.

So soft he almost didn't hear her over his own though¦

"Let's go over here and have a seat. You were looki¦
a little off so I just want to make sure you're okay," he to¦

as he steered them towards a duo of red painted
[ben]ches situated on the side of Amore between huge
[shr]ubs and a quaint little fountain.

The benches faced the water so they had a good view of
[the] waning sunlight as they sat. Drew immediately went
[to t]he far end of the first bench, resting her elbow on the
[arm] and holding her head down.

Each time, since the first time, that Parker had seen
[Dre]w, she'd been laughing or smiling or otherwise look-
[ing] as if living life was the most precious thing to her.
[She] had this kind of carefree spirit that he'd admired, at
[firs]t from afar. Whether it was her Uncle Walt or the
[gro]up of older men who sat at his counter for a good part
[of t]he evening shooting the breeze and joking with her, or
[Na]lia and Pia having drinks with her—as they had the
[nig]ht they'd spent together—she always looked to be en-
[joy]ing herself. And others looked as if they enjoyed her
[com]pany. Parker had wanted to be part of the number who
[we]re lucky enough to spend time with such an affable and
[attr]active female. Especially since he felt lately like his
[life] was on a downward spiral.

[H]owever, Parker did not like the look Drew had now.
[Sh]e was breathing deeply as if each breath was a struggle
[and] tiny beads of sweat had peppered her forehead, caus-
[ing] the wisps of hair there to stick. And when she looked
[up] at him, her eyes were wide, excitedly, but her shoul-
[der]s sagged like she was carrying a tremendous weight.
[He] was confused and he was worried and he wanted to
[kno]w what the hell was going on with her.

[S]till standing, Parker moved until he was in front of
[Dr]ew. Squatting, he lifted her hands into his again and
[spo]ke softly, "You can tell me what's wrong, Drew. If
[you]'re sick I'll get Quinn or I'll take you to the hospital in
[Bo]ston. If you just need to get out of here for a while, I
[can] do that too. Just talk to me," he pleaded.

"I'm fi—" she started to say before standing abrup
"I need the bathroom."

Her words were strained and Parker stood with l
"Sure. Let's get you inside." He walked with her, mov
quickly.

When they arrived at the small entryway to Amore
guided her up the steps and into the foyer of the rest
rant. Parker held her hand this time, walking right bes
her, waving to Salvatore Gionelli, the owner of the rest
rant, as they passed by the hostess quickly.

At the doorway to the Ladies' Room, Drew pulled
of his grasp.

"I said I'm fine, Parker," she told him again with m
than a little agitation in her tone.

"You're obviously not fine," he countered, trying
keep his voice down as a few other people had come i
the restaurant behind them.

Drew dragged her hands over her face and took
other deep breath. "I'm trying to go to the bathroom a
you're on my back like you intend to go with me," she s
through gritted teeth.

"I'm worried about you," he admitted.

She shook her head. "Don't be. I can take care of i
self."

"I know that, but I'm still worried," he admitted, tak
a step closer.

"I'm fi—" she started to say once more but Parker
his hand up to her lips to stop her.

"Don't tell me you're fine again. You definitely are
fine and I'm not leaving you alone until you tell me wh;
going on," he told her, growing steadily impatient.

"You want to know what's wrong, Parker?" she as
almost defiantly. Her shoulders had squared and she v
staring into his eyes like she was ready to haul off a
slap him.

"I do," he admitted with more than a little caution.

Parker was almost positive Drew wasn't going to hit
1. Physical violence didn't really fit her personality.
ll, her eyes were looking a bit wide, her face still too
e, and she was now clenching and unclenching her
s at her side. But he refused to back down because
v, more than ever, he was certain there was something
ng on with her.

"I'm pregnant, you idiot!" were the last words Parker
rd her say before she turned and pushed into the
dies' Room.

e was the idiot. A raving, nervous, sweating idiot!

Drew wanted to run to her car, to get inside and start
ignition and drive to her house, or possibly off the
arest cliff. She wanted to sink so far into the floor Parker
ild never see her again. She wanted to disappear and . . .

Another pressing need prevailed and she moved quickly
o the nearest stall where the nausea she'd been feeling
the last fifteen minutes finally took over. Minutes later
ien she was certain she could stand up straight and that
ere was nothing left in her stomach to revolt and/or es-
pe, Drew stood up straight, then leaned against the stall
or, trying to steady her breathing.

Her words played over in her mind as did Parker's, and
e couldn't help but groan. This was not the way she'd
inted to tell him. It wasn't what she'd rehearsed. In fact,
vas just about the worst possible scenario come true.

"If you stay in there any longer, I'm coming in."

Oh hell, was he really talking to her through the Ladies'
om stall? Of course he was, he was Parker Cantrell,
iich meant there was absolutely nothing that he didn't
lieve he could do and get away with.

"Perhaps you missed the sign that said 'Ladies'. It's in
g white letters on the door," she snapped.

She almost stomped her foot she was so angry w
herself for not following her plan and at Louisa and Ma
belle for holding her up so that she ran into Parker bef
she was absolutely ready. And, of course, at Parker for
well, for being Parker!

"I know what the door says, Drew. What I'm rea
interested in getting a replay of is what you said just
fore you barged through the door."

He was speaking in a really calm voice. It didn't ha
the hint of laughter that his voice normally held. It v
still deep and sexy as hell regardless.

A part of her wanted to retract her words and wait p
tiently until he believed her and left the bathroom befo
she came out of the stall. There were two problems w
that scenario: 1. Parker wouldn't believe her, and 2. Sh
never been a coward before, she wasn't about to start no

So taking a deep breath, Drew turned and slid
latch on the stall door to the side. Pulling on the door, s
watched as Parker moved his well-built body back t'
steps, allowing her space to move forward. Drew gra
fully took the space and headed directly to the sink whe
she switched on the water and leaned forward to rinse I
mouth. When she finished, she was surprised to look i
the mirror and see Parker standing behind her offering I
a paper towel.

For what felt like endless seconds, they only stared
each other. Then she turned to face him, accepting t
paper towel and drying her hands and mouth. When th
was done, Drew accepted that she had no choice but
look up at him once more.

It really wasn't a great hardship to stare at Park
Cantrell. He had a golden complexion, his hair so clos
cut he almost looked bald. His eyebrows were dark, ey
even darker, jaw strong, chiseled arms like a wrestler, a
chest and abs like a bodybuilder. Today he wore jea

weren't tight, but fit his muscled thighs and legs per-
tly, and a black T-shirt that hugged all the amazing
tours and ridges of his upper body. The short sleeves
a portion of his biceps and his lower arms, roped with
k veins, bare. He looked like a biker, a bad-ass biker
who was trying his damnedest to keep a tight rein on
control.

Drew took a deep breath and asked, "Do you remem-
that night we were together?"

If it were possible, his eyes darkened even more. "I can't
m to think of anything else" was his reply.

She clasped her hands in front of her and, in an effort
hide her nervousness, silently dared them to move
in.

"I doubt either one of us will ever forget that night,"
said quietly.

"What are you trying to tell me, Drew?"

Parker crossed his arms over his massive chest so that
looked even more opposing. Only Drew wasn't intimi-
ed by him, not in the least bit. Instead she was more
n sorry to realize she was still unabashedly attracted
him.

"I'm trying to tell you that on that night, that hot sum-
r's night . . ."

"We lay beneath that big old oak tree, staring up at the
mmer's moon and decided to sleep together," he fin-
ed for her.

Drew nodded. That's precisely what they'd done after
y'd left Charlie's. He'd driven them down to Fitzgerald
rk on his motorcycle. It had rained earlier that evening
the air wasn't as thick with humidity, but the grass was
ll damp from the quick summer shower. Parker had
ried her shoes in his hands as she walked around, wig-
ing her toes against the cool blades of grass. They'd
pped at the oak tree and kissed. The kiss had turned so

desperate they'd ended up falling to the ground in an
tempt to get each other undressed. Then she'd cracked
eye open and that's when she saw it. Just over Park
shoulder the summer's moon had shown so big and brigh
He paused to see what had grabbed her attention, and the
stared up at the moon together.

Then she'd invited him back to her house.

"That night I wished on the summer's moon that y
would make love to me," she told him.

"And I did," was his response.

"And we made a baby," she said simply. "I'm pregn
with your child, Parker."

There, she'd told him. Then she held her breath w
ing for his response. Instead the Ladies' Room d
opened and in came none other than Louisa Kirk. W
out a word she raised her arm and slapped Parker over
shoulder with her purse.

"You haven't changed a bit, Parker Cantrell. Still ch
ing girls into whatever dark corner you can get them i
do your deeds. Shame on you!" she yelled.